Kisses in the Rain

OTHER BOOKS AND AUDIO BOOKS
BY KRISTA LYNNE JENSEN

Of Grace and Chocolate

The Orchard

Falling for You

Love Unexpected: With All My Heart (contributor)

Kisses in the Rain

a novel

Krista Lynne Jensen

Covenant Communications, Inc.

Covenant®

Cover image: *Romantic Couple* © boggy22, courtesy iStockphoto.com

Cover design copyright © 2015 by Covenant Communications, Inc.

Published by Covenant Communications, Inc.
American Fork, Utah

Printed in the United States of America
First Printing: June 2015

21 20 19 18 17 16 15   10 9 8 7 6 5 4 3 2 1

ISBN 978-1-68047-239-4

For my great-aunts Ruth, Viola, and Betty. I miss your sweet souls.

For my aunts Jackie and Barby; thank you for introducing me to Camano and the tulip fields. I didn't get to come nearly enough.

Love you.

Acknowledgments

THANK YOU TO MY READERS. Thank you for the e-mails and reviews, and thank you for your encouragement. Hearing that you love my stories and that they've touched you in some way is one of my favorite things.

Thank you to the writing community, my crit groups, and my friends. Special thanks to Jenny Moore, Ranee Clark, Annette Lyon, Luisa Perkins, and Robison Wells for your sharp story sense and feedback for *Kisses*. Writing Friendzy, Bear Lake Monsters, LDStorymakers, where would I be without you? Probably living some kind of normal life, whatever that is.

To those at Covenant Communications, including Kathryn Gordon, and my editor, Samantha Millburn, my deepest gratitude for taking chances with my ideas and helping to make my dreams come true.

Thanks to Colonel Dan Fuhr of the UHP, who answered all of my motorcycle questions and has always been one of the nicest guys I've been blessed to know.

Thank you, Suzy G, for being there. Shiny.

To my family, I just really, really love you. Thank you for your support and hope and cheerleading. I will never be able to express how much it means to me. And I'm a writer, so that's saying a lot.

To Washington State, thanks for being my home, you big, diverse, productive, beautiful hunk of earth. I missed you.

Thank you, Brandon, for pushing me to finish this book amidst the most chaotic year of our lives together. Keep doing that heroic stuff. Me likey. Love you.

The only three things a guy should want to change about a girl:
her last name, her address, and her view of men.

Chapter 1

Jace Lowe never had cared for blondes. That was a lie. His leg swung over the seat of his motorcycle, and he jerked his helmet over his head a little too roughly. Brenna, blonde and beautiful, still watched from the window of her apartment, along with Brad What's His Name, so Jace fired up the gratefully angry engine beneath him, let go of the throttle, and peeled out on the wet roadside, spraying Brad's Lexus with mud. He allowed a grin as he glanced in the rearview mirror, catching Brad storming out, yelling words Jace couldn't care less about not hearing.

After a few miles of weaving in and out of Seattle traffic, though, his smug attitude faded. He shouldn't have lost his temper like that. But this whole time he'd been played. Just a lure to bring back the one who got away. He'd believed Brenna's smile was for him when it had really been for her successful planning. He was bait. And he'd completely fallen for it. She hadn't even denied it. She'd just stood there crying. In Brad's arms. Brad, who had actually thanked him. *Thanked him.* Jace revved the engine and leaned forward into the freeway traffic, no longer enjoying the clear day as he had on his trip into the city.

How had the guy said it? *Thank you for helping me see how much Brenna really means to me.*

The heat of humiliation churned Jace's gut. He'd spent a year—over a year—dating Brenna. He'd looked at engagement rings. He'd hinted with Brenna wrapped in his arms. She'd been coy. She'd rebuffed his questions playfully, and she'd somehow let Brad know it was now or never. Brad had chosen now.

What had Jace been thinking? *Chump.* He passed a sedan and crossed three lanes to the empty carpool lane, eliciting a few honks, then opened the throttle. Though it was nowhere near commuter traffic congestion, the midmorning travel in the regular lanes was still too slow for his need right now: speed.

Of course, that ended with flashing lights. He keenly felt the rush and zoom of each passing car as he sat on the side of the highway, waiting for the officer to dole out his punishment, which ended up being a $200 ticket. But when Jace thanked the officer under his breath, he meant it. It should have been worse.

Less than an hour later, Jace pulled into the shared carport of his fourth-row hillside duplex facing the water. Puget Sound stretched out past Whidbey Island to the open water beyond. When the weather was clear enough, a misty view of Canada provided a beautiful backdrop for the scene. Today it was clear.

A friendly bark greeted Jace's ears as the motorcycle engine cut.

"Hey, Kitsap."

The Aussie-shepherd mix bounced up and down behind the chain-link fence at the back of the carport. Jace put his helmet on the back of his bike and opened the broken refrigerator where he kept the dog food. After Kit's bowl was filled, the dog could barely contain his excitement, his entire body wagging at the gate. Jace let out a reluctant laugh. "I've only been gone a couple hours."

He unlatched the gate and gave his dog a hearty rub. He pulled Kit's ears straight back, stretching his eyelids into slants, then scratched his neck. Kit's eyes, one blue and one gold, watched his owner with contentment. All was right in his world. *Easy, for a dog*, Jace thought. Kit yawned, satisfied, and turned his attention to the bowl. Jace stood and opened the side door to his home. "Holler if you need me." The screen door shut behind him.

Jace didn't worry too much about Kit wandering off. As soon as the old dog finished eating, he'd drop down in the sun somewhere on the small property and wait for their walk. That was how they'd met. Jace had been in his house on the island less than a week when he'd opened the front door to check his mail and found the dog lying in the rare sunshine. It hadn't taken long to determine that the dog was completely harmless—though hopelessly matted—and would do anything for a Nilla wafer.

Jace had taken him all over Camano Island, including a long walk up and down the west shores and Port Susan on the east, and he'd even put an ad in the paper, reporting a lost dog. No one ever claimed him, so before a trip to the vet and getting a license, Jace had looked up a little Seattle history. He named the dog Kitsap after the leader of a historical indigenous Indian tribe, then he'd determinedly bathed and brushed Kitsap and deemed him the brother he'd never had—the shorter, hairier brother that didn't say much and was always happy to see him. There couldn't be a more satisfying partnership anywhere on the island.

"Dogs are easy," Jace said to himself, eyeing his phone. "It's the creatures who smell good you've got to watch out for." He checked his messages. He'd missed a call from his dad during the drive home. He opened his voice mail and listened.

"Jace, this is your father. Just wanted to tell you we have the date for your sister's graduation. Hope you can make it. Your mom doesn't want you on that bike if you're gonna make the trip. Talk to you soon."

Jace set the phone down on the kitchen counter and rubbed his face. He opened the fridge, removed a Styrofoam container and a Vernor's ginger ale, and warmed up some lunch. He didn't want to call his dad yet. He was still pretty knotted up inside and would probably say something he'd regret later. He and his dad didn't exactly agree on his . . . anything.

He shook his head, taking a steaming bite of the fried cod he'd shoved into tartar sauce. His sister Addy was graduating from high school this year. He should be there. It was still a ways away, and he had time to plan. He wouldn't be spending any money on girls for a while, so he could save there. He downed a hard swallow of the ginger ale and broke off another chunk of fish. The tartar sauce needed more pepper, fewer pickles.

He decided to ignore his dad's "subtle hint" about his motorcycle. He could stop stressing about getting a car. He'd been considering it because he'd wanted to take Brenna out when it was raining, which happened often, but his old Honda Shadow had been great for school in Nevada, and the gas mileage was awesome. It got him where he needed to go just fine, even if it wasn't ideal for dating around the wet Puget Sound.

No, he wouldn't be worrying about that again for a very long time. He sat up. "Man, the speeding ticket." That would set him back. He kicked back the last swallow of Vernor's and threw his trash away, tossing the empty can into the recycling bin with a crash. He ran his hands under warm water in the chipped sink and glanced at the picture of him and Brenna at the zoo, stuck to the fridge with a Space Needle magnet. Peeking out from beneath the picture was a pair of theater tickets.

"Aw, crap." He dried his hands and grabbed the tickets, ignoring the magnet and photo as they dropped to the floor. He'd bought the tickets last week after Brenna had expressed interest. Some play called *Shipwrecked: An Entertainment.*

Ironic.

He'd bought them as a surprise. He rubbed his chin. Maybe his boss would be interested. Maybe one of the guys from the ward. Maybe Mrs. Feddler, his landlady. He shook his head and blew out a breath of exasperation. He threw the tickets into a random drawer, grabbed his phone, zipped up his jacket, and opened the door to the carport, frowning.

"C'mon, Kit. Let's walk. This sunshine isn't supposed to last long."

* * *

Georgiana Tate rested her chin on her hands and stared at the view out the window, battling the dull but persistent pain in her head. Misty rain dimpled the salty waves of the small bay, and shifting clouds of varying grays weighed the world down, enclosing the island of Camano in a fold of cold wet wool. A single gull bobbed on the waves, mottled white against the dark teal waters of Puget Sound, its head tucked under its wing.

"Have you seen the whales yet? Any sign?" Her aunt Faye leaned forward above her, searching the water. Technically the house belonged to Faye and her husband, Dar, but Faye's sister lived with them too, so Georgie had grown up referring to the cottage as "the aunts' house."

Georgie lifted her head and peered farther out over the waves. "No. Should I?"

Her aunt Faye shook her head. "Mm, maybe not today." She sighed. "Not today, but you can see them out there this time of year. Of course, this weather isn't helping visibility. Wait till it clears up again. You'll see the Olympics then." She dried a bowl from lunch with a flour-sack towel tied around her waist like an apron.

Georgie's eyes found the gull again. It had been three days since she'd arrived at the aunts' house on Camano Island, which wasn't completely an island. A narrow slough, a shallow ditch of salt and river water, separated the island from the mainland state of Washington, and a single land bridge crossed it. The Sound surrounded the majority of the ear-shaped island rising in tree-covered hills, allowing its luckier residents a view of Mount Baker, Mount Rainier, and the Cascades from the east and the Saratoga Passage and San Juan Islands from the west. Her aunts lived on the northwest side, facing the bay, or channel, or whatever it was called.

Three days it had rained steadily. The earth soaked it up like a hungry sponge.

"Would you like to read? We've got lots of books. Novels, mostly. Some really good ones that even a twenty-something like yourself would enjoy, I think. What do you like?"

Georgie paused. "No, thanks." Since the accident, it often hurt to read, though it had once been one of her favorite pastimes. She'd spent summers in her bedroom reading *Little House* and *Ramona* and, later, everything by Louisa May Alcott and Meg Cabot. Her mother had introduced her to Jane Austen and Georgette Heyer, and in high school she'd been buried beneath American and world lit titles, eking out time for novels she actually *wanted* to read. Having to set aside her romances in college, she'd analyzed Ulysses, Don Quixote, and others. But she hadn't read for pleasure in a long time.

Faye touched her shoulder, her gray eyes perceptive. "Maybe later?"

Georgie nodded and focused on the gull again. Books. Part of who she'd been.

"I'm fine, really." Her head throbbed. She absently reached for what was once a swollen black-and-yellow bruise on her arm. Her cast and braces were long gone. Nothing much to show for the injuries now.

Faye stood, unsure. "Can I get you some Tylenol?"

Georgie knew Tylenol wouldn't touch the ache, but Faye looked so concerned she gave in and nodded.

Faye turned and removed the towel. "We could go to a movie later. I'll call to see what's playing." The sound of her footsteps faded as she left the room.

Movies. Movies and books and dances and music and parties. Books and school and speeches and good posture and confidence. Confidence. Friends. Leadership. College. *That* girl. She had been that girl. And in one year, it had all changed.

Now, here she sat, staring at a gull, terrified that if she looked away too long something would come up from the deep, dark water and engulf it, drag it down, a wing trailing behind, reaching for light, soundless.

Fly away.

A wave rose, and Georgie gasped as the gull disappeared.

A voice from behind interrupted her alarm. "Sometimes I wonder why they don't just fly to shelter. Stupid birds. Ridiculous."

Georgie exhaled as the gull appeared again, unharmed.

Aunt Tru, Faye's twin sister, looked out the window with her hands on her hips as she scanned the sky. "It was bright and sunny last week. You should've been here. But it'll come again. Look at that darn bird sittin' freezin' in that cold water." She shook her head. "Stupid." She gestured with her arms as she talked to the bird. "Hello? You've got wings. Fly." She gave her arms a flap and then shrugged.

Georgie had learned long ago to be patient with Aunt Tru's quirks. Her father had taught her at a young age about Tru's mild intellectual disability caused by a blockage and lack of oxygen at birth. Georgie had also been taught how to see a *person* beyond the disability. Even with her quirks and brash manner, Tru had a big heart.

And heaven knew Georgie had brought a whole catalog of her own quirks. She watched the gull. Maybe the bird was just too wet. Too tired.

Faye bustled back into the room. "There's a matinee at two. The new Gerard Butler movie. Georgie, what do you think?" She handed Georgie pills and a cup of water.

Georgie took the pills and didn't answer about the movie.

Faye raised her eyebrows. "You don't like Gerard Butler?"

Yes. Yes, she did. "I love Gerard Butler." She was safe here. She could say what she liked. She could say Gerard Butler was hot if she wanted.

"Oh—there he goes." Tru watched through the window, and Georgie turned again. The gull had lifted and was flying toward the trees down shore. "Not so stupid after all."

"What do you think, Tru? Want to see a movie?" Faye asked her sister.

"I'm reading a book, and I've got some laundry to fold." Tru turned to leave. "Besides, I'm betting Gerard is not a flannel man." She walked away and slapped the backside of her pajamas.

Faye laughed at her sister, shaking her head, then came to sit next to Georgie on the window seat. "We'll have Tru go digging for clams and have chowder for dinner tomorrow. Would you like that?" A hand touched her shoulder again. "Georgiana?"

Georgie blinked. "What?"

Faye shook her head and dropped her hand in her lap. "Is there something you need?" She reached her fingers just far enough to brush Georgie's blonde hair away from the scar above her eye. "Do you want to talk?"

Georgie shook her head, her gaze unfocused. It had been nine months since the accident and seven since she'd left the hospital. She knew she still came across as slow, though her mind seemed in a constant mode of trying to find the next word, the next thought, the right response. Fight or flight. Most of the time, though, she just didn't want to engage. But she'd come here to change that.

"All right, then." Faye gave her a patient smile but didn't move to leave. She only leaned against the window and rubbed her arms a little. "The rhodies love this. Look at that color."

The mist turned to heavy drops on the glass outside, and the thick rhododendron leaves bounced under the rain.

"You have a job interview next week?" Faye asked in her encouraging way.

"Yes. Thanks for spotting the opening." Georgie was grateful, but a knot tightened in her stomach. A restaurant on the island was hiring, and she knew she had to go for it, though it was taking all of her nerve not to back out. Getting a job was on her list of things to get her moving forward.

They didn't say anything more for several moments, but Georgie felt words pressing to get out. It almost hurt keeping them inside, but her aunt's calm presence encouraged her. "I'm sorry."

"For what, honey?"

She swallowed, and her nose stung with emotion. "Everything. Needing to come here."

Two warm hands lifted her face. "You are welcome here. It warms my heart knowing you chose this place of all places. What happened wasn't your fault."

"None of this would have happened if I hadn't gotten involved with Ian. And he would still be—"

Alive. Ian would still be alive. No matter what kind of person her fiancé had been, he hadn't deserved to die in that car crash.

Faye shook her head. "I'm going to be bold and tell you there's no point in beating yourself up over that. You put your trust in someone and something, and sometimes . . . well, things happen we can't possibly see coming. You didn't know what he was. Even your parents were fooled."

"Deacon wasn't."

"Your brother is protective of you, maybe more so than even your parents."

"I should have listened to him."

"Aw, honey, the heart hears what it wants to hear." Faye pulled away and reached for the tissue box on the TV console. She handed a tissue to Georgie. "It's a tragic thing. It truly is. But you did the right thing coming here. We're happy to have you, and don't you think otherwise. Understand?"

Georgie blew her nose and nodded.

But the accident had been her fault, in a way. If she hadn't broken things off with Ian that night, if she'd been more careful with the timing or figured out a way to let him down easier . . . But nothing had ever been easy with Ian Hudson. He was charming to his hot core. And his temper, she'd discovered too late, was volcanic. She didn't even remember getting into the car or his speed or—

All she remembered was waking up and knowing she couldn't be with him anymore. A decision she should have made a lot sooner. And then she'd learned that Ian had died in the crash.

So much time had passed, and still the guilt and the questions haunted her. She'd finally stood up for herself, for her mangled heart, and the result had left her numb and directionless. And despite her parents' worry, despite the comfort she'd felt at home, she'd left. She'd come here to Camano Island to find direction. To remember. And maybe to feel again.

She hoped to be able to feel again. And that had to count for something.

Later that evening, after the movie, after Uncle Dar had come home from work on the mainland, after dinner had been made and eaten and cleaned up, after Aunt Tru had been tucked in on the couch to watch a reality show and Faye and Dar had retired to their bedroom, Georgie pressed her fingertips against the dull pain above her eye. Though her headaches had become less frequent, they weren't any less painful, and the medicine only helped a little bit. She lay back on her pillow and remembered the gull.

She hadn't married Ian. She'd flown away. But the guilt over Ian's death pressed on her like a boulder, as it did every night.

She curled up in a tight ball, trying again to pinpoint when things had changed in their relationship. She tried to determine if the change had been over days or months and tried to remember why she'd fallen so hard for him so fast. She wished she'd succeeded in changing him. No. She wished she'd found a way to be who he wanted her to be.

No. That is wrong.

She wished she could figure out how to be her again. That was all that mattered now.

* * *

Dishes clattered along with called-out orders and sizzling food. The hum of chatting dinner patrons and low background music rose and fell as the kitchen door opened and closed with the coming and going of waitresses and waiters. Georgiana hurried to arrange the salads and garnishes, squirting balsamic vinaigrette in a swirl and dots. "Three." A ruddy-skinned, college-age boy with a shock of red hair and a determined look hurried to collect the plates on a tray.

"I need a tuna on three. And I need blue cheese crumbles on the side," he said.

Georgie spooned the cheese into a small ceramic cup and placed it on the salad plate.

The boy left with the salads.

Georgie turned. "Tuna with the sword and prawns on three."

The chef nodded. She detected a sigh and hoped she wasn't the cause of frustration.

Peter & Andrew's Fishery had been her place of employment for three days now, and she was treading water to keep up with the pace of the popular restaurant. She'd never worked in the food service business, but she needed this job. It was on the island, minutes from her aunts' house, and that meant she didn't have to venture out into the sea of people or the traffic on the mainland. Job opportunities on the island were pretty scarce. Besides, she'd always enjoyed *eating* food. She'd watched cooking shows and wasn't shy about trying new things. Even so, she really only felt confident *preparing* simple things, like cookies and scrambled eggs. The menu at Peter & Andrew's was definitely on a different level, but she'd make this work.

Her head hurt.

She pulled the next ticket off the cable and began another set of salads. As expediter, she provided a buffer between the dining room and the kitchen. The position allowed her distance from both customers and staff. She worked mostly with the head chef, Reuben Blanchard, who had hired her to keep traffic organized and pleasant and to relieve the sous-chef of the smaller tasks of carrot rosettes, shaved chocolate, and aioli.

Reuben was an older man and had been owner and chef at Peter & Andrew's for a little over a decade. He was professional and commanding in a quiet sort of way. His control of the kitchen eased Georgie's nerves, and his outward respect for the staff earned what trust she could offer him. He was a large man with thick arms, and she sensed a sort of comfort around him that she liked. She didn't read too much into it; she only knew her tension in the kitchen eased a little when Reuben arrived and took over.

She couldn't say the same about the sous-chef.

"Jace, grab these rangoons when they're done, will you?" Reuben asked. "And get on that tuna for three; the sword is almost done. I've got to see to the prime." Reuben wiped his hands on a bleach-water towel, called out, "Seven," and moved to the ovens. "Georgie, more bread."

Georgie glanced behind her as Jace stepped past her. She stiffened as his arm grazed her elbow, and in her haste to back away, her other elbow knocked one of the salad plates off-kilter. Her hand shot out to grab it, and she returned the plate to safety.

"Careful." Jace continued at the fryer.

She grabbed a tray and hurried to the large walk-in refrigerator where they kept the small loaves of bread waiting to rise in the bread ovens. As she reached for the loaves, the door shut, blocking all noise but the hum of the fridge. Georgie closed her eyes and took a deep, cool breath, then let her fingers rest on the shelf in front of her.

Pull yourself together, girl.

The door handle turned, and the sudden sound of the kitchen made her jump as the door opened. She shook off her nerves and pulled down six loaves for the bread oven.

"Here you are. Jace says two key limes and a torte, quick."

"But—" Georgie looked between Mai, a waitress just coming on shift, and the loaves of bread piled on her tray.

"Here, let me." Mai finished tying her apron, took the loaves, and turned, holding the heavy door with her foot, and Georgie pulled the desserts from their shelf. Joanie, the pastry chef, came in early and made the desserts for the day. Georgie was continually amazed that the guessed amount was always so close.

She followed Mai out, watching Mai's spiky black hair with blue highlights. The small tattoo on the back of her neck read "*alis volat propiis,*" each word underlined by stacks of small square Chinese characters. The tips of a pair of small wings peeked out just above the neckline of her black T-shirt. Time and again, Georgie's eyes had been drawn to the tattoo, and she'd had to bite her tongue so she wouldn't ask about it because she wasn't sure if she should. It perplexed her, as she wasn't one to stare at things like tattoos, and fascinated her, because the simple Latin phrase was a beacon to her.

She flies with her own wings.

She'd helped her brother Deacon study Latin for a college class. It had become a game to them, using what they'd learned whenever an opportunity presented itself. This phrase she knew.

Caleb, a station cook, brushed past her carrying a black iron pan. "Watch it."

She lifted the desserts up high to avoid the pan of sizzling sauce—some sort of reduction. Was that the right word? She knew more about Latin than she did about cooking, despite watching hours of Food Network during her recovery.

She caught up to Mai, who was shoving loaves of already rising bread dough in the oven.

"You need to keep this going, or Reuben'll blow a gasket."

Georgie turned to prep the desserts. "Thanks."

"You're welcome. Looks like I've got the upper room. See ya."

Mai left the kitchen, her wings following her. Plates of seared tuna, grilled swordfish, and battered prawns arranged next to steamed asparagus, red potatoes, and basmati were slid in Georgie's direction. The reduction spilled over the edge of a plate, and she reached for a bleach towel. "Three," she called and wiped the spill just as the redhead swept the order onto a tray and disappeared again. Everything was so fast here. Before she could move, the desserts were pushed toward her and someone held the whipped cream in front of her in a piping bag.

"Keep up."

She quickly turned her head toward Jace and took the cream. She avoided him in general, but he wasn't usually this impatient. "I'm trying," she said, though it was really more of a whisper, and she silently chided herself for not being more resolute.

He shook his head, scowling. "You're fine."

Georgie pressed her lips together and garnished the desserts, then reached for the next order. Jace was about her age, she guessed. Maybe older. Maybe his dark, curly hair made him look younger than he actually was. His intense hazel eyes and full mouth might have made him attractive in that scruffy, unshaven sort of way, but he was sullen, his eyes shadowed, and everyone around him gave him space. She couldn't help but be reminded of Ian's temper.

As he turned from the fryers to make his way back to the gas range, Jace nearly growled. "The *bread*."

Inside, she recoiled from his tone, but she wouldn't shrink. "The timer hasn't gone off," she said.

Reuben had just returned to the front. "Take it easy, Jace. I remember your first week." He turned to Georgie. "After you take out the bread, call that next order to the back and start the salads."

She nodded, knowing the heat she felt in her face probably registered as bright splotches from her cheeks down. But Reuben's firm, gentle voice had worked, and she calmed. The timer on the bread buzzed. She grabbed the plate-size spatula and moved to the bread oven.

"There's a timer," she murmured, "so I'm going to wait for the timer." She peeked over her shoulder at Jace, and when she found him watching her, she turned back to the bread.

By the time she'd sliced several loaves, arranged them in baskets, and returned to the salads, Jace had temporarily removed himself to the office. Georgie called the next order.

"Hey, seventeen up yet?" Mai smiled, her black-framed glasses accentuating her dark eyes.

Georgie placed a small cup of butter next to a baked potato. "Nearly."

"Hey, you okay? You're all splotchy."

Reuben added a plate between them. "Good to go." He knocked on the counter and took the next order back. "A bowl of the bisque, Georgie, for fourteen."

"It happens"—Georgie lowered her voice and fingered the ladle in the soup—"when I get flustered." And she remembered something, like tiny particles gathering from the outer edges of her mind and becoming a solid thing. Ian had referred to them as her *hot spots*. She'd hated that term. It had been funny at first. A flirtation that had made her flush even more. After a while, though, it was laced with his disapproval.

"Hey," Mai leaned over the counter and touched Georgie's arm. "You're doing great. Reuben wouldn't have hired you if he didn't think you could handle it."

That was true. She knew it. She'd headed up the National Honor Society's annual Habitat for Humanity service project two years in a row because she could handle it. She'd won all-state in speech her senior year in high school because she could handle it. She'd been asked to TA a humanities class last semester at the Y because she could handle it. She'd mustered up as much of that part of her as she could for the job interview, and Reuben had seen it.

She just wished she felt like a *part* of those memories. The accident had given her two things: a second chance and a fractured identity. For a long time, she'd molded herself to be who Ian had wanted, and after breaking that mold, and her head, and dealing with Ian's death, she desperately needed to find herself again.

"Rib eye and king for two, table ten," Jace said, appearing suddenly and reading from the next order he'd pulled off the cable. He gave her an impatient look and left.

Georgie held her breath as he turned away. No, she didn't like him.

"Cheer up, Jace," Mai called after him. "You're bringin' the place down." She shook her head, gathering up her order. "Poor guy got dumped last week." She picked up her tray and turned to go but stepped back again. "I'll take that soup to fourteen."

"Thanks." Georgie placed the soup on the tray with a basket of bread.

"And don't be flustered. You'll get the hang of it. This is as busy as it ever gets." She smiled again and left.

Georgie reached for the next order, then quickly readied six salad plates as she called it out. "Fried oysters, two prime, medium, one fettuccine with scallops, one tuna, one mahimahi, and one fish-n-chips." She held the ticket out to Reuben, who caught her eye and gave her the slightest of smiles.

"And get that bread out." He put his hand up to stop her puzzled protest and pointed at the bread ovens just as the timer buzzed.

She folded her arms. "*How* do you do that?"

He grinned and went to work.

Georgie turned from the salads with the spatula and caught sight of Jace. A slight scowl turned the corners of his mouth down, and he seemed to be turning the steaks with excessive force. She turned away, not a doubt in her mind as to why someone would break up with him.

And, of course, he rides a motorcycle.

She shook her head but sighed. That wasn't fair. Was it? Lots of people rode motorcycles.

As she placed the bread in baskets, Georgie glanced again at Jace's scowl. So he didn't smile. *Maior risus, acrior ensis. The bigger the smile, the sharper the knife.* Deacon had said that after meeting Ian, who was all smiles when it served him.

Jace paused and ran a heavy hand over his face, revealing fatigue and, for a brief moment, what looked like pain. He straightened his shoulders, wiped his hands clean, and continued working. Georgie turned back to the salads.

Chapter 2

DOWN ON THE BEACH, JACE watched a break in the clouds. The wind gusted off the water, and he breathed in deeply, smelling salt and sea algae and the tang of a dead fish somewhere. He'd walked down to the rocky stretch with Kit, thinking it would bring some clarity. On the way home from work a few nights ago, the idea had struck him that maybe his dad was right. He wasn't sure he was going anywhere either. Sure, he had a place on Camano. An old rental in need of new paint, floors, and appliances, to start. The carport leaned from years of exposure to sea air and rain. Moss grew in the split beams supporting the metal roof. His car was a bike.

His job was—No, he loved his job. Reuben was rolling around the idea of retirement, which was why he'd hired the expediter to give Jace a bigger role in the kitchen. Jace wouldn't wish Reuben out, by any means, but he was in a good position if retirement should come. Reuben would still own the place, but Jace would run it as executive chef.

He lifted his face to the sky as the cloud break moved on.

Returning to Seattle after serving his mission here had seemed ideal. He'd loved being in an area filled with so many trees, mountains, and lakes, as well as the ocean. It had been so drastically different from Boulder City, Nevada, home of Hoover Dam and a lot of crickets. By transferring to Le Cordon Bleu culinary school in Seattle—a city teeming with interesting people—he was given a chance to return to a place with good memories and great experiences. During school he'd shared an okay apartment with some okay roommates. Almost immediately, he'd met Brenna at the singles ward. He'd graduated, and after a good word from Jace's adviser, Reuben had called Jace for an interview. Within a year he'd worked his way up to sous-chef. Things couldn't have gone more perfectly.

Kit barked, and Jace looked down to find a small piece of driftwood at his feet and the dog watching him expectantly. He picked it up and tossed it down the beach. Kit ran after it, and Jace wondered briefly if the dog would return it this time. The cool breeze kicked up, making Jace shiver.

Last fall he'd grown tired of the commute from Seattle to Camano. He was making more income, so he'd hunted down the little duplex apartment on the island. It was significantly more than his rent in Seattle, and he'd ended up making the commute to the city three to four times a week anyway to see Brenna, plus attending church with her on Sundays, but he was finished with those trips. He'd called the bishop last week just to let him know he wouldn't be attending there anymore. That had been awkward. But he was grateful he'd chosen to call instead of show up in person on Sunday.

"I hear congratulations are in order!" the bishop had cheerfully proclaimed over the phone.

No. They weren't. He'd tried to keep his tone light when he'd told the bishop he was free to save his congratulations for Brenna because he wasn't the man involved. He'd tried to laugh it off to save the bishop further embarrassment, but the man was terrible at hiding his confusion.

Jace tried not to think of the murmuring that must have run through the chapel as Brenna and Brad had walked into sacrament meeting together. At least he hadn't had to be part of that humiliating scene in person.

But as Jace had driven home in the rain a few nights ago, he'd seen the island rental he'd been so proud of for what it really was—a run-down dump far from home, surrounded by strangers. Had he loved Brenna because she was company? Because she was part of a vision? He shook his head. Every memory with her was now tainted with the question: had it been *real*? He'd thought it was. But put him next to Brad and his Lexus and med school and was her choice any mystery?

A question surfaced in his mind. Which still hurt more: the humiliation of Brenna getting engaged while he was dating her, or losing her?

He realized the answer with a jolt. He no longer missed Brenna. But the humiliation knotted his gut.

Jace reached down and picked up a wet, smooth stone the size of a golf ball, nearly black, shining like a seal. The beach was made up of rocks like this of all colors—green, red, translucent white, orange, yellow, gray, and black—worn smooth and rounded by the pounding waves. Occasionally bits of frosted blue, brown, and green sea glass would wash up. Less occasionally, glass float balls would come ashore. A film of green algae marked the slow tide line, layering everything the water covered as it rose and receded. The lower the tide, the more barnacles and mussels took over. Jace squeezed the rock in his hand and frowned.

This rut he found himself in was affecting his cooking. Just yesterday Reuben had asked him to come up with four original dishes for the menu to update it for the spring season and the Tulip Festival tourists. Jace knew he couldn't botch this opportunity to show his boss that he was invested.

If only he could pin down something original to present. He had four weeks to come up with four dishes. Maybe he'd have to visit some of his favorite spots in the area again. Or something.

Jace felt completely uninspired.

Kit barked at gulls now, the piece of driftwood forgotten. He smoothed the stone in his fingers, remembering his one family trip to Disneyland when he was a kid. They'd visited the beach and tried to guess how long it took rocks to get to shore with the tides. Weeks? Years?

Jace threw the rock out past the surf. "There," he mumbled. "Start over." He set his hands on his hips and stared out at the waves for a long time.

* * *

Georgiana flickered her eyes open at the sudden brightness assaulting her from a window in her bedroom. Faye opened the other set of shutters, and Georgie pulled the thick blankets over her head.

"Time to get up. You've got an hour to get ready."

"For what?" But Georgie knew the answer.

"Church, silly. It's time you go."

Georgie groaned. Warmth enshrouded her, and she snuggled further into the covers. She felt the weight of her aunt sitting on the edge of the bed.

"Georgie, stop this. Your mother's worried, and frankly, I don't understand either. How is not attending church helping you move forward?"

This was Georgie's third Sunday with her aunts, and she'd stayed in bed the last two. Of course Faye was right. Not going to church had less to do with starting over and more to do with the fact that by Sunday, Georgie was exhausted. She didn't want to put on a face and pretend everything was happy and normal and exactly what others expected it to be. The interaction at the restaurant was more than enough socializing.

"Georgie."

She sighed under the covers. "I'll go next week."

"You said that last week."

Georgie sat up and pulled the covers off her head. "Fine, I'll go. But can I come home after sacrament meeting?" Three hours of church seemed insurmountable.

Her aunt paused. "Why don't we just play it by ear."

"Fine."

Faye stood and closed the door behind her.

Georgie brushed her hair out of her eyes and took in the pretty room washed in sunlight. She hadn't visited her aunts for years and didn't remember what this room had been before, but when she'd arrived, they had led her here, and she'd had trouble fighting the cheer it offered ever since.

From the robin's egg–blue walls to the old iron-framed bed to the painted sign hung above the headboard—*HOPE*—the room radiated cheer. Georgie pressed her hands into the substantial quilt printed with birds and branches of blossoms. An old bubble-glass lamp she did remember from a childhood visit to the house sat on the table next to the bed, along with a bowl of seashells and a picture of Christ calming the storm. The walls were covered with paintings in old frames. Floral still lifes, sailboats, and children with rosy cheeks.

Georgie took a deep breath, and a small smile graced her lips. Cheer won.

An hour later she pulled a cardigan on over her dress and picked up her scripture bag. She felt a pang of guilt. Her scriptures had stayed in their case since she'd arrived. She'd read them every night since she'd begun seminary as a freshman in high school, but she'd abandoned them as of late. Her fingers moved to the scar above her eye. Her headache hadn't returned for a few days. Maybe reading wouldn't be such a struggle, though the headache was only part of that.

A voice called from down the hall. "You ready, Georgie-girl?"

Ah, a childhood nickname.

"Coming, Tru."

As she entered the kitchen, she was met with smiles.

"There she is." Tru leaned forward. "You put makeup on?"

Georgie smiled patiently. Aunt Tru had never married, had refused to date even when asked out and, aside from working three days a week in the kitchen of a retirement home, was a recluse. She watched movies and reality TV and daytime talk shows. Her daily attire consisted of loud flannel pajama pants and big T-shirts. She never missed church, though, and made sure she was dressed up and looking her best for that. Her skirts and blouses were quite pretty and her lipstick bright. Why couldn't Tru find a place between pajamas and lipstick for everyday? It took very little effort for her to look more like . . . well, Faye.

So maybe that was why. Tru was definitely Tru.

"You look beautiful, Georgie." Faye pulled her in for a spontaneous hug. "I'm just so glad you're here."

Tru put her hands on her hips. "Well, what am I, crab bait? I'm wearin' makeup too."

Faye let Georgie go and shooed her sister away. "You know what I mean."

"I'm sure I don't. Now let's get going so your husband doesn't give us *the look* when we walk in late. I swear that man gets meaner with every passing year."

As Faye fluttered out the door, Tru threw Georgie a wink. Uncle Dar was about as mean as a daisy in a glass of water.

Georgie held out her arm. "C'mon, Crab Bait."

Tru chuckled and took her elbow. "Was that a joke, Miss Gloomy Buckets?"

Georgie shrugged and smiled to herself.

* * *

Jace accepted a program from the fairly wrinkled old man and stepped into the Stanwood chapel. The small town was situated on the other side of the slough separating Camano Island from the mainland, and it was the location of the area's only LDS Church building. He scanned the back rows for an inconspicuous spot and found an empty bench on the far back side. Taking his seat, he glanced around. The bishopric hadn't come in from their meetings yet, but organ music played and a couple of speakers sat nervously in their seats. Parents arranged their children, and folks visited quietly.

He knew about the singles branch in this stake but needed the atmosphere of a family ward for now. He wanted a chance to get to know people living their lives in his own community. He didn't need to be gawked at.

The bishopric took their seats behind the podium. He recognized one of them as a neighbor and watched him walk up to sit in the clerk's chair on the stand. The man then gave a small wave in Jace's direction. Jace turned as three women walked past. Two older women he'd seen before were followed by a younger woman with a ponytail. She turned her head to the side, and Jace's brow lifted.

The expediter from work. The one Reuben had hired. At least, he thought it was her. Georgie. She always wore a ponytail, but it was different today, low and loose. Something else was different. Maybe it was the dress. She glanced around, and before she spotted him, he opened the program and concentrated on reading names he didn't know. He hid behind the paper until the meeting started.

He hadn't paid much attention to her, but he had full recollection of how short-tempered and impatient he'd been at work last week. After closing last night, Reuben had pulled him aside and very gently told him that if he didn't either pull out of his slump or leave the broken heart at home, he'd put him on full-time bread duty and have him mopping up bisque until he couldn't stand the sight of it.

Jace had winced at that. There had been a particularly messy spill that evening when he'd carelessly rushed past the new girl, who'd been carrying a bowl of soup she had just filled. He hadn't looked at her, only gone for the mop while she'd tried to clean up her station, and then he'd scrubbed the oven, feeling pretty lousy. By the time he'd finished, she'd replaced the salads and was quietly eating one of the less-ruined desserts in the back corner while Reuben covered for her.

Now that he saw her again, he realized she might even be a little afraid of him.

He hadn't been able to look at her. And Reuben hadn't looked at him. Until closing.

Jace felt a nudge on his shoulder and was startled to see the sacrament bread tray held out for him by a little boy whose family had taken up the rest of Jace's bench. He looked around at the bowed heads. When had they sung the sacrament song and said the sacrament prayer? Guilt washed over him, and he took the bread. The boy grinned and handed the tray back to his father.

Jace needed to snap out of it. The last thing he wanted was to look like a brokenhearted sap. He glanced over at Georgie. No, the last thing he wanted was for someone to be afraid of him.

After sacrament meeting, he considered going home. He watched Georgie out of the corner of his eye. She spoke to the women she'd come with, they hugged, and she left them, heading his way, watching the people and the floor in front of her. A member of the bishopric caught up to her and shook her hand, then asked her questions. Georgie answered with a small smile and gestured toward the women she'd left. He couldn't remember seeing her smile before, and he watched for the expression to reappear. There it was. It changed her whole mouth into something . . . worth watching. With the greeting done, the man moved on, and Georgie turned—to catch Jace staring.

He quickly looked away, but that was stupid, so he turned back. She stood frozen; he couldn't read her expression. She was much prettier than he remembered. Whisps of her honey-blonde hair fell softly around her face, and he noticed her blue eyes for the first time—like looking-at-the-earth-from-outer-space blue. But they weren't friendly.

He gave her a quick nod of recognition, and she blinked, then moved out through the chapel door.

Great.

He stood to follow her out, thinking that now would be a good time to apologize, but he felt a hand on his arm.

"Welcome. I'm Dar Silva, the ward clerk."

Jace took his hand. "Jace Lowe."

"What brings you here today, Jace?"

"I, uh, live on the island. I've been attending a ward in Seattle with . . . some friends . . . and thought it was time to come to my own ward."

The clerk looked at him a little harder. "Jace Lowe. Do we have your records? Are you here with the Burches, or . . . ?" He glanced at the couple who had occupied the rest of his bench during the meeting and who were now hurrying their kids to Primary classes.

"Um, no, to both questions."

"Well, where can we make a request to get your records here?" The man was friendly and only doing his calling. Jace imagined they didn't get many people moving into the ward.

"I gave my bishop in Seattle the information before I left."

"Good, that makes things easier. Where do you live?"

"Off West Camano Drive. I think we're neighbors."

Dar grinned broadly. "Fantastic. We'll have to come pay you a visit. You'll be coming here regularly now, right? Or . . . did you know we have a singles branch? They meet at one."

"Yeah, I know. But I think I'll be coming to this ward."

"Great." The man slapped Jace's arm. "Good to have you here. Sunday School meets in the gym."

Jace nodded and let Dar move on.

Jace walked down the hall and even peered into the gym, searching halfheartedly for the girl. With no luck, he pushed the glass door in the foyer open and walked outside. He breathed in the cool, wet air laced with the scent of pine and mulch he'd come to love. After a quick look around for any sign of her, he pulled his keys out of his pocket and fingered them. He spotted his bike, then dropped his head and took long strides in that direction.

* * *

Georgie sat in the car, her scriptures open on her lap. She'd begged off having to sit through Sunday School alone. It was ridiculous, she knew, but with Faye teaching a youth Sunday School class and Tru in the Nursery and even Uncle Dar taking his place in the clerk's office, Georgie didn't feel like sitting alone in a room full of strangers just yet. She promised to meet Faye in Relief Society for the third hour.

But she stared at a page, not reading. Seeing Peter & Andrew's sous-chef in her aunts' ward had thrown her. She never would have expected to see Jace Lowe here. He'd looked just as surprised to see her. She couldn't help but wonder why.

She'd learned the hard way that there were all kinds of people in the Church. Some had their own way of keeping the commandments, of interpreting the order of things and where they were placed in God's kingdom on earth, even judging the faults of those around them and making it their mission to "fix" what was imperfect. As if they knew what perfection was.

Ian Hudson had had his own way of making sure life around him was his definition of perfection.

A lump grew in her throat, and she realized her fists were clenched.

She had to stop this. She had to stop thinking about Ian and move forward. She was alive and had a new chance, and she had good people helping her. The accident had definitely changed her, and she wanted to move forward, stronger, but her progress stalled whenever she remembered Ian and then attached him to the events around her.

A movement in the parking lot caught her attention, and she pressed against her seat as Jace crossed the lot to his motorcycle. A motorcycle just like Ian's.

She wondered if Jace was an active member. He wasn't staying for the rest of the meetings. It didn't surprise her.

As his motorcycle growled away into traffic, she felt more guilt for judging him over leaving church early when she had wanted to do the same thing that morning. And now here she sat in the car skipping Sunday School and resenting judgmental people. People who would judge a person by their chosen mode of transportation. She rolled her eyes. This was the downside of the new Georgie: jumping to conclusions about things and people. The change was one of the main reasons she'd had to leave home. Too many people she loved were trying too hard to bring the old Georgie back, and she'd hurt them in her struggle to figure out who she was now. She'd had to go where no one knew her. Even her aunts hadn't really known who she was before. Her father was quite a bit younger than his sisters, and Georgie's interaction with them while she'd grown up had been rare. The Georgie they were getting to know was pretty much all they knew, and except for nudging her to go to church or a movie, they weren't trying to "fix" her. And she needed that.

She readjusted her scriptures on her lap and vowed to concentrate.

Chapter 3

"What do you mean 'somebody's coming over for dinner'?" Georgie tried to keep the distress out of her voice.

Faye tied her apron around her waist. "It's been three weeks since you've come to stay with us. You've said very little about what happened. I respect that and pray you'll be able to find peace here and that I'll be sensitive to your needs, but because you won't or can't talk about it, I have no idea how you're coming along, although I have to say you look improved. But Dar and I have a tradition of inviting people over for Sunday dinner, and, frankly, you're putting a crimp in our style."

Georgie's eyes grew wide with the idea of being such a disruption.

Faye smiled. She touched Georgie's hair. "I already have one recluse in this house. As much as I love my sister, it hurts to see her spirit and beauty holed away in her room or sat down in front of that TV. Now, she has her reasons, just like you do, but let me tell you right now that holing yourself up hurts nobody but yourself and those who are delighted by your presence."

Georgie looked down, but Faye lifted her chin. "I don't know if it's right to say, but the world does go on. Life goes on. You're alive. And by no small miracle."

"I know."

"I'm glad to hear it. But that doesn't explain why you went white as a sheet when I mentioned dinner guests."

Georgie hesitated and tried to gather the right words. "I . . . calling off the engagement, the accident, losing my memory . . . Meeting people brings questions, questions I don't have answers to. I feel like I'm in limbo, like a kid lost at a bus station. And I'm not sure how that comes across to strangers. I've gotten some odd looks at work."

Faye's brow wrinkled. "I do understand that in a way."

Georgie nodded. "It's a little better now, but those first weeks after the accident were kind of a nightmare, especially when I couldn't remember what had happened. All I knew was that I didn't want to be anywhere near my fiancé. Then he was . . . gone." She rubbed her forehead. "And now, so many things keep reminding me of Ian and how he made me feel. I want to move on, but his memory keeps dragging me back, and I can't shake it."

Faye patted Georgie's leg as they sat on the bed in silence. Finally, she spoke. "I can only imagine how confused you must be at times. Maybe you're reminded of him as you try to move on because you don't want to make the same mistakes again. It's a protection thing. But, honey, you live in a world full of people, good and bad. You can't hide from all of them. It's not fair to you, and it's not fair to them." She shook her head. "It's not what you're here for."

Georgie couldn't look away. A spark ignited in the empty space she felt inside. It wasn't that long ago when she thought she knew what she was here for. She missed that naïve certainty. A lot had happened since then. She had lost trust in herself—and in others. Even in the idea of falling in love, something she had always imagined would be definite and sure, like all those romance stories. But it wasn't definite. It could be frightening. Deceitful. In a world full of black and white, right and wrong, she'd found herself engulfed in gray.

It's not what you're here for.

Maybe Faye was right. Maybe thoughts of Ian kept haunting Georgie because she didn't want to lose herself like that again. Maybe it was a defense mechanism.

Faye looked at her. "You can't hide. Even on this secluded island."

Georgie took a deep breath and let it out, nodding. After another moment, she asked, "So, who's coming to dinner?"

Faye smiled and stood. "That's what I like to hear. I've invited the Gordons." Just as she left the room, she said, "They have a daughter—I believe she's sixteen—and a son about your age, fresh off his mission. Good looking too."

Georgie groaned and flopped back onto the bed. "Faaaaye." A setup?

"Oh, I know better than to push anything on you right now. Maybe later, but not right now." She winked. "Give your aunt a little credit. He's just a good kid. They both are. You need good people around to restore your faith in humanity."

Georgie pulled herself back up. "I guess I'm a little on the defensive side."

"I don't blame you. Will you be all right?"

She groaned. "They sound nice."

"Glad you approve. Now come help me with the salad."

Later, a couple about the same age as Georgie's parents followed Faye into the main room. George could hear Dar in the entry, still hanging up jackets and giving welcomes. She gave the salad a couple tosses and set the big bowl on the table, then slowly moved toward the group.

Faye began introductions. "Earl, Karen, this is my niece, Georgiana Tate. She's my baby brother's youngest. Georgie, meet the Gordons." Georgie stepped forward to shake their outstretched hands.

Earl Gordon shook her hand with confidence. "Georgiana? Or just Georgie?"

"Georgie is fine."

Karen reached for her hand. "Georgiana is a beautiful name. So old-fashioned."

Georgie smiled. The comments about her name were not the first, and she didn't mind responding. "I was named after my great-grandfather."

Earl wrinkled his shiny forehead. "His name was Georgiana?"

Georgie muffled a laugh.

A young man and woman stepped into the room, followed by Uncle Dar.

"Georgie," Faye said. "This is Tyler and Megan. Tyler just got home from his mission in Japan."

Tyler pushed his hand toward Georgie, and she took it. "Kobe, Japan. Nice to meet you, Georgie."

Georgie couldn't help recognizing the eager look in his eye, that gleam that said, "I'm looking for eternity. Could you be the one?" She'd seen that look a number of times from fresh-off-the-plane elders.

Before she could reply, Faye said, "Tyler gave the best talk last week. It's a shame you missed it, Georgie. The Spirit was so strong."

Tyler ducked his head. "Thanks, Sister Silva."

With his blond hair, deep brown eyes, and lingering missionary glow, Georgie guessed it wouldn't be long before Tyler Gordon found his eternity. He was undeniably adorable. With a jolt, he seemed to remember his sister. "This is Megan."

Megan smiled. "Nice to meet you. Please ignore my brother's stare. He's not used to being so close to pretty girls." She giggled.

"Thanks a lot, Megan." Tyler scratched his head. "Guess you'll be walking to work tomorrow."

Megan didn't look threatened at all.

She turned to Georgie. "I was telling my mom that you should volunteer at the hospital. You're not in school, right?"

Karen broke in. "Megan, that's not really the best way to approach somebody." She shook her head and looked apologetically at Georgie. "We were discussing the need for volunteers, and apparently she's not bashful about asking for them."

Megan shooed her mother aside. "My mom is a counselor, and I volunteer. And I think you should too." She grinned as though she'd asked Georgie to help her run a concession stand at the fair.

Georgie felt her own smile fading and her pulse quickening at the idea of being in a hospital again. "I don't know. I work most days at Peter & Andrew's."

"I love that place," Tyler said.

"But that's just afternoons and evenings, right?" Megan asked.

Karen put her hand on Megan's arm. "My goodness, Megan. Give the girl a moment to get to know us first."

How old had Faye said Megan was? Sixteen? Georgie could've easily considered Megan's forwardness obnoxious, but she reminded Georgie too much . . . of herself. Sixteen was a long time ago.

Thankfully Karen changed the subject. "Something smells wonderful, and I don't know about you, but I'm starving."

Tyler rubbed his hands together. "It does smell good. Is that pork chops?"

Faye beamed. "Yes, with mashed potatoes and gravy."

"Mmm-man I missed that smell. Japanese food is amazing, but I missed food from home. It's been one of the best parts of this week."

Faye grinned. "Everything is ready and waiting on the table."

Karen looked around. "Where is Tru?"

"She's in her room. She chose to eat earlier."

Dar motioned for everyone to sit down, and after they were all arranged, he blessed the food.

After the meal, they went for a walk along the rocky shoreline. Georgie, Megan, and Tyler walked together behind the older adults until Karen enlisted Megan in looking for white rocks. It was amusing but not surprising that Megan had led the conversation to that point. Tyler was walking two good arms' lengths away. That was fine with Georgie. He seemed to gain his confidence when others were around, but alone, well, they were both at a loss for words.

"What are your plans?" Georgie finally asked.

He seemed to appreciate the opening. "I have to find a job or two to save up. I'll be going to the Y in the fall. You've been there, right?"

Georgie nodded. "Yes. But I'm not sure I'll be going back."

"Why not?" His question was innocent, off-the-cuff. Still, Georgie flushed as she tried to find an answer.

"Because I was in a car wreck. I'm still recovering, actually, and I'm deciding what to do next." She drew her jacket around her. "But I don't think BYU is in my future."

A look of concern crossed Tyler's face.

"It's a wonderful campus," she said. "I loved my classes. And my roommates." She wasn't sure what more to say. It all sounded so superficial. "The accident was bad. My—a guy—died. It's complicated." The words had tumbled out in a pile of awkward oversharing.

Tyler slowed. "Oh, wow."

"Yeah. So I'm not sure what I'm doing yet." She gave him an encouraging smile. "You'll love it there."

He nodded and smiled back.

Megan moved in a zigzag ahead of them on the rocky beach. "Megan's probably happy to have you home."

He laughed. "She won't leave me alone. I was gone a long time, and a lot of things changed, but she's still the same old Megan. Still driving me crazy. I can't believe she's dating and driving and all that." He watched his sister hop up and down at something his mother said, grinning, hanging on her elbow. He took a deep breath and blew it out. "I have three older siblings, but ever since she could walk, you'd think she was the boss of all of us." Tyler chuckled.

Georgie grinned at that. Her brother, Deacon, had always called her Boss since they were little, even though he was older.

"Tyler!" Megan hurried to them. "Faye said Georgie hasn't been to Deception Pass yet, and you haven't been since you got home, so we should go together. I'll bring Brian." She grinned and took his hand, swinging it in both of hers. "It'll be a date."

The color left Tyler's face, and Georgie could only look between the two.

Tyler turned away from his sister and took a few mindless steps. "Aw, man, Megan." He gave Georgie a tortured look and scratched his head again. "See, she's still just . . ." He dropped his hand, and a small laugh escaped Georgie's lips. He straightened and faced her, his hands on his hips. "Um, Georgie? Would you like to go with me and my sister *and* Brian to Deception Pass sometime?"

"On Saturday," Megan interjected, practically bouncing with glee.

Tyler sighed, unsuccessfully trying to hide his smile, barely meeting Georgie's eyes. "On Saturday. It's always been one of our favorite places. And Megan's right; I haven't been since I got home."

Georgie looked at the pair, who waited for her response. Her hesitation was habitual. But she hadn't felt afraid of Tyler all evening. She nodded.

"Woohoo!" Megan spun around and ran back to her mom and the other adults. "Mom, it worked! Tyler has a date!"

Georgie again tried to hide her concern while Tyler looked like he wanted to hide under a rock.

He watched after his sister, his arms crossed over his chest. "Well, that was smooth. Very smooth."

Georgie nodded. "I've heard of Deception Pass. It's up at Whidbey Island, right?"

"Yes."

"Should be fun."

"Really? You're okay with it?"

"Sure." She was, kind of.

Tyler grinned and wrung his hands. "Great."

Georgie wished all men were as easy to read as Tyler. And she wished he didn't look quite so eager.

* * *

Jace wiped his hands on the bleach towel and hung his white chef's coat on a hook. It was time for his break, and he wanted to spend it outside. The clouds had broken up earlier that afternoon, and the sunset would be incredible. He pushed the back door open and walked to his bike, taking the seat far more comfortable than the concrete steps or the weathered old picnic table next to the employee parking. As he opened his water bottle, the back door opened again. He looked behind him.

"Hey." He turned back to the sunset.

"Hey." Mai stopped next to him.

"I'd offer you a seat, but my car only has one."

She smiled and playfully kicked a tire. "Compact."

"Mm-hm."

"Such a gentleman."

He shrugged.

"You doing better?"

He peered at her as he took another swallow. "Than what?"

"Than whatever that was last week."

He looked down, slowly twisting the cap back on the bottle. He shrugged again and looked up at the color slowly spreading across the sky, bouncing off scattered clouds. Three days had passed since Reuben had given him the ultimatum.

"Look, it's none of my business, but it's nice to have you back. At least some of you."

He glanced at her. "Thanks."

"You were pretty unbearable. I wondered if you'd started drinking."

He lifted his water bottle in a salute, and she laughed. She grew quiet, and they both watched the sky turn from orange to purple.

"You know, you were pretty hard on Georgie."

"I know."

"Well, you need to know."

He set his jaw. "I *do*."

Mai folded her arms. "Good." She raised her eyebrows, looking at him over her glasses.

"Great." Was she done yet?

"That just wasn't like you."

"I know."

"*She* doesn't know." She turned. "See ya back inside."

"Yup." He heard the door close, and then he growled, knowing what he had to do.

Once back inside, Jace continued to do his best to be positive. He could sense the staff breathing easier around him. The realization of the influence his mood had in the kitchen left him shaking his head at himself, vowing not to let his personal life affect his work again. He wasn't completely back to his old self, but the atmosphere in the kitchen encouraged him. He tried especially to ease any tension he had created between himself and the expediter.

The bread oven buzzed, and he looked around. Georgie had entered the fridge in the back, and the door had closed behind her. Jace reached for a bread spatula and began removing the loaves. He had enough time to slice a few up before he needed to turn his attention back to the grill. He placed the bread in baskets and wiped his hands before moving on. As he turned, he met Georgie, her tray filled with more loaves. She looked anxiously at the baskets of bread he'd just prepared. "I could have done that," she said.

"I had a minute. Here." He took her tray, sensing her pull away from him as he did. Sheesh, how hard had he been on her? He slid the loaves into the oven and stepped back. "There you go." He moved to the grill again, feeling the weight of that old warning: *You never get a second chance to make a first impression.*

* * *

Georgie twisted thin slices of lemon and laid them gently on the salmon steaks. A sprig of dill on each finished the plates. "Ten." The plates were picked up, and she reached for the last ticket on the cable with a sigh. Mondays were not particularly busy, but that made time go slower. "Crab cakes, the special, and a fettuccine." She pulled the squeeze bottle of chipotle aioli they served with the crab cakes closer and played with the spoon in the blue cheese crumbles. The bread was hot and ready in baskets, and the busboys had already closed down three areas out front.

Mai sauntered in with a dessert order. "Almost done. I love Mondays."

Georgie couldn't disagree. She checked the small dessert fridge up front and pulled out a slice of key lime pie. "I need a bread pudding for the oven."

"I'll get it," came a voice behind her.

Georgie turned. Jace was already walking to the big fridge to get the dessert. She looked at Mai, who seemed pleased.

"He's trying."

"Trying what?"

"To make it up to you."

Georgie flushed and looked down. "What do you mean?"

"Oh, come on. The way he's been acting was hard on all of us, but you got the brunt of it. I was worried you'd quit, and you can't do that because look how great you're doing."

"It's a slow day."

"Slow days are the best days to get the routine down, don't you think?"

Georgie conceded with a nod but glanced behind her. "You said, 'The way he's been acting.' He's not always like that?"

Mai frowned and opened her mouth to speak, but before she could say anything, Jace returned with a tray and slid the bread pudding into an oven, then placed a small tray of crab cakes in front of Georgie. Instead of leaving, he waited. "Well?"

With the realization that he was going to observe her work, Georgie tried not to flush as she reached for a clean plate and the aioli. She picked up the tongs on the tray.

"Aioli first." His tone was gentle and unnerving.

She bit her lip and set the tongs down. Of course she knew that. She took the bottle and squeezed the creamy red chipotle sauce in a generous swirl, then laced the edge of the plate. Her arm wavered, unsteady with nerves. The result wasn't perfect. She placed the golden cakes on the sauce, squeezed one more dollop of sauce on them, then arranged two green blades of chive and a twisted lemon slice on top.

He nodded and looked at Mai. "Make yourself useful."

Mai took the appetizers. "Careful, Jace. Your charm is showing."

He chuckled, but Georgie backed away, needing distance. She had braced herself for his criticism, and even though he'd approved, she still found her stomach in knots. "I'm taking some of these to the back." She gathered the small stainless-steel containers of ingredients that she wouldn't need anymore and walked away as quickly as she could without attracting attention. She reached the walk-in fridge, closed the door behind her, and gripped the handle. After a deep breath, she turned and began emptying carrot slices and cucumbers into plastic baggies. Her fingers trembled, and she exhaled in frustration.

Her mother's words came back to her. *He's a charmer, that one.* She poured croutons back into the larger container. Georgie shook her head. Here she was trying to recover, trying to trust people, and Jace had her on edge and second-guessing her every move, even when he was being nice. Just like Ian. She stacked empty pans and rested her head against her hands gripping the edge of the shelf, tired.

You live in a world full of people, good and bad, and you can't hide from all of them. She nearly laughed out loud at her recollection of Faye's words, here, hiding in an oversized refrigerator. She whispered the rest. "It's not what you're here for."

The door opened, and Reuben stepped back, his fist on his hip. "Do I need to bring a chair in here? Maybe some books?" He winked.

Georgie shook her head and shivered. "A space heater."

Reuben laughed.

She managed a smile. "I'm sorry. My mind wandered." She reached for the pans. "Did you need something in here?"

He shook his head. "Just you. To help close up tonight. Jace will show you how."

Any remaining warmth left her. "Oh." She stepped past him as he held the door open.

"John and Rhea will be closing the front. And Anders is here, of course. I've got to take off early."

She nodded. At least she wouldn't be alone with Jace. Really, everyone on shift stayed and took a job, but those assigned to close were the last to leave, making sure everything was in its place. She took the stacked pans to the station where Anders manned the giant sprayer suspended on a metal hose over a rinsing sink, and she stacked dishes into the stainless-steel commercial dishwasher. Reuben waved as he left, and the back door closed behind him. His departure left the kitchen feeling hollow.

Closing commenced before the last diners asked for their check. Georgie cleaned up her station and readied everything for the next day. The dishwashing station made the most noise at this point, with clanging and spraying, though as soon as the diners were gone, Caleb changed out the disc and fixed the music so it could be heard through the kitchen speakers too. The waiters counted up their tips, and the hostess closed out the cash register. Any leftover food was put in take-out boxes and offered to anyone who wanted it. Georgie usually brought something home for Tru.

"See you tomorrow," Mai called out as she tossed her apron in the laundry basket. Her wings were obscured completely by a bold black-and-purple plaid raincoat, and as she stepped out, she flipped her hood up. "And it's raining again. Hey, Jace, your bike's getting soaked."

"Aw, crap." Jace threw aside the spatula he was using to scrape down the grill, shoved the chef's coat onto a hook on the wall, and ran outside past Mai, who pressed herself against the doorframe to avoid being run over.

"You should have parked it under the eaves!" she called into the dark after him. Georgie heard a yell in reply, but it was muffled by distance and rain and the sounds of the kitchen. Mai turned to see Georgie watching. She grinned. "He usually parks it under the eaves. Looks like somebody will be driving home with a wet backside tonight." She raised her eyebrows mischievously and stepped out the door, closing it behind her.

Georgie waited another moment. She'd always gone home at this point of closing the restaurant down, heading out the door with the waiters and station cooks. She turned to the grill and picked up the spatula Jace had been using. The ice and water he had poured over the hot, flat surface had dissipated and left a swirl of simmering drippings and charred bits. She poured a little more ice from the pitcher and gently scraped the steaming mess toward the grease trough.

She heard the door open behind her. Jace came in soaking wet and grabbed a dry towel. He rubbed it over his head and arms and face, then tossed it in the laundry basket. He gave his hair a final shake and began moving in her direction, returning Anders's light jab to his arm with a smile.

She blinked away as his eyes met hers, then she stepped aside. "I wasn't sure what to do."

"You're doing great." He motioned for her to continue scraping. "Just don't force it."

She peeked at his dark curls falling forward over his brow, needing to read him somehow. Needing to read her own heart pounding with discomfort. She looked back at the grill and swallowed. "Why ice?"

"Minimizes steam burns. Straight water sends up a bunch of steam when it hits that hot surface. Ice mellows it a bit, brings down the temp sooner. Just don't use too much. You want a gradual cooldown. Make sense?"

She nodded and continued to scrape until the grill was clear, trying to ignore the tension his presence added. He poured vinegar onto a wad of paper towels and smoothed it over the surface. The pungent fumes stung her nostrils, and she turned her head. He immediately followed it by rubbing in a few drops of vegetable oil. "Now you know." He motioned to the next grill. "Let's do this one."

Georgie saw no trace of malice, no impatience in his manner, but she kept her guard up, saying little. As they worked on the next grill, the vacuum cleaner stopped its hum up front and John, the redhead, returned to the kitchen, stowing the vacuum in Reuben's office. Rhea appeared and dropped the bleach towels in their own laundry basket.

"Done up front." She traded her apron for a jacket and followed John out. "Don't have too much fun, you guys," she teased, opening an umbrella.

The door closed again. Anders leaned with his back against the now-empty sink. He was a lanky man with muscular, tattooed arms; blond, spiky hair; and a nose ring. Georgie had wondered what had led him to a dishwasher job, as she guessed he was several years older than she was, but he did his job well and was always quick to smile. "Do you want me to wait until this cycle is through, or . . . ?" He thumbed at the noisy dishwasher.

"Nah," Jace said. "Go ahead and take off. We'll finish up."

Georgie's heart pounded in her throat. Why had everyone finished their jobs so quickly? Didn't they know not to leave her alone with Jace after last week? What was wrong with these people?

Anders had already leapt for his jacket and was out the door in a flash. *I wish that were me.*

"So," Jace said, already wiping with vinegar, "after the grills, all we really have left are the counters and floors and getting the laundry going." He pulled back and motioned to her. "Go ahead and oil this while I wipe up, then we'll do floors. Broom or mop?"

He blinked, waiting, seemingly unaware of her discomfort, his hazel eyes wide and expectant. She swallowed and concentrated on the bottle of oil. "Broom."

"Great." He left her side, and she worked at taming her nerves as she rubbed oil into the black surface.

She had to get over this. What if Jace wasn't like Ian? What if he'd just had a bad week? Mai had said he'd had a bad breakup. He'd been impatient and short-tempered, but she hadn't seen that for a few days now. And the staff seemed to respond to the change immediately, without suspicion or intimidation.

Maybe she'd been wrong. *Wouldn't be the first time*, she thought bitterly.

After finishing the grill, she pushed the broom around and under, and he followed behind with the mop. She found a smaller broom and dust pan and swept up the debris. They worked in silence, except for the music, and though she preferred it, it seemed the longer they went without speaking, the more tension grew in the room. She washed up, and he finished switching the laundry, checking lights, and collecting the remaining garbage bags. She thought about slipping out, but his hands would be full when he took out the garbage, so she put the clean pots and pans away and returned a tray of clean glasses to their stack. Jace locked Reuben's office with his own key, pulled on his motorcycle jacket, then hefted the garbage bags, nodding at her as she held the door for him. His smile was gone.

* * *

Jace knew he had to apologize to Georgie, and there had been plenty of opportunities. She hadn't said much, but she'd worked hard. He had the feeling she was trying not to make him mad, and that made him feel pretty lousy. He had almost approached the subject a few times but had bitten it back, unsure how to start. Now, here she was holding the garbage bin lid up for him so he could toss in the bags. It was raining, it was time to go, and he didn't want to do this all over again tomorrow.

She closed the lid and wiped her hands on her black slacks.

"Uh, Georgie?"

She looked up at him in the dim light coming from the one street lamp behind the restaurant. The rain had turned to a drizzle, and everything was wet and cold. Her blue eyes were grayed, shaded by her jacket hood, but she seemed to be searching him, and he had to continue.

"I need to apologize." He wiped the dampness from his face. "I think I made your first weeks here . . . harder than they should have been." She looked down. "I'm usually not such a jerk. I've just"—he shook his head—"It doesn't matter. I'm sorry, and it won't happen again."

She bit her lips, still looking down. She nodded and raised her eyes, searching him again. Maybe he shouldn't have been surprised, but he saw doubt. She didn't believe him?

He breathed out a laugh. "Listen, I feel like you're actually kind of scared of me, and I really don't blame you, but I'd like to change that. What can I do?"

She looked like she wanted to say something but was trying really hard not to say it. Finally, she said, "You don't need to do anything." Then she turned away.

He couldn't leave it like this. He was trying. He reached for her arm. "Hey, wait—"

"Don't touch me!" With a wrench, she twisted violently from his touch, jumping away as if he'd struck her. He held up his hands in defense. Her reaction seemed to have startled her as much as it had him. She was holding her hands over her mouth, her eyes wide.

"Whoa," he said, trying to defuse the buzzing tension. "I wasn't going to hurt you."

She nodded, stepping back.

He stayed put. "Hey, I'm really sorry. I didn't know—"

"No." She was shaking her head now.

What had he done?

She continued to back away from him. "I'm sorry. Please, just . . . I'm sorry. Thank you."

She turned and walked quickly to her car. He stood, waiting as she fumbled with her keys and finally pulled out of the parking lot and down the hill.

It was funny how a drizzle could soak a person as thoroughly as a downpour. It took a little longer but left him as chilled to the bone.

Chapter 4

GEORGIE PULLED UP BEHIND FAYE and Dar's camper in the side driveway but let the engine run. She realized the radio was on and quickly turned off the annoying song, leaving her alone with the irregular patter of raindrops on her car and the swish-squeak of her windshield wipers. She sat staring at the Winnebego emblem lit up by her headlights.

Jace was not Ian. Jace was not Ian. Jace was *not* Ian. Right?

She reached her right hand to her left arm and held the place Jace had touched. The humiliation of her actions hit her with intensity, her face crumpled, and she dropped her head as a buried memory surfaced.

"I don't think we should get married," she'd said, her voice quivering. She'd said it right there as she and Ian had left his parents' house and walked down the long drive to his car parked farther down the street. "I'm sorry. It feels wrong. I want to be excited about it, like your sister up there at the house." They'd been to Ian's sister's wedding reception and had stayed later to help clean up. The cars that had once lined the drive were gone now. She'd considered what she was going to say to him all through the reception, and her resolve had only strengthened as she'd observed the people around her. Ian's family members were spirited people. The kind who said "Look at me" at every social opportunity. They could be fun, the life of the party, but at times she felt run over, manipulated, even patronized. And for a while now, Ian had been using those qualities against her, turning his "playful" cutting remarks on her in front of people *and* when they were alone. Deacon had witnessed it a couple of times. He'd wondered out loud why she just took it.

Georgie had defended Ian, but the look on Deacon's face had made her step back and see. She'd been cut down so subtly and so often that it was Ian she sought to please, and when he told her she'd never find anyone else as good as him, she believed him. She *believed* him.

And that look from Deacon had been enough to finally make her see that this was not a relationship she wanted to be in.

It was lousy timing, after the reception, but she couldn't keep her feelings hidden from Ian any longer.

"Ian, it was just too fast, and I think we want different things from a marriage. I've realized—"

He laughed. "Again? I knew I should have just taken you to Vegas." He pulled her close. "We want the same thing. Trust me." He kissed her, his hands roaming a little farther than usual.

She gently pushed him away and looked him in the eyes. "I don't like the way you treat me. I don't like the way you treat people."

His expression cooled. "Babe, everybody likes me. Do you know how much competition you have? How many girls are wishing they were you?"

She said nothing but thought she saw a trace of fear shadow his ever-present confidence.

"But I don't want them, do I? I want you."

"But I'm not sure I want you." The words were little more than a whisper.

She couldn't read his expression, but she thought she saw anger flash in his eyes. He laughed and nodded. After glancing around, he took her arm, and as they walked, his grip tightened. His fingers dug into her muscles.

"Ian, you're hurting me." She spoke quietly. Why? Why was she so quiet? He didn't seem to hear her. He was lifting her arm now, her weight, pulling her along. She could feel her blood pulse past his vise grip, the pain in her upper arm focused and intense, and her fingers began to feel fuzzy.

He opened the car door, released her arm, and motioned her in.

"Ian, I'm sorry. I had to tell you." The flesh of her arm burned. She pulled the ring off her finger and held it out to him, a little shaky but surer than ever.

He nodded, even a little contritely. He took the ring and looked at it. "You're tired." He lifted his gaze and touched her cheek. She stiffened. "You look tired," he said. "Let's get you home."

She sat in the passenger seat, and he shut the door.

And she knew. She knew she'd done the right thing. Only she should have waited. She should have waited to tell him. She should have gotten out of the car.

The memory darkened and slid into place in the shelves of her mind as she sat in the car in her aunts' driveway. Tears ran down her face as rain coursed down the car windows. She rubbed her arm. "Jace is not Ian. Jace is not Ian."

After she calmed herself, she turned off the car. She got out and numbly walked to the front door, wiping her face with the back of her hand. She closed the door behind her as quietly as she could, hoping the front room would be empty so she could just steal down the hall.

"Georgie-girl's home!"

Georgie kept her head down. "I'm not feeling well. I'm—" Her words stuck in her throat. She knew she looked horrible, but what bothered her more was that she didn't want to make her family worry about her, and she was going to fail.

Faye was already there, followed closely by Tru and Uncle Dar.

"Georgie? Honey, what's the matter? Here, let's sit down."

"No, no, please. I just want to go to my room." She felt the tears ready to return, and she really didn't want to get into that again. "I'm just tired."

The sisters glanced at each another. Tru put her hands on her hips. "Georgie, what happened?"

Faye handed her a tissue.

Dar adjusted his glasses. "You look spooked. Did something scare you?"

Georgie blinked at this entourage of well-intentioned custodians. But Dar's question reverberated through her soul. As did the answer. *Yes. Something scared me.*

She blew her nose in the tissue. "I think I have to quit my job."

"What?" Faye asked. "Why, honey?"

Georgie shook her head and attempted a laugh. "Because I'm so lame."

"Oh, now. Here." Faye put her arm around Georgie. "We'll get you back to your room. Tru? Could you make some of that chamomile tea?"

Faye handed her a clean tissue and led her down the hall to her bedroom. Georgie shook her head at how pathetic she must look to draw this much sympathy.

She wanted to crawl into the bed, all the way under the covers, and sink into the mattress. A little rabbit hole like the one Alice had fallen down, right in the middle of the bed. Wonderland sounded like cake to her at this point.

Faye sat her down, and Dar kept a protective distance.

"Does this involve somebody at work?"

Georgie took a deep, slow breath and let it out. "Kind of, I guess. I don't know."

Tru entered the room with a mug and a plate with a roll from dinner. "What did I miss?"

Faye gave her a shake of her head but turned expectantly to Georgie, as did the others.

Georgie blinked back at them and then burst out with a little laugh. Dar raised his eyebrows. Georgie let out another small burst and covered her mouth. "You're just all staring at me, and I'm so . . . so lame. I think maybe"—tears threatened again, but she pushed through them—"maybe I'm broken."

"Georgie, if you're broken, I'm shattered." Tru handed her the mug, and Georgie took it in both hands.

She gave a shake of her head, already feeling the mug's warm, calming influence. "Thank you."

"I put in honey and vanilla. I always make mine that way." Tru took a bite of the roll.

Georgie brought the mug up to her lips and carefully sipped. She nodded as she swallowed. "Thanks."

"You're welcome."

"Do you want to tell us what happened? Do you want us to leave you so you can call your mom?" Faye asked with quiet concern.

Georgie blinked at the worried expressions surrounding her.

Tru moved first. "Well, I'll go. *The Bachelor* is on. Let me know if you need anything."

Georgie nodded, attempting a smile.

Tru turned and left the room.

Dar lowered his tall figure in a crouch to look Georgie in the eyes. "You'd tell us if somebody hurt you, right? You've got people on your side."

Georgie nodded. Dar was only semiretired from his law firm. "It was a misunderstanding."

Dar looked in her eyes as if to confirm her honesty, then gave her shoulder a squeeze and leaned over to Faye and kissed the top of her head. "See you in a bit." He turned and left.

After a minute, Georgie looked down into her teacup. "You're all so good."

"We're family. Now, did you want to talk to your mom?"

Georgie shook her head. "It's late. She'll be asleep. I'll call her tomorrow." The truth was Georgie wasn't sure she could talk to her mother. Her mom always got so emotional and analytical at the same time, insisting it would be better for Georgie to come home. Georgie always found herself feeling protective of her own choices and ended up spinning their conversation into what she knew her mother would want to hear. She was too tired for that.

"Okay. Well . . ." Faye started to leave, but Georgie put her hand out. "Can we talk for a minute?"

Faye stilled, then settled into the space next to Georgie on the bed.

Georgie gripped the mug. "I think it might be easier to talk to you first. Maybe because you're a little bit more removed. Does that make sense?"

"Sure it does. To sort through it."

"Yes." She sighed, relieved her aunt understood. "Remember I told you I needed to figure things out so I can move on?"

Faye nodded.

"Well, tonight . . . someone showed me that all I've been doing is pretending to move on, pretending that if I try hard enough, it will go away, it will heal, that I will heal. But after tonight . . ." She looked up at the ceiling and let out a shaky breath. "After tonight I wonder if I'll ever be able to be myself again."

"Of course you will."

Georgie shook her head, flushing with shame. She took a sip of tea, and it was difficult to swallow.

"If you think it will help to talk, I can listen. It may be all I can do, but . . ."

Georgie nodded and sniffled. "I think it might. Help, I mean."

Faye reached for a blanket at the end of the bed and pulled it around Georgie's shoulders. "Whenever you're ready."

She blew out a soft breath. "You know we met at school. Ian and I. One of his roommates wanted to ask my roommate out, so we doubled. It was like the stupid, sappy, love-at-first-sight scene in the movies. He was this gorgeous older RM who was doing his roommate a favor, and I was the young sophomore thinking, 'Oh my gosh, I can't believe Ian Hudson is asking me out.' And then . . . he fell for me." Georgie lowered her eyes. "I really believe he did. You know how powerful that is, to have someone like that fall hard for you? It was intoxicating."

Faye nodded and rubbed Georgie's arm.

"Everything and everyone disappeared when I was with him, and he spent any free time making sure we were together. It was flattering . . . something from a book. The first few months were a dream. He met my family over Thanksgiving. His manners were perfect. He impressed the heck out of my parents. We had fun. I was so gone for him it was ridiculous."

"Mm, I remember your dad mentioning it on the phone."

Georgie nodded. "After we were back at school, he began saying things. He told me I was laughing too hard at his roommate's jokes, and when we'd walk on campus, he'd jerk my hand and ask me where I was looking. I didn't know what he meant, but I realized that if we were passing other guys, he would watch me to see if I was, I don't know, checking them out. I'd just be walking with him, enjoying the day and holding his hand, and then, *bam*, he'd jerk my hand and ask me where my eyes were. I laughed at first and told him that was ridiculous. That was a mistake. I started walking with my eyes down."

Faye shook her head. "You've always been so precocious. So confident. Even when you were little, your eyes were up, looking around you."

Georgie leaned her head to the side. She couldn't disagree. She remembered that little girl and, once again, couldn't connect the dots between that person and who she'd become with Ian. "I wasn't one of those girls, Faye, in need of authority or desperate for love. I have a good relationship with my dad. The guys I grew up with were my friends. I just didn't see it coming. I keep remembering my Mia Maid teacher drilling it into our heads to marry a *returned missionary*. To date a *returned missionary*. Why would I keep my guard up when his values and morals matched mine, right?" She shook her head. "I'd heard him teach, bear his testimony. It was beautiful." She reached for a pillow and rested it on her lap, absently running her fingers over the ruffled edge. She frowned. "He began insisting on driving me everywhere I had to be. He became very critical of how I looked, accusing me of trying to impress others. But in front of people, he was attentive and happy."

"Which was confusing to you, I bet."

She nodded. "And did I stand up for myself? Did I tell him he was making me uncomfortable? That he was going too far? That his distrust was nonsense because I could still get lost in his eyes when he gave me that look? No. No, I just started simplifying my makeup and what I wore. I didn't want him angry. I didn't want him to think I was trying to impress other people. I was in love with *him*. Or maybe I wanted him in love with me."

She took another swallow of her tea and shook her head. She couldn't stop now. She'd never been able to talk like this. Guilt over Ian's death had kept her quiet, but this part was real too. Overcoming this part had as much to do with healing as the accident did. He still had a hold on her. Why?

She brushed her hair behind her ear. "I became sensitive to Ian's rules, the things that upset him, and I molded myself around them to keep us happy." Georgie straightened up, her voice growing stronger. "And when he started talking about temples and kids and rings, something in me knew . . . I would hesitate."

That was it. That was the turning point. "He began to lose his temper more often. He'd always follow it with an apology, gentle hands, declarations of his inability to live without me. And I'd be caught between not liking who I saw and knowing I could change him. I'd turned into one of those girls— the girl who stayed because she knew she could change him. He needed me."

"It sounds to me like he needed to control something, and you were the one he chose."

Georgie shrugged, looking down at the mug in her hands. "I made it easy."

"Oh, Georgie, there are so many kinds of love. And facsimiles of it."

She nodded. "I haven't been able to remember the accident or what happened just before. But tonight . . . I remembered something."

Faye was quiet but asked, "Do you want to tell me what it was?"

Georgie set down the mug on the side table and folded her hands in her lap. "I knew I broke off our engagement that night, but I couldn't remember how it happened or how he reacted. He tried to hide it, or pretended to hide it, but he was angry. Really, *really* angry."

Faye tried to mask her concern. "Oh?"

Georgie nodded. "I never understood how women could stay with guys who are jerks. But I see it now. The world I was in with Ian was very small, very confining—and he made it so wonderful in the beginning. I felt like an animal in a very beautiful cage. And the more I obeyed his rules in order to remain in the cage with him, the more I believed I could be who he needed."

Faye shook her head. "What he needed was control. And the more you changed into a girl he could control, the more you were no longer that self-assured girl he was first attracted to. It's like removing a fish's fins and getting frustrated that it can't swim, so you remove its tail too. *Control* is the thing. People like that don't know love. Foolish boy."

Georgie considered her words. Faye might have just nailed it.

"But that's not all, is it?" Faye asked.

Georgie looked at her, fighting the tears welling up again. She shook her head.

Faye took her hand. "You didn't expect that foolish boy to die, did you?"

"No." She shook her head, pressing her lips together as if that would contain the hurt. She placed her hand over her mouth, and Faye squeezed her other hand. No. She hadn't expected Ian to die. She hadn't expected her decision to end their relationship like that.

"Would you consider talking to Karen Gordon?" Faye rubbed Georgie's arm. "She's a counselor at the hospital. Maybe she could recommend someone to talk to. A therapist?"

Georgie rubbed her hands over her face. "Maybe," she said.

She'd had a therapist during her initial recovery to help her sort out the physical and emotional results of her injuries. They'd worked on visualizing her memories as files on the shelves of her mind and putting things where they were supposed to go. The points of trauma, the things that were stuck, were in a large bin she'd labeled "Lost and Found."

Faye leaned over and kissed Georgie's temple. "Blaming yourself, blaming others . . . Sometimes I think we humans feel obligated to root out the source for every negative occurrence. Sometimes it's just action and natural consequence." She sighed. "I know that's easy to say." She smiled and lowered her voice. "But, Georgie, no matter what happened with Ian, you were meant for better things. No cages. If you believe that, there's plenty of hope." They were quiet for a moment, then Faye asked, "Now, what happened at work?"

Georgie's stomach knotted again at the mention of work. She shook her head. "I have to think about that for a while."

Faye put her arm around Georgie's shoulders, and they sat that way for several minutes. "Thank you for talking to me. You couldn't have paid me a higher compliment." Faye stood and walked to the door. Before she closed it, she turned. "You'll be all right, Georgie-girl. Give it time."

The door closed quietly.

The sound of a motorcycle roared down the street as Georgie curled up on the bed.

* * *

"Hey, Mom, sorry it's so late."

"No problem. What's up?"

Jace hesitated, hearing the fatigue in his mother's voice. But this couldn't wait. "I need to ask your advice. But first, Brenna and I broke up."

"What? What happened?"

Jace leaned back on the couch, and Kit joined him, resting his head on Jace's leg and blinking up at him. Jace rubbed the dog's neck. "Long story short, she dumped me for someone else, and they're getting married."

It took a moment for his mom to respond. He should have called earlier.

"I'm sorry, Jace. How are you holding up?"

"I'm fine. I'm not. Mom, something happened, and I have no idea why or how or—" He blew out a breath of frustration.

"Start at the beginning, please."

That was what he loved about his mom. She listened. His dad lectured and speculated and tried to finish Jace's sentences before they were finished, but his mom listened. Jace filled her in on the last few weeks' events. He got to the part where he was left stunned behind the restaurant.

"I rode around the island for a while, trying to figure things out. I really think she believed I was going to hurt her." He ran his hand over his face. "I don't know what to do."

"And you're sure you didn't pull her in a way she'd think was threatening?"

"No. I barely grazed her arm with my fingers when she turned. I was apologizing."

"What do you know about this girl?"

"I don't know anything, really. She's quiet. Kind of down."

"Is she one of those emo kids?"

"No, Mom." He had to smile. "She's just a nice girl who's scared of me. Actually, she's staying with some people in my ward."

"She's a member of the Church?"

"I don't know. I've been so wrapped up in my own problems I didn't even ask. But she seems normal. I mean, I guess if I had to describe her, I'd say she was . . . sad." Jace closed his eyes and rested his forehead on his hand. He remembered her eyes, searching, as if she wanted to know something.

"And she just moved to the island?"

"I think so."

"Well, maybe she's been through something."

"You think somehow I'm making it worse?"

"Could be."

He leaned forward, suddenly on edge. The possibility that Georgie might be recovering from something difficult had never occurred to him.

"There's a saying," his mom continued. "You never know about people. It's best to be kind because everyone is fighting some battle."

"Well, what do I do now? What about work tomorrow?"

"I'd say give her some space."

"It's a small kitchen."

"Well, don't push anything. Be as invisible as possible. I don't know; maybe you'll know better how to act by how she's acting."

"Mom, I hate that she's frightened of me. I'd never hurt a woman."

"I know that. It sounds like this goes deeper than your actions in the restaurant the last couple weeks. Just try to be yourself."

"Yeah, right."

"You know, you could always come home. I could use a fancy chef in the kitchen."

Jace rubbed his hand over his eyes. Leaving the family restaurant in Nevada had been a difficult decision, one Jace knew had hurt his father, though Liev Lowe would never admit it. "Mom, I'm here now. I need to be here." It sounded weak, but even if everything else in his life was up in the air, that wasn't. He hadn't considered leaving for a second.

"I know, Jace."

Whether she was being sincere or not, hearing her say it meant a lot.

"Your dad wants to talk to you. I love you."

"Love you too, Mom."

"Jace?"

"Hey, Dad."

"You gonna come to your sister's graduation?"

"Yeah, I'm trying to swing it."

"What kind of answer is that?"

Jace rubbed his eyes. "It's the answer I have right now."

"It means a lot to your sister."

"I know it does. I've talked to her. She knows I'll do my best."

He grunted. "Can I ask you a question?"

He sighed. "Shoot."

"Is it raining?"

Here we go. Jace pressed his lips into a thin line. "Yup."

"Thought so. Totally clear here. You should see the stars. You do remember what stars are, right?"

Jace forced a good-natured sigh. "Yeah, Dad, I remember stars. As a matter of fact, I saw an amazing sunset tonight. You know, Camano gets less rainfall than the surrounding areas." A fact the islanders were quite proud of.

"So if Seattle gets about three feet of rain every year, Camano gets what?"

Three feet of rain? Was it really that much? Jace blew out a breath. "Somewhat less than that."

His dad chuckled. "I'm just giving you a hard time."

"Yeah, I know." Giving Jace a hard time was a hobby of his dad's that had intensified since Jace had decided to serve a mission for the Church. His dad wasn't a member, and though he'd tried to be supportive of his only son giving up two years of college and time at the restaurant, he'd looked forward to Jace's coming home . . . and staying home. And that hadn't happened.

"How's it going at that four-star restaurant of yours?"

There it was. His dad liked to make it clear that he knew Peter & Andrew's was above the family diner and yet not quite the top. *You left for something better than what I had to offer, but it's not quite there, is it?* The diner had been given 3.75 stars. Not enough spread to make it worth leaving in his dad's eyes. Not enough spread to keep him away.

"It's great. I love it. I miss all of you." Jace had learned early how to diffuse his dad's attempts to get him fired up. He didn't always remember to apply it, but today he had other things on his mind, and even his dad couldn't trump them.

"Will we see you at the graduation?"

Jace closed his eyes. "I'll see you soon, Dad. Bye." He hung up the phone and fell back against the couch. He groaned and pushed away the mixture of guilt and insecurity that always gathered in a cloud above his head when he talked to his dad. He closed his eyes and refocused.

The talk with his mom had helped. Still, he kept replaying the scene behind the restaurant over and over, trying to figure out what he could have done or said differently. He pictured the time they'd spent closing up. Georgie had seemed to relax a bit as they'd worked, had even waited for him at the door.

It had to have been the apology. She didn't believe it. And then he'd reached for her arm.

He winced and let out more frustration, knowing sleep was not going to come easily tonight.

Chapter 5

THE NEXT MORNING, JACE AND Kit walked along the beach. The mist that would later burn away, if the weatherman was right, hung heavy and still in the air. Kit didn't have to run too far ahead before Jace lost sight of him. He could hear the dog, though, barking at a gull, scampering over rocks. He appeared again, panting, tail wagging. Jace tossed him a Nilla wafer, and the dog caught it and paused to crunch it thoroughly.

"Good morning."

Jace looked toward the water. A tall gentleman with a gray moustache approached him from a pile of crabbing baskets. He extended his hand, and Jace recognized him.

"Hey. Brother Silva." He shook the hand offered him.

"Just Dar. Jace, right?"

He nodded. "Right." He gestured to the dog busily sniffing the crab baskets. "This mongrel is Kit. Kit, get away from there."

"Oh, he can't do any harm. I'm just pullin' 'em in to put away. Had a nice catch this morning." He looked around. "So, you said you were on Camano Drive?" He patted Kit and gathered the ropes to the baskets.

"Yeah, just up there."

Dar turned and looked toward the mist-covered hill Jace pointed to. "Ah. Well, nice to have you in the neighborhood." Dar motioned Jace to walk with him. "And what do you do with your days?"

Jace smiled and shook his head. "Actually, I was just considering looking for something to fill my mornings. I'm a chef over at Peter & Andrew's. It's a lot of work, but my days are pretty empty now that I'm here on the island and not commuting."

Dar stopped and was now looking at him with interest. "No kidding. Well, I should have you cook up the crab. And I believe you know my niece."

Jace felt the blood drain away from his face. Dar didn't seem to notice.

"Georgiana has been working at Peter & Andrew's for a few weeks now."

Jace nodded, unsure of what to say. "Georgie is your niece?"

"Yup." Dar considered him for a moment while Jace shifted nervously and directed his attention to a piece of driftwood Kit was carrying in his mouth. "How long have you been at the restaurant?"

"A little over a year." Jace wrestled the stick from the dog and tossed it away.

"Can I ask you something, Jace?"

Jace turned his attention back to Dar. The man had set the baskets down and was rubbing the back of his neck, looking out over the water. Jace answered in spite of his desire to turn and walk away. "Sure."

"How well do you know my niece?"

"Not well at all."

"Hmm. And the staff? How is the work environment?"

"It's great. Pleasant. Occasional stress can"—Jace took a deep breath—"make things hard, but the staff is great." He knew he could say more. He should say more. "Georgie had a rough first week, but she's doing great."

Dar raised an eyebrow in Jace's direction.

"She'll get it down. Everyone likes her. Reuben is firm, but he's fair."

"That's your boss?"

Jace nodded and looked away. He felt he had no right to ask, but maybe if he knew a little more about Georgie, he could figure out how to fix what had happened.

"So has Georgie always lived with you, or . . . ?"

Dar shook his head. "Just came out a week before she started work at the restaurant. It's been years since she's been out here. I think the last time was . . . sixteen, seventeen years ago? She was just a little thing then."

"What brought her out here? School?"

"Nah, she's just been going through some tough times and needed to get away." That was all Dar offered.

"Will she stay long?"

Dar shrugged. "As long as she needs to. She seems to like being out here."

Jace nodded. "Good." Kit returned with the stick and dropped it on Jace's shoe. He picked it up. "Well, I better head back."

"You bet. Hey, we'll have to have you over sometime. Maybe for lunch. I'm semiretired and live in a house full of women. It would be nice to even things up a bit, if you know what I mean."

Jace smiled. "Three sisters. I'm in the middle."

"Oh, golly. You want to come join us today?"

Jace tapped his leg with the stick as Kit tried to get his teeth around it. "I better not. Another time, maybe." He swallowed and glanced up at the house he knew Dar was headed for.

"Count on it. Oh, hey, could you do me a favor?"

Jace looked out at the water. "Sure."

"Could you keep an eye on Georgiana for me at work? She's been going through a lot, and she just seems to be struggling a bit. It'd be nice to know she has a friend there."

Jace nodded. "You bet." He forced a smile and turned with a wave. He didn't remember much of the walk home. He was too preoccupied with the burning guilt in the pit of his stomach.

"Yoo-hoo, Jace."

Under the shared carport at the top of the stairs at her own side door stood Mrs. Feddler, his landlady, pulling him from his thoughts. She was a large woman and spent most of her days in a housecoat and slippers. Fortunately, she was an animal lover and had no problem letting Jace keep Kit. She had a yippy little Yorkie herself, which currently rested in her arms, wearing a pink bow. Pepper growled at Kit, who huffed apathetically and went to his water dish.

"Hush, Pepper. Jace, I was wondering if you'd given any more thought to my offer. I've had a few estimates by professionals, but the jobs are yours if you want them. Of course I can't pay you what I would pay a professional, but we can certainly make a deal with the rent. Spring is practically here, and, well, you know yourself how this place needs some sprucing up. If my Larry were still alive—hush, Pepper; stop that—well, keeping up the place was all him, wasn't it? And you said you knew a thing or two, am I right?"

"Yes, Mrs. Feddler." Growing up working at his dad's diner and helping at home had taught him many aspects of building repair and maintenance. But when Mrs. Feddler had approached him in the fall with an offer to do some home repair jobs, he'd been too busy in Seattle to commit to it. Now there wasn't much to keep him from taking the offer, and he could use the money off the rent. "I think I'll take you up on it."

"Oh, wonderful. I'll get you the list of projects. Now, there are some that can be started right away and some, like the exterior paint, that will have to wait until nicer weather. Wait right there."

She hurried back through her doorway. Jace looked around him with different eyes, noting the scraping that would need to be done on the trim and siding, the moss growing out over the edges of the rain gutters. He inhaled and blew out a long breath. Mrs. Fiddler reappeared with a substantial list.

"Now, as far as purchasing supplies, I'd appreciate it if you gave me a list of what was needed and an estimated cost, and then I'll give you the money you need. I think I remember you saying you don't do floors. Is that right?"

Jace nodded, taking the list she held out.

Clean out gutters
New toilet
New sink fixtures/showerhead
Paint inside and out
New shed . . .

Mrs. Feddler continued talking. "I'll have to make some calls about that, and don't worry about lighting. I'm still deciding. But the carpets are getting pretty worn. That green carpet was installed in 1977. Can you believe that?"

He could.

"Now, you can pick and choose in what order you want to tackle these, and I'll direct you in colors and whatnot, but I'll certainly consider your input. My husband had fairly good taste and was always good for helping me decide. He updated our apartment before he passed on, such a blessing—not him passing on, of course, but that he had the notion to update."

Jace hid a smile as he looked over the list. He nodded. "I'll get started in the next couple days."

"Wonderful. Now, please make yourself at home with the tool cabinet, and Larry always kept supplies, so check before you think you need to buy anything."

He glanced at the toppling pile of aging miscellaneous "supplies" in the corner of the carport. At least the tool cabinet looked like there was some order to it. "All right. Thanks."

"Oh, thank you, Jace. It's nice to have a strong young man in the apartment." She turned and sighed. "Not that the Richmans were bad tenants, mind you; they were wonderful. Such good friends. But not much help in the upkeep, being older, you know." She climbed the steps. "Although Mr. Richman did replace the towel bar Mrs. Richman grabbed when she slipped on the floor when she got out of the tub—that chrome towel bar next to the sink. June did not break her hip from that fall but did break it the following year stepping down those very steps. Then, after that, well, you know I worried about those steps being a hazard, but I don't have to worry about you, do I, Jace? No broken hips for you. Poor June though. Oh, I hope I never have to experience that injury. Tremendously painful. Enjoy your youth, Jace. Well"—she turned in the doorway, panting a little—"just let me know what you need."

"I will." He waved the list, and she nodded, saying something to Pepper about a snack, and closed the door.

He read the first item on the list.

Clean out gutters.

He groaned inwardly.

* * *

Using the long, tiny fork, Georgie extracted the meat from the cracked shell and dunked it in melted butter. Letting it drip once, she lifted the morsel to her mouth and chewed slowly. Warm butter dribbled down her chin as she swallowed. "Oh, this is so good."

Dai looked pleased and passed her a napkin.

"Would you like some lemon in your butter?" Faye pushed a bowl of lemon wedges in front of her, and Georgie squeezed one over her butter dish.

"Here, you need a few more legs on your plate." Tru dropped four more crab legs onto Georgie's full plate. "Nothing like crab legs and lots of melted butter to make you feel better."

A laugh escaped Georgie's lips, and she shook her head. It had been a good morning. The sun had burned off the pressing mist, and a blue sky had shone like it had just been created. Georgie had watched it for a good hour on the back porch, just soaking in sunshine.

There had been something freeing about the previous night. Horrible and freeing. She dreaded going back to work that evening, and there was an ever-present flutter in her stomach over it, but talking to Faye had strengthened her. And she was eating crab legs. She swallowed another bite. "You guys are spoiling me."

"Yes. And doing a bang-up job, if I do say so myself." Faye dipped her own forkful in butter. "A girl should be spoiled every so often. I think that's a commandment somewhere."

Tru snorted. "Yeah, right after the one about coveting thy neighbor's chocolate."

Georgie smiled. "I don't think that's how it goes."

"Thou shalt steal all thy neighbor's chocolate."

Georgie laughed at Tru, and Faye clapped her hands. "Speaking of chocolate, I made pudding."

"Don't let the neighbors see it." Tru cracked a crab leg open.

Dar's deep laughter rumbled through the kitchen. For the first time since arriving on Camano, Georgie felt . . . happy.

"This is why I came here." Georgie blinked as she looked at the faces around the table. "Thank you."

Faye beamed, and Tru frowned. "You came here to eat crab? Not that there's anything wrong with that."

Georgie grinned, picked up another crab leg, and grabbed the crab cracker. "That too."

Tru broke into a full smile.

After they'd significantly reduced the pile of crab legs and practically licked clean the butter dishes, Dar leaned back in his chair and stretched his arms. "I met someone you know on the beach this morning, Georgie, walking his dog. As coincidence would have it, he works at the restaurant *and* attends our ward."

Georgie slowly lowered her napkin, her pulse picking up speed.

"Jace Lowe. He says he's a chef."

The aunts were too busy clearing away empty shells and lemon rinds to notice what must have been an obvious change in her countenance. Dar, however, was watching her closely. She sucked in a breath and nodded, hoping she looked interested instead of mortified. She already felt the heat in her face though. Hot spots.

She kept her eyes wide with wonder. "Oh. He was walking here? On your beach?"

"Well, I've never claimed it as our beach, though Tru would argue otherwise, very loudly if motivated." Tru shot him a look. "And technically it is our property to the buoys, but yes, he was walking. On my beach." Dar winked at her, and she gave him a small smile. "Seems like a nice enough fella. I told him he needed to come around sometime and feast with us."

Georgie looked down. "What did he say?"

"He said he'd rather be boiled in lobster bisque."

Georgie jerked her head up, but her uncle was already laughing at his own joke. "I gotcha. Did you see that, Tru?"

Georgie breathed out, trying to enjoy his humor. It wasn't working.

Tru answered dryly. "Go easy, mister. You'll scare the girl, trying to be so funny."

Georgie laughed weakly as she watched her hands.

"We'll have to have him over sometime," Dar continued. "You should see that dog. Never seen so many colors on one animal." He shook his head and pushed himself back from the table. "Anyhow, I asked him to keep an eye out for you at work, just to—"

"You *what*?" Now her eyes were wide in genuine horror.

Dar paused. "Well . . ." He looked at Faye, who had turned at Georgie's outburst, and quickly returned to his reserved self. "I just thought . . ."

Georgie tried to recover quickly. "It's fine."

"Georgie?" Faye wore that concerned look Georgie was beginning to know too well.

"Oh, no. It's fine. I just . . ." Georgie wrung her napkin under the table and swallowed. "I just don't want you to think I need supervision or anything like that." She tried to keep her voice steady. "I mean, I know after last night, well, that was just a little bit of a setback, but"—she scooted her chair back and picked up her plate—"I feel better today." She reached for her water glass but knocked it over with shaking hands. She hurried to pick it up, grateful it only held melting ice. Only it slipped out of her fingertips again, and she struggled to pick it up, scooping the spilled ice back into the glass.

Tru watched her. "Oh, yeah, you're *perfectly* fine."

Georgie couldn't stop the laugh that bubbled up, and as the others joined her, it grew until she had to sit back down. She shook her head. "I'm losing it." It wasn't just the humor of her clumsiness, she knew, that had her on the edge of hysterics. It was also the fear of what could be waiting at work when she had to face Jace, on top of everything else.

Activity picked up again, and after the kitchen was clean, Georgie excused herself to go lie down before work. She had little hope of sleeping with all the thoughts racing through her mind.

Just as she kicked off her shoes, her phone rang, and she checked the number.

Her brother.

"Deacon?"

"Hey, how's my sister holding up?"

"Hang on; let me ask her." Georgie paused, settling in against the pillows and sighing. "Beautifully. Except she seems to be suffering from a dual-personality disorder. And a severe case of overreacting."

"Uh-oh. What happened?"

She rolled her eyes. "Nothing. How are you?"

"Nope, not getting off that easy." He persisted in his light tone, and she knew this was a 'cheer up' call. "Your words are coming faster. That's something good."

"Yeah, I guess they are. It's still hard sometimes though."

"How are the headaches?"

"I don't get them as often."

"So, *how* are you doing?"

She hesitated, not knowing how to answer.

He returned to specifics. "How's work?"

"Work is fine."

"Fine?"

"Everyone is very nice." She pulled at her ponytail and absently examined the ends of her hair.

"Fine and nice?"

She gave up. "Yes. Only . . . there's this guy—"

"A *guy*?"

She rolled her eyes again. "Yes. He's the sous-chef—"

"*Sous*-chef?"

"Deacon, are you going to keep doing that?"

"Sorry."

"He's the assistant chef. Second in command."

"Like Spock."

She made an exasperated sound. She really didn't need her older brother's attempt to make her laugh with his geek humor. "Yes, Deacon, if the restaurant were the USS *Enterprise*, he would be Spock." She ignored his muffled laughter. "It's a wonder you're single."

"Spock is awesome. Is *your* Spock awesome?"

"He is *not* my Spock. He isn't *Spock*. He's just this *guy*, and I can't figure out if he . . . if he's good or bad or if I'll spend the rest of my life afraid of what I don't know or what I'm susceptible to because I can't seem to trust my own instincts or see what is real or what is . . . my own paranoia." She swallowed and rubbed her hand over her pounding heart. "Not that I'm even remotely interested in this guy or any guy or . . ." She trailed off.

Deacon let her breathe a minute. When he spoke again, his tone was more subdued. "Is this guy . . . pursuing you?"

"No. No, not at all. Are you kidding? I'm a basket case." Deacon made a sound to argue, but Georgie continued. "It's just . . . he tried to apologize for something, and I went completely psycho on him. I mean, it was nothing, it was so nothing, and I freaked out. It was like he was Ian and—"

"Whoa, what?"

How did she explain that? "He just did something that reminded me of Ian, and I flipped out. It triggered a repressed memory of the night of the accident. It scared me."

"What was the memory?"

Georgie pulled out the newly filed memory in her head and explained the scene to Deacon.

After she finished, Deacon was silent for a few seconds. "That's . . . a really crucial memory, Georgie."

"It wasn't pleasant. And I think when Jace touched my arm, I wanted to fight back. Because I didn't before."

"I think you're right, but that wasn't my point. Ian was that angry and physically hurting you? I knew he was a jerk, but this . . . Did you remember any more?"

"No."

"Hmm. Well, keep me posted if you do. Putting what happened that night together might help you bring some closure to this."

She shuddered. "Yeah, maybe. It would be nice if I didn't freak out whenever someone reached for me."

He paused. "Georgie, is this sous-chef guy really bothering you? Because you can find another job. I can call your boss. Uncle Dar could—"

"No."

"No?"

"No. It's me." She took a deep breath and blew it out. "He looked just as startled as I was. That was definitely *not* like Ian." She remembered Jace's expression. He hadn't meant her any harm. "Faye suggested I get some counseling. But I'm not sure. I'm not sure about a lot of things."

"That's not a bad idea."

"Yeah, I know."

"I'm trying to work out when I can come spend some time over there."

She couldn't help smiling. "That would really be great, Deacon. Thanks."

"Sure. Do you still believe the island is the best place for you right now?"

"Yes."

"That sounds pretty solid. I thought you weren't sure about anything?"

"I said I wasn't sure about a lot of things." The island felt safer than any other real option she had. "They're taking good care of me."

"Okay, then. I'm praying for you, sis."

Georgie was struck with a sudden longing for home. For Sunday night board games and caramel popcorn and family walks. "Thank you, Deacon. Do me a favor? When you talk to Mom, tell her I'm really doing well, okay? She'll believe you."

"And would that be the truth?"

She couldn't answer him.

"Well, tell Spock to be careful, 'cause you know I've got my phaser set on stun."

Georgie smiled.

"And give the aunts a hug for me."

"I will."

As she hung up the phone, she closed her eyes and rubbed her head. The headache was back. Her stomach was in knots all over again, and the clock told her she had one hour until her shift started.

Please, just let me sleep.

Chapter 6

JACE GLANCED AT THE CLOCK on the wall, then at the back door. Again he took in the expediter's organized station and the empty garnish trays. Again he fought the urge to fill them all and get the dressings ready. But he was supposed to become invisible. He glanced at the clock again. Georgie was late, and he tried to keep himself from guessing that maybe she'd quit. Reuben hadn't said as much, but he wasn't one to make those announcements. Still, he would have told Jace.

The restaurant hadn't opened for business yet, but prep was well underway, and Georgie had only a few more minutes to show before salads and soups would need dishing up, not to mention the bread ovens were already fired up and baking the first batch. He kept himself from going back to Reuben's office and asking for her phone number. He somehow felt responsible for her job or her quitting, if she had. But how invisible would that be? He tapped the counter, staring at the stainless-steel containers, willing them to fill themselves. If she didn't show, the job would be his again.

"Ah, forget it." He reached for a tray and grabbed a few containers.

"Hey, Georgie." He froze when he heard Caleb's greeting, then shoved the containers back, left the tray, and thought invisible thoughts as he turned to the grills and twisted the knobs, adjusted the heat, and inspected the spatula. And yet relief washed through him.

She hadn't quit. Or maybe she was coming to work to quit. His stomach tightened again, and as she approached her station, he held very still. She quietly collected her containers and took the tray back to the walk-in.

She wore a white blouse and the required black slacks. She'd tied her apron on. She was staying. He blew out a breath and checked his oil and seasonings and asked Haru to bring out more house fries.

Just cook, he told himself.

The evening progressed without too much difficulty. Jace found that if he imagined a bubble around Georgie and he stayed outside it, he was still able to attend to his duties and maneuver around the stoves and the pick-up counter. He avoided eye contact at all costs but couldn't help the few times when he needed something quickly and the only thing to do was ask, quietly and without malice.

He had purposely removed her name from the closing crew for the next few days. Reuben hadn't questioned it. Now all he could do was take his mom's advice and judge how to act by how Georgie acted. And just maybe things might get back to normal in the kitchen.

* * *

As the week wore on, Reuben remained up front more frequently, providing Jace with the space he needed to give Georgie. And it seemed to be working. Instead of the anxious newbie she'd been, Georgie was steadily blending in with the staff, becoming part of the choreographed chaos of the restaurant kitchen. She even seemed to enjoy her role of keeping things organized between kitchen and dining room. He had to admit, she was good at it.

He still caught glimpses of her nerves around him and couldn't help the way she flushed when he had to address her directly. A couple of times he had to stop himself from putting a hand on her arm just to reassure her. Definitely a wrong move. At times she seemed like a frightened little girl, and then there were other times . . . a look, something in her posture . . . and she wasn't a little girl.

Jace had plenty of opportunity to ponder all this in the mornings as he cleared out the rain gutters on the duplex. It was a messy, tedious job, and he wondered more than a couple of times how much it would cost to replace the entire system. He'd had no idea dandelions could grow in rain gutters. Kit kept him company, loyally stretching out on the ground beneath wherever Jace worked, rain or shine, and Jace tried not to hit him with clumps of moss and molded leaves as he threw them down.

"Kit," he said as he flung what looked like a mushroom down to the sidewalk leading to the front door and wiped his work gloves on his pants, "you're lucky to be a dog." Kit reached down and licked himself, then rolled over.

Jace brushed a mixture of sweat and mist off his brow and glanced down the hill at one house in particular. The movement of a wheelbarrow being pushed to the front flowerbeds of the house drew his eye, and before he looked away, Georgie came out to join one of her aunts. She wore a wide-brimmed hat, jeans, and gardening gloves, but he easily recognized the way she held herself. They were planting flowers. Georgie knelt down on the wet grass next to her aunt, the soles of her shoes slightly angled as she rested on them.

Kit barked. Jace scowled at him and turned back to the gutters. "Easy for you to say." He scraped the putty knife along the insides of the now-clear section he'd been working on. "You wouldn't know a nice-looking pair of jeans from a mailbox."

* * *

"Georgie, can you answer that? I've got my hands all tied up in these biscuits."

Georgie hurried to take off her gardening gloves, slip off her shoes, and pad across the front room to the landline phone near the bar. The house was filled with the aroma of Tru's chicken soup. "Hello?"

"Hi, Georgie? It's Tyler. Gordon."

"Hi, Tyler."

"Hi. I'm calling to see if Saturday is still okay for Deception Pass. The weather is supposed to be pretty good. Can we pick you up at eleven? I guess we're bringing a picnic."

A small knot tightened in her stomach. The date. "Sure. Can I bring something?"

"We're just doing sandwiches and chips and stuff. Hang on." He covered the phone and asked if she should bring something. "Megan suggested a dessert. Nothing fancy. Would that be all right?"

"Sure." Dessert. Cookies were dessert, right? "How's the job hunt?"

"I found one," he replied enthusiastically.

"Great. Where?"

"At the restaurant."

"What restaurant?"

"Peter & Andrew's. *Your* restaurant."

She heard the anticipation in his voice, but for some reason the news made her sit down on the barstool, and all she could do for a moment was twirl the spiral phone cord hard in her fingers. "Oh, that's great. I didn't know they had an opening."

"Yeah, they needed a dishwasher." His enthusiasm faded at the word *dishwasher*. "But it'll be good because I need to find a second job, and the hours will help with that."

Georgie wondered what had happened to Anders. Maybe Reuben just thought they needed a second dishwasher. "When do you start?"

"Next week."

Confused by her relief that he wouldn't start for several more days, she brightened her voice. "Well, congratulations. And I guess I'll see you on Saturday."

"You bet."

When she hung up, she sat still for several minutes. She didn't even really know Tyler. Why should his working at the restaurant make her feel so . . . She shook her head.

"You all right?"

She sat up and turned on the stool to face Tru. "Yeah, I guess. Tyler got a job at the restaurant."

"That bothers you."

"It shouldn't." She frowned.

"But it does."

Georgie nodded. Tru gave a sympathetic cluck of her tongue and slid a tray of biscuits into the oven. "Tyler's a good boy. I'm sure it'll be fine."

"I know. I know. I just . . ."

"Feeling a little like it's *your* place?"

Georgie looked at her aunt. She nodded. "I think that's it. And there's absolutely no justification for feeling that way."

"No." Tru wasn't looking at her, just steadily cutting out circles of rich dough and placing them on the tray. "But you've come here as a kind of safe place. Then you got a job at the restaurant. A little hard at first, but it's working out, right?"

Georgie nodded, listening for the insight this puzzle of a woman had to offer.

"It's become part of your safe place. The place you've let into your life after whatever trouble you've had. You know the people there, trust them enough to keep going there every day, right?"

An image of Jace flashed before her eyes, and Georgie could see where she was going. "And part of me feels Tyler's going to endanger that."

Tru nodded with feeling, still working with the dough, lips pressed in a firm line. She said nothing more, just finished the last of the biscuits and set the tray on the stove to wait for the others to be done. Looking fatigued, Tru washed her hands and dried them and, on her way out of the kitchen, said, "Tell Faye dinner will be ready in twenty minutes. I'm going to lie down."

Georgie said she would but sat looking after her aunt, realizing she understood the woman much more than she thought. And Tru probably understood Georgie as well.

And she couldn't help wondering if her coming to stay here had ever felt like a threat to Tru's safe place. And if it had, the woman had been very gracious.

* * *

Georgie looked down at the text on her phone.

Deacon: *This will be good. Just breathe.*

Georgie sat waiting in a small office that may have been larger except for the shelves lining two walls filled with books, binders, and framed photos. Crayon drawings and notes covered a bulletin board. A poster advertising a tulip festival hung above another kids' table, which was stacked with Dr. Seuss books and a small bin of Lego toys.

Laurel Cruz entered with a smile. "I work with a lot of children," she explained as she took the seat next to Georgie, ignoring the comfortable office chair behind the desk.

"Your therapist in Idaho Falls sent me your file, so thank you for signing the release for those. It was very helpful to see where you've come from. Trauma in any form can be difficult to overcome, but it can be overcome." She pulled a notepad from the desk and clicked a pen. She crossed her legs and sat back with an encouraging smile. "What would you like to accomplish here, Georgie?" Laurel watched her with kind, steady eyes.

Georgie knew she had an answer to this question, but she struggled to find it. *I want the old me back* seemed trite. Maturity told her that wasn't how things worked. *I want to start over* wasn't right either. "I want to move forward," she said. "I want to feel connected to myself."

"Those are good answers. How are you feeling disconnected?"

She played at a loose thread in the seam of her pants. "I feel like there are new things I don't know about myself, and they're as strange as the hole in my memories, and instead of being inside my head looking out, I'm watching myself from the outside. I'm not sure where I'm going anymore. I'm not sure why . . ." She paused, willing herself to rein in her emotions. "Why things ended up the way they did."

"Sounds like reconnection is a good goal. Did this disruption begin with your car accident?"

Slowly, Georgie shook her head. "It began when I met a boy."

* * *

Friday came quickly and was as busy and frantic as usual.

Jace turned his head in Georgie's direction. "That sirloin on eight was smothered, right?"

Georgie nodded.

He threw mushrooms and onions onto the grill next to the steak.

"Thirteen's up. And seven's about ready," she announced to the waiters.

Jace glanced up, catching Rhea smiling at John as they approached the window to collect their orders. John whispered something quickly in her ear before they each picked up their trays, and she laughed, bumping him with her elbow. Rhea left first as Georgie finished with the cups of tartar sauce and butter, and John watched her walk away out of the corner of his eye. He turned and caught Jace watching. Jace raised his eyebrows, and John stood up straight, covering his smile.

"John, you're set."

"Thanks, Georgie." John gave another nervous glance toward Jace.

Jace smiled and focused on the grill again, turning the pile of mushrooms with one flip. He shook his head, piled the steak and toppings onto a plate, and turned to find Georgie watching him. In one movement, she looked away, and he stepped around her to take another look at the next order up.

John and Rhea. Well, it wouldn't be the first time staffers had paired up in the restaurant. He just hoped they could handle everything that went with it. There was enough tension in this kitchen already. The bread oven buzzed, and Georgie turned her attention to removing the loaves, her ponytail swaying and bouncing as she moved.

He blinked, snapping out of his thoughts. "Haru, is that lobster ready?"

He picked up the pan of cream sauce Caleb had started for him and whisked it with energy. He slowly poured a thin stream into a pot of the simmering lobster stock he made twice a week and moved his whisk to the pot, incorporating the cream to make the base for the bisque. Jace grabbed a tasting spoon, sampled the soup, and tossed the spoon into the dirty-spoon bucket under the counter. He threw in a fistful of salt and a pinch of white pepper. Haru came over with a bowl of freshly cracked lobster meat, and as Jace whisked the thickening bisque, Haru added the lobster, sprinkling in a handful at a time. Another taste and the pot was headed for the warming tray at Georgie's station.

She turned and reached for a clean ladle with an empty bowl in her hand but paused, giving Jace space. He backed away, remembering the spilled bisque, and he couldn't help but think he saw color creeping into her cheeks and a hint of a smile. He also wasn't sure what to think of the small skip of his heartbeat as he set the bisque down. Frowning, he gave orders for the seared scallops and started two swordfish on the grill.

Behind him, Mai asked, "Are the crab cakes ready for table nineteen?"

He gasped and quickly jumped to the fryers, hoping they weren't overdone. But Georgie was there first, tapping a cake gently against the basket, the last drips of oil falling back into the fryer. She'd turned at his hasty movement, and he forgot to keep his eyes down. There she was, her tongs gripping a crab cake, her ocean-blue eyes locked on his.

His mind cried out, *Look away! Be invisible, remember?* And the more he thought it, the more he couldn't do it. As long as she held him with her unreadable expression, he had to let her look, let her search and find what he needed her to know.

That he was safe.

But her flush grew, and she blinked. The cake slipped from her tongs back into the oil as she gasped.

"It's okay. Here." Against everything he'd vowed before he stepped into the kitchen each day since that night behind the restaurant, he stepped forward and took the same handle she held and rested the basket on the hook above the oil. He felt her watching, his hand resting against hers, his heart about ready to pound out of his chest. "Did you get splashed?"

She shook her head.

He rescued the dropped crab cake. "Not even broken, see?" He felt her nod as she quickly pulled her hand away from his, and he caught a whiff of something fresh and sweet. Oranges? He turned, but she'd already gone after a plate. Her hair was a swirl of varying shades of soft pale gold, and he caught himself wondering what it would look like down.

He cleared his throat when she held the plate of the other cakes out to him. He placed the escaped cake with the others, and Georgie moved away to her station, but not before he heard her, though barely.

"Thank you."

He finally breathed.

He turned, fighting the urge to smile, and went back to work. "Caleb, where's that reduction?"

* * *

Georgie wiped down the counters with bleach water, trying not to look like she was listening in on the conversation taking place over at the grills. It was her first night to close since Tuesday, the night she'd made a complete fool of herself. It was down to her, Jace, and John, who was covering as dishwasher for closing. He was obviously done with the dishes.

Jace cleaned one of the grills. "Have you taken her out yet?"

Georgie peeked at John, who leaned against the protective bar in front of the grill's surface, his arms crossed. "That's just it, man. Every time I think I should ask, I clam up. Like an idiot."

Rhea wasn't assigned closing tonight, and Georgie had noticed the shy way she'd said good night to John, lingering long enough for him to say something more than "See ya tomorrow." It hadn't come, but she'd still left with her broad grin, her eyes bright against her cocoa skin, and a wave to everyone. Georgie had remembered that giddy feeling that had come with wondering when, not if, the guy would ask.

"Sometimes you've just got to man up and blurt it out. *Rhea, you wanna go to a movie?*"

"Yeah, I know, but," John's leg bounced, "she's so . . . so . . . I don't know, smooth. And I'm a . . ."

"A clam."

"No—"

"An idiot."

"*Dude.*"

Georgie smiled and took the towel to the basket.

As she turned to get the broom, John stopped her. "Hey, Georgie, you're a girl."

She paused. "I am."

"Yeah. So what do you think?"

She'd liked believing they didn't know she was listening. "Um, about what?"

Jace turned away and continued cleaning the grill.

"How do you like to be asked out on a first date?"

"Oh." Georgie dropped her eyes. "I don't think I'm the best person to be answering that right now."

"Why not? I'm dying here. It's *Rhea*."

Jace cleared his throat, looking sideways at John and, to Georgie's surprise, shook his head.

John wasn't going for subtleties. "What? Like you're a lot of help?" He turned back to Georgie. "What do you think?"

But Georgie was still trying to read Jace's attempt to keep John from questioning her.

"Is it that bad?" John asked.

Georgie blinked and focused on John. "*No*. No, I just . . . The timing isn't great." How could she give advice about something she'd lost faith in?

"You think I should wait?"

"No, that's not what I meant. I meant I'm just not—" *Why* was this so hard?

He looked ill. "I'm making a fool of myself, aren't I?"

"No, not at all. I just don't think . . . that I—"

"Maybe Georgie's uncomfortable giving you an answer," Jace broke in. John and Georgie looked at Jace.

"Why? What is Rhea gonna say?" John turned to Georgie. "What do you know? Oh, man, she totally hates me, doesn't she?" John pushed his hands through his red hair and began pacing. "I *am* an idiot."

"What do you mean uncomfortable?" Georgie watched Jace, waiting for an answer that didn't include the words *insane* or *unbalanced*.

Jace shifted nervously. "You just seemed to struggle, that's all. You know what? You can go home if you want. You've done a lot. John and I can finish up."

"Why would I go home?" She looked around, knowing what was left. "There's plenty to do still."

"Wouldn't you like to go home?"

She straightened up. He had somehow touched a nerve. "Only after I've done my job here." She wasn't going to have another meltdown, if that was what he thought.

"Well, you can leave now, if that's more comfortable for you. It's no problem." He poured vinegar on a wad of paper towels and turned away.

The image of her overreaction the other night pained her, but it bolstered her determination to fight her insecurities and whatever prejudices she had assigned to Jace. The more she was around him, the more she realized how out-of-control her fears had become and how she couldn't let them paralyze her.

"I'll sweep." She glanced over at John, who had his hand over his face, mumbling something about "goddess" and "What was I thinking?" Georgie took a deep breath. "After I fix that." She walked over to John and folded her arms. "John."

He turned in her direction, worried.

"I'm sorry. I don't know how Rhea feels about you, but I can guess." His brows rose.

"I don't think she'd mind at all if you asked her out."

"Really?"

"Really. And Jace is right." Confidence raised its weary head. "Just ask her out. Be yourself. Don't worry about looking a little nervous; some girls like that. But just . . . be real." She nodded as his expression changed to a look of hope. "Be. Real."

John smiled. "I can do that."

She smiled back and left for the broom closet but then turned. "Oh, and if you want to wow her just a bit, you know, be *smooth*, find out her favorite flower, and then give her one when you ask her out."

John became serious. "Okay. Um, just one?"

"Just one. One you can hand her. Trust me." She quickly retrieved the broom and began sweeping. It was her mother's story, and she'd heard it since she was a little girl. Her father had asked her mother's roommate to find out what her favorite flower was. Her mother said the single sprig of lilac had melted her right on the spot. Her father always said he was lucky it was spring when he asked her out.

She hadn't thought of that story in a long time. She swept the debris into the dustpan. Ian had given her so many bouquets of roses. Too many.

She turned from the garbage can and jumped when she found Jace a foot from her.

He stepped back, a sudden look of concern on his face. He swallowed. "Sorry. I just needed to get the mop. You really can go home now if you want. John and I will finish up."

She nodded and raised her eyes. He looked cautious, probably afraid she'd go mental on him again. "Thanks." She tried to convey sanity.

She put the broom and dustpan away, then stopped in the bathroom to wash her hands. She reached back to pull out the band holding her ponytail in and sighed as she rubbed her scalp where her hair had been pulled tight. Her fingers moved to her temples, and she wished the headache would go away. It was only faint, but it hadn't left her all evening. She finger brushed her bangs down over her scar.

When she was done in the bathroom, she made her way back through the kitchen to do one more check of her station so everything was ready for tomorrow and then headed for the back door.

As she pulled her jacket on, she heard Jace behind her.

"You gonna wear that home?"

She turned and looked down. She still wore her apron. "Oh." She flushed. *Dang it.* She reached around back and tugged at the knot. Turning, she set her jacket down on the counter and reached back with both hands.

The more she tugged, the tighter the knot seemed to get. She looked at the ceiling, hoping Jace was busy mopping the floors, wishing the knot would just undo itself and let her go already.

"Do you need some help?" John was tilting his head, looking at the knot behind her.

"No, thanks. I think I can get it." She bit her lip. "I think it got wet."

After another few unsuccessful seconds, he asked, "Sure you don't want any help?"

She blew out a breath, giving up. "All right."

He tugged. "This is some knot. How'd you do this?"

She blinked, looking up, just wanting to go. "I just tied it the same way I always do."

"Man, I don't know. Jace, get over here."

She turned abruptly. "You know what? I'll just wear it home and wash it there." Jace was approaching, trying not to look amused.

"I'm afraid all aprons need to be accounted for every night." He folded his arms.

"Seriously?"

He nodded, his eyes touched with humor.

She narrowed her eyes. "So is there a high rate of apron theft on the island?"

John still tugged at the knot.

Jace smiled then. "Only since the restaurant was featured in *Sunset Magazine* in 2011. We could hardly keep the kitchen stocked that year."

She peeked at John. "He's kidding, right?"

John shrugged, still at work.

"It settled down some after The Great Grill-Off of 2012," Jace said.

"The *Great Grill-Off*?" Even as she spoke, she realized this was the most they'd ever said to each other in all their weeks working side by side.

"It was a thing of beauty. Island-wide, grill masters came to pit their skills against one another, and, of course, where there are grill masters . . ."

She folded her arms. "There are aprons?"

"Six Peter & Andrew's aprons were worn that day."

"That's incredible. What happened?"

He shrugged. "We figured it was good publicity. But we've guarded our aprons closely ever since."

"Can't you just buy them up front?" Just inside the customer entrance, a display case showed T-shirts, aprons, and umbrellas with the Peter & Andrew's logo.

John gave the knot one last tug and dropped it. "I give up. You may have to cut it." He placed earbuds in his ears, lifted a tray of clean glasses, and walked away. "Good luck."

Georgie lifted the neck strap over her head and brushed her hair back out of her face. She shifted the apron around backward and began attacking the knot at her waist again, this time able to see where the loops needed to be worked at. "I can't believe this," she muttered.

"You'll get it."

"Thanks, but I'm not sure I should believe anything you say after a story like 'The Great Grill-Off of 2012.'"

"Smart lady."

She peeked up at Jace, whose gaze shifted from the mess of hair around her face to her eyes. He stepped forward, and she stepped back, suddenly alert to his every move. But he slowed and reached past her, flipping off the switches to the music and lights over her station up front. As he pulled back, she caught the scent of him above the bleach . . . a woodsy lemon scent. He met her eyes again, pausing just inside the edge of her comfort bubble. He searched her face. "How old are you, Georgie?"

She blinked and swallowed, not having expected the question. Her hands felt behind her for the counter she leaned against. "It's not polite to ask a woman her age."

"I've been trying to guess."

His directness was a little disarming, and she wasn't sure she liked being disarmed. "Why would you be trying to do that?"

He shook his head, a smile at the corner of his mouth. "You don't have to tell me."

She lifted her chin. "Twenty-two." What about him provoked her?

He studied her in an unnerving manner, and she steadied her breathing, allowing her thoughts to linger on his features since he was so close. His eyes were the lightest hazel she'd ever seen.

She glanced at his mouth and gripped the counter. "I'm not one of your apron thieves, if that's what you think. I don't fit the profile. I don't even cook, let alone grill."

His eyes narrowed at her admission. "Hm." He watched her a bit longer, then nodded and turned, pushing the mop and wheeled bucket toward the broom closet.

Georgie collected herself. "Th-that's all?" She stepped away from the counter, having pressed herself uncomfortably against it. Her fingers began to work at the knot again.

"Yup."

"No. There's a reason you asked."

He paused again, then turned, folding his arms as though considering whether or not to say anything. Then he nodded. "Mostly I was just curious. But sometimes you look older, that's all."

He turned toward the laundry.

"Gee, thanks." What every woman wanted to hear.

He chuckled. "It's not a physical thing." He peeked back at her over his shoulder, then continued starting a new load. "Something in your eyes."

She blinked. What had he seen in her eyes? "Well, how old are you?"

"Twenty-five."

She didn't know how to respond to that but watched him now as he shut the broom closet. A loop finally budged in her fingers, and she was able to work the remainder of the knot loose.

"See? I knew you'd get it."

She looked up, and he gave her a small smile.

"You're free to go, Miss Tate."

She pulled the apron away, nodding, and tossed it into the basket. Feeling his eyes on her, she reached for her jacket again and turned to him. "About the other night—"

He stilled.

"I, uh . . . It wasn't about you."

He listened.

"I'm just trying to get over some things and . . ." She shook her head, her heart pounding. "I know you were just trying to apologize."

He leaned against the counter, his hands in his pockets. "You were terrified of me."

"I didn't mean to be."

He nodded and looked down. He glanced over at John, who was busy humming, bouncing his head as he cleaned the other grill. He went into an air guitar solo. Jace pushed away from the counter, squaring himself a small distance in front of her, and she couldn't help withdrawing a bit. His expression grew earnest. "I'm safe, Georgie. Okay?"

She pressed her lips together, wishing he didn't have to feel it necessary to make that clear to her. And yet, here he was, telling her what she wanted to know. Now she had to choose to believe him or not.

She gave him a small nod. He nodded with her.

"Thanks." He looked like he might extend his hand, but instead he reached up behind his neck and rubbed. "Okay, get out of here."

"Hey, Georgie!"

She turned toward John. He held an earbud in his fingers. "Will you help me find out her favorite flower?"

She nodded.

"Thanks! Tomorrow!"

She lifted her hood and reached for the door only to have it opened for her.

"'Night."

She stepped past Jace, subdued and careful. "'Night."

She hurried to her car, breathing easier once she heard the back door close behind her.

Chapter 7

GEORGIE CLOSED HER SCRIPTURES AND looked out the window. The view from her room wasn't the expansive bay; it was the neighbor's dogwood trees, but the sunlight played with the pale bark and the hint of pink in each hard little bud. She watched a small bird busy in the branches, and she couldn't help smiling.

A knock sounded at her door, though it was open.

"It's a beautiful day," Faye said.

Georgie had to agree. It was the kind of day that proved the weatherman's forecast of 'mostly sunny' an understatement. "I'm kind of looking forward to getting out."

"Good. When are they coming?"

"Eleven. I need to pack up the pie. I can't believe Tru." Georgie had woken this morning to a heavenly smell only to find that Tru had been up early baking.

"She makes the best lemon meringue pie. And lucky us, she believes that if you're making one pie, you might as well make two."

Georgie smiled. "She'll have to teach me. I've never made pie. Only cookies, and cakes from a box."

"I'm sure she'd be happy to teach you." Faye glanced at the scriptures on the bed. "Find anything helpful?"

Georgie looked at the worn brown book with the faded gold-edged pages. "Nothing specific. But just reading the words helps settle my nerves."

Faye smiled. "Nervous?"

Georgie swallowed. "Yeah, a little."

"Well, that's all right. Heaven knows Tyler will be too."

Georgie let out a small laugh. "I'm glad Megan is coming."

"That should certainly help." Faye turned, and Georgie followed her out, grabbing her jacket and purse on the way.

After finding a suitable container for the pie, Georgie checked her hair in the hall mirror. She'd grown tired of wearing it up all the time, and since she wasn't at work, where wearing it back was required, she was wearing it loose.

"You look very pretty."

"Thanks." Georgie lowered her eyes and checked her purse. "Where is Tru? I wanted to thank her again for the pie." Truth be told, she needed Tru because the sisters had become a comfort to her, and she was very nervous.

"She's down at the water, looking for shark eyes."

"Looking for what?" Georgie turned to the back window of the main room, but the doorbell rang before she could spot her aunt.

"Oh, there they are. Have a great time, sweetie. Be safe." Faye gave her a quick hug and whispered, "You can do this."

Faye stayed close as Georgie answered the door. Tyler looked sheepish.

"Hey, hi."

"Hi, Tyler."

He rocked on the balls of his feet. "I, uh, have some bad news. Megan's sick."

Faye spoke behind her. "Oh no."

"Yeah, she came down with something just before we were going to leave."

"I'm so sorry," Georgie said, her stomach dropping.

"Yeah, me too. I, uh . . ." He looked at the car behind him, still running in the driveway, "I was going to call, but she insisted I come and we go without her. Is that all right? Because if you'd rather reschedule . . ." He looked both hopeful and mortified.

Georgie looked at Faye, who gave a slight nod and a pushing motion with her hands. Georgie looked back at Tyler, suddenly more aware of how little she knew about him. She fought the sudden need to ask Faye if she'd come with them.

Tyler scratched his head and took a step backward. His cheeks flushed. "We could go some other time. I should have called. I'm really sorry—"

"No, it's all right." She glanced at Faye again and then back at Tyler, wincing. "I just . . . haven't been *out* in a while."

Tyler nodded, his ears turning red. "I know. Me neither."

Of course he hadn't. He hadn't been out on a date for at least two years.

"But you know," she said. "My aunt Tru made us pie." She looked at the sky. "And it would be a shame to waste this weather."

Tyler broke into a grin. "Yeah. And Deception Pass is pretty amazing on a clear day. So you don't mind?"

Georgie glanced at Tyler's car in the driveway and pushed down the knot of fear in her stomach. "No. Let's go."

"Okay, then."

She followed him to the passenger side of the car.

"Have fun, kids!" Faye called.

* * *

Georgie squinted, gripping the rail separating her from a two-hundred-foot drop to the deep blue water. The sunlight bounced all over, and she lifted a hand to shield her eyes.

"One of the things I missed about this place," Tyler said. "When the sun comes out, it's everywhere."

She nodded, looking out at the sparkling waves, the pure blue sky, the vivid colors of the pines on the islands. Even the cars passing them on the bridge seemed to glow, reflecting a brightness she welcomed.

"Why is it called Deception Pass?" The drive north had been mostly quiet, though Georgie had made an effort to make light conversation. Tyler seemed more relaxed now that they were out in the open.

He leaned over his folded arms to look at the channel below. "Well, there was this explorer, Captain Vancouver, who thought Whidbey Island was a peninsula. The discovery of this channel told him he was wrong."

That certainly explained the name. Believing something only to find out you'd been fooled. Georgie peered over the railing and felt the vertigo she experienced at great heights. The swirling water below taunted her, and gravity seemed to double its pull. She suddenly felt very small and breakable. Her grip tightened on the rail.

"They always say, 'Don't look down.'" Tyler must have noticed her reaction.

She laughed weakly. "There's really nowhere else to look, is there?"

"Just look out." He pointed. "Look out there to the island. See the trees? And the . . . boats?"

She laughed. There were plenty of trees and boats.

"Better?"

She nodded, feeling foolish.

"Want to go eat?" Tyler asked.

She nodded again. She still clung to the railing as they made their way back across the bridge, but she looked up at the sky and glanced at people seemingly unaffected by the frailty of their mortality.

They reached what she knew was solid earth—no steel girders supporting wire and concrete over air but dirt compacted on rock, strengthened by tree roots reaching downward from centuries-old sturdy trunks. They followed the paved walk back to the parking area in silence. She glanced back toward the bridge, now obscured by trees.

"Are you okay? You looked a little pale back there." Tyler held the door open for her.

"Yeah, I'm fine. It was incredible. I'm just a wimp."

"Nah." He grinned. "We'll eat at sea level."

"Perfect."

As they wound down through the trees, she tried to shake the feeling that by getting dizzy she had done something wrong.

They pulled into a little park on the water. Tyler handed her a quilt from the trunk and grabbed the food. He led her past the picnic tables and down to the beach. The rocks here were smaller than on Camano, and the thick quilt she laid out made an adequate cushion for sitting. Tyler pulled out plates, sandwiches, and a bag of chips, and Georgie found apples and bottles of Squirt. Seagulls swooped nearby, calling other birds for the possible feast.

Georgie zipped up her jacket. Down by the water, the sun shed more light than heat.

They sat facing the waves, their plates on their laps, still saying little.

"What were you studying at school?" he finally asked.

"I was still deciding between English and humanities." She bit her lip. "Or maybe even law. I was TA-ing a literature class. That was fun." She had never been sure or felt the spark that some of her roommates had felt about their majors.

Tyler swallowed the bite of apple he'd been chewing. "So after the accident, did you have to drop your classes or are you finishing them long distance or what?"

"I had just finished spring semester. I stayed a couple weeks longer for a wedding." She gazed back out at the water. "The accident happened after that. I wasn't ready to go back in the fall." She still wasn't. She wasn't comfortable with where these questions were going. But, awkward as the date had been so far, she realized she wasn't trying to impress him. And that was a relief.

They set down their plates, drawing the attention of the hovering gulls. Georgie wrapped her arms around her knees as Tyler threw the crust of his sandwich down the beach, causing an uproar of flapping wings.

A question came to Georgie's mind, one that would certainly lead to fewer questions about herself. "What was Japan like?"

He took the change of subject gracefully. She played with some rocks at the edge of the blanket, letting them fall through her fingers as he shared a few stories about Japan. He talked about missionary experiences and then classes and what he expected from school.

"You could go back to BYU though, right? If you wanted? Just reapply?" He looked at her, hopeful. "You could have a fresh start." He averted his eyes and threw a rock into the waves.

She smiled, knowing what he was asking and appreciating the direction of his thoughts, but if she went back, it wouldn't be a fresh start. Somehow it would be going backward. But she didn't want to explain that to Tyler. "I have time to decide."

He nodded. He brushed off his hands and stood, then held them out to help her up. "C'mon. I think we can still see some tide pools."

She looked at his hands, pale, steady, undemanding. She gave him one of hers, stood with his gentle pull, and let go. She suspected he would have preferred to hang on, but he smiled and walked by her side to the tide pools, pointing out anemones, sand crabs, and sea urchins. Gradually Georgie relaxed enough to enjoy the wonder of her surroundings.

By the time they returned to the blanket, the seagulls had cleaned her plate and emptied the bag of chips, and Georgie was smiling, winded, and ready for pie.

* * *

When she entered the back door to the restaurant, she felt lighter than she'd felt in a long time. Which was why she immediately sensed that something was very wrong.

"What do you mean I'm *fired*?" Anders yelled at Reuben.

Directly in front of Georgie, Anders's back was to her when he grabbed a tray of cutlery and pulled it to the floor with a crash. Georgie jumped back, avoiding a paring knife spinning across the floor. She took in the few staff members already in the kitchen, frozen where they were. Reuben stood in the doorway of his office, filling it up with his size, his hand on the doorknob as if he was just inviting Anders in to talk.

Reuben appeared calm. "We can talk in here, or you can leave now. Those are your options."

"My options? What are my options if you fire me? *Huh*?" He stepped toward Reuben, lifting his arm in front of him, a knife in his fist.

Georgie drew in her breath with the others, and someone to her right pulled her closer.

"How am I supposed to feed my kid, *huh*?"

Reuben let out a sigh. "Anders, you knew the rules—"

"*Forget the rules*! I come here, I work"—the emotion in Anders's voice pitched—"I do my job and you . . ." He inched closer to Reuben.

"Stop," Georgie whispered. "Please, stop."

Anders flicked a look her way, desperate, hate-filled, his eyes red-rimmed and wet.

She felt herself being pulled back. Jace stepped in front of her. "Anders." Jace held his hand up in a calming gesture. Anders turned quickly, swinging the knife around toward Jace. Jace backed up half a step into Georgie. "I thought you were going to quit that stuff, man."

Anders fought to steady himself. He gritted his teeth. "I tried." He shook his head. "I need this job."

"You need to put the knife down. That's not helping anybody," Jace said.

The veins in Anders's neck bulged with strain. "Who's gonna help *me*? Huh?" He seemed on the verge of breaking, giving in to emotion, and the knife lowered. Jace took a step forward at the same time Reuben did; Anders's eyes grew wide. The knife came back up.

"*Who's gonna help me*?" he shouted.

He lunged at Jace, but Reuben grabbed him from behind, wrenching Anders's hand so the knife fell to the floor. Sirens approached from the distance, and Reuben pushed Anders to the wall. He whimpered as Reuben and Caleb kept him secure.

Jace had turned, completely shielding Georgie as tears ran down her face. She jerked her gaze from the scene to his eyes. He reached for her but paused. "Are you all right?"

She nodded, trying to lie, but she knew he could see right through her, so she gave up and shook her head no and gasped for breath.

Mai pulled her into a hug. "It's okay, Georgie. Shhhh." Mai shook too.

Long after the police had recorded everyone's statements and taken Anders away, and after Reuben had taken a vote on whether or not to stay open, and staying open won, Georgie hung on to the feel of Mai's hug and Jace's protective stance when Anders had turned her way.

No matter how weak or inadequate she'd been, they'd given her exactly what she'd needed. They'd made her feel safe. Mai . . . and Jace.

After everyone was somewhat settled again, Jace returned to keeping his distance, asking only the essentials of her. She found herself oddly strengthened by this. Even after what had happened, she could handle her job, keep up with her responsibilities, help the restaurant run as smoothly as possible on their busiest night of the week. She felt shaken but not coddled or frail.

Only a few times did Jace meet her gaze or she his. Only a few times did she wonder what had changed between them. Because something definitely had.

She stepped out into the cool night air for her break and caught a whiff of cigarette smoke.

"Mai?"

Mai turned, stepping on the butt. "Hey, Georgie. You okay?"

"Yeah. I didn't know you smoked."

"I don't. Begged it off Haru to calm my nerves."

Georgie nodded. "Want to sit?"

They moved to an old picnic table under the eaves. Jace's bike gleamed in the weak light. Georgie yawned, and Mai leaned forward, dropping her head between her arms. Mai's wings peeked over the top of her T-shirt's neckline.

"Can I ask you a question?"

Mai rubbed her temples. "Sure."

"Your tattoo. She flies with her own wings, right?"

Mai looked back at her, a slow smile coming to her face. She sat up. "Yeah. Something my mom taught me. A long time ago. An old story from China."

Georgie waited for her to continue.

Mai rolled her eyes good-naturedly. "You want to hear it?"

Georgie nodded.

"Well, maybe we deserve a story after today."

Georgie rested her chin on her hands.

"The story is about an emperor's daughter. She had food and fine clothes, but the one thing the emperor wouldn't grant her was freedom. He feared for her safety, didn't trust her to make decisions about her future, and only allowed her to study art and flower arranging. She was beautiful and kind and wanted to please her father, who kept her in a tower of jade and golden bars. She could see the world from her window but couldn't be in it. She wanted to learn more. So she studied from books smuggled to her by her handmaid: history, philosophy, architecture, and science. She learned to play instruments her father hadn't assigned. She taught herself to weave silks, embedding them with the magic of the earth: the warmth of fire, the cool of water, and the lightness of wind."

Georgie watched the stars and then glanced at Mai, who smiled as if she thought storytelling on break in the lot behind a restaurant was silly.

"Keep going," Georgie said, nudging her. "It's helping."

Mai continued. "She kept everything hidden from her father, but one day his steps were quiet, and the instrument she played drowned out the sound of his entrance. The books, the music, it was all out for him to see, everything but the silks, which the handmaid kept behind a loose jade tile in the wall. In his rage over her defiance, the emperor ordered everything destroyed and her feet bound, and then he pronounced her engaged to an aged, wealthy suitor who was known to be miserable and cruel, the kind of man her father had tried to protect her from."

"Oh no."

"Oh yes. And as a final display of her dishonor, he took the handmaid, weighed her down with chains, and paraded her through the world, anywhere visible from his daughter's window."

The back door opened, and both girls turned.

"Mai, they need you up front," Reuben called.

"Just a couple more minutes?" she asked. "Please?"

He paused. "All right." The door closed.

Mai leaned closer to Georgie. "Okay, so, the emperor takes the old guy she's going to marry to see his daughter, only she isn't there. While he's been gone, she's used her knowledge and courage and the magic silks and escaped. Her father's rage builds so much that he goes to strike the old man, who is laughing. As the emperor raises his hand, the old man transforms into a beautiful, terrible dragon. The emperor freaks out, of course, but the dragon says, 'Fool. You've caged what was meant to soar, and now she flies with her own wings.'"

Georgie stared.

Mai blinked. "Was that too anticlimactic? I sort of rushed the end."

Georgie shook her head. "No. I really liked it."

"I'd better go in." She looked at her watch. "You've got a few more minutes, huh?"

Georgie nodded, still dazed.

"Okay. See you inside." Mai walked away but then turned back. "I forgot. The emperor's daughter rescues her handmaid, and the dragon is really a handsome sorcerer who'd heard stories of the girl in a cage. He finds her and her handmaid, and they live happily ever after exploring the world together." She shrugged with a grin and hurried to the door, where she paused again. "Oh, hey, Jace."

Georgie quickly turned to face the parking lot, hearing the door close and Jace's footsteps halt. Then they continued toward her, and her pulse quickened. He sat on the bench, which made the old wood creak. He set down a Styrofoam takeout container filled with bisque.

"Do you mind if I . . . ?"

"No, of course not." She looked down, running her hand over her slacks to her knees.

"Would you like some?"

She turned her head in surprise. He held out a second spoon.

"You're offering me bisque?"

He shrugged. "It's been a long night." When she didn't respond, he leaned closer. "I'll try not to spill any on you." One corner of his mouth came up, and she couldn't help matching it.

She reached for the spoon, but he pulled it just out of her reach, and when she reached farther and grabbed it, he broke into a smile that she wasn't sure she could look away from. He let her have the spoon and pushed the container closer, offering her the first taste.

Georgie hadn't realized how hungry she was, but with the smell from that container out in the crisp air, she was suddenly famished. She lifted a spoonful to her mouth. The warm, sweet cream and salt of the seafood passed over her tongue. She couldn't help it. Her eyes closed, and she sighed, which she immediately cut short, her eyes flying open, and then she choked.

"Is something wrong?" Jace asked as she got her coughing under control.

She swallowed and shook her head. "It's perfect."

"Are you sure? You don't seem to be enjoying it . . ." His look was teasing.

"No, it's good. Just went down the wrong tube." She'd recovered and dipped her spoon back into the cup.

"Hey, hey, save some for me." He pulled the bisque closer to himself and took a spoonful. "Mm. That is pretty good."

She nodded. "It's not bad in the pie either."

He looked at her and laughed. She reached for one more spoonful. His expression changed, no longer teasing. She found she was okay with that look too. A very long moment drifted between them, their eyes still locked.

Finally he blinked and looked away. "Are you sure you're okay after what happened in there?"

She nodded. Though they'd all been shaken, she'd been the only one to shed tears, a fact she was glaringly aware of. "It just caught me off guard. What about you?"

He shrugged, concentrating on the container in his hand. "It was weird. Anders has been around a lot longer than I have. I liked him, for the most part."

She'd observed that herself. "He needs help, doesn't he?"

Jace took another spoonful and swallowed. "Reuben was giving him help. He had to come to work clean. Strike three." He offered her another taste, and she took it. "But, yeah, he needs help."

"Does he live on the island?"

He shook his head. "Marysville. I think you and I are the only islanders on staff." He watched her. He wasn't one to avoid eye contact when speaking. Yet she had the feeling he'd been trying to do just that all week.

She looked down at her spoon in her fingers. "Thank you. For what you did." She raised her eyes to his.

"No trouble at all."

A smile reached her mouth before it did his.

Then he blinked and furrowed his brow. "Isn't your break about up?" He looked down, stirring the bisque.

She glanced behind her. "Yeah, I should get back. Reuben's kind of a mess without me."

He laughed out loud, and it startled her. She frowned. "What, you don't think so?"

He passed his hand over his mouth, attempting to straighten out his smirk. "Oh, definitely."

She stood, brushing off her pants. "Listen, Mr. *Sous-chef*—"

He stood as well, closer than she'd expected. "Yes, Miss *Expediter*?"

The back door swung open. "Georgie, I need you in here. It's a mess." Reuben looked past her. "You too, Romeo. Move it. Break's over." The door swung shut behind him.

Georgie turned back to Jace, triumphant, though her heart was pounding a little too hard. She folded her arms. "A *mess*."

Jace stepped even closer, and she couldn't cover the small catch of her breath in time. "The last bite." He slowly waved his spoon filled with the bisque under her nose, his eyes locked with hers. She inhaled, refusing to look down but opened her mouth just a little. His eyebrow arched up, and he brought the spoon to his own mouth and swallowed. "Mmm. That is so good."

Her mouth still hung open. He tipped the cup up to his mouth and tapped down the last drops, licked his lips, then tossed the container in the trash as he walked past.

She watched him open the door.

"Hurry up." He thumbed toward the kitchen and mouthed the word, "Mess." The door closed behind him.

Georgie stared, not knowing whether to laugh or growl. Or hide. Because Jace's charm was definitely showing.

She looked at the container in the trash can and tossed her spoon in.

"Dumb bisque." She bit her lip. She hadn't felt so much like herself in a long time.

Chapter 8

JACE RAN HIS HAND OVER his face.

What was he doing? Yes, she'd been vulnerable standing in the doorway with Anders going off half-cocked, and yes, he'd been the nearest to her. Of course he'd shielded her.

His focus came back, and he realized he was staring at the *Employees must wash their hands* sign on the mirror over the sink. He blinked and turned off the water, grabbed a paper towel, and dried his face and the back of his neck from the splashing he'd just given himself.

To heck with the invisibility thing. He was no good at it. And why would he tease her like that? Her uncle had said she'd been through some tough times, was trying to get away. He shook his head. After coming inside, he'd just about turned right back around to apologize. Again.

But the look in her eyes . . . There was something there that didn't require careful handling. Something he'd seen the other night as well. A spark she didn't show often enough. A spark, he suspected, that if he wasn't careful could ignite into something he really didn't need right now. Nope.

He was just watching out for her. Like her uncle had asked. She could use a friend.

The clatter outside the door reached through his thoughts. He shook off his stupor and opened the door to the chaos of the kitchen. He found Georgie washing her hands in one of the kitchen basins. A bit of her hair had escaped her ponytail, and she tucked it behind her ear, where it curled against her neck. She turned and caught him watching, then glared at him.

As she stepped past him she said quietly, "Next time I'm bringing my own bowl."

Despite every warning screaming inside his head, he countered, his voice low, "Next time we won't be interrupted."

She missed a step and whipped her head around, her mouth opening as if to say something she'd forgotten. The look changed to the beginnings of a smile, drawing a chuckle from him, and then she walked calmly to her station, where Reuben turned over a number of salads to her care. The red was already creeping into her cheeks.

Jace set his hands on his hips as Reuben brushed past him.

"You thinkin' of working tonight?"

Jace's brow furrowed, and he turned toward the grills.

At ten o'clock, things started slowing down. They stopped taking customers, and attention turned to pleasing the remaining patrons and keeping up with the dishes. It was still a full house, and drinks and desserts kept the waiters busy.

"Hey, John," Jace said.

The waiter looked up at Jace from a loaded tray Georgie had just helped him with. "Yeah?"

Jace passed Georgie a lobster plate. "You don't close tonight, do you?"

"No, tomorrow."

"Be sure you talk to me before you take off."

John gave Jace a curious look but nodded. "Sure." He glanced at Georgie and looked around, then leaned in. "Georgie, did you find out yet?"

Georgie shook her head, squeezing a swirl of chocolate sauce over the torte plate. "Been a little busy. I'll get it, don't worry." She slipped the torte onto the plate and arranged the raspberry garnish on top. "Mm. This would be really good with a crème fraîche," she muttered to no one in particular, then turned to check on the bread oven.

"Hey, Romeo."

Jace blinked.

Reuben pointed at the grill. "Is that rib eye supposed to be well done?"

Jace jerked back into action, throwing a fresh steak on the heat, knowing he'd be buying a well-done rib eye to take home. But he was still distracted, considering crème fraîche. And making a mental note to ask Reuben to stop calling him that.

* * *

"Could you use some help?" Georgie knelt on a chair next to Rhea's, who was rolling silverware into cloth napkins.

"Are you sure?"

Georgie nodded, not sure. She'd hurried to clean up her station and knew she was expected to help in the kitchen, but she had a mission. She folded the burgundy napkin on the diagonal and grabbed a salad and dinner fork and a knife and rolled them up. "You know what I miss?" She placed the roll in a bin and started over.

"What?"

"Flowers."

"Mm-hm. I'm so ready for spring. My mom's crocuses are about to pop."

Georgie nodded. "Thank heaven for crocuses. Is it crocuses or croci?"

Rhea screwed her nose up. "Croci? That sounds awful."

"Mm, like a frog."

Rhea laughed.

"No frog flowers?" Georgie asked.

"No, thank you. For now I'll take crocuses, daffodils, and tulips, please."

Perfect. They busied themselves with more napkins. "So, what *is* your favorite flower?"

Rhea leaned her head to the side. "Canna lilies. My nana grew them in her garden in North Carolina."

Georgie nodded at her silverware, smiling. "Pretty."

"What's *your* favorite?"

Just then, the door of the kitchen swung open, and Jace stuck his head through. "Rhea, have you seen—"

Both girls lifted their heads. Rhea finished his question for him. "Georgie?"

Georgie tossed her last rolled napkin in the bin. "Coming. See ya, Rhea."

"See ya, Georgie."

Georgie walked past Jace. "Girl talk."

"Great."

Jace let the kitchen door swing shut behind him.

She looked around. "Is John still here?"

"Yup. Waiting outside."

Georgie made a beeline for the back door. As soon as she stepped out, John pushed away from leaning against his car. She jogged over to him.

"Canna lilies."

"What?"

"Canna lilies. C-A-N-N-A. Not to be confused with calla lilies."

"Calla?"

"Right. Not *calla*, *canna*. *N* as in Nancy. They're tall with lots of bright-colored blossoms. If they're white, they're callas. Which you don't want. Got it?"

He nodded. "Canna. *N*. Bright colors. Got it. Just one, right?"

"Right. Call the florists first; ask if they have them."

He grinned. "Thanks, Georgie."

"What are you doing? Dinner and a movie?"

"Didn't Jace tell you about the tickets?"

Georgie furrowed her brow as he dug in his pocket and pulled out two tickets. "He gave me these. It's a play in Seattle next weekend, supposed to be good. He bought them for his ex just before she got engaged to some jerk. He just gave them to me. Cool, huh? What do you think? Smooth?"

She looked over the tickets. "Very smooth." She smiled.

"I'm asking her on Monday." He put the tickets back in his pocket. "Canna, right?"

"Right. It'll be great."

Back in the kitchen, Georgie stole a glance at Jace cleaning his grills. His ex-girlfriend got engaged. While they were still together? She reached for a bleach towel, not quite understanding the flare of irritation that flashed through her. It would certainly explain his mood that first week.

Reuben walked past with the money bag. "Georgie, could you finish up on dishes?"

She looked around at all the other jobs already underway. Served her right for leaving the kitchen. "Sure." She dropped the towel and approached the stainless-steel box, eyeing the boa constrictor–sized sprayer hanging down from a bar looming over the sink.

She picked up a pot and grabbed the sprayer head, aimed, and sprayed the pot. And herself.

"Careful with that aim. The pressure's pretty strong." Jace continued past, pushing the broom. Probably smirking.

She pressed her lips together and ignored the water soaking the front of her apron. She tipped the pan away from her and briefly considered aiming the sprayer in his direction. "I'll try to remember that." She eyed the pile of pans and dishes and wished Tyler well with his new job.

By the time she finished the last load, most of the lights had been turned off and the dryer hummed with the load of bleach towels. The cleaning service's bin of burgundy napkins sat ready for its morning pickup, and Jace was locking the office door. Everyone else had gone. She wiped everything down with a dry towel. *She* needed a dry towel.

Jace stopped and looked at her with a crooked smile. "You all right?" That was the second time he'd asked her that today.

"Can you give me a minute?" she asked.

"Sure." He leaned against a counter and folded his arms.

She pulled at the damp bow on her apron, and it gave with a little effort. No more knots.

Exhaustion had hit her about halfway down the third giant stack of plates. It was hard to believe she'd been on a bridge over Deception Pass that morning. She threw her apron in the empty basket and walked to the washroom, pulling out her ponytail on the way.

Using paper towels, she patted at her shirt and arms and blotted her face and the waterproof-but-flaking mascara. She ran her fingers through her humidified hair, finally pulling it all back in a damp, messy bun. It was enough to get her home and into bed. A flicker of self-consciousness made her grimace, but Jace had already seen her, and this was the best she could do. Of course, *then* she spent a moment convincing herself that she would have felt a little self-conscious about her appearance if it had been anybody waiting out in the kitchen, not just Jace.

She exited the bathroom. Jace was turned away from her, his jacket on, reading something. She couldn't help noticing the way his jeans hung on his hips just right. He turned, and she looked up.

"Ready?"

She nodded.

He tossed some junk mail on the counter. "Do we call it a tie?"

"Hm?" She had no idea what he was talking about.

"The battle between you and the sprayer."

She breathed out a sigh. "I'm not a very objective judge. I just don't want a rematch."

He chuckled and opened the door for her as she grabbed her jacket. "The new dishwasher starts on Monday."

"I know. Tyler. He'll be great."

"You know him?" He hadn't stopped at his bike but had continued walking with her toward her car. To her surprise, it didn't bother her.

"His family is in our ward." She peeked at him. They hadn't discussed their shared membership in the Church at all.

He only nodded. "Good. I doubt he'll have the issues Anders did."

She pulled her keys out of her pocket. "He's a squeaky-clean RM."

"Perfect job for him, then."

She shook her head, suppressing a laugh.

"I'll see you tomorrow at church."

She nodded. "See you tomorrow."

He backed away and held his hand up in a sort of wave, then turned. She opened her car door and watched him a second longer, then got in and started the engine. She watched him again in her rearview mirror as he put his helmet on and kicked up the kickstand. The motorcycle roared to life over the sound of her little Kia, and Jace revved the engine a few times. He pulled out but waved her on, and then, to her surprise and confusion, he followed her nearly all the way home, turning left off the street and up a hill just before she pulled into her aunts' driveway.

She got out and looked behind her to the few lights still on among the trees. Shaking her head, she turned and walked into the house.

* * *

Georgie sat down on the church pew next to Faye and looked around. When Jace walked into the chapel, he seemed to spot her immediately, a smile growing on his face. He headed in her direction.

"Georgie," someone else said.

She turned. Tyler made his way down her row, followed by Megan and their parents. He grinned as he sat down next to her.

"Hi, Tyler."

"I wasn't sure if you'd be coming here or going to the singles ward. I'm glad you're here."

Megan leaned forward. "Hi, Georgie."

Georgie smiled. "Are you feeling better?"

She shrugged. "I guess. Must have been a twenty-four-hour thing."

"Glad to hear it's over."

Megan sat back, and Georgie glanced behind her to find Jace sitting a few rows back, studying the program.

She turned to Tyler. "Why aren't you at the singles ward?"

He shrugged. "Family wants me to come with them for a few weeks more. I don't really mind. I guess they missed me."

"And he's substitute teaching my Sunday School class for a couple weeks," Megan said. She leaned forward and whispered loudly, "They're going to eat him alive."

"Excuse me?" Tyler said. "I've been teaching for the last two years. I've got this."

Megan leaned back. "Oh, now, see? That's the right attitude."

As Tyler reached for a hymnbook, Megan looked at Georgie and drew a finger across her throat.

Georgie muffled a laugh as the prelude music began.

Tyler turned to Georgie. "You should come to class with us."

Megan leaned forward. "Yeah, to watch him get *eaten alive*."

Tyler shook his head and looked at the ceiling. "You know, sometimes I really miss Japan."

They settled down as a hush fell over the congregation and a member of the bishopric stood to welcome them to the meeting. Georgie looked behind her again. This time she caught Jace's eye and smiled.

He winked.

She turned quickly, her smile widening.

Faye must have noticed her expression because she looked behind her, searching but apparently not finding. She leaned over. "You seem pretty chipper this morning." She gave a pointed look toward Tyler.

Georgie frowned. "Shhh. Just sing."

Faye laughed silently as Georgie handed her the open hymnbook. Georgie didn't dare take another glance behind her during the song. Slowly, though, the smile returned.

After the meeting, she visited with the Gordons for a few minutes, waiting for the pew to empty on either side so they could exit. Out of the corner of her eye, Georgie found Uncle Dar greeting Jace with a welcoming handshake. The two made their way to the end of her pew. Dar was already introducing Jace to Tru and Faye, and he motioned for Georgie to join them.

Tyler was in conversation with a man in the pew behind them, and Megan was already making her way out of their row on the other side. Georgie walked toward Dar and Jace.

Dar opened his arm to her, and she stepped in. "Look who I found."

Jace smiled. "Good morning, Sister Tate."

She ignored Faye's penetrating gaze. "Good morning. Nice tie."

He glanced down at his orange tie, then up at her. "Thanks. You too. Nice tie, I mean."

She muffled a laugh.

"Would you like to join us for dinner this afternoon, Jace?" Faye asked a little loudly. "We love having new members of the ward over."

Georgie quickly looked to her aunt, eyes wide.

"Um, yeah, thanks." Jace seemed flustered over the sudden invitation and peered at Georgie as he ran a hand through his dark waves. "If that's all right."

Faye didn't even bother looking at Georgie for confirmation. "Of course it's all right. We try to ask someone every week. Isn't that right, Dar?"

Dar nodded. "Of course." He looked at Georgie and smiled. "Every week." He turned to Faye. "You do know this guy's a chef, though, right?"

"Chefs eat sloppy joes, don't they?" Tru asked.

Jace nodded. "Yes, ma'am, they do."

Faye looked after her sister, who was already leaving for her class. "Oh, Tru, I'm sure we could do better than sloppy joes." Tru waved her hand without looking behind her. Faye turned back to Jace. "I have to admit I'm feeling a little pressure."

Georgie interjected. "Faye, you're a wonderful cook. So is Tru."

Jace put his hand up. "Please don't feel any pressure. Really. I look forward to the company *and* the meal. And if it's all right, I'll bring dessert."

Faye brightened. "Oh, now, I think I can deal with that."

Dar rested his hand on Georgie's shoulder. "Well, now that that's settled, shall we go to Sunday School?"

Georgie looked at Jace. "Are you staying?"

He arched a brow. "Why wouldn't I stay?"

"Georgie."

She turned her head. Tyler stood back at the center of the pew, looking at her expectantly. Dar hadn't noticed and was pulling her along. She shrugged helplessly and pointed to her family. Tyler, looking a little deflated, nodded, waved, and exited the other side of the bench.

She turned and found Jace watching her with veiled curiosity. She gestured toward Tyler's retreating figure. "The new dishwasher."

Jace's eyebrows rose a fraction, and he nodded. "I see."

"I'll have to introduce you."

"Looking forward to it."

Faye left to her own responsibilities, and Dar herded Georgie and Jace to the gym for Sunday School.

Chapter 9

JACE RANG THE DOORBELL AND tugged the edge of his pant leg down to the heel of his shoe. He checked the box inside the bags he held again just to make sure no damage had been done on the walk over. The door opened.

Once again he couldn't help looking at Georgie a little too long. He saw her so often in her black slacks, white shirt, and apron, her hair back, that it still took him by surprise to see her this way: jeans and a gray sweater, her hair down around her shoulders.

"Hi," she said, looking a little uncomfortable.

"Hi." He bounced on his feet, feeling unusually nervous. "Um . . ." He reached absently for a leaf on the shrub next to the doorway and tugged, saying what he had prepared in his head on the way over. "Listen, if this is too weird, I could just . . ." He swallowed. "You could tell them I wasn't feeling well or—"

"Is that dessert?"

He looked down at the box and various containers inside the bag he carried. "Yes."

She stood back, opening the door wider. "Then you better come in."

He stepped in, shaking his head. "Why do I have the feeling that's the only reason you're letting me in?"

"That's not the only reason. They said that if I didn't let you in, I have to do all the dishes. And you know how I feel about doing dishes."

"Ah." He took off his jacket, which she hung on a peg in the small enclosed entry room, and then she led him into a long, narrow main room with a kitchen and dining area off to the right. Old pictures lined the walls, and the furniture looked comfortable but far from the shabby stuff in his living room. All of the windows at the back of the house looked right over the sound.

"This is nice." He inhaled. "And something smells really good."

Georgie smiled, glancing at the kitchen. "Sloppy joes." She padded in her socks to a stereo in a large entertainment center against the long wall and turned down the Mozart to conversation level.

"It's been a long time since I've had sloppy joes."

"Tru made her homemade rolls, which are absolutely amazing, and Faye made mandarin coleslaw, *and* she got out a jar of her homemade bread-and-butter pickles, which are like gold around here, *so* . . ." She gave him a look, warning him to be impressed.

"*So*," he answered her look, "when do we eat?"

"Hello, Jace!" Sister Silva emerged from a hallway opposite the kitchen. She too was without shoes, and he suddenly wondered if he should have taken his off at the door. He'd walked over from his place and hoped he hadn't dragged in mud or gravel. Had he wiped his feet?

Sister Silva took his hand in both of hers. "We're so glad you're here. I didn't hear your motorcycle."

"I walked."

"Oh, it's nice you're so close. And it's a beautiful day too, though we're supposed to get rain later." She let go of his hand. "Is that dessert?"

"Yes. It was key in getting past the guard." He glanced at Georgie. She shook her head, but he thought he detected a smile.

"Here, let's set it over here. Does anything need to be refrigerated?"

He followed her to the counter and pulled out one tall and one short container. "These can go in the fridge. The rest should be fine." She peeked around him, but the remaining dish was covered securely.

"Any hints?" she asked from behind the refrigerator door as she found a place for the containers.

He shook his head. "I just hope you like it. Dinner smells really good, by the way." He spied a baking sheet of mounds covered with a flour cloth. The rolls.

"Thank you. Dar should be out in a minute. He had a nice nap after church. Georgie? Why don't you open the bays a little and let some fresh air in here. I'll go see if Tru would like to join us." She was already headed down a hallway off the kitchen.

As soon as Jace thought Sister Silva was out of earshot, he turned to Georgie, who was tugging on one of the bay windows. "Should I have taken off my shoes?"

She yanked. "No, you're fine."

"Do you need some help?"

"No, I've got it—aaugh." Her hand had slipped up as the window gave, hitting the frame. She grimaced, shaking her hand.

"You all right?"

"Yes." She wrinkled her nose. "Just banged it." She stuck her finger in her mouth and crossed to the kitchen sink.

"Sticky windows?"

She nodded, turning on cold water and running her finger under the stream. "This house is about eighty years old."

"I like it." The arched entries to the halls. The rock fireplace and textured walls, the built-in bookshelves.

"Me too." She turned the water off and dried her hand on a hanging dish towel. "It feels loved."

She'd said it off-the-cuff, but he considered it and agreed.

They were quiet, looking at the old house surrounding them. Finally she said, "This does feel a little weird. You know, not being at work. You being here. Where I live."

He raised his brow. "Maybe not weird. It's . . . different."

"Yes, different." She tapped the counter. "Because I keep looking at you and thinking that I need to be putting a garnish on something and wondering why you don't have your chef's coat on."

He smiled at her. "I could go home and get one if—"

"No, you're totally fine without it." She paused and covered the grin that came, then turned around to face the window.

"Totally fine?"

He saw her fist clench, then relax.

"Well, thank you." He didn't have to hide his smile from anyone; he leaned, a bit more relaxed, against the counter. "I noticed you weren't wearing an apron."

She looked down, then turned around, her face a little pink. "I'm going to go see what's taking Dar so long."

He nodded, and she hurried across the room.

A few minutes later, Sister Silva invited them all to the table. "Tru isn't up to joining us. She sends her apologies."

Jace took his seat next to Georgie, and Dar asked Georgie to bless the food. She did, her voice soft.

"We're thankful to have Jace here with us. Please bless his dessert that it will do our bodies much good."

Jace grinned, his eyes closed. She finished, and Faye firmly said, "Amen."

Dar picked up the bowl of coleslaw. "No pressure there, right, Jace?"

"No, not at all."

Georgie smiled as she split her roll.

"I know this is a simple meal," Faye said, "but I like to keep it simple for Sundays. We do a bit fancier on fast Sunday."

Jace shook his head. "This looks wonderful. I grew up on my dad's very traditional, very good cooking. When he didn't cook, it was my grandma, who raised my dad, so . . ." He shrugged, taking the sloppy-joe filling from Georgie, "this feels like home to me."

Faye passed Dar a roll. "Your mother doesn't cook?"

He took the bowl of coleslaw. "My mother was sick for a lot of my childhood. My dad ran the diner, and she did what she could to keep the books."

He felt Georgie's eyes on him.

Faye leaned forward. "Oh, I'm sorry. What a very hard thing."

He nodded, spooning out a pile of coleslaw and setting the bowl down. "It was. But we had a lot of support. And she's a lot better now, thank goodness." He grinned. "Terrible cook though." He glanced at Georgie, and when he winked, her expression brightened as he'd hoped it would. "So between that and helping out at the diner, I had a lot of opportunity to mess around in the kitchen. I liked it."

The subject naturally moved to questions about Nevada and his schooling.

"So," Dar asked, reaching for another roll, "what made you choose Seattle?"

Jace finished chewing and swallowed. "I served in the Washington Everett Mission."

Dar paused with his fork in the air. "You're kidding."

"Nope."

"And you came back?" Faye asked.

Jace shrugged, scooping up some fallen meat with his fork. "Yup." He glanced at Georgie, who was resting her hand on her glass and gazing out the window where raindrops had just begun to fall, making plinking sounds on the porch roof.

"I loved it. Loved the green and the mountains. Loved the people."

Georgie turned and looked at him.

"Loved the rain."

She smiled. Dang.

She lifted her glass, and he wiped his mouth with his napkin.

"And I already had a year at the Cordon Bleu in Nevada, so I just transferred to Seattle."

"But did you ever serve here on Camano?" Dar poured more water in Faye's glass. "We usually feed the missionaries that come to the island."

"No, never out this way. Lynnwood, Bothel, Shoreline, Monroe. I had a few companions who served up here though. Elder Stringham? And Elder Moore."

Faye clapped her hands. "Oh, we remember Elder Moore, don't we, dear? He had a beautiful singing voice. Ate with us several times and at Christmas." Dar nodded. "But I don't recall Elder Stringham."

"He wasn't here long. Little guy," Dar said. "I helped him and his companion put a new roof on Rita Holmgren's house. That was some time ago. Four, five years?"

Jace nodded. Yes, it was.

Georgie shook her head. "It's a small world."

"Sister Silva, this coleslaw is perfect. I think people forget what a touch of sweet can do to cabbage."

She beamed. "Thank you, Jace. And call me Faye."

A little while later, Faye stood. Dar and Jace followed. "Well," she said, "we usually go for a walk after dinner. Would that be all right? Then we'll come back for that dessert you're keeping a secret."

Jace smiled. "Sounds good." He followed the rest of them, helping clean up the dinner table.

Dar suggested taking a few umbrellas, which became necessary as they walked the beach. The rain pelted the black nylon above Jace's head, but they didn't turn for home. It was one of the things Jace admired about the people of the Pacific Northwest. Rain didn't deter. At least not often. He'd seen walking commuters, picnics, days at the zoo or the beach go on as planned. Enjoying life didn't stop because of a little rain. He zipped his jacket up a little higher. People just . . . adapted.

He and Georgie walked behind Dar and Faye, who shared an extra-large umbrella.

"You were a missionary," Georgie said, her red umbrella bobbing with the slow rhythm of her steps.

He nodded, raising an eyebrow. "Yes. Best two years and all that."

"Huh." She watched the ground in front of them, for good reason. It could get tricky if a foot landed on a bigger rock or a loose piece of driftwood.

"Huh, what?"

"Nothing. I'm just trying to imagine you in a suit." He'd worn khakis and a white shirt to church. No suit. She glanced at him. "And a haircut."

He ran a hand over the trimmed whiskers along his jaw. "Yeah, that was me. It was great that they let us ride motorcycles though."

She stopped, her mouth open. "They did not."

He chuckled and shook his head. "Of course not."

She rolled her eyes and began walking again. "And your family?"

"Mom, Dad, three sisters."

"Younger? Older?"

"Two older. My younger sister's a senior in high school." He blew out a breath, remembering he still needed to talk to Reuben about that.

"And you're close?"

He nodded. "I guess you could say that. We kind of raised each other with mom so sick."

"What kind of sick?"

"MS."

"Oh."

He recognized that tone of compassion in her answer that he'd heard so many times before.

"She's doing great right now though. The last several years have been good. Meds are working to keep her strong."

"That's good. And your younger sister will be graduating?"

"Addy." He picked up a shell, not really looking at it. "She used to call me Sammich."

"Sammich?"

"Yeah, as in *make me a sammich*."

Georgie laughed, and he absently handed her the shell.

She paused, and his thoughts of his sister crashed as he realized he'd handed her the shell as he'd always handed Brenna shells. She'd collected them and was always on the lookout for more. He almost pulled the thing back, feeling stupid, but Georgie had taken it, her fingers just brushing his, sending a current through his skin.

She looked at the shell as he stuck his hand in his pocket. He didn't get embarrassed often, but the memory affected him. The current affected him.

"This is full of holes." She gave him a funny look, holding up the shell. "What?"

"The shell—it's full of holes. Look." She held it closer, and he leaned forward, seeing what he hadn't before. Dozens of tiny holes along the spiral, as if they'd been drilled by some angry little sea creature.

"Oh yeah. Sorry, I didn't see that."

She shrugged, looking down at the shell. "It's all right. It's interesting." She held it up to her eye. "And you can see through it."

"That's helpful."

She laughed again. He liked her laugh a little too much, and that bothered him.

"What's your father like?" she asked.

They'd stopped walking, reaching the end of the stretch of beach, where a copse of soaring pine trees took over. Eagle nests crowned two of the trees, and he wondered if the birds were huddled inside. He took a deep breath of ocean air mixed with wet pine. It cleared his head. "You're full of questions."

She shrugged and looked away. "You're interesting."

He glanced at the shell in her hand and felt oddly pleased.

"My dad," he said, "is a hard, stubborn, devoted man, and we knock heads all the time."

She gave him a curious look, then blinked and looked away.

"He thinks I should be home."

She nodded, kicking at some rocks. "So does my mom," she said quietly.

She didn't say any more, and he had the impression she would when she wanted to. He looked over at Dar and Faye, who were closer to the water, in deep discussion.

Georgie had stopped walking and was searching the hills behind them. "You're . . . a lot different than I thought you were."

He turned. "What did you think I was?"

She gave her head a shake. "I'd rather not say."

He caught the change in her, the small frown line along her brow. He recognized it but hadn't seen it on her for days. "That bad, huh?"

A smile started at the corner of her mouth, and she peeked at him.

He put on a serious face. "It's probably my fault."

"Probably. But not completely."

"Well, I know something that will prove you wrong in every way."

She gave him a challenging look, her tone skeptical. "Really? What's that?"

"Dessert."

* * *

Faye set out five of her pale aqua dessert plates, then stepped out of the way and watched. Georgie had her arms folded on the counter, leaning forward. From the tall container, Jace pulled out a filled pastry bag. He squeezed several large dots of a heavy white cream across each plate. Then, slowly, he uncovered the cake, and even Dar *ahhh*ed.

"What did you make?" Faye asked, breathless.

Jace ran a knife under hot water from the tap. "Its very unimaginative name is flourless chocolate cake. It deserves better." He sliced cleanly into the round of the most decadent dessert Georgie had ever laid eyes on.

"Is that frosting?" Georgie asked.

He nodded. "Ganache."

"It looks like soft chocolate."

"There's some cream in there. Laced with a little orange liqueur." He raised an eyebrow and put his finger in front of his lips. "Shh."

She smiled. He was enjoying this. It was no wonder. Jace slid pieces of moist cake off his spatula onto the plates, then picked up the white cream again. He squeezed another large dot on top of the ganache. Then, from the short container, he pulled out what looked like paper-thin slices of candied orange, cut in half to form sparkling semicircles. He set a slice upright into the cream on top of a piece of cake.

"That's beautiful," Faye said.

Georgie had to agree.

Jace continued with more orange slices for the remaining plates, then pushed two of them gently toward Georgie and Faye.

Faye shook her head. "Tru has to come see this. If she wants a piece, she'll have to come out." She left the kitchen with purpose. "Don't start without me."

Georgie watched her leave, silently wishing her success. When she looked back toward Jace, she found him waiting, holding out a fork. She went to take it, but he pulled it just out of her reach. Her eyes widened, and she grabbed the fork on her second try. He laughed and pushed a plate to Dar, who grabbed his own fork.

"I knew inviting you was a good idea." Dar eyed the dessert. "I may need another walk after finishing this."

Georgie ran her fork along the edge of the "cake," a cross between the gooey center of a brownie and chocolate mousse. She moved her fork to the point of the slice and pushed through the dense ganache, nearly half an inch thick, then down through until it touched her plate.

"Your aunt said to wait for her."

She raised her eyes. "I don't think she'd blame me."

Dar chuckled over by the window, shaking his head. "I hope not," he said, his mouth full.

Jace's brow rose a fraction, and Georgie lifted the fork to her mouth. Her eyes closed, and she let the texture and flavor melt in her mouth. "Oh my." She sighed. Her fork found the next piece, and she ran it through the white cream. With this bite, she recognized it. The consistency of sour cream, but milder, and sweetened to perfection.

She looked at Jace, who watched her closely. "Crème fraîche."

"Do you like it?"

She nodded, running her fork through the french cream and picking up another bite. "One of my favorite restaurants at home serves it with fresh raspberries."

"And what do you think of this version?"

She swallowed. "Better." She pushed her fork into the cake, getting a bit of orange this time.

"You said something about it the other night. It started me thinking. My thoughts ended in this."

Her fork paused midair. A second ago there was nothing anyone could have said to keep her from taking another immediate bite of that decadence. But he said she'd started him thinking, and it had resulted in this. His eyes became a stronger distraction than even the cake.

A small commotion broke their gaze.

"I don't know why you had to make me get out of bed when I was perfectly—" Tru stopped, her mild tirade coming to an abrupt end at the sight of flourless chocolate cake and ganache with crème fraîche and candied orange. "Oh, heavens."

And in her flannel pajama bottoms and Navy Seals T-shirt, Aunt Tru joined the dinner party.

* * *

Faye opened the front door to the steady downpour outside. "You're not walking home in this. Georgie, tell him he's not walking home in this."

"It's only a few blocks." Jace shrugged on the jacket Georgie had retrieved from the peg.

"You'll be soaked through. Even with an umbrella," Faye argued.

He looked out the window. It was coming down pretty hard. The street gutters ran in little streams. He looked down at his shoes.

"Georgie—" Faye turned, pleading to her.

"Me?"

"Yes, you. Get out to your little car and zoom him up to his house."

Georgie chuckled. "*Zoom* him?"

"Yes."

Georgie turned to Jace. "Would you like me to zoom you?"

"By all means."

Dar laughed with his hand over his mouth but stopped when Faye whapped him lightly on the arm. "Stop that. You know what I mean."

Tru called from her chair in front of the TV. "If somebody doesn't drive him home soon, I'll take him." It was followed by a murmured, "Any boy who cooks like that, I'd carry him up the hill on my shoulders if I had to."

Jace smiled, looking down.

"Well, I guess I better drive you, then," Georgie said in mock agitation. "We wouldn't want Tru to throw out her back."

He nodded, zipping up his jacket. "The hill is pretty steep."

Faye nodded, pushing him and Georgie to the door. "Yes, it is. And slick. Georgie, put your hood on."

Georgie hid her laugh and pulled on her jacket. "You sound like my mom."

Faye sighed. "Just wear it to the car. Then I don't care what you do."

Jace lifted his eyebrows at Georgie, and Georgie held back another laugh.

Faye ignored the exchange. "Jace, it was wonderful having you over. Please come again real soon." To Jace's surprise, she reached up and gave him a quick hug.

"Thank you, Faye. I had a really good time. And again, thank you for dinner. It was delicious." He raised his voice. "And the rolls were perfect, Tru." She raised a hand, not taking her eyes off the screen.

"Jace." Dar reached out and shook his hand firmly. "What did I tell ya? This was a good idea."

"Yeah." He glanced at Georgie. "It was. Thanks."

Georgie grabbed a key ring off the hook and zipped up her jacket. She looked down at the keys, fingering them as Jace picked up his bag from the sideboard. He'd left the rest of the cake for them to enjoy and was bringing home empty containers. He loved that feeling. As a cook, it was satisfying. It was the whole point.

"Ready?" Georgie asked, pulling her hood on.

He nodded, and they were out the door, dashing for her car. She had an orange Kia. He'd learned to expect its presence in the restaurant employee parking. The lot felt oddly boring without it.

"Do you like your car?" he asked once seated inside.

She nodded. "My brother helped me buy it from a friend of his."

"The color kind of stands out. The orange in all this gray."

She frowned. "It's *burnt* orange."

"I meant that I like it."

She looked sideways at him as if deciding whether or not to believe him. He laughed.

Her windshield wipers worked like crazy as they drove up the hill. "This one here."

She pulled up into the drive and shifted into park. She'd been quiet for the short trip. He gave his place a once-over, looking past her, and groaned on the inside.

"It's nice." She turned back to him.

"It's a dump."

She tried not to laugh at his abrupt summation. She looked in the rearview mirror, then turned a little in her seat to look out the back window. He could smell her perfume again. Or maybe it was her shampoo.

"It has a great view."

He turned and looked. "I can't argue with you about that." The low clouds didn't quite conceal the bay, and he could still see Whidbey stretching out across the water.

"Faye says sometimes whales come."

"They do. I have a friend on Whidbey who gives me a shout out if he spots them first. If I hear anything, I'll pass it along."

"Thanks. Hey, you can see the house from here." She turned back to him, closer now that they were both leaning toward the center.

He nodded, hit with a pulling in his stomach, not unpleasant. Her eyes were a deep, clear blue in the evening gray, with islands of burnt caramel just around the centers.

"I, uh, had a good time." He watched for her reaction, not knowing what he wanted to see.

She looked down and sat back in her seat. Nope, that wasn't it. "Me too. We all did." She took a deep breath and lifted her chin. "Not so weird, huh?"

He sat back. "Not so weird. But you got to ask all the questions."

She narrowed her eyes. "What do you mean?"

He looked out at the awful scraped siding on his house. He could see Kit's head in the dark of the front window, could picture his tail wagging behind him. "I mean you know a heck of a lot about me, and all I know about you is your name, where you work, who you live with, and that your brother helped you buy a car."

"And the crème fraîche."

"Yeah, and that."

She lowered her eyes and played with the key ring dangling from the ignition. "That's a lot more than I want most of the population to know about me," she murmured.

He watched her for a second, curious about what she hid when she withdrew like that. She didn't offer anything more on the subject, so he changed it. "Do you think the cake would be a good addition to the dessert menu? It would replace the torte."

Her brow lifted in surprise. "Oh. Yeah. The torte is really good. But that cake . . ."

He smiled. "Great. I'll let Reuben know."

"Do you get to change things on the menu anytime?"

He shook his head. "No. He asked me to come up with some changes a few weeks ago. Freshen things up for the new season. It's an opportunity to show what I can do. I just haven't had much . . . inspiration."

She turned and looked out her window.

"So, when is it my turn?" he asked hesitantly. "To ask the questions?"

She lifted her hand and ran it along the steering wheel.

Enough time passed that he knew she was uncomfortable. "Another time, then?"

She met his gaze. "Maybe."

He nodded. "Thanks for the zoom."

She rolled her eyes. "Anytime."

He popped his door open. "I might take you up on that."

She muffled a laugh.

"Tell your family thanks again." He hopped out but ducked his head back in the doorway. "I'll see you tomorrow."

She nodded. "See you tomorrow. Hurry; your back end's gonna get soaked."

He grinned, and she shook her head, laughing again.

"Go."

"Bye." He pulled himself out into the rain and ran to the front door, not wanting to draw attention to the dismal carport. He unlocked the door, stepped inside, and turned just in time to see her wave, and then her car disappeared down the steep hill before reappearing farther down.

Don't stand here watching like some creep. When her car reached the main road, he turned and closed the door. Kit greeted him enthusiastically as he set his bag down on the small table and collapsed on the couch. The dog went to the back door and waited to be let out.

"Give me a minute, buddy." Jace ran his hands through his hair. "What am I doing?" He looked around at the threadbare place and shook his head. He checked the clock on the wall and felt the silence. She'd had to drive him up here because it had rained. And he only had a bike. "You're a real piece of work, Jace."

He reminded himself that he was trying to avoid these very pressures with his declared single status.

He imagined her laugh. She'd said he was interesting. Like a seashell full of holes.

He couldn't help smiling.

Chapter 10

"Jace, I need to talk to you for a few minutes." Reuben motioned to his office. It was just the two of them, an early Monday as usual. They used this time to plan, go over supplies and ingredients, make orders, that kind of thing. Jace yawned. He'd spent the earlier morning hours scraping siding.

Reuben sat at his organized mess of a desk, and Jace sat in the usual chair across from him and waited. Reuben folded his hands.

"How are you coming on the new menu items?"

Jace leaned forward with interest. "I have a new dessert. It's a flourless cake with a ganache. Crème fraîche from Golden Glen Creamery. Orange twist."

"Replacing the torte?"

"Yes." Most of the menu items were Reuben's own, so the assignment had an added hazard. He didn't want to offend the man. The torte, however, was not Reuben's. "Had a chance to test-drive it yesterday."

"I gather it passed. Can't wait to try it."

Reuben, of course, would have the final taste on all the dishes, but Jace was confident about the cake.

Reuben rapped his knuckles on the desk, his telltale sign the subject was about to change.

"We've had some publicity stemming from Anders's outburst the other day. I can't decide if it'll hurt or help us." He pushed the newspaper next to him forward. "It's not much, just the police reports. Facts about the disturbance and the arrest."

Jace looked it over and had to agree he didn't know if or how it would affect the restaurant. "Well, maybe a few more people will know we're out here, eh?"

Reuben smiled at Jace's half attempt at humor. "Right. And people are curious. But the faster we get the restaurant back into a more positive light, the better, no matter how small this is. So. . ." He leaned back in his chair. "I want the new menu written up next week. We start getting word out now, get the ingredients ordered so we're in full swing April first when the Tulip Festival hits. People talk. Local markets make suggestions. Bloggers . . . blog. Or whatever. I'm hiring a guy to get a website up for us, nice and shiny. My gut still turns about Anders. I wish he'd been able to fight it out. We all have demons. But this is a business. And we cover the bruises."

Jace remained quiet but nodded his head.

"I know what I'm asking. But you can do this, Jace."

He'd felt the pressure to turn in four dishes in as many weeks, but three in one? Jace hadn't even considered entrees yet. He decided he didn't have time to be cautious. "What do you think is weak on the menu?"

Reuben pulled the menu over. "Well, let's have a look."

When they finished taking apart the menu, Jace had three entrees *and* a new appetizer to come up with. Four dishes.

"Great." Reuben slapped him on the back as they left the office. "Think fresh. Bright. Tulip Festival."

"You know, tulip bulbs are edible," Jace offered.

"They are?"

"Yeah. But they taste like mud."

"Ha. Right. Thanks, Jace." Reuben checked his watch. "About time for the crew to start showing up. New dishwasher today."

"Oh, right. Georgie will be happy." He remembered her damp emergence after her turn at the sink.

"Will she, now? Things seem to be improving in that department." Reuben kept his expression one of general observance, but Jace had worked with his boss long enough to know when the man was hiding a thought.

"Yup." No way was he telling his boss he'd had dinner with Georgie's family.

"How 'bout that?"

Jace folded his arms and shrugged.

Reuben pursed his lips. "Well, keep tolerating each other. I like her."

Jace nodded. "You bet."

Reuben passed with a smirk and greeted Caleb, who'd just entered through the back door. Jace narrowed his eyes. *Tolerating.*

He'd like to think they'd moved beyond that. Hadn't they?

He turned to the bread ovens and flipped them on, remembering his new assignment. *Something new. Something fresh. Something not seen on every menu along the Washington coast.*

"You bet," he repeated with not a little sarcasm.

Almost an hour later, the new kid showed up for work.

"Everyone, this is Tyler, our new dishwasher. Make him feel welcome, crew." Reuben arched a brow in Jace's direction, and Jace couldn't help but roll his eyes. Just because he'd been a jerk about Georgie didn't mean he'd give all the new employees the same treatment.

To prove this, Jace approached Tyler as Reuben retreated to his office with the website guy. He stuck his hand out. "Tyler, Jace Lowe. I saw you at church."

"Yes, Jace. Good to see you." They shook hands.

"We really appreciate our dishwashers, so don't think you've got the low job on the totem pole. Without someone to man the beast over there," Jace nodded toward the sink and sprayer, "things get mucked up really fast. Just keep things cycling through. You'll be fine."

Tyler smiled. "Thanks. I'm sure I can handle it."

Jace patted him on the shoulder once and reached for his chef's coat hanging on its hook. He turned to the staff as the kitchen started that familiar hum. "Okay, people. Let's make them want to come back."

A couple of whoops came from the crew.

"So when does Georgie come in?"

Jace looked back at Tyler. "Any minute."

Tyler grinned. "Great."

"Georgie's station is up front." Jace motioned with his head as he buttoned up his white jacket. "You won't be seeing much of her."

Where did that come from?

Tyler nodded. "Sure. Great. Thanks."

"Good luck." Jace turned just as Georgie came in the back door. "Oh. Hey," he said.

She gave him a reserved smile. "Hey."

Jace suddenly couldn't think of anything more to say.

"Hi, Georgie." Tyler gave a wave from behind Jace.

Her smile widened. "Oh, hi, Tyler. First day of work."

"Yup."

Georgie hung up her jacket and picked up an apron. "I guess we'll be seeing a lot of each other, huh?"

Tyler's grin widened. "Yup."

Georgie pulled her apron on and tied it as she passed Jace, who felt like an idiot but wasn't going to show it.

"You gonna just stand there and let the customers fix their own food?" she asked.

Jace scowled. "No. I'm not."

* * *

"Prawns and the special for fifteen," Georgie called. "And coconut shrimp for table eight."

Jace turned to her. "Coconut shrimp. Okay, if you didn't have that in front of you on the menu, what would be satisfying to see in its place?"

Georgie stared. "Uh. I don't know . . . some sort of other . . . kind of shrimp?" The bread timer went off, and she turned most of her attention to that.

He chuckled. "You're a lot of help."

She heard the sizzle as he flipped steaks. "It's an odd question." She pulled hot loaves out and replaced them with loaves that had been rising. "Why are you asking about the coconut shrimp?"

"We're replacing it."

"What?" Her bread knife slid easily through the loaves. She could get just the right width on each slice now so each loaf had six slices. "Why replace the coconut shrimp? Everybody loves that appetizer."

"Yeah, and everybody can get them at almost any restaurant around here." He set the plates of steak down in front of her, and she drizzled them with clarified butter, sprinkled the top with minced parsley, and sent them on their way. He shook his head. "I need to kick it up a notch."

Georgie frowned in concentration as she put together a couple of wedge salads. "Kick coconut shrimp up a notch," she murmured. "Hmm."

Jace turned back to his pots.

The shrimp were crunchy and light, even though they were fried. And everyone loved the garlic aioli sauce they were served with. "Maybe a new dipping sauce?"

Jace turned and lifted his spatula to gesture with it. He did this often, she'd noticed, while talking or making a point while at the grills. "I've been considering that."

"Maybe change up the dip with something local?" She pulled an order off the cable. "Fish and chips, planked salmon, and a kids' number two," she called. "And two bowls of clam chowder," she added, picking up the ladle.

"A dip with something local," Jace mumbled.

"Yeah, something sweet," she said. "The aioli's amazing but not sweet."

"So . . . sweet and zingy."

"Yeah, zingy. But then the shrimp can't be too sweet."

"Eleven's up!" they both called, and John appeared.

He leaned forward to both of them. "Thanks for hiding the canna in the cooler, Georgie."

"No problem. It's gorgeous. Great color."

John had chosen a stem with orangey coral blooms and deeper orange throats. Georgie had a feeling Rhea would be grinning before John even got the words out.

Looking nervous, John left with the food. Georgie rapped her knuckles on the counter and reached for the next order.

Jace laughed to himself.

She faced him. "What?"

"The way you knocked on the counter just then. That's Reuben rubbing off on you."

She shook her head in disbelief, but he was smiling at her in a way that reminded her she liked to be smiled at.

Then his brow furrowed. "Help me."

She frowned, her face feeling warm. "Help you? With what?" She glanced around the kitchen and lowered her voice. "Is there someone you want to ask out too?" She pulled out salad plates and picked up the tongs.

"No, that's not it."

She busily started filling plates with greens.

"Georgie."

She paused and ignored the way her heart sped up. "What?"

"I need to come up with four new dishes by the end of the week. Reuben wants a menu overhaul. Will you help me?"

She looked at him. He was serious. She glanced around again. "Why me?"

He shook his head. "I don't know. Maybe because of the way you influenced the chocolate cake recipe."

"All I did was mutter 'crème fraîche.' Like a crazy person. Who mutters 'crème fraîche'?"

He smiled crookedly. "I just have to follow my gut, and I'm asking you."

She pulled out the dressing cups for each plate, wondering what in the world she was supposed to say.

"Please?"

Slowly, she nodded, not sure what she was getting herself into. "Who's crazier, the person who mutters 'crème fraîche' or the guy who listens to her?"

He breathed out a sigh of relief. Or of exasperation. She couldn't tell. "Thanks," he said. "We'll talk later."

She nodded again and finished the salads. But she peeked over at him as he tended the lobster broth he was making. He barely measured. Just added the ingredients with relaxed concentration, or confidence, she guessed.

Yet, he was worried about these new dishes. The chocolate cake idea was a fluke. How in the world would she be able to help him come up with brand-new items for the menu?

A voice in her head surprised her by asking her why in the world she would hesitate. *Help me*, he'd said so quietly. She swallowed hard and went to the bread oven just before the timer went off.

* * *

"Hey, Georgie."

"Hey, Tyler. What's up?" She dusted the dessert plates with powdered sugar for the key lime pies.

"I'm on my break and just thought I'd come see what you do up here."

"Excuse me, Tyler."

Tyler moved as Jace passed with a tray of halibut steaks.

"Well, as you can see, I pretty much run the place."

Tyler chuckled. "Yeah, I see that."

"Excuse me, sorry."

Tyler moved as Jace passed off the empty tray to Haru.

"Two primes, fried oysters, and a mahimahi," Georgie called, then she murmured, "Two baked potatoes and a house salad for me." She pulled out the appropriate plates. "How's your first day, going?"

"Great. Wet. Listen, I was wondering if you wanted to catch a movie tomorrow. A matinee."

"Oh—"

"Excuse me, Tyler." Jace set down two plates of food between Georgie and Tyler. "Four," he called. "Georgie, could I see you for a minute?"

She glanced at him. "Give me a minute." She placed a cup of dressing on the salad plate and finished with the potato toppings. "Tyler, tomorrow isn't good for me, but I have Wednesday off."

"I work my other job on Wednesday and Thursday. Friday?"

"I promised Faye I'd go to Edmonds with her on Friday morning, and then I work."

Tyler looked down.

"We'll have to figure something out," Georgie offered. "A late movie or something."

Tyler's brow rose, and he looked hopeful again. "Yeah, sure."

"I'll check my schedule." She gave him an encouraging look.

"Okay."

Reuben joined them to remove the prime rib from the oven. "Tyler, take your break in the back or outside. Sardines are not on the menu."

"Yes, sir. Sorry, sir." Tyler grimaced at Georgie and removed himself from the front.

With Reuben busy with the prime, Georgie looked over at Jace. He peeked over his shoulder at her from where the halibut sizzled on the grill.

What? She mouthed at him.

He hesitated, glancing at Reuben, then motioned to the walk-in fridge. He called Haru to come take over the halibut for a few minutes and made sure he saw the order. Then he walked into the fridge.

"Georgie, I need sides with these prime," Reuben said.

"Of course." She went to work and arranged the plates, which would wait for the other two entrees on the order.

She glanced at the bread ovens. "We need more loaves." No lie. She wiped her hands again and hurried to the fridge.

She entered and closed the door behind her. When she turned, she found Jace contemplating a glass container of aioli. He set it back on the shelf and searched another shelf. She felt compelled to whisper, but loudly. "What couldn't wait until my break?"

He spoke quietly, not looking at her. "I needed you to understand something, and it seemed a little more urgent at the time than it does now."

She wrinkled her brow. "What?"

Apparently unable to find what he was looking for, he turned to her. "When I asked you to help me with the new menu items, I meant I needed you to . . ."

"Yes?" She glanced behind her, inexplicably nervous about somebody coming in while she stood in the walk-in with Jace.

He scratched his head. "Well, it means a lot of time. A lot of brainstorming, a lot of searching ingredients, a lot of going to restaurants and trying to get . . . inspired. And cooking. Lots of cooking. I just wanted to make sure you understood that before the dishwasher guy—"

"Tyler."

"Yeah, Tyler—scored a date with you."

"*Scored* a date with me?"

"Yeah, but it sounds like it won't be a problem after all. At least not this week, so—"

"At least not *this* week?" She folded her arms. "Will it be a problem next week?"

He blinked. "No. No, I guess not." He paused, then asked, "Are you dating this guy?"

She opened her mouth to answer, but Jace put his hands up. "Sorry. That's not my business." He closed his eyes and shook his head at himself. "Look, this is all coming out kind of *weird*."

"We're in a refrigerator. It's already weird. And Tyler isn't *scoring* a date with me. He's already taken me out once. We're friends, if you must know, sort of. I'm not *dating* anybody."

He watched her a moment. "I shouldn't have said that. I'm sorry."

"It's okay." A corner of her mouth lifted. "Weirdo." As soon as she said it, she wished she hadn't. It had just come out naturally. Ian had put an end to any kind of playful banter. He didn't like it.

Jace covered a laugh. "I just wanted to give you a heads up about this week without making it awkward out there in front of Tyler. Or Reuben."

He hadn't even flinched at her teasing. Georgie relaxed a bit. "And you couldn't tell me this out there once Reuben was gone or Tyler had moved to the back or I was on my break because . . . ?"

He set his hands at his hips and studied her again. She lifted her chin, not wanting to appear to be trembling, whether or not she was.

His voice came out more calmly. "I told you. Because I didn't want it to be awkward."

She swallowed. "Too late."

"And because I like your idea. Something local. Something sweet."

She saw a glint in his eye, but he was somehow calming her. "That still doesn't expl—"

"I guess I'm impatient to get started. You said you had something tomorrow morning?"

"Kind of." She hesitated, not wanting to tell him she had a therapy session. "But it's not until two."

He paused. "So you lied." He was teasing, but it riled her. "You lied to that poor boy."

"I didn't know when a matinee would start, and I guessed it would interfere with my appointment."

He nodded, that infuriating glint still in his eye. "Can we meet tomorrow morning, early?"

She growled. "Yes."

He grinned. "My place or yours? You choose."

She'd already agreed to help him. She still didn't know what good she'd be, but she'd never seen him like this. And she had to admit, she was intrigued. "My aunts' place. Eight o'clock."

He nodded and smiled. "Great. Now get back to work. We need bread."

He reached for the door behind her and opened it as she moved to the bread shelf. The door closed behind him. She picked up a loaf and looked at it. "What just happened?" she asked it.

No response.

Dumb bread.

Chapter 11

Jace watched John and Rhea out of the corner of his eye. He scraped the grill down but listened to her laugh. John held the flower behind his back, waiting for the right moment to give it to Rhea.

"C'mon," Jace whispered. "Now."

Georgie kept sneaking glances too, taking more time with the broom than usual.

Finally, John held the flower out in front of Rhea. Her eyes grew large, and she stopped laughing.

"There's a play. I hear it's good. I was wondering if you'd want to come with me. We could grab dinner. Maybe."

Jace felt a tug on his arm and looked down. Georgie gripped his rolled-up sleeve as she watched them. Jace held very still, watching Georgie's face. She wasn't grinning or hopping up and down like some girls would. She appeared truly concerned. He turned back to John.

Rhea's eyes went to the flower, then back up to John. She broke out in the widest smile Jace had ever seen on her face. "I'd like that," she said. He saw the relief in John's shoulders as Rhea took the flower and gave him a hug.

Jace looked down at Georgie's fingers as she let go of his shirt. He detected a smile on her lips as she went back to sweeping.

She'd touched him. Kinda. That was good, right? It showed some form of trust, even after his crazy-talk in the walk-in. Or . . . she was just excited to watch John ask Rhea out, with the flower and all. But she wouldn't have done that to someone she was scared of. He'd take it.

Before John and Rhea left, John gave Jace a thumbs-up, then he and Rhea ducked out into the rain.

Jace took the laundry back to the washing machine and passed Tyler, who still had a large stack of dishes and glasses. "You doing all right?" he asked.

Tyler nodded.

"It'll go faster as you get used to things. Music helps. You get in a rhythm. We usually turn some on back here, but the sprayer's loud. The guy before you usually had his earbuds in."

"I wasn't sure that was allowed."

"For the dishwasher? You bet."

"Good to know. Thanks."

Jace continued to the washing machine. Half an hour later, Tyler had the last load of dishes running and Georgie was almost done mopping.

"Okay, Tyler, you can go." Jace flipped off lights in the front. "We'll see you tomorrow."

"Thanks." He tugged off his apron. "I've got to wait for my sister to pick me up. Not enough cars."

"I'll give you a ride, Tyler," Georgie said as she returned the mop to its bucket.

"Megan's already on her way. But thanks for the offer."

Georgie leaned on the mop handle. "How was your first day?"

Tyler shrugged. "Great. About what I expected."

A car beeped outside.

"There's my ride. Check your schedule about that movie." He opened the door.

She smiled. "I will. Tell Megan hi."

"I will." He ran out into the rain.

Georgie wheeled the mop bucket back to the utility sink. "Well, that was pretty great," she said.

Jace wasn't sure what she was referring to. He helped her lift the bucket and drain the water. "That he got a ride from his sister?"

She rolled her eyes at him. "No. John and Rhea."

"Oh, right. Yeah, that was pretty great." She wasn't referring to Tyler at all. "You were right about the flower."

She gave him a satisfied sort of look and removed her apron.

He switched off the light in the utility closet. "Do you have an umbrella? It's pouring out there."

Thunder rumbled, and both of them looked toward the door.

"Do you think we could see the lightning?" she asked. She grabbed her jacket and pushed right out the door.

Of course he followed her. She stood on the landing just outside the door, looking out over the sky, getting soaked. Sure enough, lightning flashed, and he watched her lips move as she silently counted. One-one thousand, two-one thousand, three, four, five—

Thunder rumbled, and then she grinned. Lightning flashed again, closer, and she gasped. It was just a little sound next to the thunder that followed. Another flash lit the whole sky, heavy with clouds, and again she counted. One-one thousand, two-one thousand, three—

The rumble shook through Jace.

"That was huge," she said. "I haven't seen one of these since before the accident."

"What accident?"

She looked up at him, blinking in the rain. Her smile had disappeared, and she rubbed her forehead. She just shook her head. Then another stab of lightning flashed, and she watched, the grin coming back. She pulled her arms around herself, though, and shivered. He opened his jacket and raised his arm over her head to try to shelter her.

She lifted her hand. "No, it's okay. Let the rain fall."

He lowered his arm, studying her. What accident? Why wouldn't she tell him? Was that why she had come here?

The storm and the lightning drifted farther away, and the rain slowed to a drizzle.

Finally she said, "I used to be afraid of that. When I was little. My dad said it was the only thing that scared me."

"But not anymore."

She shook her head, still watching the storm move away. "Not anymore." She bit her lip. "Now everything else does."

He frowned. She turned and looked up at him. Then she shrugged.

He had to ask. "Are you still afraid of me? Because you don't have to help me with the menu. I ca—"

"I want to help."

She hadn't answered his question. But maybe he didn't want to hear the answer.

"Okay, but you tell me if it gets too crazy, okay?"

She nodded. "Speaking of crazy, you're soaked."

He broke out into a smile. "Yeah. Somebody wanted to stand in a downpour and watch lightning."

"Didn't *you*?" she asked.

After another moment, he nodded. "Yeah."

She pulled her keys out of her jacket pocket.

"I still need to lock everything up," he said lamely.

She nodded. "I'll see you in the morning, then."

He nodded and watched her walk to her car and drive away.

After asking her to help him and talking to her like a maniac in the walk-in . . . and the Tyler thing—whatever that was . . . and just now watching her watch the lightning like a kid . . .

The less he knew about her, the more he wanted to know. Just . . . like a friend.

* * *

Georgie answered the knock at the door, wearing jeans, a hoodie, and bigfoot slippers. A gift from Tru. Comfy and warm. Jace stood holding his motorcycle helmet, looking like he'd been up for a while already.

"Oh, good," she deadpanned. "You're a morning person." Maybe that wasn't the right thing to say.

It didn't seem to faze him. "I had this idea so I need to take you somewhere. Won't take long, not even an hour, and we'll come right back."

She slowly processed what he'd said. "Somewhere?"

"On the island. I'll explain on the way. If you'll come." He looked at her hopefully.

"I'm going to need more info than that," she said. "Don't take it personally."

He gave her a nod. "Okay. We're going berry picking." His brow lifted.

"Berry . . . picking?"

"Yup. Kinda."

She considered berry picking with Jace Lowe on the island. At eight in the morning. On a Tuesday. In April.

She shuffled out the door. "Okay. But let me text Faye so she won't worry."

"Are you going to wear those?" he asked, looking at her Sasquatch feet.

She turned right back around and kicked her slippers off into the entry, then pushed her feet into a pair of nearby gardening boots and shut the door behind her.

"Better?" she asked.

He chuckled.

She wrote the text as they walked. Then she looked up. Jace had straddled his bike, his helmet was on, and he was holding another helmet out to her. She looked at the bike. Black with blue shiny parts. A small soft-side cooler was strapped to the rear.

"Wait, we're going on your motorcycle?"

"Yeah. It's not far, and I thought . . ." He paused and pulled his helmet off again. "If it's a problem, we can—" He glanced over to her car but looked away quickly. "Crap. I should have asked."

"No, it's okay. I actually like motorcycles. I just don't like jerks who think riding them makes them bigger men." Whoa. She'd just blurted that right out.

His eyes widened, and he sat down on the seat. "Wow."

She could feel her face turning to a full flush. She breathed out unsteadily and shook her head. "I didn't mean that."

"It really sounded like you meant it."

"No, I just—" She reached for the second helmet in his hand and pulled it out of his grip. She brushed her hair back with her hand and shoved the helmet down on her head. "I just knew a jerk once." She lifted her leg over the back section of the seat, sat, and waited.

He looked back at her, incredulous.

She lifted her shoulders. "Don't mind me. I'm a basket case. Come on. Let's go pick berries on your motorcycle. In April."

He shook his head. "We get off the motorcycle, *then* we pick the berries. You *are* a basket case." He put his helmet on, then started the bike.

The engine growled, and despite the turn of her gut from opening her big mouth, her heart leapt in an *I'm alive* kind of way she couldn't help appreciating. He turned up the driveway, then revved the engine a couple of times.

He hadn't gotten angry at her slip. He'd made a joke.

"For the record," he called back above the noise, "driving this *motorcycle*? It keeps me humble." He checked for traffic. "Hang on."

Feeling like a jerk herself, she rested her feet on her own set of foot pegs and did as he asked. As they smoothly launched onto the main road, she both hated and loved the excuse to grip his waist. Hated because she'd just stuck her foot in her mouth and wanted to retreat. Because she wasn't ready to touch like this, to be this close to anyone, really. But loved because his waist was just there, beneath his shirt, above his jeans, and felt real beneath her hands. Just real. Somehow that was important. Somehow she'd placed her hands on his waist and hung on.

They drove the main road around the island for a few miles. This morning the sky was clear blue. Everything sparkled after the storm from the night before.

When Jace slowed to turn, Georgie spoke loud enough for him to hear. "I'm sorry about what I said."

He reached and patted her hand firmly, then made the turn.

Georgie breathed a sigh of relief, surprised at how much she needed that simple gesture.

He followed a narrow road toward the center of the island, past a few homes tucked farther and farther back in the trees. After a dip, he pulled onto a turnout and parked.

"Are those . . . ?"

"Blackberry bushes," he said. He put down the kickstand and took off his helmet.

Georgie did the same and got off the back of the bike. Like dense, tall hedges, blackberry bushes lined the road, barely budding with green leaves along the weeping canes. The bushes continued up the road as far as she could see.

"Well, they're prolific," she said. "But they don't have any berries on them." She gave Jace a questioning look.

"You are correct. Berries won't come on until July."

She arched her eyebrow. "So . . . how are we going to pick them?"

Jace shook his head. "We aren't. Yet. But I woke up at four this morning thinking about *local* and *sweet*, and it occurred to me that blackberries grow all over the island. Just like this. Along the roads, edging the fields."

She nodded, thinking now. "The coconut shrimp. With blackberry sauce?"

"Too sweet." He dismounted the bike and joined her. They stood in front of the tangled branches, and he rubbed his neck. "We've got to lose the coconut. I'll use a crispy panko crust for the shrimp. But, yeah, a blackberry sauce. It's local, it's fresh, and I'm not sure I've seen one yet. When the berries do come on, we can pick local for the season and play that up. Maybe even bottle our own sauce for the off-season."

"Wow. That's kind of genius. And what about the zing?"

He looked at her. "Not sure about the zing yet. People like the garlic because of the kick. But we can start with this. What do you think?"

"I think it's a great idea. But where are you going to get blackberries if they aren't in season?"

"A magical place."

She frowned, but he motioned for her to get back on the bike.

A few minutes later, they pulled up in front of the grocery store.

"Oh," Georgie said.

He chuckled. "Hooray for California."

Jace picked out a carton of juicy-looking blackberries, a bag of limes, several large lemons, and a small bunch of parsley, and then he rested his arms on the grocery cart handle. "Now, what about the zing?"

Georgie looked around and shrugged. "The citrus will be zingy. But maybe something spicy?"

"I considered that. It's possible."

He rolled the cart over to the chili selection and chose a few different kinds and dropped them into bags.

"Garlic would still work too, wouldn't it?"

He nodded, choosing a few bulbs.

"Are you adding these to the sauce or the coating?" she asked as they moved the cart slowly along the produce section.

"I haven't decided yet. But it's a good question. We don't want to complicate the sauce. But we don't want to turn the shrimp into buffalo wings either."

"So bring out the flavor of the shrimp but add a little something extra."

"Exactly."

She considered a moment. "My friend's mom makes this appetizer. I hadn't even thought of it because it's not with crunchy shrimp. She just puts the raw shrimp in the oven for a while. But it's all pepper. Everyone loves it."

He stopped the cart. "What do you mean?"

"The zing. She pours melted butter over whole shrimp in a casserole dish, then sprinkles enough black pepper over them to make an elephant sneeze."

"That's it?"

"That's it."

She watched him thinking as he rubbed his neck. "It's simple. And with the lime . . . that would be a great combination. But black pepper in the sauce might overpower it."

"Could you put it in the crust?"

He looked at her, his brow furrowed, still thinking. She decided she liked watching him think. She liked watching him consider her ideas.

He lifted his hand, the same way he held a spatula when he had an idea. "Put the lime in the blackberry sauce and black pepper in the crust."

She paused. "Well, my mouth's watering."

He smiled. "Let's get some pepper."

They chose fancy pepper berries she'd never heard of, picked up a grinder and a few more spices, grabbed a few pounds of fresh, peeled shrimp at the seafood counter, some bottles of peanut oil and safflower oil, a bag of panko bread crumbs, and a carton of eggs, and headed for the checkout lines.

"It'll take a few tries," Jace said. "It's mostly a guess at first, getting the right amounts and combinations."

"I don't know how you just make stuff up."

He smiled as they unloaded the ingredients onto the conveyor. "You just did it yourself. Basic recipes are everywhere. Like your friend's shrimp. And after you know what a bunch of stuff tastes like, after you know the chemical reactions that certain combinations of ingredients or applied heat bring on, you just take those basic recipes and tweak them. And hope."

"So it's science."

"Yup." He paid the cashier, and they took the bags.

Georgie had never thought of cooking as science before, but she considered her chemistry classes in school. Following directions, measuring chemicals, applying heat and exact timing . . .

They walked outside. "So, to you, the kitchen is one big chemistry lab," she said.

Jace began packing the cooler on the back of the bike. He nodded. "And today we're mad scientists. You're sure it's okay with Faye that we use her kitchen? We can go to the restaurant instead."

"Would you rather be at the restaurant?"

"Not really. Not when I'm making stuff up."

"Let's go to Faye's. I think she's looking forward to it." She pulled on her helmet.

He pulled on his. "Let's not disappoint her."

Chapter 12

Jace pulled all the ingredients out of the bag while Georgie found an assortment of mixing bowls and saucepans and a deep fryer. Jace hadn't thought of bringing his deep fryer, so he was glad they had one. They could have used a heavy pan, of course, or a wok, but for experimenting, the deep fryer was the most convenient. He did bring his own food processor, however, and unpacked it along with his notebook. He'd keep an exact record of the amounts used and the adjustments made so he could replicate their results on a larger scale—which was a whole other experiment—but a small batch was the best way to start.

"All of your recipes are in here?" Georgie asked, gesturing to the notebook.

He shrugged. "The newer ones. I have a few more notebooks at home."

"May I?"

He nodded, and she lifted the cover of his beat-up ninety-nine cent composition notebook as if it were made of glass.

He couldn't help watching her as her gaze lingered on the pages jammed with his notes and ideas, recipes he'd imagined during the commute to Seattle, a solution to a wrecked paella he'd let get too complicated, a sandwich idea . . . her finger absently touched the notes in the margins, and he found himself suddenly nervous, caring what she thought of what he'd laid out on the lines.

She lifted a page and paused. She looked up. "Is this—?"

He leaned over her shoulder, daring to close the space between them. His heart hammered with nerves, and he reminded himself that though she seemed to be comfortable trying different foods and flavors, she was unfamiliar with the art of actual cooking and probably wouldn't be too critical. He just wished he'd been more organized with his scrawl.

"The bisque," he said. His words came out kind of breathy, and she looked up at him.

Dang, she was close.

"It doesn't say anything here about dumping it all over the expediter," she said.

He still wasn't used to this eye-contact stuff with her. A split second passed, and he saw the humor in her eyes fading.

He blinked. "Well, that's because that particular experiment was unintentional." He grabbed the pen and scribbled a note with an arrow. "There."

He pushed the notebook toward her.

She read. "'Spilling bisque on expediter not recommended. Improvement of flavor minimal.'" She frowned. "Well, *that's* debatable."

He laughed and closed the book.

The excitement that came with creating something new buzzed through him as he became familiar with the space: the stove, the bar, and Georgie restacking a set of bowls so they nested large to small.

"Knives?" he asked.

She opened a drawer full of an assortment of knives next to him. He chose a chef's knife and a small parer.

"Cutting boards are below."

He selected a couple of those as she added oil to the fryer so it was ready to heat up.

"Okay," she said. "What now?"

He pulled out two aprons from the cooler and shook them out.

She narrowed her eyes. "I thought we couldn't take those home."

"We can't. I bought these. Employee discount."

She shook her head but grinned and reached for one. He pulled it from her, and she made an exasperated sound.

"Say thank you."

She folded her arms. "Thank you."

"Say thank you, *Jace.*"

She paused and looked away, biting her lip, and he thought maybe this time he'd pushed it too far. But maybe her comment about the bike this morning had stung, and maybe he wanted a thank you.

She turned back to him and set her shoulders, meeting his gaze. "Thank you, Jace. That was really thoughtful. And I'm glad you didn't steal them." She smiled as he handed her an apron.

Maybe he'd wanted that smile too. Maybe.

"Good morning," Faye said, entering the kitchen with a paperback tucked under her arm.

"Good morning," Jace and Georgie answered, tying their aprons.

"Well, don't you look official? Did you two get breakfast?" Faye opened a pantry door and pulled out some bread.

"I had a yogurt this morning." Georgie answered. "Jace?"

He shrugged. He hadn't thought of breakfast. Ironically, when he had a new recipe idea in his head, he seldom thought about eating. "I'm good."

Faye stayed out of the way as she made toast and poured some orange juice, eyeing them with a smile. "I'll be reading out on the porch if you need me."

"Don't you want to watch?" Georgie asked.

Faye nodded. "I'll check in from time to time."

"It's your kitchen," Jace said. "You're welcome to stay if you'd like."

Faye picked up her breakfast. "I appreciate that." She headed to the door, and Jace heard her mumble, "I'll let you two warm up a bit." The back door closed behind her.

He blinked, unsure he'd heard right, then turned to Georgie. "Do you have a colander?" He opened the package of shrimp.

Georgie quickly retrieved a large colander.

"Where's your other aunt? Tru?"

"She works at the retirement home today. Dar dropped her off on his way to his law office this morning."

He nodded. He liked the aunts, and he didn't mind anybody watching them work. But he felt a measure of relief that he and Georgie would be mostly alone.

Less pressure, he told himself.

They washed the shrimp and patted them dry, then Jace separated them into small bowls and put them in the fridge. They'd be attempting the sauce first.

"Could you rinse the blackberries and add one cup to the processor?" Jace asked.

Georgie emptied the carton into the colander, and Jace peeled and minced several cloves of garlic, his chef's knife quick and precise.

"How do you do that?" Georgie asked.

"Practice." He washed his hands at the sink. He chose a small saucepan, set it on the stove, and turned on the heat. "Let's figure this thing out."

He made notes as they measured out honey, garlic, and lime, adding each ingredient to the blackberries. He looked at Georgie, his fingers on the food processor's power button. "What do you think?"

She shrugged. "Go for it."

He turned on the processor, and he and Georgie watched the ingredients blend to a pulpy purple-black. He hit a button, and the blade stopped.

"Now what?" Georgie asked.

"Now"—he grabbed a spatula—"we scrape this mixture into the saucepan and cook it." He'd removed the processor lid and lifted the bowl. He sniffed the mixture. "Mm, smell this."

Georgie leaned forward and sniffed. "Oh, wow."

"What do you think the odds are that we hit this on the first shot?"

She smiled. He scraped the mixture into the pan, and it sizzled at first, then mellowed out as it filled up. "Now we stir it as it simmers so it will thicken and the flavors incorporate. Here." He offered her the spatula. She hesitated at first but then took it and gently stirred the sauce as he'd shown her.

"When did you know you wanted to be a chef?" she asked.

He frowned. "I'm not sure exactly. We weren't allowed to get too creative at the diner. That menu's been in place for forty years." He adjusted the heat under the pot. "But I got to try pretty much anything at home. Most of my experiments centered around hamburgers." He smiled, remembering.

"What was the best burger you ever made?" she asked, concentrating on her stirring.

"I made this one burger with brown-sugar-caramelized bacon, avocado, tomato, sweet onions, and BBQ sauce. I spread peanut butter on the top bun."

Georgie made a face. "Peanut butter?"

He nodded. "My sisters called it my sweet bacon peanut burger." He laughed at that. They'd made a game of giving all his experiments names. He didn't remember most of them now, but he remembered that one. "We all took turns taking a bite of that burger until it was gone."

She shook her head. "Peanut butter on a burger . . . What did your dad think?"

Jace shrugged. "He never tried it." He took up his pen and wrote down the cooking time so far. "It's beginning to thicken."

He turned, and she was watching him. "Keep stirring," he said. She did.

"Did your dad try your other experiments?"

He frowned and kept his eyes on the sauce, now bubbling gently. "He mostly just made sure I could make the diner stuff. If I nailed the chili fries, he was pleased."

"Did that feel stifling?"

He looked at her and cocked his brow. "They were amazing chili fries."

She smiled then. For a moment, he forgot his dad. And the sauce.

He quickly checked the time. "Take that off the heat, and we'll let it cool." He wrote down the time as she moved the saucepan and turned off the burner.

He poured enough to taste into a small bowl, covered it, and put it in the fridge.

She wiped the counter where they'd assembled the sauce. "When did you know you wanted to move beyond hamburgers and chili fries?"

He leaned on the counter and folded his arms. "Aren't you full of questions today."

She threw the rag in the sink. "You don't have to answer." She looked at him, though, as if she was issuing a challenge. He couldn't help thinking how it would go if their roles were reversed. He didn't know a thing about her, really.

Maybe it was the idea that if he answered her questions, it would be his turn to ask, or maybe he was pleased that she wanted to know about his career, but whatever the reason, he answered her. "I was sixteen when I realized I was experimenting with the burgers and the french toast and the sandwiches in hopes that someday my dad would want to put something of mine on the menu. At the same time, I realized that probably wasn't going to happen. Stupid, maybe, putting so much importance on what goes on a diner menu. But I knew what my dad wanted of me, what his plans were for me. Work at the diner, run it when he was done. Keep it constant in a world moving forward. Which is kind of noble, right?"

She nodded. "Right . . . but not for you?"

He shrugged. He really didn't know. He admired his dad's devotion to the diner. "I just . . . let go of the idea that Dad would put something on the menu and started experimenting with other things. Other dishes, other regions." He chuckled. "I even applied for a job at an Asian restaurant. Man, my dad found out and hit the roof." Jace pushed himself away from the counter and pulled out the cooled sauce from the fridge.

He set it down on the counter and removed the cover. With a clean spoon, he stirred it to cool it further. "Ready to taste this?"

She nodded, but the questions came out in a stream. "What did your sisters think of all this? Did they work at the diner too? Did he just expect you to take over, or were there expectations for them as well? And if you did take over and maybe added the sweet bacon peanut burger or whatever to the menu, what could he say?" Here she began to pace in front of him. "I mean, the fact that you wanted to cook and you have this talent at all should mean something to him. What if you'd been born without a care for how food was cooked, just as long as somebody made it for you? What if you'd wanted to be a doctor or a computer programmer or a fireman or a . . . a ballroom dancer?"

His brow rose at her outburst. "A ballroom dancer?"

She threw out her arms. "It could happen."

He hid his laugh, appreciating her sudden loyalty to his craft. He reached for a box of crackers and spooned some sauce onto one and handed it to her. She took it, a little out of breath, and took a bite.

"This is good. This is amazing," she said and took another bite. "I want to dip shrimp in this."

He busted out laughing.

"Cut it out," she said, looking hurt but not really.

He calmed his laughter and shook his head. He spooned some sauce on a cracker for himself and took a bite. "Hm. That is good."

"Did we do it? On the first shot?"

Where did this enthusiasm come from? This version of Georgie was so different from the quiet girl who had started at the restaurant, afraid to step in somebody's way. Afraid to step in his way.

"Maybe," he said. "I think we should make a couple more batches just in case we can hit something better."

"That will be hard to do. I want to put this on chicken and pork and biscuits and—"

"Ice cream?"

Her eyes grew wide. "Yes. Ice cream."

He grinned. "Well, before you call Ben and Jerry's, I think we should try it with a little more citrus and again with some chilis. Just to see."

She nodded. "You're in charge."

They began the process from the start, and he noticed her questions had stopped. He opened his mouth to ask her about her own family, but just as he did, she spoke.

"I'm sorry about what I said before. I didn't mean to be disrespectful to your dad. Sometimes I just . . . say stuff."

He looked at her. "That's okay. It's just one of those family things. It seems kind of silly on the surface. But there's a lot of . . . baggage behind it."

She nodded and pushed the cutting board closer to him. He sliced another lime in half.

"You know what you said about my dad not appreciating the fact that I like cooking?" he asked.

"Yeah?"

She sounded so contrite he almost didn't continue. But he liked talking to her. He seemed to be able to work out his ideas better with her bouncing them back at him. He continued. "I think he did and still does appreciate that. So much that he put a lot of hopes on me taking over the diner. And then I didn't. If I'd wanted to do those other things . . . ballroom dance or whatever . . ."

She smiled.

"He wouldn't have banked on me and the diner." He looked at her, regarding her expression. What Georgie Tate thought of him was becoming increasingly important.

She frowned and considered his words. "So I guess he knows what he's losing."

He stilled at that perspective.

She dumped a cup of blackberries into the processor. "You're lucky. Not many people understand that until it's too late." She looked up at him.

"You're suggesting it's not too late."

She shrugged and added the measuring cup of lime juice to the blackberries. She scratched her forehead and sighed. "He's still alive, right?"

He didn't answer, and she picked up his pen. "Write the amounts down in your recipe journal thingy."

He did.

Half an hour later they had three blackberry sauces cooling in the fridge and were preparing to make the shrimp.

Jace couldn't help observing how cooking with Georgie was different from cooking with Brenna. On the occasions when he'd cook for Brenna, he did all the preparations before she arrived, or Brenna sat in the other room while he worked in the kitchen.

"I'll just be in your way, babe," she'd say, then get on her phone and text or read. Now that he thought about it, even when he'd asked her to help, she'd seemed bored or impatient.

And it occurred to him how little he thought of Brenna anymore.

He watched Georgie sort through the ingredients for the next phase of their experiment, noticing a small splotch of blackberry pulp on her neck. He had the fleeting temptation to say something but chose not to. Then he surprised himself by imagining kissing her there, tasting the berries.

Followed by her punch to his gut.

Yeah, that was all he needed.

She turned, catching him watching. With a jolt, he grabbed the stack of bowls, and she quickly focused on the egg carton. She popped open the lid. "Do we have everything we need?"

He surveyed the ingredients, taking a deep breath. "Looks like it. We're flash-frying so the shrimp stay light and crunchy without getting too greasy." He slid one of the small bowls to her. "Would you crack an egg in here?"

Georgie cracked an egg, immediately diving after a small piece of shell. He smiled to himself and scooped flour into the second bowl and then a handful of panko crumbs into a third. He minced the washed parsley and poured the peppercorns into the grinder as Georgie wiped her hands on a towel. She set the towel down and waited.

"Well?" she asked.

"Well, now we figure out the seasonings." They studied the array before them.

He raised his eyebrows at Georgie, and she shook her head.

"Don't ask me. Until a few hours ago, I didn't even know that panko bread crumbs were a thing."

He nodded and reached for the salt. Pinch of that. Garlic. Minced parsley. He made notes as he went.

Faye wandered in to get a sweater. "Something smells good in here," she said.

"We made blackberry sauce," Georgie said with pride.

"Mm, heavenly. I thought about giving you some instruction in the kitchen, Georgie, but I'll admit you've found a more interested teacher." Faye winked at Jace, pulled her sweater on, and excused herself once more. "Let me know when it's ready," she called behind her as the back door shut again.

After Faye left, Jace found himself trying to look anywhere but at Georgie, and Georgie seemed to be doing the same.

She spied the ingredients. "What are those?" She pointed to a small glass jar.

"Black sesame seeds," he answered, grateful to get back to the task at hand. "I thought they would add to the crunch and the look of the shrimp."

She nodded, and she actually seemed eager, so he added the sesame seeds.

Then he lifted the pepper grinder. "How much black pepper did your friend's mom use?"

"She sprinkled the heck out of them. Kind of made your lips burn."

He kept himself from smiling. "Do we want our lips to burn?" He watched her gaze flicker to his mouth and back up, and the action made him strangely nervous.

She looked down and shrugged, tracing a dark vein in the granite countertop. "I guess it depends on what you want," she said. "If you're going to sell them as lip-burning spicy, then customers who like that will order them."

He nodded. "Like buffalo wings."

"Right. But if you want to appeal to a wider base, keep them on the milder side."

"Which do you like?" he asked casually. "Lip-burning spicy or a slower heat?"

She looked up at him quickly, and her cheeks colored. "I . . . don't—"

He considered teasing her, but something told him not to. Maybe it was that nervous hammering of his heart again. He was anticipating how this experiment would turn out, that was all.

He grabbed another small bowl and started grinding pepper like a mad man. "We'll figure it out. The addition of the sauce will also be a deciding factor." After filling the dish with a small mound of cracked pepper, he reached for a quarter teaspoon. Always start small.

"You tell me when," he said.

"Me?"

"We don't have to get it right the first time. We have plenty of tries. But you know what the pepper on the butter shrimp looked like."

After three spoonfuls, she stopped him.

"You sure?"

She peered into the bowl. "Maybe one more?"

He added more, made a note, and mixed the crumbs a few times with his hand to blend the seasonings. He showed her the mix. "How's that?"

She shrugged, nodding. "I guess."

"Good enough for me," he said. "Grab a bowl of shrimp from the fridge."

As he washed his hands, Georgie brought out a bowl of four shrimp. He returned to the counter, and she set the bowl down in front of them.

"Our first victims," he said.

"Bless their little shrimp bodies."

"Amen."

She grinned.

He showed her how to dredge the shrimp in flour, then egg, then the bread crumbs. She followed perfectly.

"Good. Now we fry them."

They added the shrimp to the fryer basket, and Jace lowered them sizzling into the hot oil.

He got out the sauces from the fridge, and Georgie set up paper towels on a plate for the hot shrimp.

The shrimp quickly turned crisp and golden, even heavily flecked with black pepper. Jace lifted the fryer basket and let it drain. Then, with tongs, he transferred the shrimp to a plate.

"Those look great," Georgie said.

He had to agree. But even after the blackberry sauce, he knew successful first tries were rare. "Okay, when you taste these, I want you to consider your very first impression of that first bite, then what you think as you chew, and then what you experience after you swallow. Imagine yourself at a restaurant and trying these for the first time."

He held the plate out to her, and she chose a shrimp. He chose his. She went to dip hers in the first sauce.

"Wait. Taste them without it first. We need to make sure they can stand on their own."

"But they don't have any feet."

"Ha, ha." He held his shrimp up, and she mirrored him. "Here's to good ideas."

"Cheers."

They bit into their shrimp with the exact crunch he wanted to hear. He watched her as they chewed.

And then the heat hit.

Her eyes grew wide. Jace drew in a breath but choked. She waved her free hand near her mouth and hurried to the cupboard for glasses.

"Milk," he cried, knowing water wouldn't do much.

Georgie poured milk. They grabbed the glasses and gulped, then both gasped.

"The crackers," Jace said.

Georgie attacked the box and shoved a few in his hand.

He bit into a couple and chewed. After wiping tears from his eyes, he asked, "What do you think?"

She nodded, finishing off her milk. "The first impression was perfect until, you know, my mouth ignited in flames." She shoved a cracker in her mouth and talked around it. "Swallowing left a trail of pepper lava. My ears hurt. But we're close."

He grinned, still choking a little. "You want to try them with the sauce to see if that will help?"

She shook her head. "Not even with ice cream."

"No Ben and Jerry's? No *My Lips Are on Fire Ripple*?"

Georgie laughed. "I'm so sorry," she said, sobering a little.

"It's not your fault. Experiment, remember? You've taken mad scientist to a new level. Fresh cracked pepper is always stronger than preground. I should have remembered. But now we know where to go from here."

"We do?"

"Yeah," he said. "Less pepper."

She smiled and sipped more milk.

Three more tries later and Jace knew they were getting it. They held their crunchy shrimp in front of them in anticipation.

"Third time's a charm," he said.

"Smells good," she offered. Their glasses of milk stood at the ready.

He smiled warily and took a bite. She followed.

As they chewed, Georgie's eyes closed.

The burn was subtle, allowing the earthy flavor of the pepper to come through without overpowering the buttery sweetness of the shrimp.

"I like the lemon," she said, her eyes still closed. "It's not lemony but just a little . . ." She opened her eyes and studied her shrimp. "Lighter."

"And the burn?"

She swallowed. "It's good, but I can't wait to try it with the blackberry sauce."

That was exactly what he wanted to hear. He pushed the first bowl of sauce in front of her and spooned some onto her shrimp. She bit down and chewed.

"Mmm, that's good. That's really good."

"Yeah?"

"Yeah." Georgie spooned a little more sauce on her shrimp and pushed the bowl toward Jace. "Try it, sous-chef."

He spooned deep-purple sauce over his shrimp, lifted it to his mouth, and took a bite.

Georgie nodded slowly, and Jace raised his hand to her, palm open for a high five.

She returned the gesture, her smile open and without caution. Her carefree expression was fleeting. She lowered her gaze and turned to the other sauces.

"We need to try these too, right?"

He nodded, feeling the triumph settle in. "This first sauce is going to be hard to beat though."

"Definitely."

With this boost of confidence, he no longer wished to be the only one giving answers. "Georgie, where do you come from, and how is it that you've never cooked before?"

Georgie bit her lip just as Faye came in from the back patio.

"How's it going in here? It smells wonderful."

Georgie gave her her full attention. "We just finished. Try this." Georgie held the plate out to Faye.

Faye helped herself, and despite Georgie not answering his question, that small thrill of expectation ran through Jace. One of the best things about cooking was when he knew he'd hit the nail on the head and he got to share the first tastes.

Through Faye's sounds of approval, Georgie invited her to help them choose the best sauce. It didn't take long. They were all tasty on their own, but with the shrimp, it was clear.

"It's unanimous," Jace said. "The first sauce is the best."

Georgie and Faye nodded in agreement.

"Incredible," he said.

Georgie grinned. "So we're done? We did it?"

He paused. "That depends."

"On what?" she asked, opening the fridge.

He leaned against the counter. "On whether you were satisfied or you were left wanting more." He glanced at Faye, who winked at him. He couldn't help chuckling and offered her the fourth shrimp. She didn't even hesitate.

Georgie pulled out the remaining bowls of raw shrimp. She set them down on the table with a clatter and lifted her gaze to his once again. "Let's make more."

Slowly he grinned.

Chapter 13

Jace picked up his helmet. "I'll see you tonight at work."

She nodded and folded her arms.

"Tomorrow we'll explore a bit more. We've got to get a main dish. Start that brain of yours thinking in that direction."

"No problem," she answered, heavy on the sarcasm.

He grinned. "You have the day off tomorrow, right?"

She nodded.

"I think we should head over to the tulip fields. Maybe hit a few restaurants for inspiration."

"Oh . . ." Worry suddenly clouded the lightness she'd felt in their success. "I'm not . . . I don't . . ." Restaurants, tulip fields. It sounded like a—

"Don't worry," he said. "It's on the restaurant's bill. Research."

The sensation of foolishness immediately took the place of her sudden nerves. He wasn't asking her out. This was work. "Of course."

"But there's the matter of . . ." He looked down at his motorcycle. "Do you mind taking the bike again?"

She felt herself shaking her head no. She didn't mind.

"I mean, I didn't want to ask you to drive—"

"We can take the bike," she said, recoiling at how eager she sounded. "Or I could drive."

He nodded, studying her. "It might rain."

She flung her arms out. "Whatever. Let's just take the bike."

He seemed to enjoy her awkward display. "Okay, then." He pulled the helmet on, kicked up the kickstand, and got it started. "Thanks!" he called above the engine.

"For what?" she asked.

He just shook his head and pulled out of the drive.

Georgie watched him leave, his motorcycle growling away and up the hill, and she fought the smile tugging at her mouth.

She'd had no idea what to expect. She'd had no idea what kind of help she'd be or if Jace would be impatient or if he would do all the work. But he had been patient, and they'd worked together, mostly. Now they had their—his—appetizer for the menu. And there was something more.

She hadn't felt incompetent, inadequate, or extra. She'd had fun. All morning. Cooking with Jace was fun.

She folded her arms, and her smile faded. She'd made that horrible comment about men and motorcycles, and then she'd managed a small tirade about Jace's dad. At least he'd taken it well. Even, she sensed, with some amusement. At least about his dad. And when Jace had flirted with her—she was pretty sure it was flirting, despite her rants—the thump of her heartbeat had not been unpleasant. She'd struggled to downplay it. They were friends. After Uncle Dar admitted he'd asked Jace to keep an eye on her at work, she'd noticed Jace often went out of his way to draw a smile from her. And today she realized she appreciated it.

She pulled out her phone for the first time since that morning. Twelve thirty.

Her therapy appointment was at two. She sighed. The day had been great so far. And though the therapy was helping, it wasn't fun.

At all.

Laurel Cruz leaned forward in her chair, her elbows on her knees. They'd gone through the pleasantries, and now Georgie felt the lightness of her morning dim and deflate. She wasn't in therapy for pleasantries.

"I've had a good day," she said.

"Wonderful. What made it good?"

Jace. She pushed that answer away. It wasn't Jace. Not all of it. "I was trying new things. I felt a lot like myself. It was distracting . . . from everything."

"I'm glad you were able to have some distraction. I don't think you've allowed yourself very much of that; am I right?"

Georgie nodded. She wanted more of that distraction—more feeling . . . real.

"Where would you like to go from here? Why are we here today?"

That was a loaded question, but Georgie knew what Laurel meant. "I feel guilty. Just . . . guilt. Most of the time. I jump on things and people

. . . Tons of questions keep floating around in my head, and I don't know how to shake them or answer them."

"What questions?"

Georgie sat on the edge of the chair and rubbed her forehead. "Should I have waited to break up with Ian? Why did I let it get so far? How was I attracted to someone like that in the first place? What caused the accident? Why did he have to *die*? How can I prevent something like that from happening again?" She rolled her eyes and fell back against the chair, realizing her tone had become urgent. "You know, just the usual."

Laurel smiled patiently. "Do you think it was a mistake to break up with Ian?"

"No."

"So, if you're sure that wasn't a mistake, why should it matter when it happened?"

Georgie dropped her hand and leaned forward. "Because he *died*."

"But you don't know what caused the crash. You don't remember."

"He was very angry. Really angry. I made him angry."

"What are some general reactions when people break up with each other?"

"What?"

"Let's just list some common reactions that occur during breakups." Laurel stood and pulled the lid off a whiteboard marker.

"Um, okay. So, anger."

Laurel nodded and wrote *anger* on the board.

"Sadness."

Up the word went.

"Confusion. Heartbreak. Relief."

Laurel wrote all these down and popped the lid back on the pen.

"Good. Now, you said Ian was angry. Why, of all of these emotions, do you think he chose to be angry?"

Georgie blinked, unsure of how to answer.

"Let's try this." Laurel tapped her pen at the words on the board. "We tend to attach the value of somebody's romantic feelings, or love, to the type of suffering at breakup. What do you think of that?"

Georgie considered and leaned back in her chair again. "I think that when people are sad, really sad, it's easier to believe they truly loved. Or thought they could truly love."

"And what about when they choose to be angry?"

"It's a little different. Maybe they're hiding their feelings. Or maybe they're mad because it wasn't the plan. Maybe they'd invested a lot in the relationship." *Or they're narcissistic psychos*, she thought.

"Go on."

Georgie rubbed her forehead. "Maybe insecurity?" She remembered what Faye had said, "The need for control? He got mad easily. About a lot of things."

"What kinds of things?"

Georgie closed her eyes and pressed her lips together, visualizing Ian and the ways he'd lost his temper. "When he couldn't get cell service. Or his steak was too done at the restaurant." She frowned. "He'd get upset if my opinion didn't match his. He hated being teased." She paused, thinking of Jace. "Playful banter made him mad." She wondered how she could have ever been with someone like that. They'd had instant chemistry at the beginning. But it had soured so quickly. She had only ever wanted something good and true. Why had she hung on?

"How are you feeling right now?"

Georgie hadn't realized her fists were clenched. She found it hard to breathe. "Like I want to call Ian a jerk for treating me that way. Like I want to tell him all the reasons I would never marry him. Like he was a controlling egomaniac." A tear squeezed out the corner of her eye. "But then I remember I shouldn't say those things."

"Why not?"

Georgie wiped the tear. "Because he died, and that's worse than anything I could say."

Laurel watched her for a moment. She laid the pen down. "Georgie, you're talking like you believe that Ian dying in that car crash was his punishment. A sentence too harsh for whatever happened between the two of you."

Georgie blinked, wondering if that was true.

"Let's say, for the sake of figuring this out, that you hadn't broken up with him yet, that you'd decided to wait until he pulled up to your apartment that night to drop you off. Let's say that on the way home the car still hit a curve going too fast and you sped down an embankment and crashed and Ian still died. What then?"

Georgie ran the scenario through her brain. She still would have been quiet in the car. He would have been teasing words out of her. He didn't like it when she was quiet, but he might not have been angry. If he'd taken the curve too fast—if he'd still died—

After a minute, she said, "I guess I would have thought of it more as an accident. A life taken by circumstances. And less the other way."

"What other way?"

She paused, gathering her courage to say the words. "Thinking that the accident was my fault."

"Would you still have felt guilty?"

"No, not as much."

"Why not?"

Georgie sighed. "Because I would've known his last moments of life weren't spent upset with me. I would have known the accident wasn't my fault."

"What if he had been driving recklessly because he was happy or showing off for you?"

Georgie couldn't argue those possibilities down.

"What if you hadn't been in the car, and upset or happy, he'd just decided to race through the canyon?"

Again Georgie didn't have a response. These were real possibilities with Ian, possibilities she hadn't considered in all her nights spent awake and weighed down.

Laurel continued. "As I understand it, if there had been no accident, you still would have called off the engagement, even knowing how angry he would become."

Georgie nodded, her thoughts spinning. "I couldn't have married him."

"No. You couldn't." Laurel sighed and removed her glasses. "You mentioned control. What if I suggested to you that Ian became angry when you broke up with him because he felt loss of control?"

"That . . . actually makes sense." He hadn't become angry—or sad or heartbroken—because he'd lost her love. He'd become angry because he'd lost control.

"Georgie, you and I share the same belief system, right?"

"Yes."

"Do you mind if I incorporate that here?"

"Go ahead."

"We believe in an afterlife. What do you think that is for Ian right now?"

The thought was not new to Georgie. She'd often begun to wonder only to shut the ideas down. She was too close, too hurt, too upended, and she'd decided to leave the judging to God. "I've been telling myself that's between him and Heavenly Father."

"That's wise. It is. But I want to try something. Now, excuse the visuals. This isn't scripture here, but I'm trying to simplify. Close your eyes and picture Ian standing in front of the gates of heaven; imagine his life laid out before him like a movie."

Georgie did that.

"Now imagine one of the officials—let's just say Peter—sets his hand on Ian's shoulder and turns him to look back on the earth, to look at you."

She imagined it. Her heart pounded.

"And because he's been shown his life from every angle, he understands. He knows why you called off the engagement. He knows exactly why."

A sensation Georgie couldn't identify formed in her center and slowly worked its way outward. Her breathing quickened, but it wasn't from fear. Because if he knew why . . . if he understood why . . .

More warm tears formed along the seams of her closed eyelids.

"Georgie," Laurel spoke quietly. "There's a chance Ian is past holding you accountable. You need to do the same. You need to forgive yourself."

The warmth continued to spread to her limbs and fingertips and to spill out of her eyelids.

Ian, if you know why I couldn't marry you, then you also know that I would have never wished for you to die. I would never wish for anyone to die.

* * *

Jace watched Georgie with concern. She'd come to work wearing dark sunglasses, and when she'd taken them off, he'd seen that her eyes were puffy and red. She'd said it was just allergies, but her smile hadn't come after several lame attempts to coax one from her.

Something had definitely changed since earlier that day when they'd cooked together, laughing and smiling. A lot of smiling.

He'd left her house just after noon and had taken advantage of the dry weather to start priming the duplex for painting. He'd used that time to brainstorm food. A fresh spin on the halibut with some kind of salsa. He couldn't wait to run ideas by Georgie and was even considering asking her to stay at the restaurant with him after closing to plan the trip for tomorrow. But now she looked exhausted.

If he was honest with himself, he'd say she looked like she'd been crying. He wondered if this had something to do with her appointment or why she'd come to the island in the first place. Once again he wished he knew more about her.

Since his first few attempts to engage her lighter side had failed, he decided to try another tactic. She'd gone to the walk-in fridge for something, and he followed. She barely turned when he entered.

"You again?" she asked with mild sarcasm.

He smiled at that. "We've got to stop meeting like this."

As she loaded her tray with bread, he pretended to look over their supply of cream. He tried to sound nonchalant. "Are you okay, Georgie?"

When she didn't answer, he turned.

She stood staring down at the loaves. She nodded.

"What if I don't believe you?" he asked.

She shrugged. "I'd say you were an observant guy."

He wanted to go to her and take the tray and brush her hair off her forehead. "What if I don't believe you have allergies?" he asked instead, reaching for a pint of cream and pretending to read the label.

"What if I don't believe you need any cream?"

He paused. "I'd say . . . I find your lack of faith disturbing."

And then she smiled, slowly shaking her head, but she smiled. "That's something my brother would say."

He smiled back. He took a couple steps closer. "And what would your brother say if he found you so down after he knew what kind of victorious morning you'd had in the lab?"

She lifted her gaze to his. "He wouldn't say anything. He'd just . . . put his arm around me and . . . wait until I felt better."

Jace rubbed his chin. "That's it?"

Her eyes widened. "That's *it*? That's the best. That's . . ." Her eyes turned glassy, and she looked away.

Crap. He hadn't meant to make it worse. He began to reach his arm out, but then as she looked back at him, he scratched the top of his head instead, like an idiot. "Do you wish he were here? Your brother?"

She nodded and took a couple more loaves of bread. "I miss him. He's coming though, next week."

"Oh. Good. From where?"

"School," was all she offered.

"Well, I'm glad."

"Yeah." She looked up at him, her expression only slightly brighter. "Thanks, Jace. I'm just tired, and I've got a lot on my mind. I'll be fine."

He nodded. "Good. It doesn't . . . it doesn't have anything to do with this morning, does it? Because—"

"No." And then she did smile. A real smile. "This morning was great. Incredible, I mean. I can't wait for tomorrow. I mean—" She looked down and shook her head. "I mean, to see what you come up with next for the menu."

"What *we* come up with next."

She glanced up and rolled her eyes.

Jace swallowed. "Georgie, I was thinking that tonight—"

The door to the cooler opened with a blast of kitchen noise. Caleb called loudly behind him. "Here they are!" He faced them as Georgie hurried past with her tray. "What the—? Guys? One of you goes, fine, but both of you? It's chaos out here!"

Jace held up his carton. "Just getting cream." He thumbed back toward the other cartons. "A couple of those are expired."

"Yeah. Tell that to Reuben." They exited the fridge.

"Reuben isn't here tonight."

"Oh, yes, he is." Caleb pointed. "He came in to pick up a bill and saw how crazy it was."

Jace turned and saw Reuben furiously turning steaks and manning a lobster plate with Haru while Georgie hurriedly pulled out two—four—s— eight salad bowls and several side cups.

"Crap."

Reuben looked over and pointed at him with his tongs. It was not a delicate gesture.

Jace started to move but halted, looking down at the carton of cream still in his hand. He didn't have a clue what to do with it. *Nice, Jace. Nice job.*

* * *

Georgie worked through her break time. If Reuben had noticed she was skipping her break he would have said something, but the restaurant was packed, and the kitchen clattered and sizzled with nonstop activity, and Reuben was in his element. After being caught in the walk-in with Jace, she had no desire to claim her break while they were so busy.

Jace, however, noticed. He simply began helping make salads while she sliced bread. "Take your break, Georgie," he said quietly.

She would have argued with him, but she was exhausted, and he'd offered the perfect opportunity to slip away while he took over her station. She gave him a quick look of gratitude and pulled away from her counter, wiping her hands, hung her apron on a hook, and headed straight for the back door. She pushed it open and took a deep breath as if emerging from deep water and kept walking to the old picnic table. She didn't sit. An evening rain had come in off the water, and though the table was partially covered, she stood and lifted her face to the sky. Her eyes were closed, but she blinked as drops hit her lids.

You need to forgive yourself.

The words had been going through her head since her session with Laurel.

But I made him angry. I made him angry. He was angry. She automatically reached for the place where her arm had been bruised. He'd been very careful to let her know of his anger and appear calm at the same time. That was his way. To threaten and reassure at the same time. That was his power over her. The simmering volcano.

And she'd learned to be careful around that. To bow to it. To appease it. Because the reward was his charisma. His charm. His pride in her.

His *love.*

She shook her head.

It wasn't love.

Somehow, on that drive home, he'd lost his power. He'd lost control of the car. She'd failed to be careful around the volcano. But that didn't make his death her fault, did it?

"Georgie?"

She turned abruptly and found Tyler holding an umbrella.

"I'm on break too, and I saw you come out here." He stepped forward and held the umbrella out so they were both sheltered from the rain. "It's really coming down, huh?"

She hadn't minded the rain. "I hardly noticed. I guess I was getting pretty soaked."

He frowned. "You're shivering."

She focused on the ground. "I'm fine." They were silent for a bit. Then she said, "Thanks, Tyler."

He shrugged, looking out at the unimpressive lot behind the restaurant. "No problem." He remained quiet and seemed to be deciding what to say next. He got up the nerve to speak again. "Is everything okay? I mean you seemed kind of sad when you came into work, and I just wondered if everything was all right."

"I'm good. Everything's fine. How's dishwashing tonight? Nonstop, I bet."

He looked down, and she knew her attempt to change the subject would fail. "Georgie, I have sisters. I could tell you'd been crying. Is there something I can do? Is this about the accident? Or work? Is someone . . . bothering you?"

His frankness caught her off guard. "Is someone bothering me?" She clenched her fist, nearly laughing with contempt. Her thoughts spun. *Well, let's see. I had a therapy session that pretty much knocked the wind out of me, and I keep talking to a dead guy I used to think I loved, but now I can't even understand how I was with him, even though I'm mourning his loss, which, by the way, has also been the source of humongous guilt on my part because of the accident I can't remember . . . and I'm kind of angry because I think I've realized that I could have avoided all this—all of this—by simply keeping my head and not falling for some charming guy who could captivate a whole room and me with his smoldering looks and bold confidence.* She turned away from the umbrella. *He was attractive and popular. Popular. And I seriously allowed a potential eternity to be based on that. Because he was a returned missionary. And that was supposed to make it okay.* She let out a sound of disgust. "No *offense*, Ian," she yelled at the sky.

She turned and caught the bewilderment in Tyler's expression before he hid it. She rubbed her forehead, slightly out of breath, trying to recover from her small and slightly insane inner monologue. "I just yelled that out loud, didn't I?"

He nodded, eyes wide. "Who's Ian?"

She shook her head. "Someone I used to know. Look, Tyler, you're right. Somebody's bothering me. But it's not who you were thinking."

Tyler's cheeks reddened, and he watched the ground.

She felt remorse and nausea. "Tyler, I'm sorry. I've just got . . . I've got weighty . . . *things* going on, and I'm trying to work them out, and I guess . . . I guess today has been a rough day."

He gave a nod and kicked some gravel. When he spoke, it was quiet. "Was this what you were talking to Jace about in the cooler?"

She rolled her eyes. "Seriously? That was about food."

"Food?"

"Yeah, the new menu. And . . . cream. But he did ask me if I was okay."

"And did you . . . you know . . . freak out like you did just now?"

She blinked and shook her head. "My freak-outs seem to be random and unpredictable. I'm blaming the head injury. You are today's lucky winner."

A corner of his mouth lifted in a smile, to her relief.

"I am sorry. I promise I used to be totally normal. My biggest worry used to be my calculus final."

He shook his head. "That explains a lot."

She twirled her finger in the air next to her ear.

He chuckled but sobered. "Were you talking to the guy who died in the accident?"

"Shouting at, you mean? Yeah, I kind of didn't want you to know that. Gives off a *crazy* vibe."

He hesitated, and she knew he was thinking it was too late for that anyway. "If you ever need to talk or, you know"—he made an exploding gesture—"you know where to find me."

Georgie looked at the ground. "Thanks. Hopefully I won't be exploding anytime soon."

He laughed uncomfortably, and then they both stood in the rain, he under the umbrella and she still getting wet.

"So about that movie . . ."

Was he serious? "Tyler, you don't have to—"

"Don't worry. I can see you have a lot going on. I was thinking of asking you to see a late show tonight, but it sounds like you need sleep more than sci-fi."

She nodded, relieved.

"You'll need an escape sometime though."

An escape. That was one reason she'd come to the island. To escape but also to begin again. "Yeah, sometime."

Mai came out the back door in her rain jacket, signaling to Georgie.

"Looks like my break is up. Thanks, Tyler." Georgie meant it. He'd only been trying to help. But she walked away with that empty, queasy feeling that came with revealing too much to someone.

She passed Mai. "Hey, Wings," she said.

Mai smiled. "Hey there, Rain Girl."

Georgie freshened up in the bathroom and retied her damp hair back. The morning with Jacc seemed like a long time ago. A week. She looked in the mirror.

"Hey there, Rain Girl," she whispered.

With her apron back on, she walked to her station. As she passed Jace, he looked up and followed her.

"Have a good break?"

"The best," she answered.

He gave her a funny look. "Great. Feel better?"

"A little."

He helped her switch the bread loaves, which was completely unnecessary.

"I can do this," she reminded him.

"I know. I just . . ." He put his hands on his hips, then leaned forward. "Listen, if you don't want to go tomorrow—"

"We're going." She wanted to go to the tulip fields. She needed to go.

He stepped back. "Okay." He smiled cautiously. "We'll go."

"Duh." She held up the next order in front of him. "Now go over there and grill a steak or something."

He shook his head, laughing quietly, and did as she asked.

Chapter 14

Tru looked up from her *Bachelor* show. "Is that Jace person coming to dinner again?"

Georgie turned the page of one of Faye's magazines. "Why do you ask?"

Tru turned back to her show. "That cake was good. He needs to come back and bring more cake."

Georgie had just come home from work, and though she longed to go to bed, Tru had asked her to sit down and watch with her. That had never happened before, so Georgie thought she should accept the invitation, at least for a few minutes. "Well, he's picking me up in the morning to go to the tulip fields. But I don't think he's bringing food this time."

"He must really like you."

Georgie flushed. "Why do you say that?"

"Because the tulips aren't even going to be blooming yet, and he's driving you out there. Why else would he do that?"

"Tru, it's not like that. It's for the restaurant. And the daffodils are blooming." Daffodils were blooming all over the island now. There would be fields of them out at the bulb farms.

"Because he wants to spend time with you."

"He wants to figure out the next dish for the menu. We're just friends. Now stop it, or I'm going to bed."

"Don't you sass me. It's just like this show."

Georgie eyed the TV, where a good-looking guy sat casually with three women obviously vying for his attention with cleavage, makeup, and flipping hair. "What do you mean?"

"I mean the guy never sees. He never sees the girls who are nice and the girls who aren't. We see because we see all the girls living together. We see them real. And I see Jace likes you."

Georgie stood and went over to Tru. "You don't make sense, but I love you." She kissed her on the forehead.

"Oh, stop," Tru said as she brushed Georgie away.

"I'm going to bed. You watch too much TV." She walked toward her room.

"You need to watch more. You could learn something."

Georgie bit back her retort. *What good has it done you?* she'd almost asked. *What good does it do to learn a lesson if it scares you out of trying?* Fatigued, she stopped at the bathroom and brushed her teeth. *You never see the ones who are real and the ones who aren't.* She spit. *Jace likes you.* She mentally wrestled to put that last thought into a box and onto a shelf.

Once she reached her bed, she crawled under the covers and prayed that she could bypass the inevitable insomnia.

* * *

Jace texted Georgie from the front porch, not wanting to wake up everyone in the house if they were still asleep.

You ready? I'm outside.

As he waited for her response, he watched the sky. Clouds hung low and still, but rain hadn't started yet. Early-morning mist had wet everything; the world was green and dripping. He wished for a breeze to push the clouds on to the east. He looked at his phone, but just then the door opened and Georgie stepped out. Again he was struck by her casual appearance. She wore jeans, and she was zipping up a blue rain parka. He looked down and smiled. "New boots?"

She nodded. "Faye and I went to Bothel last week, and she said I needed to get myself a present. I found these." She raised her foot and inspected the rain boot. Colors swirled in different patterns and graphics on the shiny black plastic, and printed on the ankle was a large white wing reaching upward. It had a match on the other foot. "They're for flying," she said, almost to herself.

"Perfect," Jace said.

She nodded, still looking down. Sometimes she said the most unexpected things.

"We can grab breakfast in Mt. Vernon before we get started, if you're hungry. It'll be a couple of hours before we hit the lunch menus."

"Great," she said. She looked up. Her eyes widened. "You shaved."

He shrugged. "It'd been a while." He kept his beard cut close but hadn't shaved clean for over a year. He felt her inspecting his face and suddenly became self-conscious. He rubbed his chin. "I just felt like starting the beard over."

She nodded, stepping off the porch and walking to the bike. She glanced at him again. She didn't say anything, and he wondered what she was thinking. Did she like the shave? Did she prefer the whiskers? He had no idea. He had no idea why it mattered. Except he recalled the point at the bathroom sink where he'd wondered, just briefly, if Georgie would prefer a clean-shaven look, and then he'd slathered on the shaving cream. He winced at that. He joined her at the bike and climbed on. She was already buckling her helmet. He put his on and started the bike.

Her light touch at his waist made him pause. *Geez, heart, calm down. This is nothing. Just friends. She's a basket case. You're a bachelor. You're not getting into this again. Focus. Recipes.* The quick starts or sudden accelerations he'd used when he was younger, when girls had ridden on the back of his bike, just so they'd pull their arms around him tighter crossed his mind. He rolled his eyes at himself.

He eased the bike out of the drive, onto the road, then onto the main drive off the island. Towering pines lined both sides, and the air smelled wet. Georgie's hands stayed just above his hips. Where they should be. Where he wanted them to be because he'd sworn off girls and dating and complications.

He navigated traffic north toward Mt. Vernon for about twenty miles and took Exit 226. He slowed at a stoplight and placed his feet on the ground. Glancing behind him, he asked, "You okay?" She hadn't said a word during the trip.

She nodded and gave him a thumbs-up. "It's beautiful."

"The freeway?"

"All of it. It's saturated."

He laughed. "That's a good word for it." The mist had mixed with fog the farther north they'd come. You couldn't even see the mountains, which was a shame. Maybe it would burn off later. "The Farmhouse is just up here a bit. Nothing fancy, but breakfast is good."

"As long as they have pancakes," she said.

He smiled, revving the engine out of habit as it idled.

"I never thought I'd like the weather here so much," she said. "It's kind of poetic."

He turned and looked at her.

"Like Prufrock," she said.

"Prufrock."

"Yeah. T. S. Eliot. Which is, of course, perfectly normal to bring up on the back of a motorcycle." She rolled her eyes at herself beneath her visor.

He shrugged. "Why not?" He turned back, vaguely remembering having to pick apart the poem in English lit in high school. Maybe he'd have to take a look again. After all, he liked the weather here too, and he was curious about how it related to a forgotten poem. But more importantly, whatever had caused her so much trouble yesterday didn't seem to be bothering her this morning. And that made him glad. He looked down at her boots. She'd tucked her jeans into them, and he thought that they were the sexiest pair of rain boots he'd ever seen.

"You like my boots, huh?" she asked.

He nodded. "Yup." He revved the engine again, and the light turned green.

* * *

Georgie pushed the last bite of pancake through the syrup on her plate and stuck it in her mouth. Pancakes were comfort food, and she was spending the entire day alone with Jace Lowe, talking about food she didn't know how to make. They had miraculously worked. For now.

"So," Jace said, looking over a piece of paper he'd unfolded. His omelet was long gone. "I made a list of foods usually associated with spring. Maybe as we explore we can keep these in mind. If you can think of any others, say something."

She put down her fork and nodded. "Springtime foods. Right."

He raised his brow at her and smiled. She returned the same look, and he read. "Asparagus, because that's a given."

"Of course."

"Lemon or citrus—"

"Like in the shrimp."

"Like in the shrimp," he agreed. "Let's see . . . crab."

"Crab?"

He nodded. "It has seasons. Spring is one of them."

"I had no idea. I just thought they were always kicking around under there at the bottom of the ocean."

"Well, they are. But there are crabbing seasons, and they're the right size at the peak of those seasons."

She lifted her mug. "Learn something new every day."

He watched her.

"Go on," she told him and sipped the creamy cocoa, wondering how in the world he expected her to be any help.

He looked back down at the list. "Uh, parsley, cilantro . . . tarragon . . . fennel. Any fresh herb, really. Spinach, lettuce, cabbage . . . rhubarb." He set the list down. "That's all I've got." He didn't look inspired.

She set down her mug. "Well, it sounds to me like you could just create some sort of asparagus, lemon, parsley-rhubarb-tarragon-stuffed crab, and you're set." She watched him expectantly.

He wrinkled his nose.

She smiled and sipped her cocoa. The waiter brought the check and cleared their plates. As Jace placed his credit card with the bill, Georgie felt a twinge of nerves.

"Are you sure I can't just pay for my breakfast?"

"Oh, I'm sure you can. However," he flipped the card around so she could see it. "This is the restaurant card, and today is work. So as long as you don't order every pancake in the house, this is covered."

"I'll try to control myself."

He nodded and pushed the bill to the edge of the table. "Very wise. We've got a lot of tasting to do later. Now, about the list of spring foods, did anything else come to mind?"

"Umm, chocolate bunnies?"

He leaned back and stretched. "It's going to be a long day."

"I blame the cocoa." She grinned.

He stood and offered her a hand up.

She hesitated half a second, and she could immediately see his realization that he may have done something he shouldn't have. At the moment he started to pull his hand away, she reached for it. He gripped her hand firmly and pulled her up, and once they stood facing each other, she let go at the same time he did. The waiter brought back the check, and Jace signed it, but as he did, Georgie clenched her fist and turned, watching out the windows at nothing, because his hand had been warm and a little rough and nice.

"You ready?" Jace asked.

She nodded and forced a smile. *No*, she thought, *I'm not.*

* * *

They left town and traffic behind. Georgie drew in her breath and patted Jace's arm. "What are those?"

An entire pasture was filled with large, white, resting birds. Had their necks been longer, she would have thought they were swans.

Jace looked where she pointed and turned onto the road that would take them just past the field. He slowed to a stop but didn't turn off the bike. "Snow geese," he called.

"Snow geese," she repeated. "There are a ton of them."

He nodded. "They migrate through here every year. Thousands." He reached for the bike's horn and beeped.

Like a down blanket being settled over a bed, the geese lifted as one, flapping their wings and settling once more.

Jace and Georgie watched for another minute, and then Jace turned the bike. In another mile, down another rural road, another field came into view, only this field was a blanket of vivid yellow.

"Daffodils," Georgie whispered. The surrounding emerald fields would be filled with tulips in a few weeks, but right now, under a canopy of gray mist, the daffodils had the floor.

Jace pulled off the road and parked. He cut the engine, and silence settled—that silence of a field or a lake in the morning: a few birds, whatever sound fog made; it made a sound, like snow makes a sound.

Georgie stood at the edge of the damp field, her motorcycle helmet in her hand, and gazed over row upon row of the yellow heads. Occasionally a flower would bob. Duck. Sway.

"Are we allowed to walk in there?" she asked Jace as he joined her.

"Sure. If we don't disturb anything."

Georgie walked carefully along the edge of the furrows, her boots sinking a bit in the soft, wet earth. She crouched down and touched a few of the thick, waxy petals. "Do I dare disturb the universe?" she asked quietly.

"What was that?" Jace asked behind her.

She glanced at him. "Prufrock: 'Do I dare disturb the universe? In a minute there is time for decisions and revisions which a minute will reverse . . .'" She trailed off at the end, looking back down at the flower cradled in her hand. She hadn't thought of that poem in a long time, and now she'd been reminded of it twice in one morning. Strange how something from so long ago could come back and suddenly mean everything.

"The Love Song of J. Alfred Prufrock," Jace suggested.

She smiled. "Yes. A crazy old man aging and loving and questioning a whole lot of stuff."

"So you can relate."

Georgie shrugged. "You mean being crazy?"

"I meant the old-man part, but whatever." She laughed and stood. She took a picture of the field with her phone. "I'm surprised I could remember even that much of the poem. My brain hasn't been working right for a long time. Maybe it's getting better."

She bit her lip and took another picture. Should she have said that? Did that sound crazy? Holy cow, would she always be second-guessing herself? Even while declaring herself improved?

"Maybe it is getting better," he said. "Maybe recalling Prufrock has tipped your brain to genius levels."

He was teasing her. "I don't hear you recalling any poems."

He grinned. "Well, that's because my brain is subgenius."

"That explains why you asked me to help you cook."

He nodded, studying her.

She looked away, focusing on the fields. "This is gorgeous. I can't wait to be here when the tulips are out."

Jace looked out too. "It's pretty amazing. Acres of them."

"I've seen photos online. I looked up the Roozengaarde website." The bulb farm was the biggest and most popular farm in the area.

"Have you seen paintings?" he asked as though he had a secret to share.

"No."

He motioned toward the motorcycle. "C'mon, Alfred."

They stood in the open doorway of an old barn where some light construction was taking place.

"Hey, Jace. Good to see you." A man in a cowboy hat and canvas jacket approached with his hand out.

"Hey, Dean," Jace said as he shook the man's hand. "How are you?"

"I'm great. You're a little early, aren't you?"

Jace shrugged. "Just a couple of weeks. Took a chance on you being out here getting ready for the art show. This is Georgie. She's a friend of mine. Works at the restaurant."

Dean removed his hat. "Nice to meet you, Georgie. Dean Stroud."

She smiled and shook his hand. "Hello."

Jace surveyed the work being done. "We're looking for inspiration for some new menu items."

"And you came here?"

Jace shrugged. "The new dishes are to celebrate the festival. Spring. New. Fresh."

"Ah." Dean nodded in understanding.

"Reuben wants them ready to go ASAP, so we're up here for the day. Georgie's never seen the tulip fields in bloom."

"We'll have to remedy that," Dean said. "In the meantime, we can help with a preview."

"I was hoping you'd say that."

"Follow me."

As they followed Dean farther into the barn, Georgie gave Jace a questioning look.

He answered it. "I met Dean and his wife on my mission. Every year they invite the elders to a prefestival showing."

"Of what?" Georgie asked.

Dean opened a door of an office space built onto the inside of the barn. "Delia, we have visitors. Jace brought a girl."

"Oh!" came the exclamation from inside. A woman with long silver hair appeared at the doorway, smiling and wiping her hands on a cloth. Her large hoop earrings dangled as she moved. She wore a large men's button-up shirt and jeans, and her sleeves were rolled up to her elbows. The shirt was messy with smears and splotches of paint, and the office had the tangy smell of paint supplies mixed with a hint of patchouli.

"Welcome, welcome! Jace, it's good to see you. You brought a girl—wonderful!"

"I brought a coworker," Jace said and glanced at Georgie.

Georgie nodded as if he needed her witness to the statement.

"Is she a girl?"

Jace glanced again at Georgie. "Well, yes. A woman . . . girl."

Georgie muffled a laugh.

"So I was right," Delia said.

"I'm leaving you in good hands," Dean said with a smile. "Delia will answer all of your questions. I've got some work needing my attention." He leaned down and kissed his wife on the cheek. "Be good," he said, then headed back toward the front of the barn.

She grinned innocently at Georgie. "Would you like to see the collection so far? They've started coming in from all over just the last couple of days."

Georgie nodded like she knew exactly what she was talking about.

"I'm Delia," the woman said, linking her arm in Georgie's. "You have an interesting aura. What was your name? Jace, you didn't tell me her name."

"Georgie," Georgie answered before Jace could.

"Now is that one name, like Sting or Madonna? Or do you have another to go with it?"

Georgie bit back another laugh. "Tate. Georgie Tate."

"I see. And is Georgie short for something?"

They'd left the office and were walking toward several tables and vertical display boards set up against a stack of hay bales. A couple of young men were hammering boards into what looked like more standing displays.

"It's short for Georgiana."

"Lovely. Mr. Darcy's sister."

Georgie smiled. "Actually, nobody's made that comparison before. But, yeah."

"Unbelievable. Sweet girl. And that horrible Mr. Wickham. Ugh." She patted Georgie's hand and looked her in the eyes. "But you share more than just a name, there, don't you? A betrayal of the opposite sex." She squeezed her hand.

Before Georgie could stammer a reply, Delia let go of her and pulled a large cloth off a pile of boxes.

"Here we are."

Georgie's attention went from the woman's eerily insightful comment to what she'd thought were boxes beneath the sheet.

They were, in fact, paintings. Framed reproductions of the tulip farms during bloom season. From faraway scapes to sunny windmills to macrolens close-ups. Fields, still lifes, petals. From abstract to folk to finite realism. Oils, watercolors, mixed media. And all tulips.

"We've got some beauties this year," Delia said. "And more than we've ever had before. Once a year this amassing of creativity gives the barn a whole different energy. Can't you just feel it?"

"Which one is yours?" Jace asked, looking around.

"Oh, let's see." She shuffled through the stacks to a framed oil of a larger-than-life red tulip painted against a black-and-white diamond background. "Here's one. Apeldoorn. The queen of Roozengaarde tulips."

"That's beautiful," Georgie said. The neoclassical style contrasted with the rustic surroundings of the barn. "It's striking against the others."

"Thank you. She wasn't going to be shy, this one. Bent on making a statement. I've got another piece in the studio I'm not quite finished with yet. I'm still thinking her through. She's close though. Wanna see?"

They followed Delia back to the office, which was apparently a studio, and she led them to a large easel.

"This is Gander's Rhapsody. She's more demure than Apeldoorn, though she has every right to flaunt. Alas, I'm struggling a bit with balancing the background with the fore. But isn't she pretty?"

Georgie nodded. "Very." Pretty was not the word. Full creamy petals were finely speckled with red on the exterior of each. And the inside of the petals were somehow brilliant, solid reddish-pink, as though they'd been spray-painted from the inside and the overspray had settled on the outside. "I've never seen a tulip like this one before. It almost glows from the inside."

"She's a surprise for the viewer," Delia said, her eyes twinkling. "I'm so glad you like her." She looked at Jace. "You're awfully quiet."

Jace had been frowning at the picture but started at the comment. "What? Oh, no, it's gorgeous. Yeah."

Delia considered the painting. "Well, like I said, I can't figure out the background. I had originally planned a bokeh thing back there in greens, but now I think it might be too much. What do you think?"

"Bouquet? Like more flowers?" Jace asked.

Georgie wondered the same thing.

"No, no, no. B-O-K-E-H. Like, out of focus spots of light."

They all studied the painting.

"No," Delia said after a few moments. "It would be too much. If she's going to demand anything, it'll be simplicity."

"Why not the gray?" Georgie asked. The background was already brushed with gray matte paint, and the tulip had been painted realistically on top of it. "It's like the mist."

Delia nodded slowly. "It doesn't overpower the tulip. And the bloom does pop against it, doesn't she? Sort of a trompe l'oeil. Hm. Mist-gray concrete? Maybe add a crack or two." She clapped her hands. "Wet concrete. Yes, I like that very much. Thank you, Georgie." Delia studied the painting as though lost in it.

Georgie glanced at Jace, who was watching her with a small smile. "What?" she whispered.

He shook his head. "You're doing it again."

"What?" Georgie looked from Jace to Delia, who grinned. "What is he talking about?"

Delia laughed soft and rich. "I have no idea." She winked at Jace. "But you know what you're doing bringing her along. Be careful with this one."

"Yeah, yeah." Jace checked his phone and sighed heavily. "Time to go." He started to leave the studio. "Thanks, Delia," he called.

"What?" Georgie asked. "Why do you bring me along?"

Delia laughed again behind her. "Where are you both off to next?"

"La Conner," Jace called over his shoulder.

"La Conner is one of the top-five best places to kiss," Delia called back to him. "In the nation."

Jace kept walking, and Delia laughed.

But Georgie was still stuck on the previous subject. "Why does he bring me along?" she asked Delia.

Delia sighed. "He'll figure it out eventually. Thank you for coming, Jace! Don't stay away so long next time." She took Georgie's hand in a quick but firm grip. "You come back. Don't miss the tulips. They quiet your soul." She smiled. "I'll see you again."

The way Delia spoke, it was as if she wasn't just guessing.

"It was nice meeting you," Georgie said. *And a little odd*, she thought. But who was she to talk?

Jace was up ahead, already saying good-bye to Dean. Georgie jogged up to them as Jace thanked him.

"Georgie," Dean said, "you're welcome back anytime."

"Thanks. I'd like to come back once the festival is going."

"Don't you miss it," Dean said. "You two stay dry. Good luck with the menu." He patted Jace on the arm and headed back to the studio.

Georgie watched Jace turn and head back to the motorcycle.

"Hey. What was that all about?" she called after him.

He waved her off, and a knot coiled in her stomach. She clenched her jaw and walked to the motorcycle. "Hey."

Jace looked up from his keys.

She folded her arms. "Don't brush me off. I don't like it." She wouldn't just take it anymore. "What was that all about?"

But Jace only looked amused. "Don't be angry. Don't. Delia's just . . ."

"Yes?"

"She's kind of a mystic."

"I got that."

"She tends to read people."

"A lot of people do that."

"No, I mean *read* people, like their auras, their laugh lines, and the patterns of color in their eyes. She says it's a gift."

"Oh." Georgie calmed a fraction, not really seeing the humor in that. "So?"

Jace picked up her helmet from off the back of the bike. "So I didn't really want to stick around to hear what she had to say, that's all." He held out the helmet to her.

She put her hands on her hips. "Why not?"

He rolled his eyes and stepped closer to her, lowering his voice. She swallowed. "Because I could tell where she was going, and I didn't think either of us would appreciate it." He lifted his brow and waved his finger back and forth between the two of them.

"Ohh." Georgie felt a blush coming on, and she took her helmet and stepped away. *That's what that was about. Connection. Romance.* "Well, that's ridiculous," she breathed out. She went to smash the helmet on her head but paused, remembering what had upset her in the first place. "Wait. What did you mean back there when you said I was doing it again. Doing what?"

He rubbed his head. "I don't know."

His hair stuck out a bit, and she tried not to stare at how great it looked. "Yes, you do. You said it."

He pressed his lips together and looked out at the fields.

"Well?"

He glanced at her, then threw out his hands. "I don't know. It's like you're a walking muse. The way you throw out ideas. The way you just say stuff and . . . things come together." He shrugged. "That's why I asked you to help."

Her blush deepened, and she couldn't look at him.

"That's all," he said.

"Well . . ." She bit her lip. "Thanks." She pulled on her helmet.

He nodded and got on the bike. He started it up, and Georgie climbed on the back.

"Which was your favorite?" Jace asked, putting on his own helmet.

"Favorite what?"

"The tulips. The art."

"Oh." She recovered from the abrupt change of subject. "Uh, I really liked that Rhapsody in the studio."

Jace nodded.

She put her hands at his waist without hesitation because that was what friends did. They were friends.

And he'd just called her a muse.

He kicked up the kickstand, and they were off.

Chapter 15

SOME OF THE FOG AND mist had dissipated while they were in the barn, and the daylight had brightened some. Georgie couldn't get over the tranquil beauty of the emerald bulb fields, even without the blooms.

Jace spoke over the noise of the engine. "I thought we'd loop down south to La Conner and up to Anacortes. By then, maybe it will have cleared enough to see the mountains up at Samish Bay. Or, you know, it could be pouring."

"Perfect."

"What?"

"*Perfect*," she said loudly enough for him to hear.

"I don't think you're being sarcastic when you say that," he called behind him.

"I don't think I am either," she said. "Is that weird?"

He shook his head.

She took a deep breath. It was weird. Normal people wanted to go inside when it rained. "I *would* like to see the mountains though," she said, looking north-ish. "Is it far to La Conner?"

"Not too far. But we'll take the scenic route. I'm guessing you're still full from pancakes."

She smiled.

Jace was true to his word, leisurely winding between more fields of daffodils, green tulips, and clumps of iris getting ready to burst. It was like reading the blurb on the back of a paperback but not getting to open the book yet. A glimpse. An expectation. A taste.

Jace pulled to a stop at an empty intersection, and a bee flew past her helmet and paused. Georgie cringed away and ducked.

"What are you doing back there?" Jace asked.

"There's a bee."

"Well, hold still."

"Why . . . do people always . . . say that?" She swatted at the bee. "Ah, it's behind me."

"You've got a helmet on." He was chuckling. Of course he was.

"It doesn't cover *all* of me." The bee returned, and she swayed.

"If you'll hold still, we'll just drive away."

She grimaced but stilled. "Okay, go, go, go."

Jace accelerated. The bee followed them for a mere second and then disappeared.

"Is it still there?" Jace asked from the front.

"It's gone."

She turned her focus from the bee and froze. Her arms were wrapped around Jace, her hands clenched just over his abs. And she was leaning into him. She could smell his aftershave. She didn't know, biologically, how blood could drain from her face at the same time her face filled with heat, but it happened. She carefully pulled back, then moved her hands to his hips.

"You okay back there?" His tone was light. She appreciated that. And hated it. Because he was trying to be light. Because she'd glommed onto him like hot gum during the bee attack and then moved away like he had cooties. Or something.

"Yeah, sorry," she said lamely.

"Are you allergic?"

"To bees?"

"Yes, bees."

Of course he meant bees. "No, it's just that fear thing again."

"Oh, right. Everything but lightning. I'll try to steer clear of any more bees."

"Thanks." She tried to think of something else light to say because to say nothing would leave a silence, and silences were filled with pondering things like abs and aftershave. "I guess there would be a lot of bees out right now because of the daffodils and stuff."

His helmet bobbed. "Lots of bees. Lots of pollinating."

She bit her lip, needing to keep talking. "Do farmers out here keep bees too?"

"I wouldn't be surprised."

"Honey could be on the springtime food idea list."

He glanced back at her. She couldn't read his expression.

He turned forward again. "Yeah, it could."

The awkward dread she'd felt eased. Somewhat.

* * *

Jace's thoughts began turning. He'd tried not making too much of the embrace he'd found himself in as Georgie had fought off the maniacal bee. She probably had no idea what she'd done. Just a reflex, pressing against him for safety. And then, just like that, she'd mentioned honey.

Something local. Something sweet. The same phrase that had stuck with him and led him to the blackberry sauce returned to him now. *Something sweet.* Georgie had wrapped her arm around his waist without hesitation and pulled him closer—

Snap. Out of it. What had she said?

Honey.

He needed a surf dish and a turf dish. He'd been considering a pork chop for the turf. He laughed, daring to pat her hand. "Georgie," he called. "You're brilliant." He picked up speed as they left the bulb fields, and he didn't hear her muffled response, though her grip definitely tightened at his waist. He liked that too much.

Neither of them had been hungry when they'd arrived, so she and Jace had walked up and down La Conner's First Street and the Marina, stopping in shops and watching boats come and go under the Rainbow Bridge. La Conner was known as "the best small town in Washington." And it was small. But because of the large marinas the town had built on the long Swinomish Channel and the enthusiastic calendar of events centered around the community's artists, industry, and agriculture, the local restaurants took great pride in feeding their many visitors fresh, tasty food.

Jace and Georgie now perused their menus at one of the grills along the Marina.

"I don't understand," Georgie whispered, glancing behind her. "Are we looking for ideas to copy? Because that doesn't seem right."

Jace glanced around as well and leaned forward, his voice low. "As often as that does happen in this business, no, we're not looking to copy.

We're doing the opposite. Sort of a process of elimination." He leaned back, enjoying this conspiratorial tone.

A waitress came to fill their water glasses. Jace took a sip as Georgie leaned forward, whispering again as soon as the waitress left. "So we want what they don't have?"

He gave her a nod and winked. She sat back, resting her chin on her hand and looking over the menu. "Well, that makes more sense. Look, they have coconut shrimp. It's not even an appetizer either. A main dish?" She rolled her eyes, and he stifled a laugh. He happened to know the coconut shrimp here was a favorite, and with good reason.

He scanned the menu. "I don't see halibut steak *or* pork chop. That's a good sign."

"But we already have halibut steak on our menu."

He nodded and grimaced. "I know. But Reuben wants me to rework it. Make it new."

"Fresh," she said.

"Right."

The waitress returned to take their order. "You ready?"

"Yes," Jace said. "We'll split the coconut prawns and the seared rock fish."

The waitress smiled. "Great choices." She took their menus and left again.

Georgie watched him, and he waited for her question. He was beginning to recognize the look in her eyes, the look of gears turning in her head just before she asked him questions.

"Why did you order that? We already have something different than coconut shrimp."

He nodded. "You're right. But they have a crushed almond breading as the base for the coconut shrimp that I'm curious about for the pork chop, and I'm considering searing the halibut over grilling it, and they've done that with the rockfish. And while I'm looking to see how they did it, I'm also looking to see, as I've said, how I can do it *differently*."

She watched him steadily, and he decided not to break her gaze. She finally looked away, playing with her straw in her glass of water.

"Did you have something else you wanted to ask me?" he ventured.

She gave a slight shake of her head and pulled her glass closer. "It's just that you seem to try hard to do things differently."

He grinned. "Is that bad?"

She looked away again. "No. No, it's not."

"Then why are you frowning?"

She pressed her mouth in a line, and for a moment, Jace thought he'd asked another question she wasn't going to answer. But then she shrugged.

"It's just that a lot of people are bent on doing everything the same. The more same, the better. And we talk ourselves into pursuing that. There's a little hierarchy: *my same is better than your same* . . . but how dare we deviate. As if two equally intelligent or talented people can't think of two different ways to do the same thing. So many times *different* is interpreted as *wrong*. It's . . . it's frustrating. It's frustrating to have your different be dismissed as wrong. All the time. Different can still be *good different*. Maybe my different feels better to me—safer or something—than your different, because it's mine."

He watched her warily. Her right hand trembled slightly as she raised her glass to take a drink. She quickly set it down and pressed her left hand to her forehead.

"Are you okay?" he asked quietly.

Georgie squeezed her eyes shut and nodded. "Yeah, I'm fine. I'm . . ." A laugh escaped. "I'm different."

He lifted his brow and gave her a nod.

She sighed. "You know what I mean, right?"

"Of course I do."

She paused and looked at him curiously, her eyes almost green in this light.

He clarified. "I mean, with my dad, his way or the highway." Something told him his experience with his dad and the diner was small beans compared to whatever she was talking about. "But I don't think that's exactly what you're describing. Did someone make you feel like that? All the time? Wrong because you were different?"

"I wasn't different," she whispered.

He looked up at her, and she stared out the window as light broke through a cloud and temporarily lit up the boats moored outside.

She dropped her hand and picked up the paper wrapper to her straw. She crumpled it in a little ball and rolled it around and around between her hands. "I was the same. More and more the same until I wasn't different anymore." She dropped the paper ball and flicked it to the side. It hit the salt shaker and fell. "And I was still wrong." She frowned, then rolled her eyes. "It doesn't matter anymore. Forget it." She shook her head and made a face. "Sorry."

But it did matter. "It was wrong that you were made to feel that way," he said, ignoring her attempt to dismiss the subject. "There are plenty of people who don't do that. Not intentionally or over and over. I mean, can you imagine squeaky-clean Tyler making anybody feel like they don't matter?"

She slowly smiled and shook her head. "No."

"That kid stops the sprayer a dozen times a shift to open the back door for the people going outside."

She laughed quietly. Again she looked out the window.

Carefully he asked, "Do you think I would treat anybody that way?" He held his breath, waiting for her answer.

She looked down and picked up the wadded-up wrapper again. "At first I thought maybe. But it turns out your heart was just broken. We do really lame things when our hearts are breaking. Did you know that?" She peeked up at him. "I'm in therapy."

Again his brow lifted. That was a big thing to share. "From your heart breaking?"

She leaned her chin on her wrist. "I'm not sure. Partly."

"What lame thing did you do while it was breaking?" As soon as he asked it, he wished he hadn't. She'd answered so few of his questions. He hadn't even had the opportunity to ask her very much.

But as she considered his question, her eyes became moist and she bit her lip. She turned back to the window.

Nice going, Jace.

The waitress appeared with their order, and Georgie sat up, brightening her expression. "Looks good."

He nodded, but he had little appetite. He smiled his thanks to the waitress, and after she left, he leaned forward. "I didn't mean to upset you."

She looked at him and brushed her hair off her forehead. He noticed the thin pink scar above her left eyebrow. He'd seen it before when she'd pushed her hair out of her eyes, but now he wondered how she'd gotten it. He met her gaze, hoping she believed him.

"I know you didn't mean to," she said. "As you've witnessed, I get upset fairly easily. It's part of my charm."

Jace noted her sarcasm, but the gleam had returned to her eyes, and that encouraged him. He thought about what she'd said. That she was in therapy.

He was glad she was getting help. He wasn't sure what else was spinning around in that head of hers, but some of it had to be pain.

Georgie picked up a coconut shrimp and dipped it in the mango sauce. Before she took a bite, she asked, "What do you think makes your dad, or anyone, think that their way is the only way?"

Jace shook his head, not sure what to suggest. His dad wasn't a jerk. Or an egotistical blowhard, though Jace had known a few of those in his lifetime. He had to answer because he thought she'd dropped the subject, but here it still was. "With my dad . . . I think he's just stubborn. He takes a lot of pride in doing things exactly how they've always been done. Maybe he feels the thing he works so hard for is threatened when something new is introduced. Like . . . a change will topple the tower, you know?"

She nodded. "Like Jenga. I used to play that game all the time as a kid. I can hardly stand it now." She took a bite of the shrimp and chewed. "Mm. That's good." She swallowed. "Not as good as crunchy black pepper shrimp with lime and blackberry sauce."

He smiled and lifted his fork to taste the rockfish. He was looking for a crispy edge. Not dry but lightly caramelized. Halibut was meatier, denser than rockfish, so it might hold up to a more intense flame than the rockfish. He chewed. It was tender but missing the crisp edge. Maybe grilling would be better.

His mind turned to what Georgie had said about Jenga. Somebody—someone controlling—had made her feel that her ideas didn't matter, that her way of thinking was wrong. But she was here now. And from what he'd observed, she'd surrounded herself with people who wouldn't treat her that way.

He helped himself to a shrimp. "I invited you along today, this whole week, because I think your ideas are really good. And different is what I need—"

She dropped her fork with a clatter as she was cutting into the rockfish.

"—for the menu," he finished, watching her curiously.

She had already picked her fork back up and was busily scooping a portion of fish onto her own plate. "Of course for the menu," she said a little breathlessly. "Glad I could help. Or whatever you call this that I'm doing. Muse—ing." Her cheeks were splotchy. "Because I know so much about"—she held up a forkful of fish—"shearing versus grilling."

He hid his grin. "Searing."

"That's what I said."

Dang, she was aggravating and fascinating and undeserving of whatever it was she'd been through. He shook his head in disbelief and leaned forward. "I'm sorry somebody made you feel—"

"Like a puppet," she murmured and took a sip of water.

He remembered the mouse she'd been when she'd started at the restaurant, but he couldn't imagine her taking something like that lightly. "What happened when you stood up for yourself?"

Georgie wiped her mouth with her napkin. She pushed a shrimp around on her plate, and the frown returned. She answered him but kept her eyes on the window. "The tower toppled." She visibly shivered and wrapped her arms around herself. "It crashed into a million pieces."

He didn't dare ask her more. Something in her tone warned him he'd come close enough.

* * *

Out the window, Georgie watched the clouds swallow up the sun. A new boat maneuvered along the moorings and glided toward a spot just beyond the restaurant's outdoor deck. She held her breath as the captain steered the boat into place, stopping as the buoys compressed against the wood dock, cushioning the impact. A woman jumped out and expertly tied off the boat as the man shut things down and locked things up. He met the woman on the dock, handed her her bag, and kissed her, and arm in arm, they strolled away, heading for shopping or lunch.

"Georgie?"

She turned and found Jace standing with his hand held out to her. She glanced at the table, now cleared of their plates. The bill was signed and waiting for the waitress to pick it up. A mint sat on the table directly in front of her. She grabbed it, unwrapped it, and popped it in her mouth.

Where had she been? She ran a hand over her hair and reached for her jacket on the seat next to her. "Did you find any inspiration?" She didn't remember eating the rest of the food.

"A little. Let's walk. I'd like to take a look at a few more menus before we head back to the bike."

She looked again at the hand he held out for her, and again she took it before he changed his mind.

He helped her up and this time didn't step away, so for a moment, they stood with only their arms pressed between them.

"Are you okay?" he whispered close. He searched her eyes, concern etched in his brow. His lashes were short and curled up.

She nodded. "I liked your beard," she said. "It made you look more like you."

A slow smile came to his face. "It'll grow back. Come on." He didn't drop her hand, and he kept her close, guiding her out until he got the door for her and they exited the restaurant. Once outside he shoved his hands in his jacket pockets and motioned with his elbow for her to keep up. She did.

"I decided not to go with a breading on the pork chop. Maybe a glaze." He peeked at her. "A honey glaze."

She smiled at the ground. "And the halibut?"

"Still haven't decided yet. Let's see what we find in Anacortes."

Georgie glanced around as they walked. "Why do you think this place is on the top-five-kissing-places list? How do you even make a list like that?"

Jace stopped and looked at her like he didn't know what to think of her.

She felt the heat rising in her face. "I said that out loud, didn't I?"

He laughed. "Come on." He grabbed her hand and pulled her to the south.

Her heart pounded, not knowing what he would do to answer the questions she'd posed. "I was just wondering. It doesn't matter."

"Oh, but it does. You're questioning the very roots of tourism in this part of the world, and the city must answer."

He was almost jogging, and she was barely keeping up. They came to the east side of the Rainbow Bridge, a red metal structure spanning the Swinomish Channel. He continued across, hardly pausing.

"Where are we going?" she asked, looking back toward the side they had just left and then down at the water. Not anywhere near as high as Deception Pass, thank goodness.

"I'm not sure. I'm just having a look."

She was getting winded. "This is having a look?"

"You bet."

They approached the far side of the bridge, and he stopped. They turned to look back at the main part of town, catching their breath. They stood significantly higher than the marina.

It mostly looked like a little, quaint, gray fishing town, but where the sun poked through the clouds, splashes of color lit up masts and ship flags, baskets of flowers and shop signs. Beyond the town nestled in pine trees, the mist veiled acres of green fields, and then beyond that, a large mountain rose from a forest of dark, obscured woods painted with glaciers of white.

Storybook. That was the description that came to her mind. *Once upon a time.*

"So, I guess," Jace said between breaths, "imagine this at sunset. And there you go."

She held her hand very still in his, not wanting an involuntary movement to give him any encouragement . . . or discouragement. "All it needs is a couple of swans," she murmured.

"Trumpeter swans come through a little later in the year."

She stifled a laugh. "Of course they do. What mountain is that?"

"Baker."

"So . . . top five, huh?"

"Yup."

After a couple more long minutes, he squeezed her hand and said, "Well, let's get back."

His tone was light, but he studied her face, and she wasn't sure she wanted him doing that because her pulse was already racing. And she was pretty sure her ears and nose had blossomed into a brilliant pink.

She looked down, and they began their long, quiet walk back to the other side of the channel. As they walked and stopped at restaurants to pick up menus and made small talk, Georgie couldn't help but notice all the places, all the corners and waterfronts and flower-selling kiosks, where a kiss might be perfect.

Curse you, Delia Stroud. And your patchouli.

Chapter 16

THE TRIP TO ANACORTES WASN'T that long. Jace took Reservation Road up from La Conner. The landscape changed several times, from dense woods to farmland to a stretch of auto dealerships, and then, through more trees, they saw glimpses of water.

"Is this the way to Deception Pass?" Georgie asked behind him, above the sounds of the highway.

He nodded. "If we dropped south, here in a couple miles, we'd eventually end up at Deception. But we're going north. Did you want to go there?"

"No. I just recognized it."

"Did your family take you?"

"No, Tyler did."

"That sneaky little dishwasher." It was a joke, but he couldn't help the pang of jealousy that rose up.

Georgie said nothing. He had no idea what she was thinking, but he was having a hard time not considering things he shouldn't be considering. She'd brought up that kissing thing, and it had somehow opened up a surge of . . . challenge? How was he supposed to consider kissing as an unapproachable subject—an unapproachable anything—now? She'd brought it up. He'd walked away from Delia and shoved it aside as unapproachable. And now it was all he could think about. He turned north. He didn't think Anacortes had any "best of" lists. No "top-ten places to make out" or "best parking in Washington, if you know what I mean." Not that they could park with his motorcycle. Not that they should.

Not that he should be thinking about this.

He shook his head, even more aware of Georgie's light grip. He'd let go of her hand soon after they'd turned around on the bridge, sensing her uneasiness, and he'd told himself he needed to be more careful with that. It had just seemed so natural. And not a big deal, really, to take her hand.

He cared about her, and she'd been treated poorly, and maybe he wanted to remind her that not all guys were like that. Maybe he just needed to prove that for the sake of his gender. Maybe he was protective of her.

But maybe she didn't want him to be. And if she didn't feel comfortable when he took her hand, then he wouldn't. And he wouldn't kiss her.

And here he was again at kissing.

Thanks a lot, Delia.

He continued through the town of Anacortes onto Commercial Avenue. About six blocks up, he found a place to park and cut the engine. He took a deep breath to clear his head while Georgie got up and stretched.

She removed her helmet. "Swell Food for Salty Dogs," she read out loud.

He removed his helmet and looked at the sign above the windows of Adrift, the restaurant he'd been wanting to check out for a while.

"Are we salty dogs?" she asked.

He smiled and stowed their helmets, locking everything up. "Let's find out," he said.

They walked up to the old pale-blue building with white trim, and she brushed her fingers through her somewhat tangled hair. He tried not to let it distract him.

"The storefronts on this street all look like they were built in the 1800s," Georgie said.

He nodded and held the door open for her. "The building is old, but the menu here is pretty creative."

"Fresh?"

"Really fresh. I hope you're still hungry. " There were several dishes on the menu here he wanted to try, that he wanted her to try.

"I'm starving," she answered.

"Good." She'd hardly eaten anything at the Channel Grill when she'd withdrawn into herself. He'd try to avoid subjects that made her do that.

After they were seated and had placed their order for sodas and enough food to feed six people, he decided that for conversation, focusing on the new menu might be best.

But she had other ideas. "John told me the girl you were dating got engaged while you were dating her."

He'd been reaching for his drink and paused. "Is there a question in there?"

She rubbed her fingers over her brow. A habit when she was unsettled. "I just wondered if that was true. Because that would be awful. I mean, how serious was it? Because you were not yourself that first couple of weeks at the restaurant."

He looked at her, wondering why she got to ask the hard questions. But he wasn't going to not answer her just out of spite. "Yeah, it was kind of serious. But I'm over it. So." He hoped that would be enough to drop the subject.

She looked at him expectantly. Man, she was infuriating.

"Here's the deal," he said. "At the time, it seemed like the end of the world. I felt used and humiliated. I mean, how do you not know your girlfriend doesn't actually want you? We were making plans." He shrugged. "But now . . . I guess I'm kind of relieved. It all seems pretty superficial looking back."

"Why is that?"

He stared at her, wondering how in the heck he was supposed to answer. He had his ideas, but he wasn't ready to voice them. "I don't know. You look back on something and realize things happen for a reason."

"You believe that?"

He shrugged again. "Mostly. Maybe some things happen because you've got a billion people on this planet making a billion choices and life is just life. But I don't know; putting a reason to something really tough . . . somehow makes it easier to let it go. You know?"

She sipped her cola. "Seven billion."

"What?"

"There are over seven billion people on the planet making seven billion choices."

"I stand corrected."

"You're sitting."

He rubbed his hands over his face.

"I was on the debate team," she said.

"That explains so much."

She smiled. And her eyes lit up. He wondered how much therapy she needed.

"Why are you suddenly so happy?"

She shook her head, her smile still plastered on her face. And he had to smile too because it was ridiculous. He'd gone philosophical on her, generously answering her questions, and she was grinning like a kid dumping out Halloween candy on the floor.

"I forgot how much I like that," she said.

"What? Guys needlessly spilling their guts to you?"

She pressed her lips together. "No. Not that. I'm sorry. I liked what you said." She frowned. "I'm sorry."

"It's okay," he said, not wanting her smile to fade. "I'm kind of getting used to your erratic mood changes. They're endearing."

A corner of her mouth lifted. "I'll remember you said that."

He leaned forward. "Now, tell me what made you so happy just now."

She began to tell him about debate team. About going to state. About the topics she'd had to address and ideas she'd had to prove with facts and witnesses. He watched her use her hands, watched the animated expressions on her face, and she didn't even slow down when they brought the food. She told him about her trips to D.C. and how she'd considered going into law.

"Well, why don't you?" he asked. He had no idea how much school she'd had or where she'd gone.

She dropped her eyes, picking shredded cabbage off a fish taco. "I don't know. I was told . . ." She leaned her chin on her wrist. "I was told it wouldn't be worth getting a degree for something I would never practice."

He frowned. "Who told you that?" It didn't sound like something a guidance counselor would say. Her parents?

She grew quiet, but this time he didn't feel bad that he'd asked. He just waited.

Eventually she spoke. "You know how you said that attaching a reason to something hard helps you let it go?"

He nodded. She had been listening, then.

"Well, I'm really having a hard time doing that with something. But I'm trying. And this . . . *someone* who told me that is part of it all."

She looked at her plate and took a bite of crab cake with lemon avocado sauce. She made a face.

"Did you know what branch of law you wanted to study?" he asked.

She shook her head. "It was just an idea I was throwing around. With lots of other ideas. I'm kind of off the radar for school right now anyway."

She pointed her fork at the side of her head and twirled it around. "My brain is a little off, and sometimes I say stuff I probably shouldn't say. Don't know if you noticed. Like *that*. I don't know if what I just said should have been said. I'll regret it later, I'm sure."

"It is an adventure," he said, managing to keep a straight face. This may have been the most she'd ever spoken to him at once.

"The mango stuff with this fish taco is amazing." She took another bite of the cabbage-less taco and spoke with her mouth full. "Didn't you say something about a salsa with the halibut?"

He started to laugh. It grew, and he laughed more. He kept it quiet, of course, but he laughed until he leaned sideways and wiped moisture from his eyes.

And she watched him, bewilderment on her face. "What is so funny?" Her brow wrinkled, and she set her taco down. Her cheeks pinked.

He reached across the table and grabbed her hand, and she looked at it.

"You're just funny. You are. And you're good to talk to. And I just realized I never *ever* laughed like this with Brenna—"

"You mean you never laughed like this *at* Brenna."

"No, I mean *with* her, and I never really thought this hard with Brenna, and when I said my relationship with her seems superficial now . . ." He chuckled again and shook his head. "It's because this—whatever this is"— he waggled his finger back and forth between the two of them—"it's like putting on 3-D glasses after walking around in 2-D." His laugh quieted.

She wasn't laughing. "Thank you," she said softly. She looked down. "You're a good friend, Jace. We're friends, right?"

He let go of her hand as she pulled it back and withdrew it out of sight, under the table.

He nodded. "Yeah. Yeah, of course." Of course they were friends. That was what he'd meant.

She rolled her eyes. "That sounded like such a middle-school thing to say."

"Don't worry about it." He gave her what he hoped was an encouraging smile.

She smiled back, but the light wasn't there anymore. "Will you excuse me for a bit?"

"Sure."

She got up and headed for the restroom.

He wiped his mouth and dropped his napkin in his lap, feeling like a deflated hot air balloon. He looked at the array of food in front of him.

What the heck are you doing, Jace?

* * *

Georgie stood in the stall with the door closed, fighting tears that insisted on coming. She leaned back against the door with her hand over her mouth, not breathing because if she took a breath, the tears would follow.

Like putting on 3-D glasses after walking around in 2-D.

That was a really perfect thing to say.

She took a deep breath and blew it out.

A tear spilled.

Why did she have to be such a mess?

I hate you, Ian. I hate you. I hate what happened. I hate that I let it happen.

She obviously needed to work harder on assigning a reason to the tragedy that was Georgie Tate and Ian Hudson.

Ian could be so fun. So disarming. His confidence had been alluring. His command had been exciting. At first. She'd trusted him with her heart.

She'd trusted him.

He'd used it like a tether ball, then turned it inside out, and then he'd left her.

And here was Jace Lowe. Unassuming, flawed, surprisingly compassionate, deep thinking, and so chemically attractive she had to try really hard to stop looking at him, to stop allowing him to be so near. He wasn't perfect. He was better.

Like he'd said: 2-D to 3-D.

And she couldn't trust him.

Another tear fell.

Not with her heart. She wouldn't do that to him. Her heart was bruised and ripped and erratic. And she couldn't trust herself with his.

So that was it. She took another deep breath, and the tears stopped. She was glad, relieved that they were friends. Friends were good. Friends could be safe. She could be close, but she kept her heart. She'd have to keep her heart.

When she returned to the table, he stood. She looked at the stack of empty takeout boxes and frowned. "Are we leaving?"

"No, not if you don't want to," he said. "I just wasn't sure, and the waiter asked if we needed boxes." He looked like he was being careful, and she wanted to put him at ease. "Are you all right?" he asked.

She'd been in the restroom for a while. "I'm good," she said. She slid into her seat and picked up her napkin. "I haven't even tried this soup thing yet. What is it called again?"

"Cioppino," he answered and sat back down. He pushed the wide bowl toward her and picked up his own spoon. "The broth is different. Kind of a tomato-citrus thing. But it's good."

She tasted it, more of a stew with white fish, clams in their open shells, shrimp, and vegetables. The taste was a mixture of sweet and tangy and salty, but it was still smooth. "Mm, I like this."

He smiled.

She spooned up another bite. "You wouldn't think of putting tomato with orange or whatever this is."

He nodded. "They used saffron, but I think they used orange zest too." He took his own taste.

"Well, maybe you could do that with the salsa for the halibut. Maybe mandarin orange salsa or something."

His eyes narrowed thoughtfully. "A Cioppino-inspired salsa for the halibut. That's a great idea."

"Well, you know," she pointed at herself with the spoon, "muse. Just doing my job."

He laughed again, and she smiled. She gradually felt more at ease as they talked about the menu ideas and finished the rest of the food. It was good. It was safe. She kept her guard up.

And it all felt a little faded.

Georgie packed the takeout box in the back of the motorcycle. "Where to now? Back to Camano?" Despite everything, she had no desire to go home yet. But the afternoon had slipped by. The sun was still setting early in March, and in a few more hours, the sky would be dark.

Jace was buckling his helmet and shook his head. "Not yet." He shifted the bike and lifted the kickstand. "We need to stop at the grocery store and pick up a few ingredients for tomorrow. And I'd like to drive out around Samish. We're so close, it's kind of a shame not to. Do you mind?"

She shook her head. She had no idea what Samish was. "The place names in western Washington are strange. Cle Elum. Hoquaim. Enumclaw.

Kittitas. My favorite is Tukwila. It kind of rolls off the tongue. Tuk-wil-la." The names grew on her. Like the weather. "Where is Samish?"

He studied her with an amused expression. "Just north of here. It's a great drive around the bay. Sometimes it's just good to get out and ride. Then we'll head home." He started the bike up.

Georgie still stood with her helmet in her hands, but the sound of the revving engine jolted her into action. She pulled her helmet on and climbed behind Jace.

He glanced behind. "Have you had a good day?"

She nodded.

"I'm glad," he said.

As he backed the bike out of its parking space, she glanced up at the sign above the restaurant windows once more. "We are salty dogs."

She felt him laugh.

The long road to Samish Bay took them past furrowed fields ready for planting, white picket fences, cows, aged red barns, and towering copses of pine trees. Only a couple of cars made an appearance as they traveled north toward low, gray mountains. Jace wasn't in any hurry and seemed to relax as he drove. Maybe this, and the picturesque setting, was why Georgie felt herself leaving the anxiety she'd felt at the restaurant behind and just watching the scenery pass by. The morning mists were long gone, and a blanket of light gray clouds covered the sky. The sun was still up somewhere, but already its light dusted everything with a pale pink. It was incredible what a mere hint of sunlight could do to a cloud-covered sky.

By the time they began to see glimpses of Samish Bay, the sky had turned apricot. Dark clouds gathered on the far side of the water, but anything green shone vivid and alive. The scenery changed from rural farmland to emerald woods on the right and vast bay water glimmering between stands of more trees on the left. Jace continued driving, leaning into the curves, meandering between shore and mountain. Sometimes it seemed the trees grew right over the top of the road, and the air would cool in those shady stretches. Georgie shivered and leaned closer to the heat Jace provided.

"Hang on," he said as they passed a sign signaling sharp curves ahead. She steadied her grip, and he maneuvered the s-curve without a problem, and when they emerged, he opened the throttle a little more. He picked up speed, and Georgie felt her grip tightening, but he steadied it out and didn't push it any faster, and after a moment, she enjoyed the pace as they wound through the trees.

After a few more miles, Jace slowed and pulled off at an overlook. They removed their helmets but stayed on the bike, and he didn't say anything, just sat watching the hidden sun play tricks with the clouds and the moisture in the air. Hazy pink, orange, and purple blended so softly she hardly noticed where one color ended and the other began.

Between watching the sunset, glancing at Jace's silhouette, and pretending she wasn't cold, Georgie hadn't felt more a part of her world. For good or for crazy, she was on this earth, and the ideas they had for the menu were good. And some of them had been hers. She was seeing things she never had before. She was learning. And she was on the back of a motorcycle with what felt like the best friend she'd allowed herself to have in a long time.

Jace turned, then, and glanced at her. "Ready?" was all he asked.

No. I'm not. She took a deep breath. "If you are."

He looked one last time over the bay and then back at her. "Are you cold?"

She shook her head and smiled. *Liar.*

He started the engine back up, and they put on their helmets. He took the same leisurely pace leaving as he had coming in. The sky was a hazy dark now above occasional street lamps. After a few tight curves, where she'd huddled into Jace, she didn't ease her hold on him. He was too warm, and the cooler night air seeped through her rain jacket.

By the time they reached the highway, rain had started to fall. Jace dropped his head and shook it. "I'm sorry," he called back to her.

"I don't mind," she replied. She wasn't lying.

As the rain fell harder, Georgie lifted her knees, trying to bring them nearer her body as if that would protect them from the deluge. She drew even closer to Jace in an attempt to shelter him as well as her. He kept his bike at a steady speed, deftly avoiding puddles if they came up. She'd learned to anticipate his leans into the curves, and her arms moved with him around his midsection as they wove through traffic.

She told herself she felt warm and solid, but, really, she felt light. Fragile. Like if she wasn't holding on to Jace, she'd float up like a lost balloon into the low clouds and the starless sky, all wet and shivery. He pressed his forearm against hers, wrapping his fingers around her cold hands, and her heart thudded.

No. No, no, no, don't love this.

She closed her eyes, feeling the buzz of the engine, hearing the sound of tires on wet concrete, and sensing that if Jace were to drive her anywhere, pull up anywhere and say, *Here we are*, she wouldn't blink. She'd say, *How did you know I didn't want to go home yet?* And he'd say, *Because I know you.*

Her eyes snapped open. *Because I know you.* It wasn't Jace's voice but Ian's that rang clear in her head.

"You'll take the ring back."

Georgie hadn't answered him, but Ian persisted. "You'll take it back before I walk you to the door and kiss you good night."

He glanced sideways at Georgie as he drove into the canyon. "You'll forgive me and take it back. You'll see. Actually, why don't we start that good-night kiss now."

"No, Ian." He'd begun to slow and pull off the side of the road. "Take me home."

He chuckled and accelerated. "Fine. But you'll beg for the ring back. Because I know you, and you'll realize you're nothing without me. You were made for me, Georgie."

Bright lights and a horn somewhere behind them on the highway jerked Georgie out of the memory with a gasp.

"Everything all right?" he called back to her.

She tried to relax her hold, but her heart beat erratically, as if someone was tugging her balloon string, threatening to break her tether.

"Yes," was all she could say.

"Do we need to stop? We can try to wait out this downpour at the gas station up here off the next exit."

"No. Keep going. Maybe slow down a little."

"You bet."

And he did. His thumb caressed the back of her hand. She knew he was concerned for her and that he'd liked the day they'd had together. He'd liked the new ideas, and he was grateful. But her head spun with the new memory of Ian, of his words. *You're nothing without me.* He'd said that before, earlier on when he'd sensed her pulling away, and had followed it up with how they completed each other, like in that movie. Two halves made a whole. And she'd swallowed his words like a pill, hoping they'd make her feel the same way. As if something was wrong with her because she didn't feel it. It was a romantic thing to say. Being nothing without someone.

But that was wrong. It wasn't romantic. It was manipulative. Selfish.

And there was the engagement ring. In the memory, it was important, but she'd never seen it again.

Sometime later, Jace pulled into her driveway. She'd tuned out her whirling thoughts by watching blurry lights go by in the dark and keeping herself tethered to Jace. But with the kickstand down and the motorcycle engine cut, she had to let him go. He was still and quiet, his hand still over hers, keeping it warm. Here the rain had slowed to barely a drizzle, and she shivered. She drew in a deep breath and slid her arms from around his waist. They removed their helmets, and Georgie got off the bike. She stowed the helmet as Jace got off the bike as well. "Thanks," she murmured to the ground.

"I'll walk you to the door."

She turned to the front walk, and he joined her, his helmet in his hand.

"You okay?" he asked again quietly. Only the porch light was on; the rest of the house was quiet.

She nodded and brushed her hand over her hair. "Just, you know, haunted."

He crooked an eyebrow at her but seemed to let it go. "Sorry about having to ride in that downpour."

"It was fine. I'm fine . . . just tired," she said.

Jace shook his head. "It's been a long day. And now you're soaked and shivering."

"I loved it."

He looked down at her as if she'd said something extraordinary. "I'm starting to believe you when you say that."

She managed a small smile.

He returned it. They both stood shivering. She broke their gaze.

"So, tomorrow morning? Eight-ish?" he said. "I think we'll use the restaurant kitchen this time. They've got some tools and ingredients there that I'll need, and that way we won't mess up your aunt's kitchen."

"Sounds good. I'll meet you there."

"Okay." He looked like he didn't want to go. Either that, or he really wanted to go and didn't know how to make a graceful exit. He shifted his weight and ran a hand over his face. "Well, thank you," he said and stepped forward, wrapping his arms around her in a warm hug. "You were a lot of help today," he said softly next to her ear. "I think we can do this."

She didn't move, just closed her eyes, smelling his jacket, letting his warmth sink in. She'd held on to him all day, but this was different. This was him holding her, and she let him for just a minute.

He let go quickly and walked away. She watched him get on his bike, and after a small wave, he drove off, up the hill.

Two halves didn't make a whole. Not with people. What good was half a person? Put two half people together and they just . . . they just toppled.

You're nothing without me.

That couldn't be true. How had she bought into that? She'd been something before Ian. With him she was . . . She wasn't sure what she was. And now she was less, but she wasn't nothing. Shouldn't people be well on their way to being *something* before they committed to giving over everything they had, laying their hearts out to be cherished or ripped apart? How could Georgie, being half—even half sounded like a lot—how could she expect to be somebody to someone if she couldn't even be someone to herself?

I'm more with you.

That was what it should be. That should be the wonder, the miracle of a relationship. *I thought I was whole, but I'm more with you.*

The thought flickered inside her, making her wonder if Jace felt like he was more with her. She shoved the thought in a box and put it high on a shelf. Those were dangerous thoughts.

Because she was half. She was less than half. And she couldn't lose herself again.

* * *

Jace lay in bed staring at the ceiling, remembering the day, remembering the things Georgie had said, the looks she'd given him, and the unknown that surrounded her.

Their trip had been productive. Enjoyable. Even deep on some kind of level. He hadn't been bored. Frustrated, yeah. Worried about her. But he'd never felt . . . inadequate or like he had to prove himself. Even on the bike in the rain. Especially on the bike in the rain. She'd been okay with it. She'd said she loved it.

The hug at the end. He hadn't known what to do. What with the hand holding and the not hand holding and the ride home . . . and the friends thing. So he'd hugged her. She'd felt so . . . right tucked in his arms.

So, yeah. Good day.

But the expression on her face when she said she was "haunted"—it wasn't a joke. This guy she'd been with had treated her like crap, and she'd left home because of that. Maybe school too. And she was in therapy. That was serious. The more he thought about that, the more ticked off he became. The more he wanted her tucked in his arms.

Because he cared about her. He cared about her a lot.

He grabbed his phone off the nightstand and Googled "The Love Song of J. Alfred Prufrock."

After reading through it a couple of times, he texted Georgie. He could do that. Friends texted. *Just read Prufrock. Measuring my life in tablespoons.* He paused, hoping that didn't sound too corny. *Thanks again for your help today.* He hit send and waited, wondering if she was already asleep. After a few minutes, he decided it didn't matter if she was asleep. She'd get the text in the morning. He set his phone back down just before it buzzed.

She'd answered him. *You can thank that stupid bee.*

He smiled. The honey was a brilliant idea. *Good night, Alfred.*

He waited again, a little uncomfortable with how eager he was for her answer. She might not answer. Why would she answer? She was probably rolling her eyes—

His phone buzzed. *Stop calling me that. I'm not a guy.*

He smiled again. *I know.*

Chapter 17

THE MORNING SHONE BEAUTIFUL AND bright, and Jace had propped the back door of the restaurant open.

Of course, he thought, looking out at the clear sky. *On the bike, rain. Working inside today, sun.*

But he hardly cared. He'd be inside cooking with Georgie. They'd start with the salsa for the halibut first. And they would try pan searing as well as grilling the halibut steaks. He pulled a heavy-bottomed fry pan from the rack and prepped the grill.

"Good morning," Georgie said. She stood in the doorway, her hair kind of lit up from behind.

Jace stood back from the grill, trying to ignore the pleasant jump in his stomach. "Good morning."

She reached for an apron and tied it on. "I'm sorry I'm late. I slept in a little bit."

"No problem."

She smiled up at him, reserved but friendly. "What are we doing first?"

"The salsa," he said.

She looked around. "Should I have tied my hair back?"

"No," he said a little too quickly. "I mean, it doesn't matter. We're just cooking for us."

"Halibut for breakfast, yum."

He moved to the cooler. She followed.

"So what do you think for the salsa?" He opened the heavy door and allowed her through, then pulled out the box of ingredients he'd separated from the others. He handed them to her as he named them. "Tomato, of course. And onion, green pepper—basic salsa." He grabbed some mandarin oranges and a little black-topped glass jar. "Mandarins and this." He shook it gently.

"What is it?" she asked, peering closer.

He handed her the jar. "Saffron."

She studied the reddish-orange threads in the jar. "But what are they?" He opened the lid, and she sniffed. "Smells sweet."

"They're the stigmas of crocus flowers. Can't get more spring than that, right?"

She looked up at him, her eyes wide. "You're kidding. Those little things in the centers of the flowers?"

"Would I make that up?" He screwed the lid back on. "They're used as a spice and a food coloring. Very subtle but worth a try if we're going for something different."

"Interesting," she said, still studying the saffron in the jar.

He grabbed a container of steamed clam meat; peeled, cooked shrimp; a bunch of fresh cilantro; and a few other ingredients. She followed him out with the vegetables.

Jace showed her how to peel and seed the tomatoes and zest the oranges. Then they went through their routine of measuring each ingredient and noting it in Jace's book. He dumped the contents of half a dozen little bowls into a pile on a large cutting board.

"Now," he said, "take one of those saffron threads and crumble it up."

She looked at him like he'd asked her to step into a bullfight.

"Here." He chose a thread from the little jar and took her hand, turning it palm up. She watched him cautiously, and he smiled. "Just gently rub it between your finger and thumb." He demonstrated, and the bits of saffron fell into her cupped hand. He held the remaining piece out to her.

She took it and rubbed the thread carefully between her thumb and finger. It didn't make much, but it was plenty for the salsa.

"Now sprinkle it on our pile here."

She did, and he added a pinch of sea salt.

"Instead of chopping each of these up individually, we're going to chop them all together, so the flavors and juices mix, and that will be our fresh Cioppino salsa. Or something close to it." He picked up the large chef's knife and began to chop swiftly, giving it a good start.

"That smells amazing," Georgie said, watching over his shoulder.

"It does. And now it's your turn."

She took a step away. "Oh, I'm not a good chopper."

"I think you might be. Look, this is about the easiest thing to learn on. It's just a pile. No grains to follow, no particular size except smallish. C'mon." He held the knife handle out to her, and hesitantly she took it.

"Okay, but let the record show that *you* are the one who handed the crazy lady the knife."

He grinned. "Don't be so hard on yourself."

She raised her eyebrows at him, then turned her concentration on the chop pile in front of her. She set the blade on the center of the pile and pressed it down slowly. She repeated the motion, moving it a little bit to the right. She repeated this action several times.

"Have you used a chef's knife before?" he asked.

Her brow creased. "Of course I have. Just not like you do." She sliced the knife through the pile, aiming for a shrimp. "You're so fast. And precise."

"I bet you say that to all the sous-chefs."

She just shook her head.

"C'mon," he said, reaching around her and placing his hand over hers on the knife handle. He glanced at her sideways, as they were almost cheek-to-cheek. He could smell her shampoo again. "You're overthinking it. Just press the tip of the blade to the surface and keep it there. Think of it as your anchor, or your pivot point."

She gave a little nod, and he felt her grip on the knife change accordingly.

"From this point, you move the knife handle up and down like a water pump, directing the blade through the pile."

"A water pump?" she murmured.

"Yeah," he said, then demonstrated the action. "Like pumping water."

"Oh, a *water* pump," she said. "I just used a water pump this morning after I made soap and milked the cows."

"Ha, ha." He smiled. "You get the idea."

She grinned at him sideways, and he shook his head, allowing a laugh. She turned her attention back to the salsa and placed the tip of the knife to the cutting surface and rested her fingers on top to anchor it like he'd shown her. Then she pushed the handle up and down, like a water pump, pivoting the angle of the knife around in a fairly even, if still careful, rhythm.

He eased off until she was on her own. "There you go. See?"

"Thanks," she said, her face a little flushed. "Next you can teach me how to hitch up ol' Bessie to the plow. And churn butter. Or—"

"I get it." He stood up straight and rubbed the back of his neck. "Let's see if we can get through the salsa first, hmm?" He watched her smile as she concentrated on the chop pile. She bit her lip a little, and he had to step back and go over the notes he'd already taken. He found himself agitated in a really good way, and he needed to focus. Something had shifted again with Georgie. He couldn't put his finger on it, but she was teasing him, and somehow that felt good.

"I'll get the fire going," he said, moving to the grill.

"I'll pluck the chicken," she said without missing a beat.

"I can arrange that."

Her knife paused, and he grinned.

It wasn't long before they sat on stools and sampled their Cioppino salsa on grilled halibut. They'd made a few adjustments to the salsa, but he thought they finally had it.

"This is good," Georgie said, making sure to scoop a little salsa on her second bite of fish. "I like how you used the grill pan for the halibut."

He nodded. In a last-minute decision, he'd chosen to use a grill pan with a little EVO and butter. It gave the fish just the right crisp-tender edge he was looking for while retaining the char marks everyone loved. "Slices of lime on the side would be good."

She nodded. "Definitely. So we did it?"

"We did it. Again." He held up his hand, and she gave him a high five. He clasped her hand quickly, not letting it go. "Thank you." He studied her face. "It was a *good* idea."

She met his gaze. "I don't even know what I'm doing," she said.

"That doesn't seem to matter." He swallowed. He felt that burn he experienced every time he touched her hand. That hum from her fingers right to the area just below his ribs.

She lowered her eyes, slipped her hand from his, and got up to scrape the remaining salsa into a container. He took a steadying breath and carried the dishes to the sink.

"So now we make the pork chop?" she asked, wiping down the prep area.

"Yup," he answered, throwing the cooking utensils a little harder into the sink than he'd intended. He put his hands on his hips. *Cool it, Jace.*

A while later, Georgie stirred the honey glaze while Jace flipped the garlic-crusted pork chops. They worked side by side at the stove, and he worked to ignore the buzz of electricity between them. He told himself he was only grateful to have someone like Georgie so interested in cooking with him. He'd had no idea that sharing his passion with someone—who seemed to enjoy it too—could feel so satisfying. He was grateful. And that had to be enough.

"I was thinking we'd serve this with a vegetable. Maybe asparagus," he said. "What do you think?"

She'd been quieter since the high five, and he found himself scrambling to say something to bring out the lightness in her again. He didn't think she was upset, but she'd been so at ease with him earlier. He wanted her to feel at ease.

"I think vegetables would be good," she said. "And it would be pretty. This is simmering. Do you want it to simmer?" she asked.

He peered over her shoulder. "Perfect. Take it off the heat, and let's have a taste."

She did as asked and retrieved a tasting spoon. She dipped it in the golden glaze—the color of her hair.

She held out the spoon, her hand cupped underneath. "You first." She had a drop of glaze just next to her nose. He pulled his focus away from her face and leaned toward the spoon.

"Careful, it's hot," she warned.

He blew a little and sipped at the spoon. "That's good." He lifted his gaze once more, and she didn't back away, only watched him with this sort of hopeful, careful look. "Really good." He reached for another spoon and touched the tip to the glaze. "Now you taste it." He held it out to her, and she blew on it softly, then, with a glance up at him, touched her mouth to the spoon. A smile played at her lips as she swallowed.

"Good, huh?"

She nodded.

He found it a little difficult to breathe as he reached and touched the drip away from her cheek.

Her brow rose in question.

"You had a drop of glaze." Carefully, he reached again, daring to brush his fingers along her cheek, soft as a peach. "Just there."

Her eyes fluttered closed at his touch, then she shook her head. She opened her eyes wide and stepped back.

She looked away, rubbing her forehead. "I'll get the vegetables out of the cooler."

He sighed. So much for making her feel at ease. "Georgie."

She was already halfway to the walk-in. "I'll only be a sec." She opened the cooler and disappeared.

Ignoring everything telling him not to, he followed. He found her with her back to him, staring at the various bunches of vegetables.

"I don't know what would be best," she said without turning around. "Don't you?"

Her head dropped a little, and she traced her fingers over package labels.

These little things, these little touches and tastes and drips of sauce and steam rising . . . they were all driving him crazy. But he wasn't sure what to do with it all. He wasn't—

"How do you know?"

Her question caught him off guard. "What?" She still faced the shelves, and he stepped toward her.

"What kind is best? What if you think you know, but it ends up being all wrong? So wrong you're afraid to even—"

He reached out and gently pulled her around. "Afraid to even what?"

She watched him with those eyes, again with that mix of hope and caution, and he stepped closer. "Afraid to even what?" he asked again more quietly. He tried not to show how hard it was for him to breathe.

"You're very close," she said, a tremble in her voice.

He moved to take a step back.

"No," she said quickly, and he paused. "You're fine. I just . . . You're very close."

He steadied himself, hoping she wouldn't break her gaze. "Since you started working here, I've been trying to keep my distance. And then yesterday . . . I don't know. How do I earn your trust if I'm across the kitchen pretending to study the grill?"

She swallowed, and he noted a tiny crease between her brows. "That's a remarkable point," she said.

He smiled.

She visibly shivered. "It's cold in here."

His smile disappeared. "You're really cold?"

She shook her head. "That was a lie to cover my uncertainty. I don't trust easily, Jace."

He dared to draw her closer, slowly reaching his arm around her waist. "Uncertainty," he said carefully. "You know, you've asked me a lot of questions, and I've answered them. You know more about me than my mom does."

She swallowed and nodded. "So ask me something."

He studied her, his heartbeat racing, feeling the electricity between them, his thoughts unable to land on a single question. It was his turn to ask a question, and he couldn't think of anything pressing he needed to know about her that he didn't already. She was unpredictable and kind and scared and brave and brash and looking at him. "You know what?" he said breathlessly. "I'll figure it out."

He closed the distance between them and met her mouth with his. She lifted her chin in response, tasting like honey and salt from the glaze. Her lips were cool for only a few seconds, and he enjoyed warming them. One-one thousand . . . two-one thousand . . . She pulled him closer, making a little sound, and any intelligent thoughts spun away from him. Kissing Georgie was like . . . kissing her was . . .

She pulled back, her eyelids heavy.

"What?" he asked, half dazed.

"Have you just been . . . looking out for me?" she whispered. "Like my uncle asked you to do?"

He frowned. "Do you need looking out for?"

She watched his mouth and shook her head again.

"I didn't think so." He lifted her up on her toes, and she seemed eager to take up where they left off. His heart pounded, and he felt more sure of himself as her arms wrapped around his neck. He pressed deeply into the kiss, bracing his arms between her and the shelves behind her. She pressed back, and he sort of forgot everything but all of Georgie—her taste, her smell, her touch—for who knows how long, when suddenly she squealed and let go, scrambling for the door.

"The pork chops!" she cried.

He groaned and raced after her. Smoke filled the kitchen, and he opened the back door as the smoke alarm went off. Georgie turned off the heat and removed the pan. Jace reached for a towel, whipping it through the air just below the alarm.

Georgie grabbed another towel and started wafting the smoky air out the door.

The alarm stopped its screeching, and Jace filled a glass with water and poured it into the pan. It hissed, and steam rose from the ruined lumps of meat. He threw a lid on it.

From behind him, Georgie began to stammer. "I'm sorry . . . If I hadn't run to the cooler . . . What am I even doing? I'm so sorry—"

He turned, throwing the towel on the counter. "I'm not." He took her hand and pulled her to him again and did his best to stop the pointless apologies coming from her mouth. Between kisses he heard her say something about burned and ruined and out of her mind.

"I don't care," he whispered into her ear, brushing his hands through her hair, kissing her cheek, knowing he'd wanted to touch her this way for a long time.

"But it was going to be perfect."

He took her face in both his hands and pressed his forehead to hers. "I'm okay with it. Aren't you?" He hoped he knew the answer.

A small smile came to her lips, and she allowed a laugh to escape. He kissed her again.

And again.

And again.

* * *

Kissing Jace was like standing in ninety-degree weather and tasting the perfect ice cream.

The perfect. Melting. Ice cream.

And the touching. She'd never been comfortable with much touching, but him? He touched her like it was new—well, of course, it was new with her, but like *touching* was new. He watched where he touched her. Watched her react. Not like slow and weird but sure and careful. Her arm. Her face. And he never once made her feel uncomfortable or manipulated or—

Jace touched her neck as he kissed her, and there was nothing she could think of to convince herself that this wasn't where she should be, which was a huge feat considering all that hazy stuff calling to her from way far away . . . something about jade cages and wings . . .

Dang, she was in trouble.

She gently pulled away from him, as difficult as that was, and walked to the open back door, breathing in fresh air. Her heart pounded, but her head cleared a little.

He'd been fine with the burned food. He'd been fine with her oddness. He'd been more than fine. And even now as she'd pulled away from him without a word, he stayed back, giving her space. She could feel him, where she'd left him near the stove.

"Are you for real?" she heard herself say.

He didn't answer, and for a second, she hoped he hadn't heard her. But for another second, she hoped he had.

"Why do you ask that?"

He sounded both amused and wary. So often she'd seen him carry off two contradicting emotions like that. She closed her eyes against the sunshine, willing herself not to compare him to Ian again. It wasn't fair to any of them. She felt Jace now, walking in her direction. He stopped a few steps behind her.

"I'm not just . . . playing around, Georgie."

She glanced behind her and was surprised to see a look of confusion on his face.

She faced the sunshine again. "Well, what if I am?"

"Are you?"

A lump rose in her throat, and her eyes began to sting. Why? Why was she attempting to brush him off? She swallowed and asked again, "What if I am?" A traitorous tear slipped down her cheek. *What if that's all I can do?*

She heard him shift his weight.

Was she testing him? To see how far she could press this trust thing they'd built? To prove him to a fault?

"I'd like to ask you a question now, if the offer still stands," he said, sounding faintly perturbed.

She shrugged and nodded without turning. It was only fair.

But he moved around to face her. She couldn't meet his steady gaze.

He carefully lifted his hand, and she must have flinched, because he paused. But then he continued and brushed her hair away just over her brow.

"How did you get this scar?" His voice had become soft again. He brushed his thumb across it like a feather, and she shivered.

"I—" Emotion stopped her words. She wrapped her arms around herself.

He stepped to her, and she stepped quickly back. She couldn't help meeting his gaze this time, and she knew he regretted asking. Maybe he regretted it all.

He dropped his hand. "You don't have to tell me," he said. "I'm sorry."

No. She wanted to tell him. She swiped at a tear. "I—" The words stopped again. She couldn't find them. The right words. She'd been able to tell Tyler. Not everything but more than just *I*.

Jace reached for her hand, and she withdrew again. She looked around for her jacket. On the peg behind him.

"Georgie, forget I asked. I shouldn't have even . . . I'm sorry—"

"*Stop saying that!*"

He flinched. She knew she'd hurt him, and pain tore through her like fire. She tried to breathe, and he moved to turn away.

"No—Jace. You . . . you have nothing to be sorry for. You've answered my questions, and I want to tell you. I—" She pressed her fingers over her scar and tried to find the words. "I . . . don't know." She felt the beginnings of panic, not because she couldn't find the words but— "I don't know how I got this scar. I don't remember." Her panic rose. "I can't remember, and I try, and I try, and I tell myself it doesn't matter, but it *does*. Because if I remember how I got this scar, I'll remember the car accident." She gasped for a breath. "And if I remember the accident, then I'll remember how he died . . ." She drew in another ragged breath. "And then maybe . . . maybe it wasn't my fault . . ."

Or maybe it was.

She wasn't shivering. She was shaking. But Jace had drawn her into his arms again. She gripped his shoulders, and he held her for several minutes, not asking any more of her. She sniffled to keep her nose from running.

"Pretty irresistible, huh?" she thought out loud. "All of this?"

Jace shushed her.

She whispered. "I told you I'm a basket case."

He nodded into her shoulder and whispered back. "I believed you."

Somehow that didn't hurt.

He pulled back, and she reached for a towel and dabbed her face.

"I don't know if I'm ready for this," she said, not without regret.

"Ready for what?" He watched her with that steady gaze of his. How was he doing that?

She pointed to him and her and the space between them and all around them in slightly manic circles. He reached and held her hand still. He brought her finger to his lips and kissed it before gently releasing it. Quietly, he asked, "Was he your boyfriend? The one who died?"

She breathed out the truth. "I had just broken off our engagement. He was driving me home. That's all I remember."

He looked down and nodded, a frown on his perfect mouth. "The guy with the motorcycle."

"Yeah. It had become—he had become . . . I had to get out. I had to. I just . . . didn't know how."

"And you were hurt? In the car accident?"

She nodded. "Ribs. Back. Arm." She took a shaky breath. "Head. I have metal pieces in me."

He swallowed hard, reaching for her, then stopped himself. "I'm so sorry. Why didn't you tell me before?"

"It's complicated," she whispered. "I think . . . I thought somehow telling you meant having to give you a piece of me. And I just—" She drew herself up straight, despite feeling like crumpling. "I just can't afford that."

A minute of silence skulked by. Jace rubbed his jaw, his brow drawn downward.

"Now what?" Georgie finally asked, though her voice came out barely above a whisper.

"Well," he said, still watching the ground. "Seeing as I've recently committed to bachelorhood, done with women and dating and all of that . . ." He paused and cleared his throat. "And you need . . ." He lifted his brow.

"The psych ward?" she suggested.

"*Time*," he offered. "Maybe I should just"—he looked around, and she suddenly missed him looking at her—"go get more pork chops and try this again." He glanced toward the cooler, his brow furrowed. "Without the vegetables."

She swallowed the returning lump in her throat, flicking a look toward the cooler, and nodded her head. "You still want my help?" She was afraid of the answer.

He turned to get her jacket off the hook and studied it for a second. He handed it to her. "Yeah. Apparently we're neighbors in Crazytown."

She took the jacket, relieved and dejected at the same time. They were going to the store. But it would be a strained trip.

Jace turned toward the door. He paused in the frame. "For the record, Georgie?" He didn't look back at her.

"Yeah?"

"I wasn't playing around."

She watched him not looking at her, and she realized with a sick feeling that he meant it. He wouldn't do that. Because Brenna had played around with him.

He was for real.

And Georgie was broken.

Chapter 18

Rain began to plop in the mosaic-tiled birdbath next to the azalea bushes. Drops slowly dotted the walk to the driveway as Georgie watched out the window of her aunts' house. The sun still shone, and Faye had opened the windows to let the fresh air in.

Georgie couldn't keep her thoughts from returning to earlier that morning at the restaurant. She and Jace had gone to the store and returned to the kitchen. They'd made garlic, honey-glazed pork chops. Reuben had come in soon after they'd returned and suggested asparagus spears as a side. Jace had simply written the addition of asparagus into his notes.

Throughout the rest of the morning, she and Jace had been quiet and careful around each other. They'd seldom made eye contact as they'd worked side by side to get the job done. Jace had become very technical about it all. Polite. And technical.

She'd kept her distance physically and emotionally, as she should have done all along. As she should do from now on.

But as she watched the rain gather strength, the heat of Jace's kiss washed over her without her permission. Her heart beat double time as though he was standing right there touching his lips to hers, drawing his hands around her waist. Georgie leaned against the windowsill, closing her eyes and inhaling the scent of new rain.

Her stomach sort of dropped at the memory of what had followed. Heat had turned to cold humiliation, which had then turned to resignation that she'd done the best thing for both of them.

After a couple of minutes, and feeling steadier, she called behind her. "Faye, I'm going for a walk."

"Okay. Don't go too far. Dinner is just about done."

"I won't." She stepped out into the light but steady rain. The south side of the house was narrow and bordered by the neighbor's fence and clusters of hollyhocks getting ready to bloom, but once she reached the beach, she kept heading south. The family usually went north on their walks, keeping to the long rocky stretch of beach, but the way south curved outward to the sea and led to towering pines and woods.

This was the direction the seagull had flown in that downpour weeks ago. She hadn't forgotten that seagull, nor the dread she'd felt watching it getting pelted in the choppy water.

She flies with her own wings.

She'd come a long way. But she was far from where she needed to be, wherever that was. She wasn't going back, but she wasn't ready to take to the sky yet either. She was still shivering in the waves.

Georgie picked up her pace as she left the rocks behind for rich soil, pine needles, and moss. She breathed deeply and picked her way through the trees. These woods weren't dense, and she could see the water to her right and homes and fences to her left. She considered that perhaps she was on private property. She didn't much care. The rain dropped on her head and face and hands, just lightly enough to let her know it was still coming down. She may have gone mental on Jace, and that was hurting more than she could admit, but she didn't feel caged.

However, she did have to show up for work in a couple of hours. Maybe she could find a different job. Maybe she was strong enough for that. Somewhere off the island. Jace would just be a neighbor. A friend at church. With a kiss between them that had turned her insides to honey. Lava honey.

Her phone buzzed in her pocket, and she pulled it out. An unfamiliar number with a Utah area code showed up on the display. She frowned but answered. "Hello?"

"Georgiana. This is Shannon Hudson."

Georgie pulled up short, turning in place. Shannon Hudson—Ian's mom. "Hello." Her heartbeat started an uncomfortable staccato in her chest. She hadn't spoken with either of Ian's parents since they had come to see her at the hospital not long after Ian's funeral. She'd barely been conscious and didn't remember most of the visit, only that the feeling had been dark and sorrowful.

Ian's parents had left her alone after that.

Sister Hudson continued in her businesslike tone of voice. Pleasant and in charge. "You're probably wondering why I'm calling out of the blue. Your mother gave me your phone number. I guess I understand you not wanting to give us your new contact information."

Georgie opened her mouth to protest. It hadn't been that she hadn't wanted to—

"No matter. Your mother says you're doing much better? I do hope that's true. At least one of you—" She paused and made a little sniff noise.

Georgie carefully answered. "I am doing better. Little by little."

"*Good.*" The word sounded forced from her throat. "I'm so glad."

The next pause seemed too long, and Georgie toed a fallen pine branch. "Is there something I can do for you?" she asked quietly. Like a mouse. She hated the mouse voice.

"Well, there is something." Sister Hudson cleared her throat, and her party-planning voice returned. "I know it's been some time, but we've been sitting on some confusing information, and I feel enough time has passed that I can come to you with questions."

She felt enough time had passed? Georgie's muscles tensed, and she began to walk, watching the ground, her arm pulled tight around her. "What questions?"

Sister Hudson took a deep breath. "Well, I'll just come right out and say it. Results from the investigation after the accident told us that Ian's car was going approximately one hundred miles per hour when it left the road."

Dread pushed through Georgie.

"Jack and I have been wondering all these months what in the world possessed you to be driving that fast, especially in the canyon."

Georgie frowned. "I wasn't driving."

The woman made an exasperated sound. "Well, I know that, but you were in the car."

Georgie's mind spun with the information and near accusations coming from this woman who had lost her son in this wreck. One hundred miles per hour? Georgie recalled how once, out on a flat, lonely highway in southern Utah, Ian had pushed the speed of his car to ninety-seven. It had been a thrill for him, but it had scared Georgie to death, and she'd begged him to slow down. He'd *reassured* her by letting her know he did this all the time on his motorcycle. A shiver ran down her spine.

"I'm sorry, but I don't remember the accident."

"Yes, your mother said that. But surely you remember what happened before it."

Georgie hesitated. While it was true she remembered some of that night, the accident itself was still a blank, including most of the drive back to her apartment and what had caused the crash. Now her head reeled with not knowing, fearing why Ian had been driving that fast when he knew they would be taking the curves in the canyon. She rubbed the place above her eye, her fingers wet.

The rain had become irritating, and she suddenly didn't like feeling damp. She turned back to her aunts' house.

"I'm sorry, Sister Hudson. I only remember our walk to the car after the wedding reception. That's all. I didn't even remember that until recently."

Sister Hudson didn't say anything right away, and Georgie could only assume she was trying to decide whether or not to believe her.

"Your mother says you're still in therapy."

Georgie clenched her jaw. What had her mother *not* told the woman? Just then Georgie's phone chimed, and a text flashed across the top. *Shannon Hudson may be calling you. Call me ASAP.*

Georgie rolled her eyes at the text from her mom. She squared her shoulders. "Yes, I'm in therapy. I'm sure you can understand that I've been climbing out of depression. I've been learning how to deal with everything that resulted from that night." She paused, searching for the next words. "I was hoping to reach a point where remembering the details didn't matter. But learning that Ian was going that fast . . . I don't know. I wish I had an answer for you." She wasn't so sure of that. Something told her she'd rather not know the truth.

She was breathing a little heavily now and realized her walk had taken on a frenzied pace. Her body had warmed with perspiration, and she felt faintly sick.

Sister Hudson paused again, probably considering why Ian had ever wanted to marry such an unstable girl in the first place.

Georgie hadn't told Ian's parents how she'd really felt about him when she'd woken up in the hospital. They'd just lost their son. She couldn't find it in her to add to their pain. Everything had been so foggy. Only her parents, Deacon, and her shrinks knew about her confusion and fear of Ian upon waking. *Oh, please, Mom. Please say you kept that to yourself.*

"Well, I hope you continue to heal, Georgiana. We're all doing our best. I do have one more question. I hope you don't take offense."

Georgie braced herself. "Okay."

"The ring."

"The ring?" Her stomach knotted.

"Yes, the engagement ring Ian gave you. Do you have it?"

"No." She didn't. The memory of that night had shown her giving the ring to Ian and his casual insistence that she take it back. Before those memories had returned, she'd assumed the ring had been lost in the accident, just like her shoe. She couldn't remember what he'd done with the ring. He'd taken it and told her she was just tired, like he was only keeping it for her until she'd had a nap. And then he'd taunted her with it and told her she was nothing without him.

Georgie wrestled with whether or not to tell Ian's mother those details. Before, keeping her feelings to herself had been out of concern for their sorrow, but now Georgie couldn't ignore the sick protective feeling building inside her. She kept her voice steady, her mind ricocheting around for the words that would keep her safe. Words that couldn't be used against her. "I promise you, I don't have the ring. If I did, I would give it to you without question, if that's what you needed."

"Oh. Well. We were more curious about where it was. I don't know that we would necessarily ask for it *back*. It was rather expensive, but it was given to you."

The half-karat diamond had been the cause of many stares. "I've never had it since that night. You could've claimed it on the insurance. But Sister Hudson . . . it was a ring. I mean . . . your son—"

"Yes, I understand. Thank you." She cleared her throat daintily. "Anyway, I ask that if you do remember what happened with the ring or the car, if you could find it in your heart to let us know why you were going that fast—"

I wasn't going that fast. I would have never gone that fast.

"—it may help give us some closure."

Georgie reached the clear view of the Sound, and a cool breeze pushed against her, causing her to stop. Her heartbeat hammered. "I'll let you know what I can." The promise was a scary one, but part of Georgie felt obligated to this woman, would *always* feel obligated to this woman. "I'm sorry, Sister Hudson."

Sister Hudson sniffled. "Well, we must forgive."

Georgie's entire body went cold.

"Good-bye, Georgie. We wish the best for you."

"Bye," Georgie whispered, then hung up. She stared at gray nothing.

I'm sorry, she'd said. Meaning she was sorry for their pain, sorry for their loss, sorry for their confusion.

Well, we must forgive.

We must forgive you because we blame you. We must forgive you because that's what we're supposed to do.

The words echoed around her.

"They blame me," Georgie whispered to the blurry space in front of her. She wiped at her tears before they dropped. No way was she going to lose it here because of that woman. Her fists clenched, and her heart hurt like it was too big for the cords lashed around it. A painful thud began above her right eye, and she pressed there. Great. The headache.

She'd liked the possibility that Ian understood, that image of Peter helping Ian see her, that she could maybe let go of the guilt over his death. Over everything. She'd found a measure of peace. It may not have helped things with Jace, but it was something. And in one cold phone call, that peace had cracked like a dropped mirror.

Georgie looked down at her phone and typed a text to her mom.

She called. She wanted to know if I had the ring. I'm fine.

She didn't know how long she stood there between woods and shore, but an eagle cried somewhere, and she blinked. Numbly, she resumed her walk home. She had to pull herself together for Faye and Tru. And work.

Move forward, Georgie. Keep moving.

* * *

Jace hesitated over his phone. He'd been working hard in the kitchen, throwing himself into the food preparation like he hadn't in weeks. It helped him focus, almost forget that Georgie was right there working as hard as he was. Almost. And the kitchen was running with precision.

He'd submitted the recipes to Reuben, and Saturday morning he would prepare each dish again so Reuben and the assistant cooks, Haru, Joanie, and Caleb, could sample and say yea or nay. He hadn't asked for Georgie's help yet, and he knew he should. A lot of the credit went to her. He just couldn't bring himself to ask. He had one day to gather all the ingredients and make a plan.

When she'd hinted that she was just playing around, toying with him, part of him knew it was only a show. He knew she was being defensive. But part of him recoiled. Some of the humiliation and resentment that Brenna had caused had resurfaced, and he struggled to shove it aside. It was a high price to pay, avoiding the things that might bring rejection simply to avoid rejection.

He sat outside on his break, finding himself winded after the busy dinner rush. He drew in a deep breath and blew it out.

He read the text from his sister again.

Know you're busy. Call me when you can. It's about Dad.

The text was from his oldest sister, Cassi. She and Addy still worked at the diner. Cassi acted as assistant manager, and her husband, Dan, often took over the books for Jace's mom when she wasn't feeling up to it.

Jace hit call back and waited.

"Hey, little brother. How's big-city life?"

Jace looked out over the darkening pines toward the darker waters of the Sound. "Quiet. What's up?"

"I'm worried about Dad," she said, cutting the small talk in true Cassi style. "Something's wrong."

"What do you mean? Is he sick or something?" Jace clenched his fist and opened it, then clenched it again. His dad was getting older. He'd always worked himself hard. He was coming up on sixty-seven years and hadn't slowed down at all.

"No, not like that."

Jace relaxed a bit. "Then what is it?"

"He's driving everyone crazy. He scowls; he yells. He snaps at every little thing, and it's having an effect on the whole place. The waiters skirt around him; the kitchen is sullen. It's making the diner a miserable place to work. Dan won't even come in anymore."

Jace chuckled.

"What's so funny?" Cassi asked, clearly annoyed that he wasn't taking her seriously.

"Nothing." He sobered, rubbing the back of his neck. "I just know what that does to a kitchen. I'm sorry. What can I do?"

"You can come back and take over while we send him and mom on a Mexican cruise and maybe try to talk him into semiretirement or even selling the place."

There was a long stretch of silence between them. She'd gone from dancing on the Lido deck to selling Dad's pride and joy in one sentence.

"Why don't you take over, Cass?" he asked.

The silence continued. "The old man was born in a different era, little brother. The business goes to the son."

He picked up on the resentment in her tone. He began to argue but realized she was right. Jace had been groomed for the job from the beginning.

"Jace?"

He cleared his throat. "Yeah?"

"He needs a break. We found them one of those last-minute saver deals on tickets. But he needs to feel the diner is in good hands before he'll agree. He needs to spend time with mom. She's not . . . she's not improving anymore. They need time together. She's asked for time with Dad."

He swallowed hard. His mom seldom asked for anything. "What about you? Dad can't trust you to handle things while he's gone? Even for a couple weeks?"

She didn't answer right away. When she did, the resentment had returned. "I can't even offer to do it right now. School is bogging me down in homework, and we're getting into soccer season. The boys are all over the place, and Dan's got his hands full with several new accounts. As it is, I'm only working part-time, and that's still enough that I'm crashing every night. If you want me snapping at everyone and running myself into the ground—"

"No." He stopped her. "Sorry I asked. What about Kelly?" His next oldest sister, Kelly, lived an hour from his family but knew the diner and the cooking as well as he and Cassi did.

"What? Jace, she's seven months pregnant with two little ones at home, and Rob is still in Afghanistan. Where is your head?"

He closed his eyes, feeling like a jerk. "Sorry, I forgot."

"Nice. Maybe you should come back, if only to reconnect with your family. No wonder Dad gets so frustrated."

Jace's stomach knotted. "I was coming for Addy's graduation in May."

"You can come now." Her tone eased. "Dad may be a grouchy, stubborn man, but you'd be a relief, Jace. He might not show it, but you'd alleviate a lot of the strain he's is carrying around. And Mom would be overjoyed to have you back."

Jace couldn't argue with any of it. And Cassi knew it. "For how long?" he asked.

"Three weeks." Her voice had picked up that certainty of winning. "Maybe more, but that would totally be up to you."

"Yeah, right." He paused. "Things are happening for me here, Cass. Good things."

But suddenly all the "things" happening for Jace seemed hollow. He'd worked hard for this chance at earning Reuben's faith. He'd worked hard to earn his own place on the island. Mrs. Feddler needed him to finish the work on the duplex. And Georgie . . . she'd needed him. At least, that was what he'd believed. The same invisible fist that had squeezed his throat when she'd rejected him returned, and he couldn't breathe.

Cassi answered quietly. "You deserve good things, Jace. I just . . . I could really use your help right now. There might be other options. But you're the best one. For now."

He knew she wasn't just saying that. "Can you give me a couple days to think about it?"

"Of course. Thanks."

"Yup."

They said good-bye, and he hung up. He stared at the shapes the trees made in the dark. The low clouds that had rolled in during the afternoon wafted lazily through the highest treetops, occasionally exposing the black sky above. An owl hooted.

His motorcycle waited for him under the eaves, calling to him for a long ride. But he studied his phone for several minutes, then stood and returned to the kitchen.

Friday morning dawned gray and drizzly. Jace threw on his jacket and patted Kit on the head. "C'mon, boy." Kit followed him out to the car he'd borrowed from John in exchange for the play tickets John was using with Rhea that night. He'd have the car back in plenty of time for the date, but Jace needed room for his groceries, and he was always grateful not to have to run errands in the rain.

"Yoo-hoo, Jace."

Jace turned. "Hey, Mrs. Feddler."

"Not quite the weather we need to paint the house, is it?" she asked, tickling the top of Pepper's head so the leopard-pattern bow wiggled back and forth.

"I'm afraid not. But we're supposed to get a break in the next few days. It's ready to go. I've scraped and primed all I can. And I fixed that lean in the carport too." He walked toward the bracing he'd put in place and pointed out where he'd reset the post as well. She oohed and ahhed.

"The gutters are in pretty bad shape. I'm not gonna lie. You probably want to look at replacing them within a couple of years." Even now as he looked behind him, the rain bore testimony of his words. Water dripped, and in some places ran, from intermittent leaks along the gutter's track. "Living here, it's just not something you can ignore for a season."

"Oh dear, I think you're right. I was hoping that cleaning them out would improve them."

"Me too. There's a spray sealant that might be a temporary fix if you need to wait. Of course, it needs to be completely dry to apply it."

She smiled halfheartedly. "Of course. I'll have to look at the budget." She sighed deeply. But then she opened her eyes wide. "Oh! The budget! I came out to tell you. I've had the flooring people out—I hope you don't mind; you weren't home—and they're scheduled to come a week from today. Carpet, tile, everything. The appliance and heating people are scheduled too, so I'm afraid your apartment will be in a bit of upheaval all at once."

"Appliances?" he asked.

Her eyes twinkled, and she leaned forward, holding Pepper even more closely to her floral polyester bosom. "Isn't it exciting? New microwave, new refrigerator, and new stove—I thought you'd appreciate that, Jace—and a disposal! An entire suite. Oh!" She held Pepper up and nuzzled him in his expressionless face. "Isn't Jace's apartment going to be so pretty? Isn't it, Pepper Popkins? Yes, it is . . ." She continued making kissy sounds with her dog.

Jace winced and scratched his head, suddenly wary of what all this renovation would mean. "Uh, Mrs. Feddler, I have to ask . . ."

"Yes?" She turned her attention from the dog.

"With all of these improvements . . . will you be raising the rent?" He held his breath, and she settled Pepper back onto her hip.

"Have no fear. I will give you ample notice of any changes in the rent. Don't forget, I'm giving you credit for all the splendid work you're doing. You're an excellent tenant, Jace Lowe." She turned to go into the house. "Just keep praying the rain will ease up enough to paint the place. Hate to see all your hard work sit stagnant." The door closed behind her.

Jace looked over the leaky, scraped, not-quite-leaning-anymore structure he called home, very aware that she hadn't answered his question.

Chapter 19

FRIDAY NIGHT HAD FINALLY ROLLED around, and Georgie was on her way home after a physically and emotionally exhausting day. By the last couple hours of work, she was fighting yawns and a desperate desire to curl up in bed with a big quilt and not think about the week she'd had, or the end it had come to.

She'd barely slept the night before, tossing and turning over her conversation with Ian's mother, mixed with flashes of her experience with Jace in the cooler and what she'd said to him after, and long, sad, lingering thoughts over their day at the tulip fields. The best day she'd had in a long time. Those thoughts exploded into fragments as Ian's voice taunted her with the engagement ring. *I know you, Georgie. You're nothing without me, Georgie. It's your fault, Georgie.*

Ian's mom. *Well, we must forgive.*

An idea had begun to take root as the most recent memory of the accident settled into place: the Hudson family were all off their rockers.

Of course, she'd shoved this idea in a box and put it high on the shelf next to a few others because she shouldn't be thinking that of other people. It wasn't right, was it? To just judge others as off-kilter because you were hurting? And who was she to call someone else crazy? Unbalanced?

It sure would make it easier to move past it all though. She shuddered at having to face another night of spinning thoughts and the wet pillowcase that came with them. Maybe her family would provide some distraction.

She entered the Silva home while the moon, or the idea of it beyond the heavy clouds, hovered above the tree line.

"Georgie's home," Faye called out and welcomed her with a hug. Her aunt briefly studied her. "You're tired. I'll get you some Tylenol for that headache." She bustled away before Georgie could ask how she knew she had one.

"Did you bring me something?" Tru asked from the couch.

"No, Tru, not today. Sorry."

"Mm." She patted the seat next to her, and Georgie took it.

Georgie leaned into Tru and rested her head on her shoulder. She smelled like Dove soap and Snickers bars.

"Hard day?" Tru asked.

"Yeah. Hard week."

Tru made an exasperated sound. "You got a little holiday right in the middle of it with your man."

"Tru—"

"Okay, okay . . . your man-*friend*. Holy Hannah, you gotta be so touchy about something so simple."

"It's not simple," Georgie argued.

"Yeah, I know. 'Cause you were hurt. And we're not supposed to talk about it."

Georgie lifted her head, and Faye appeared with a glass of water and the medicine. She thanked Faye and swallowed the pills. "You can talk to me about my injuries. I don't mind."

"I'm not talking about getting *that* kind of hurt," Tru said.

"Tru—" Faye's voice had a tone of warning in it.

Georgie looked between them both. "What kind of hurt do you mean?" Tru looked down at her folded hands, and Faye held the empty glass up to the light as if to inspect it for cracks. "Okay. Fine." Georgie pushed herself up from the couch, wincing as the headache briefly intensified.

"Where are you going?" Faye asked.

"I'm tired. I'm going to my room so you two can talk about my *injuries* all you want." It was an ungrateful, petty thing to say, but she was feeling petty and ungrateful. And awful and worthless.

"Like heck you are."

Georgie turned as Tru stood and placed her hands on her hips. The TV had been turned off, and the room had become significantly silent. Tru pointed to Faye accusingly. "She said we had to be careful with you because that boy who died in the accident was hurting you. He was hurting your heart. He was hurting your spirit. And for some reason, all we can talk about is your headaches and your broken ribs and your outsides. Well, it seems to me that we've talked a lot about those things, and those things have almost healed. You can't even see your scar anymore, barely maybe. And you get your headaches sometimes but not all the time like before." She turned to Faye. "What if we talked about her inside hurts? Her heart and her spirit. Like we talk about in church? She has a spirit in a body, and if that boy hurt her spirit—I don't care if he died, and don't you be mad at me—if he hurt her spirit, then if we talk about those hurts, maybe they'll heal faster too. That's all." She crossed her arms and set her jaw in stubborn insubordination.

Faye's arms flopped at her sides in defeat, and she shook her head. "I'm so sorry, sweetie. We're just doing what we think is best. Guessing, really." She wiped her nose with her apron. "Tru's right in some ways—"

"In a *lot* of ways," Tru corrected her.

Georgie barked a half laugh, half cry.

Faye shook her head. "Tru, Georgie *is* talking about her heart and her spirit. With the therapist." She turned to Georgie. "Right, honey? That's a private place. It's safe."

"And she's talking to Jace too," Tru added.

Georgie's head snapped up. "Why do you say that?"

Tru opened her eyes wide. "Well, who wouldn't? I'd tell that man anything. Excuse me, that man-*friend*."

Faye put her entire hand over her face and sighed.

Georgie looked to the ceiling, shaking her head. Faye moved to say something—most likely apologetic—and Georgie put out her hand. "It's okay," she said, her voice peculiarly strong considering how shaky her emotional state was. "Really, it is. I don't want you tiptoeing around me anymore. Maybe I needed that at first—I *did* need that. But I don't want it from you anymore. Any of you. If I'm supposed to get stronger . . ." She thought of the phone call with Shannon Hudson. "Even when things are still so crappy—sorry, Faye, crummy—I think I'd just as well have you ask, 'Hey, Georgie, how's your spirit doing today?' as have you ask how my headache is." She managed a smile through the wave of emotion pushing through her.

She turned to Tru. "I am talking to the therapist, and it's good. And yes, that boy did hurt me, and he died, and you don't have to be sorry. You didn't know him. I did. And it's a shame he died." She drew in a breath and wiped at an escaped tear. "But I'm learning some good things. And some hard things. But important things, I think, so that maybe one day I'll look back on all this and see . . . why . . ."

Tru nodded in encouragement.

"But it still hurts pretty bad right now, and I don't want something like that to happen ever again. So my spirit is scared."

"But Jace—"

"Jace is good. He's a friend. And maybe he's safe. But I just can't . . ."

"Your spirit is afraid Jace will hurt it," Tru said.

Georgie looked at her aunt, who saw plainly the things presented to her and then made up her mind about them.

Georgie nodded, and Faye sniffled into her apron.

Tru picked up the remote and sat back down. "Okay. I won't say things about Jace anymore. But I'll ask you how your spirit is doing. 'Cause that needs a *lot* of help."

Georgie muffled a laugh, and Faye let out a soft groan. She came to Georgie with her arms spread wide, and Georgie allowed the soft but firm embrace.

"I'm sorry," Faye spoke quietly. "Tru always tells it like it is." She released a soft laugh. "Do you know what our real names are? Our full names?"

Georgie pulled back and shook her head, curious.

Faye still spoke in a hushed voice, but her face was lit with a secret joy. "Our daddy named us *Faith* and *Truth*. Imagine that."

Georgie glanced at Tru, now absorbed in her show. She smiled. "Imagine that."

"You're going to be okay, Georgie-Girl," Faye whispered. "One of these days."

"Is that a promise?" Georgie whispered back.

On Saturday morning Georgie climbed the three steps leading to the kitchen of Peter & Andrew's Fishery. She paused before the door and stared at the handle.

The night before, Jace had sent her a fairly formal text about helping him prepare and present their dishes to Reuben and some others this morning. If they passed, the restaurant could move forward with the new menu and website. Orders would be put in for any ingredients the restaurant didn't already have in stock, like the creamery's crème fraîche.

She hadn't asked Jace what would happen if they didn't approve of a dish. Of course Reuben would like everything. Jace had taken simple ideas and brought them to life. He'd made them new. Exactly what Reuben had asked for.

And Jace had asked her to help. Of course he had. It was a lot of food to prepare, and she'd made everything with him at least once, except for the chocolate cake.

She reached for the handle and pulled the door open.

The kitchen was warm, clean, and welcoming. A far cry from what it had been those first couple of weeks on the job when she'd slunk in and tried to be invisible. She shook her head at the thought. As expediter, she could no more be invisible than the food the waiters picked up from her counter. But she'd definitely learned to help make the flow from kitchen to table smooth. Most times anyway. Especially when she was ultrafocused. Like the last couple of days.

Jace concentrated over chocolate cake sliced into pieces already and separated onto plates.

He glanced in Georgie's direction but remained focused on the tube of crème in his hands. "Hey. Come over here and help me with these, would you?" He straightened up and stretched his back.

As she walked over, she could see he'd been here for a while already, preparing sauces and readying garnishes into neat little stations.

She pulled on an apron, then went to the sink and washed her hands. "I could have come sooner."

He shrugged and motioned for her to take the pastry bag from him. "This'll be your job, so you might as well do the rest of these pieces. It's basically like the whipped cream on the key lime, but the pressure's different because it's thicker. You want three dots here, and one on the top. Not too big. There you go."

She repeated the design on the other pieces of cake, and then he handed her the candied orange slices, which she pressed into place. The smell of the rich chocolate and sweet orange reminded her of when he'd come for Sunday dinner. That felt like a long time ago, and it somehow seemed like a turning point.

But right now, in the kitchen, things were very quiet. Without the hum and pulse of the dinner rush, Georgie found herself searching for things to fill the silence. She swirled a little chocolate sauce on the plates, and Jace carried the tray of them off to the cooler to wait their turn.

"I wonder how Rhea and John's date went," she said.

He emerged from the cooler, his jaw tight. He wiped his hands on a towel and shrugged. "I don't know. I hope they had a good time." He tossed the towel out of the way. "Next we'll get the fresh garlic rub on the pork chops and let them rest. Then you can make the Cioppino salsa while I prep the asparagus."

So much for small talk. "What about the shrimp? Won't we be serving those first?"

He pointed to a neatly laid-out station of seasoned flour, beaten eggs, bread crumbs, and a glass dish of deep-purple blackberry sauce. She had an odd sense of being left out—ridiculous as that was—and stopped herself from saying something of that nature. Was she that needy? She hoped not. There was plenty more to be done. She took a steadying breath, pulled over a small dish of freshly minced garlic, and massaged a teaspoon into each thick pork chop, both sides. She set the chops aside on a plate and washed her hands with salt and soap, like Jace had taught her the first time they'd made the chops. *The salt cuts the garlic so your hands don't smell. Chemistry.* And then he had placed the chops in sizzling oil, and then they'd kissed.

She jumped as Reuben greeted her loudly from the kitchen door.

"Georgie Tate, is that you assisting the chef?"

Of course he knew she would be there, and of course he knew she'd been helping Jace during the week.

He came over, rubbing his hands together in anticipation. "We'll make a sous-chef out of you yet." He peered over her shoulder and nodded, then withdrew his large frame and surveyed the rest of the setup. He took a stool around to the other side of Georgie's expediter counter and sat. "I'm excited. I'm ex-ci-ted."

She covered a laugh, feeling her tension ease just a bit. She retrieved the ingredients for the Cioppino salsa from the cooler as quickly as she could.

Stupid walk-in refrigerator kissing place.

When she returned, Haru and Caleb had joined Reuben, and Joanie was just coming in the back door. After they'd all greeted Jace and her, Georgie went to work on the salsa, following the notes in Jace's book. Her fingers shook a little, and she squeezed her hands together tightly, telling herself she had no reason to be nervous. It was only Reuben, the executive chef, and the fry and sauce cooks, who knew how to do all of this better than she did. Carefully she pulled out a delicate saffron thread and crumbled it between her thumb and forefinger, watching the aromatic flakes fall to the waiting ingredients below like a blessing. Her hands didn't shake as much after that. Which was good, considering she was picking up the large chef's knife.

As she finished with the Cioppino, Jace clapped his hands together and addressed the gathering. He'd dropped some folders on the counter next to him. "Okay. Welcome. This morning we're offering you several dishes for the new menu. We were given the task of capturing the freshness of spring and the celebration of the Tulip Festival, and I believe we've done that. I must give credit to Georgie," he gestured toward Georgie, "who planted a lot of ideas, resulting in the dishes you'll be trying today." He paused, and the small group clapped, smiling in her direction. She could feel the heat creeping up her neck.

Jace picked up the folders and passed them out. "Here you'll find the names and small-batch recipes of each dish, along with a brief menu description and the cost breakdown of each."

Reuben nodded over his open folder, but Georgie couldn't tell if he was impressed or just wanted to get on with it. When had Jace found time to do all this?

"To start," Jace said, "we'll make the black pepper shrimp with lime and blackberry sauce." He made a little bow, and Georgie wondered if she should bow too. She gave a little nod and joined Jace at the shrimp assembly station.

"Go ahead, Georgie. You know what to do." He nodded at her to begin while he tested the temperature of the oil, set out appetizer plates, and spooned blackberry sauce into condiment cups.

She really thought the roles should be reversed, but she did as he asked, dusting the shrimp in flour, dipping them in the lemon-egg mixture, then coating them in the Panko crumbs specked with black pepper and black sesame seeds. They looked good so far, and she began to anticipate the others' reactions when they bit into the spicy-sweet crunch. After she had all the shrimp coated, Jace lowered the fryer basket into the oil and set the timer.

Reuben asked questions about Jace's plans for acquiring the blackberries and seemed amused and pleased when Jace simply listed the areas on the island where public blackberry picking was not only allowed but encouraged. "Of course, we'll have to look into codes about picking our own. And this year we'll have to wait until midsummer to pick fresh, but in the meantime, you can find a seller from California. It won't take many berries to make a larger batch of sauce. If we processed it ourselves, the jars would keep in the pantry for several months."

Reuben nodded, thoughtful, and the timer on the fryer beeped. Jace lifted the basket, let it drain for a few seconds, and then placed two shrimp on each plate. He motioned to some curls of stripped green onion. Georgie grabbed a few and placed them at artistic angles between the shrimp. Together they set the plates of food in front of the others and stepped back.

Georgie watched for their reactions, but Jace moved to the large gas range, turning up the heat under the heavy pan he would use to sear the pork chops. Reuben and the other staff commented among themselves, and although Georgie thought the happy-sounding groans were a good sign, Jace remained all business.

"Georgie, let's get the chops going."

They had to time everything so there wasn't too long a gap between dishes but also so timers weren't all going off simultaneously.

He grabbed the prepped bowl of asparagus and a mesh grill basket. "That oil's hot enough. Carefully set each chop in the pan, about one inch apart, and let that garlic brown up nice and caramelized. I'll get this asparagus on the grill."

Georgie nodded, again wondering that she should be handling the chops instead of the asparagus. She knew, though, what the chops were supposed to look like before they added the honey glaze. She also knew how they *weren't* supposed to look, remembering the charcoal lumps Jace had covered with water and a lid. Just before he'd kissed her again.

"Georgie."

Jace had said her name softly, but she still jumped. "What?"

"Turn the chops gently. Keep that garlic crust intact."

She took the spatula, still feeling a little shaky, and carefully turned the chops, only losing a little bit of crust here and there. The sizzle and smell rose up and filled her nostrils, and, again, she couldn't wait to share this dish with the people behind her. Jace slowly poured the honey glaze over each chop and then, with a heavy oven mitt, placed the whole pan into a hot oven and set another timer.

He looked at her and nodded. "Good job."

"Thanks."

"Turn the asparagus."

"Yes, sir."

He gave her a second glance. He shook his head, but she saw the twitch just at the corner of his mouth.

Just before they served the pork chops, they started the halibut, and Jace repeated similar instructions, having Georgie handle the main ingredients and taking the side dishes or garnishes for himself. He gently talked her through each one, but she found she'd watched him so closely when they'd made them together in the past week that his directions were only reminders of what she'd already learned, and now she was the one turning, testing, and judging. By the time the thermometers in the halibut steaks read 145 degrees, the pork chop dishes had been practically licked clean. Georgie carefully transferred the creamy-white fish with dark grill stripes to plates, and Jace spooned the Cioppino Salsa on top. Georgie placed lime wedges and sprigs of cilantro on each and couldn't help smiling as their audience gasped. The gleaming grilled halibut with its colorful salsa and limes made a vibrant presentation.

They were almost done, and Georgie felt herself start to relax.

"Only the cake left, right?" she asked Jace quietly as the others discussed the fish.

"Not quite. I kind of . . . came up with a surprise dish, just in case something was rejected."

Georgie's eyes widened. "Oh?" She tried to loosen the knot of emotion in her stomach. Of course he could come up with another dish without her help. Of course he'd stayed up late or gotten up early or done whatever he did and experimented without her. After all, she'd pushed him away. And that was better. That was good because they were getting too close. They'd gotten too close. And he was the sous-chef. And this had been his assignment.

"Are you okay?" Jace asked as he readied his oven mitts.

"Yeah, I'm fine. So far so good, right?" He nodded as she went to the sink. She grabbed a tissue and wiped her brow and neck, then washed her hands again and got a hold of herself.

She heard Jace address the staff. "I know you only asked for four dishes, but as I said earlier, Georgie has a way of talking and the ideas come. I'm not even sure she would recognize that she had anything to do with this next dish, so I kept it a surprise, but it was her idea too. I guess you could call it a backup plan, but I hope you can wait a little longer for dessert and enjoy it either way."

At his praise, remorse for her earlier selfish thoughts engulfed her. She wanted to crawl under a rock. But curiosity won out over her chagrin, and

Georgie made her way back to where Jace bent over the open oven door to pull out a large iron pan.

"Ohhhh." The sound reverberated through the room from every mouth but Jace's. He placed the pan on a sideboard made especially for the large hot dishes just out of the oven.

"This," Jace said, "is whole roasted crab with tarragon gremolata and butter."

Two round, shiny, red crabs steamed fragrantly on the black iron pan, along with a handful of curled, roasted lemon slices. Using a broad, flat spatula, Jace scooped the crabs onto a platter lined with lettuce leaves and set it in the middle of the gathering.

Reuben took the liberty of lifting the tops off the crab shells, which apparently were just there for presentation. Underneath lay buttery roasted crab meat, tender and flaky, laced with bits of garlic and green gremolata. Jace pushed a dish of fresh gremolata toward them. "In case you want more," he said.

They each picked up their crab forks, and with a satisfied expression on his face, Jace turned away and began wiping up the counter and gathering the remains of the morning's efforts.

"Georgie, you have to taste this," Caleb said, his mouth full. "Jace, you've outdone yourself."

She held up her finger to Caleb, signaling she'd be there in a minute, and followed Jace to the sink where he was stacking pots and mixing bowls.

"What's gremolata?" she asked.

"Basically lemon, garlic, and parsley."

She looked over at the steaming crabs. "You stuffed the crabs with parsley."

He nodded, concentrating on stacking a couple of plates among the pots. "And tarragon. Just a little so it doesn't overpower everything. I tried the rhubarb too, but—" He made a face.

She remembered her tongue-in-cheek suggestion of stuffing the crab with all the spring ingredients from his list. "But I was only playing around."

He gave a short, sad laugh. "Yeah. I know."

Georgie swallowed, catching his meaning. If her face hadn't been red before, it was now.

He dried his hands on a towel. "I'm sorry I didn't have time to show you how to make it, but I'll leave you instructions." He placed a gentle hand on her arm, looked her in the eye for just a moment, then turned away, leaving her at the sink.

She frowned as his words sank in. "You'll leave me instructions? Are you going somewhere?"

He'd already moved back to the counter where everyone was eating. She wasn't sure if he hadn't heard her or if he was putting her off until they were done with the presentation. But she was suddenly filled with a sense of foreboding. That was what he'd been teaching her all morning. How to make the dishes on her own. Why would he do that?

She turned and watched his back, seeing the easy lift of his shoulders as he spread his arms out in victory. "Who's ready for dessert?"

The small group cheered.

Georgie clapped her hands with the others, but with all of the confusing choices she'd been making lately, she didn't feel very victorious.

The voting was unanimous. All the dishes would go on the menu, and the roasted crab would be a regular Friday-night special. And although Georgie was relieved and proud of being part of something so momentous, she couldn't shake the feeling that Jace wasn't as thrilled as he should have been.

Everyone helped clean up, and Georgie made light conversation with Haru, Joanie, and Caleb as Jace met with Reuben in his office, probably to discuss the finer details of whatever it took to change a menu. She had a couple hours left until her shift started, and she was wondering if she should just go home right before Reuben called her into his office.

She avoided eye contact as she passed Jace, who was leaving the room.

"Georgie," Jace said. She turned, lifting her face to his. He paused just a second and briefly smiled. That simple act shouldn't have sent ripples through her middle, but it did.

"What?" she asked.

"I just wanted to say thanks. You did good today."

"Thanks."

He drew in a breath and let it out, looking back toward the office. "And . . . I think a person should consider opportunities to try something that makes them feel like it could be a part of them." He shook his head like he hadn't said that as well as he'd wanted to. "I mean, something that makes them feel valued and respected but also passionate. Because *they've* chosen it. Not because somebody else chose for them."

She frowned. "Okay . . ." It was a good thought, but she wasn't sure what he was getting at.

He gave up and motioned to Reuben's open door.

Inside, Reuben was putting Jace's folder down, his brow furrowed. But he looked up, and his face brightened. "Hey, Georgie. Have a seat."

She left Jace and took the chair across from Reuben at his small desk. She glanced at the certificates of his titles framed on the wall. Jace's was up there too.

"How do you like working here, Georgie?"

"Is this a trick question?" She swallowed. Had he found out somehow about her and Jace in the cooler? Is that what he and Jace had talked about in here before she'd come in? What had Jace said to her? Something about choices and respect? Oh, please, no. Nothing happened, and it wouldn't be happening again. "Am I in trouble?"

He smiled. "No. And after this morning, I don't see how you could ask that. But tell me what you think. How do you like working here?" He watched her expectantly.

She let out a sigh of relief. "I like working here." Simple as that. "I'm grateful for this job. It's on the island. The staff is nice. It can be stressful, but it's . . ." She searched for the words. She remembered how she felt that morning, anticipating the joy the food would bring to the assembled crew. "There's a buzz that happens, like everybody's kind of excited to get good food out to people."

Reuben nodded. "It's a bit contagious. Is that all?"

She swallowed. "Well, I'm learning a lot."

His brow raised a tick in interest. "Would you like to learn more?"

She couldn't guess what he was after. She went with the safe answer. "Sure?"

He reached behind him and turned back with a professional-looking pamphlet about the size of a dinner plate. He set it in front of her. "What would you think about attending Le Cordon Bleu Culinary School down near Seattle?"

Her eyes grew wide. "What?" Her heart began to race, and she wasn't sure why. Her gaze dropped to the pamphlet, though, and she had to keep her fingers from reaching for it.

"After watching you today, I consulted with Jace, as my sous-chef, about whether or not he thought you had any interest in pursuing the culinary arts. He was careful about his answer."

She lifted her gaze from the pamphlet, eyes still wide. "What did he say?"

Reuben leaned forward on his elbows and pressed his large fingertips together. "He said he thought you had a lot of potential, that you seemed a natural at putting things together once you were taught." He grinned. "That you had a knack for finding inspiration."

She rolled her eyes, but her leg bounced with her body's excess energy. She didn't even know she was coming up with ideas when she was coming up with ideas. But she eyed the pamphlet again.

"He said he thought you enjoyed the process of cooking. Of becoming a 'mad scientist' in the kitchen."

A small smile played at the corners of her mouth, but she looked away. "I didn't even know what saffron was until Thursday."

"He also said he didn't want you to feel pressured in any way because he figured you'd be good at anything you wanted to do. It's just an idea. A good one."

People should do what makes them feel like it could be a part of them. Passionate. Because they've chosen it. Not because somebody else chose for them.

Jace's words came back a little clearer now.

Reuben pushed the pamphlet toward her. "I enjoy a long history with this particular school. Jace didn't know your educational background, but he did say you're recovering from a pretty bad car accident and that you might've had to quit school before you were ready. Now, mind you, he was strictly discussing this in answer to my questions about a scholarship, and he informed me that I should ask you myself. Forgive me, but is that true?"

Scholarship? She wasn't sure whether to be angry at Jace or not. "Yes," she answered. "It's true that you should ask me yourself."

He looked at the desk and laughed. But he sobered and studied her face. "Was it bad?" he asked quietly.

She paused, then nodded, trying not to mist up.

"I'm sorry. I would never have guessed." He tapped the top of the pamphlet. "Will you think about it? They sent me Jace and Haru and a few others before them. You could move up to assistant cook . . . sous-chef . . ." He raised his eyebrow at her.

She couldn't help the smile that came. Or the eye roll. Carefully she reached for the pamphlet, placing two fingers on top of it and drawing it toward her. "I'll think about it."

"That's all I'm asking." He grinned and rapped his knuckles on the desk.

Georgie emerged from the office and scanned the kitchen.

"If you're looking for Jace, he just left," Caleb said. He pointed at the back door.

She walked that way, opened the door, and stepped out into the sunshine. She squinted and held the culinary-school pamphlet up to shade her eyes, watching the tail-end of Jace's motorcycle disappear over the rise and down the hill, its roar fading on the air.

She'd have to catch him at work later. To thank him. Or wring his neck.

But he wasn't at work.

Tyler must have been keeping a lookout for her because as soon as Georgie emerged from her car, he hurried over and joined her as she walked to the back door of the restaurant.

"Hey, I was waiting for you," he said with a smile. "Did you get my text?"

"Uh—" She checked her phone, and sure enough, there was a text from Tyler.

Want to see that movie tonight? Megan wants to see the late show. Thought it would be fun if we doubled. Escape.

He'd included a link to the movie trailer.

"Well?" he asked.

"I didn't see this." She tried to land on an answer for him. Honestly, her first instinct was to say she was busy, but that would be a lie. And then she considered that maybe a movie out with Tyler would be good for her. On the other hand—

"You don't have to look so pained over it."

She looked up at him. "I'm not pained."

He shook his head. "You don't look excited."

"I was wondering if I'd be good company, that's all. I'm beat, and I haven't even started my shift. I worked all morning helping Jace with the new menu—"

"Ah." He folded his arms and kicked the ground. "Jace."

"Yes, Jace. And I don't even want to be here right now. I want to be home under a quilt. Maybe reading a book. I like books." Yes. Maybe she'd escape into a book, where other people made decisions and faced consequences and chased dreams.

He cocked his head at her. "Well, maybe we could watch a movie at our house instead of going to one—"

She touched her forehead. "Maybe you should just ask someone else." The words, impatient and flat, were out of her mouth before she could stop them.

"Oh." He frowned and looked away but nodded. "Oh, yeah."

"Tyler, I didn't mean to say it that way."

"But you did mean to say it." He strode ahead of her, climbing the steps and opening the door for her.

Great, now two guys were avoiding eye contact with her, though one was still getting the door for her.

She paused at the top of the steps. "Whether I did or didn't, I'm obviously not good company. For anybody. I'm sorry."

He nodded, looking down. She went through the doorway, feeling like a slug.

"If Jace had asked you out tonight, would you have said yes?" he asked quickly.

She stopped, catching a few interested glances from overhearing staff, and looked at him. She lowered her voice. "I'm not playing this game, Tyler. I'm not dating anyone. I don't want to date anyone. I *shouldn't* be dating anyone." She turned away, taking off her jacket. "I'm broken," she mumbled. "Remember?"

He didn't answer.

Later, after she'd observed Tyler's extra diligence at the sink, she overheard Haru ask Reuben where Jace was.

"He asked for the next few days off. I figure he's earned it."

"Enjoying this great weather."

"Maybe. He's painting his rental for his landlady."

Haru chuckled. "He finally takes a break and paints a house." He shook his head.

That feeling of foreboding Georgie had experienced earlier returned as she added cups of dressing to the plates in front of her.

"Georgie."

"Hm?" She looked up to see Mai watching her.

"This is a baked potato. It gets the sour cream. The vinaigrette goes here." She switched the cups.

"Sorry."

"No prob." She flashed a smile and walked away with the plates.

Georgie read off the new order. "Sirloin with crab legs, rare; captain's plate; salmon plank and . . . no, sorry, salmon *grill*; and the prime rib, medium." She looked it over again with a quick glance. "Sorry, that's *two* captain's plates."

Reuben looked pointedly in her direction.

"Sorry," she mumbled. "Distracted."

"I can't imagine why." He winked. "Try to focus."

A few seconds later, Georgie stopped herself from slicing a baked potato like a loaf of bread.

It was going to be a long night.

Chapter 20

JACE HADN'T SEEN OR SPOKEN to Georgie since Saturday. Two days. He wished he could say he hadn't thought of her since then either. He'd done everything he could to keep busy. He'd been perched at the top of the ladder ever since the early sunshine had dried the house siding. He'd rented a paint sprayer for the job and was grateful for that decision. Even with all the taping and covering the windows he'd had to do, each coat was going on fast and smooth. A couple hours after he'd started, he'd also made the decision that his own home would be brick. As it was, though, he was finally on the last coat.

"Hey, dog."

At the sound of Georgie's voice, Jace's stomach made that annoying drop. He twisted on the rung of his ladder and found the source of the greeting.

She crouched, rubbing behind Kit's ears. Kit's tongue wagged shamelessly. Georgie stood and folded her arms, squinting up at him. She spoke over the sound of the sprayer pump. "Are you snorkeling?"

He pulled off his protective eye gear and let it hang from his neck.

"My mistake," she said. "Raccoons don't snorkel."

He rested his arms on the top rung. He was painting the house white, and he was pretty sure that with his goggles shielding his eyes from paint and his old dark ball cap sitting backward on his head, she wasn't far off in her observation. "No, but we're excellent swimmers. What are you doing here?" he asked. He searched for her car. "Did you walk?"

She nodded. "It's not far, you know? I, uh, didn't get to talk to you before you left on Saturday."

"I wasn't sure you'd want to," he said.

"That's fair."

"I had to take advantage of the sun and start painting."

She nodded. "Is that why you're taking all these days off?"

"Mostly." He didn't say any more, and she just blinked up at him, her hand shading her eyes from the sun.

He let out a deep sigh and climbed down the ladder to the ground, switching off the pump for the sprayer. He grabbed a damp towel and mopped himself up.

"I didn't mean for you to stop painting."

"Yes, you did."

She didn't argue with him. "It looks good," she surveyed his side of the duplex. She looked at him sideways. "You weren't at church yesterday."

"Yeah, I slept in and went to the singles branch."

She nodded. Kit brushed up against her, his tail zigzagging wildly. She patted his head. "What's his name again?"

"Kitsap."

"Nice to meet you, Kitsap. Good dog."

With the extra attention, Kit's whole body began to wag with joy as he nudged her playfully.

"Whoa—" Georgie lost her balance, laughing.

"Kit, get over here." Kit walked over to Jace and plopped down on the ground, panting as if he'd run a mile.

"His eyes are cool," she said.

Jace nodded, looking at his dog. A silence settled between them as he tried to decide if he should just come out and ask her what she'd thought of Reuben's idea or if he was allowed to ask her questions anymore or . . .

"Well," she said, "I don't mean to keep you. I just wanted to tell you that I think the culinary school idea is . . . interesting. And I'm seriously considering it."

He tempered the thrill her words gave him by crossing his arms and looking at his feet. "I'm glad."

"I mean, I might as well learn how to properly use a chef's knife."

He peeked up at her.

She half shrugged. "And all the other things."

He smiled. "Well, whatever the reason, I think it's great that you're considering it. And just so you know, it was Reuben's idea, not mine."

"What difference does that make?" she asked.

He paused. "Because I wouldn't want you to think that I was . . . trying to be controlling . . . or whatever."

"I wouldn't think that."

Jace lifted his gaze in question.

She shook her head. "Not with what you've told me about your dad."

His gaze dropped to the ground again. On the one hand, she'd told him she would trust him not to be controlling. On the other hand, she'd struck a nerve.

He took a deep breath and looked around the yard. "I need a drink and something to eat. Do you want to come inside? Or would you rather wait out here?"

She looked toward the house. "I'll follow you."

Jace offered to make her a sandwich, but she turned him down. She did take a can of Vernors, and they both sat at the small table. He rubbed the back of his neck, staring at his sandwich while she looked around at his front room and kitchen. Kit had followed them inside and had plopped down at Jace's feet under the table.

"My landlady's putting in new carpet and appliances and stuff," Jace said as if trying to make an excuse for the apartment's bleak appearance.

"Oh, nice," she said. She eyed his duffel bags in the corner, and her smile faded. "Are you going somewhere? A hotel while they do the carpet?" She reached up and rubbed the scar over her eye. "You said on Saturday in the kitchen that you'd leave me instructions so I'd know what to do. And you had me do most of the cooking. That's why Reuben offered me the scholarship. He saw me doing the hard stuff." Finally she looked at him, and her blue eyes locked on his. "Are you going somewhere?"

Slowly he nodded.

"Where?"

He pushed his plate around a bit on the table. He should have told her sooner. He'd put it off. "Home."

"To visit?"

"Sort of." He pushed his plate to the side and leaned forward, folding his hands in front of him. "My sister asked me to come take over the diner while my mom and dad work out some things. My dad won't leave it for anyone else, and they need to get away for a while."

She swallowed. "Oh."

He shrugged. "I'm leaving Wednesday morning. So I've got to get this house painted for Mrs. Feddler."

"But what about your job? What about the new menu?"

"The new menu is a sure thing. I don't need to be there for it. And Reuben is being pretty understanding."

"So Reuben knows? Why didn't he tell me?"

"Why would he?"

She opened her mouth to answer, but nothing came out. She quickly shut it.

"Look," Jace said. "On Saturday I was still thinking about everything. And when I told him I had to go, he was supportive. He'll hold my position for a while, so I can figure out what I want to do."

"What do you mean 'what you want to do?' Are you thinking . . . are you thinking you might not come back?"

She held his gaze, and he couldn't look away. "I'm not sure."

She blinked and then suddenly stood, rubbing her forehead. "So you've known for, like, two days and haven't told me? Were you just going to leave?" Her voice rose. "What about the people at work? Were you just going to have Reuben announce it? They love you there, Jace. They love you." She was breathing heavier now because she was ticked.

"I'm coming into work tomorrow after the house is finished and I'm all packed."

She threw her hand out toward the dog. "And what about Kit?"

"He's coming with me. I've got a crate for the back of the bike."

"You're taking your *motorcycle*? To Nevada? Are you crazy?"

He folded his arms. "Really?"

She folded her arms too, and they locked eyes. After half a minute, she turned away, her jaw tight, her leg bouncing. "What about the tulip fields?"

"I'm sorry about that. I may be back in time."

"Or not," she said.

He didn't say anything. It was true. She could see the tulips with her family. He'd made his decision.

"I would have to come back for the rest of my things."

Her shoulders dropped. "But you like it here." Her voice had softened. She took a couple steps toward the front window. "You like it here. And your recipes are on the menu. And you told me . . . you told me not to let other people choose what you do . . ."

"I'm helping my family when they need me. That's different."

She turned back to him. "But you might not come back." Her chest rose and lowered, and she pressed her lips together. "Not to stay."

He got up and walked to her as she turned away. He paused just behind her, close enough to draw his arms around her if he could.

"Are you going to stay here forever, Georgie?" he asked.

Her answer was muffled as she stared out the window. "I don't know."

"Can I tell you a secret?"

She shrugged.

"I'm as confused as you are."

She turned, looking down. She sniffled and nodded.

They stood there for a minute, the space between them crammed with words they weren't saying. Finally he had an idea. He reached past her to his keys on a hook. "Know what I usually do when I'm confused?" He held the keys up and gave them a shake.

She took a small breath. "Ride?"

He nodded.

"But your paint," she said.

"It can wait."

As they circled the island on his bike, they didn't speak. Georgie had put her arms around his middle and was holding on tight, resting against his back. Every so often he felt her give a little shudder and wondered if she was crying. But she made no signal for him to stop, and she didn't crumple against him. He just kept driving, feeling the sun, flying beneath the shadows of the trees, wondering how he could consider leaving this place he'd learned to think of as home and yet knowing all too well that what he wanted and what he got were seldom the same thing. Life kept hitting him on the head with that one. Sometimes he had to grow up and take whatever it was and make it work anyway.

He wondered about Georgie, so close to him on the bike. And yet the distance between them seemed unbreachable—like he was on the peak of one mountain and she was on another, and they could speak to each other across the divide, but until she healed and he figured out what his future held, all they could do was talk. And even that wasn't safe.

They completed the circuit. Jace drove her to her aunts' house and kept the motor running but dropped the kickstand. He'd been thinking of what he could say to her to say good-bye.

Go to the culinary school and maybe find more of yourself.

Never let anybody make you change.

I hope you heal, inside and out.

Call me.

They dismounted the bike and removed their helmets. She stowed hers in the seat.

He took both her hands, and she let him. He studied them, frowning, fighting with himself, wishing he was already gone and wishing he never had to leave. He brought her hands up and kissed the backs of her fingers. The scent of her seemed to decide it. He lowered her hands and pulled her to him, wrapping her up and kissing her mouth harder than he'd intended, though he hadn't intended anything. She wrapped her hands around his shoulders and kissed him back, and he eased a little, pulling her closer. The kiss softened into something he would have a hard time forgetting over the next several weeks.

Jace let go and stepped back, his heart stuck in his throat. He turned, mounted the bike, crammed on his helmet, and growled away, leaving her standing in her driveway, the Sound water shimmering behind. He didn't go straight back to the duplex. Sometimes he needed to ride just a little more.

* * *

Trying to breathe, Georgie watched after the motorcycle until she could no longer hear it, long after she could no longer see it. Long after her sight had blurred.

Blinking, she turned and walked around the side of the house, letting her feet take her where they would. She walked down the boat ramp and out on the rocks and stopped just short of the water's lapping edge. She didn't know how much time had gone by when some level of consciousness stirred enough to hear her own hushed voice repeating, "I'm so broken. I'm so broken. I'm so broken. I'm so—"

She drew in a deep, sharp breath to silence herself. She blinked at the water, drawing her arms close around her in the cooler air, feeling numb. *I'm so broken.*

"Yes, I know," she answered, her chest aching.

She looked down at her feet and didn't think, because thinking would lead to feeling, and feeling hurt too much. Feeling caused a lot of problems. Feeling stunk.

She lifted her gaze, watching the sliding, rhythmic movement of the bay water. She let it soothe her, pull her into a waking trance with its soft sounds, the birds crying in the distance, the lapping noise at her feet.

Suddenly she gasped as something in the distant waves spouted. "A whale," she whispered. She clasped her hands over her mouth and watched as a dark body rose slowly out of the water and spouted again. It repeated, rolling a large fin up in the air, and then a second whale spouted stronger and higher than the first.

"Two of them." She wished she knew what kind of whales they were. She automatically turned to search for Jace's house and wondered if he could see them from the hill or if she should call him—and then her stomach dropped, and she turned back to the whales.

Feeling hurts too much.

She watched for several more minutes until the whales swam beyond her view.

He hadn't wanted her to think that going to culinary school was his idea. And he'd wanted her to make the decision without him. Did she want to go because Jace was a chef? Did she want to go to please him? Because that wouldn't matter now. She would go to the school and come back, and he wouldn't be here.

She remembered how she'd felt about the brochure when she'd finally pulled it toward her in Reuben's office, and she realized she hadn't been thinking of Jace at that moment. She'd been thinking of what she could do. What she could be. Could she be?

"In a minute, there is time," she whispered to the sea. "For decisions and revisions . . ."

She heard soft footsteps on the rocks behind her and turned her head. Faye came, holding one of the big quilts they kept in baskets around the house in case anyone felt chilled. She opened it up and set it around Georgie's shoulders.

Georgie shuddered as warmth began to seep in. Instead of comforting, though, the warmth seemed to melt all the frozen emotion inside her, and all that feeling started spilling out in tears she couldn't seem to stop.

Faye put her arms around her. "My dear, what is the matter?"

Georgie sucked in a deep breath. "He's going back to Neva—da."

"Oh no," Faye said.

Georgie nodded, sucking in another breath. "And I'm going to the Cor— *hic*—don—*hic*—Bleu . . ." She dissolved into Faye's arms, who continued to pat her gently on the back, most likely bewildered.

Chapter 21

On the day Jace left for Nevada, Deacon came.

Georgie couldn't have been more grateful for the distraction. They spent hours talking on the back-porch swing, sharing the food Faye kept bringing out to them. Georgie told him everything. Well, almost everything. She left the details of the kissing to herself. After sharing the things Tru had said the other night, she told Deacon about remembering Ian and the engagement ring, and Shannon Hudson's call, and then Reuben's offer to go to culinary school.

She smiled at Deacon's supportive enthusiasm for that last part. "I'm scared to death." She had no trouble admitting it.

"That's good," Deacon said, grinning.

"Why is that good?"

"Because when you graduate and you're all chopping onions with one hand behind your back and drizzling beef medallions with béarnaise sauce, you'll totally appreciate it. You'll be your own conquering hero."

"Do you drizzle beef medallions with béarnaise sauce?"

"It sounds right. I watch Food Network, so I'm sort of an expert."

"I'll be sure to call you for the really hard homework."

He leaned back on the swing, lacing his fingers behind his head. "Anytime."

"Maybe I should start watching Food Network again," she murmured. "I watched it in the hospital."

"Wouldn't be a bad idea."

Georgie considered getting Tru hooked on a new TV channel, one that didn't involve a man riding up on a horse and thirty women throwing themselves at his feet.

Deacon watched the sparkling bay. And Georgie thought again that he really couldn't have picked a better day to show up. "This is an incredible view," he said.

She nodded. "I saw whales the other day."

"Awesome."

"It was. I wish I'd been out there closer. I didn't even have binoculars."

"This coming from the girl who was afraid for a little seagull on the waves?"

She'd shared that story with him, hoping it didn't sound crazy, asking him if he thought it was. His answer was no. "A boat is bigger than a seagull," she said.

"And whales are bigger than boats." His eyes lit up as he teased her.

"Not all of them."

He smiled. "True."

They grew quiet again.

He spoke. "You know, Mom and Dad are pretty worried about you." He glanced sideways at her and leaned forward, his elbows on his knees. "They feel like you . . . cut them out of your life."

A knot of defense tightened itself in her chest. "I had to leave. I had to get away and figure out how to . . . start over."

He nodded. "Still, they're worried."

"I know. I know. But . . . I had to leave, Deacon. There was no moving forward at home. It was all back. They'd say, 'It's okay. It's going to be okay. You'll be yourself again. It will come back. Everything is going to be okay.'" Georgie frowned at the white, puffy clouds floating in the sky. The dogwood tree, the azaleas, the lilacs were all blooming now. "But it wasn't okay," she said. "No matter how hard I tried. And them telling me that over and over was making me feel like I was doing something wrong. Like I was failing."

"They love you."

"I know that. They're doing what they should be doing: worrying, caring, reassuring. Saying, 'Everything will be okay.' But I don't need reassuring. I don't need to be told that everything being okay means everything goes back to the way it was. Because it won't. After the—abuse—from Ian—and after the accident and all the physical therapy and psychological mumbo jumbo and putting things in boxes and filling in the gaps of my scrambled memory and carrying blame—yes, blame—for so long, nothing will be the same. And don't tell me faith and forgiveness will wipe it all away. There's something missing in that way of thinking. Nothing will ever be the same, and part of me mourns that every night . . . but most of me grabs on to it and defends it to the death because I never, never want anything like that to happen again."

Her fists clenched on her lap. "Forgiveness is one thing, but trust? *We must forgive*, yes," she quoted Shannon Hudson. "But nowhere does it say I have to trust those who hurt me. Love your enemies, but don't invite them into your house." She gulped a breath. "Especially when you can't seem to tell between your enemy . . . and your friend."

Deacon reached and pulled her in so her head rested on his shoulder.

"I lost myself with Ian," she said, her voice shaking with emotion. "He pushed me down until there was barely a trace of me."

"I'm sorry, Georgie," Deacon said quietly.

"You knew. You knew he wasn't any good. And I didn't want to see it."

Deacon made a dismissive sound.

After a deep, cleansing breath, she felt stronger. She sat up and looked at him. "I'm trying to figure out this new me. And I know this new me will completely consider your judgment."

He gave her a small smile. "No pressure."

She sat back and kicked the swing into motion. "None whatsoever."

They settled into silence.

"Georgie?"

"Yeah?"

"What is it you blame yourself for?"

She didn't answer right away. She was tired of this question and of looking at it from every angle. Tired of being told it wasn't her fault. "Sometimes it's about the accident. But sometimes it's anger at me, and humiliation; what was wrong with me that I let myself get into a relationship like that?"

He remained quiet for a minute as the swing rocked back and forth. She waited for the lecture.

"Call me crazy," he began, "but when I think about it, my question is, what was wrong with Ian? That he needed to break someone as trusting and alive as you? All you did was trust someone with your heart."

She turned to him, taking in his words. He'd just explained the anger she'd been directing at Ian, the anger she'd felt so much guilt over. And the clarification felt good. It felt . . . liberating.

"Ian would have done this to anybody," Deacon said. "He would have run anybody right into the ground. He probably already had. What makes you so special is . . . you called him on it." He turned to her.

After a moment, she wiped away a tear. "Thanks, Deacon. You're the best."

"You have to say that because I'm your brother."

She laughed.

The swing continued to sway, and Deacon turned to look at her again. "You know, I don't think Mom or Dad would have a problem with you not wanting to go through any of that again. As a matter of fact, I'm sure they'd be grateful if you never got close to anyone like the Hudsons ever again. And if that means accepting changes in you, even the way you need to protect yourself, I'm pretty sure they'd be all for getting to know you again."

Georgie sighed. "I just . . . have to figure out who I am first."

"*Igne natura renovator integra.*"

She frowned. "I don't know that one."

He leaned toward her. "Through fire, nature is reborn whole. You're like a phoenix."

She studied him and decided she liked it. "You're such a nerd."

He sat back, unruffled. "You could start including Mom and Dad in that process. I could talk to them. Tell them what you just told me."

"I don't—"

"You just said you'd completely consider my judgment from now on."

She covered her face with her hand, then let it drop. "I did say that, didn't I?"

"Mm-hmm."

"Okay, I'll consider it. But, Deacon?"

"Yes?"

"Don't tell them about Jace. It wasn't that . . . significant."

He arched a brow at her, and she felt her face warm up.

"Please?" she asked.

He nodded. "Sure. But I hope this new self of yours realizes that some things can't be hidden with words. *Veritas vo liberabit.*"

She knew that one: "The truth will set you free." She grabbed his pathetic attempt at growing a goatee while on vacation and said, "*Barba non facit philosophum.*"

"Ouch," he said.

She smiled.

"A beard does not make one a philosopher."

But she glanced at him, then out over the water, and thought about what he'd said. Maybe the beard did help a little bit. "Thanks for coming when I needed you."

He looked at her. "That's what families do."

* * *

Jace had ridden twenty hours. Twenty hours from Camano to Boulder City, Nevada. Twenty hours of nothing to do but ride and stop for gas, food, and to let Kit use a patch of ground every so often. And think. He'd done a lot of thinking.

He turned the corner into his parents' neighborhood—his neighborhood growing up—and the undeniable feeling of coming home set in. He'd been able to hold the feeling off as he'd bypassed town and the diner to get to the old house in the dark. But here he was, where he'd ridden his bicycle and swum at his friends' houses and snuck his first kiss. He'd come home for Christmas during his freshman year of college and then had missed it during his mission. Then he'd come home again with his plans set in his mind and heart to leave it altogether.

He pulled up in front of the low stucco house lit by the front porch light. A big old catalpa tree shaded a square patch of lawn to almost black. The rest of the yard was neatly paved in crushed sandstone, including the driveway back to the side of the house. His mom's favorite spiky greens still lined the path to the front door, where an old half barrel overflowed with red geraniums. An occasional bug swooped past the porch light.

He cut the engine on his bike and lowered the kickstand. Chirping crickets filled the quiet left behind. "Just a minute, Kit. Let me tell them we're here." Not telling his parents he was bringing a dog with him might have been a mistake, but he didn't feel like walking an emotional tightrope with his dad over it. "We work long hours," his dad had always said. "We can't give a dog what it needs." Well, the dog was here. They'd make it work.

He walked to the front door, his boots crunching on the gravel, mixing with the sound of the crickets. He passed the mailbox and noticed the *E* had fallen off, so it read LOW. He reached down and picked the dirty letter off the ground, brushed it off, and stuck it back on, hoping it stayed in place until he could replace it.

When he reached the front door, he paused. He never knew if he should knock or just go on in. It was late, but the entry light was on inside, and they were expecting him.

He knocked and waited. He peeked through the side window as his mom turned the corner into the small entry hall. He stood back, and she opened the door.

"Jace." Her grin couldn't be any wider.

"Hey, Mom." He bent down to hug her and noticed the cane she was using. "How are you?"

"I'm wonderful."

He smiled and breathed in her smell, then pulled her to him, pressing his face to her wavy dark hair, barely streaked with gray. He released her, and she motioned him to come farther into the house.

"How was your trip?" she asked.

"Not too bad." He followed her past the galley kitchen and into the main living room. A drinking glass lay on the floor, its contents darkening the carpet.

"I was so excited when I heard the motorcycle that I knocked over my water," she said, chuckling at herself. "Good thing it was nearly empty." She moved to head to the laundry room.

"I've got it, Mom. You sit." He took three strides to the laundry room, really a large closet with bifold doors, and grabbed a towel from a freshly folded pile on the dryer. He worked at the spill while she sank carefully back into her chair with a sigh.

"Where's Dad?" he asked.

"Oh, he stayed at the diner, tying up some things. You know how he is. Hates to leave anything undone."

Jace nodded, then threw the towel in a basket on the washer. It occurred to him that it might be better to bring up the dog now instead of later.

"Have a seat, Jace." She motioned to the sofa next to her easy chair.

"Actually," he rubbed the back of his neck. "I have a surprise, sort of. I brought my dog. He's on the back of the bike—"

"Kit? Oh, bring him in. Heavens, you don't need to leave him on the bike. That couldn't be very comfortable for such a long drive. Does he jump? I think I'll do just fine as long as he doesn't jump."

Jace grinned. "He doesn't jump. He can sleep with me or outside if you want him outside."

"We'll figure it out; just go get him. He might be scared."

Jace went out front and unpacked his dog and duffel. "Be good. No jumping."

Kit wagged his tail.

Inside, Kit didn't jump but greeted Jace's mom in his usual manner, tongue hanging out, tail zigzagging. He heard his mom as he took his duffel down the hall to one of the guest rooms—his old room.

"There now, aren't you a sweetheart? Are you a good little dog? Yes, you are."

The basics of his room were the same: full-size bed, stocky chest of drawers painted brown, one of those box-kit desks and a folding chair. The quilt was different, and instead of his motocross posters and a framed print of a vintage Harley Davidson Fatboy, his mom had hung up desert sunset pictures and one of Hoover Dam, which was just a few miles down the road. Over the bed's headboard, his mom had hung a picture of the Las Vegas Temple. Jace's dad might not ever join the Church, but he had never gotten in the way of his mom's adherence to the religion. Jace was pretty thankful for that.

Jace heard the front door open and his mom talking to Kit, he assumed. "Oh, Grandpa's home." Jace smiled at the thought of what his dad would think of being referred to as a dog's grandpa. Still, he hurried back out to the front room. He wasn't going to leave his mom to face the consequences.

"What the—"

"Hey, Dad," Jace said brightly as he entered the room. "We made it."

"So I see," Liev said, eyeing Kit. "He goes outside."

Jace nodded. "Outside, then. Nice to see you too." Jace could already feel the tension in his body.

"Oh, Liev," his mom said, "he's harmless. You're a sweet dog, aren't you?" Jace watched Kit lick his mom's chin and almost laughed.

"Well," his dad said, still frowning at the dog. "How long you here for?"

"As long as I'm needed."

His dad grunted and moved to the kitchen. His gait was slower than normal.

"Liev," his mom called after him. "Jace has come all this way to help you. The dog is fine. Aren't you, Kit?"

Kit seemed to smile, wagging his tail harder at the sound of his name.

His mom hushed her voice. "Go in there and talk to him. He really is glad you're here."

"That is a happy little world you live in up there, isn't it?" He gently tapped the top of her head, then leaned down and kissed her forehead.

She beamed up at him and shooed him toward the kitchen.

Jace entered the kitchen and folded his arms as his dad poured himself a glass of water and took a couple of Advil. Jace hadn't been afraid of his father for a few years now, but the man was still intimidating. Though Liev had always seemed like an imposing figure, with his broad shoulders and heavy brow, Jace had reached him in height and was more muscular.

Jace noted how his dad's skin seemed to sag off him a little, like he'd lost weight. And yet, what this man said and did affected Jace like no other human being on the planet. Most times, though, Jace could guess what he would say or how he would react, and that helped. It had helped when he'd left for Seattle. Some.

Liev took a seat at the little square dining table. "You came here to help me."

"Cassi said you were so impatient in the kitchen, they're taking bets on who you'll fire first."

"Paco. Tomorrow, if he's lucky."

Jace paused, then caught a glint in the old man's eye. "Paco's made it this long, huh?"

His dad grunted and sipped his water.

Jace pulled a chair out at the table and sat. "Cassi also said you and Mom need time together."

His dad set his drink down, and he seemed to steady his hands on the tabletop.

"And," Jace continued, "that you wouldn't leave the restaurant in anybody's hands but mine."

His dad raised his gaze to Jace's. Jace held his ground, feeling like if he moved he'd be forfeiting some kind of victory. *Freedom*, a voice inside him cried. *Freeeedom. Hold on to any you can keep.*

Finally his dad cleared his throat and flipped his hands over, palms up. He looked at them. "Your mother . . . wants time with me. And while I'm trying to figure out why the—"

Jace cleared his throat.

"—why she would want that, I'm realizing time with her wouldn't be such a bad thing . . ."

Jace lifted his brow.

His dad continued. "Kelly doesn't want the diner. She's got enough to handle with Rob deployed. Cassi's working her tail off for this business degree. I think she might actually consider taking it over if Dan gave the nod, but . . ." He shook his head. "She's got enough to handle."

Jace wondered how much truth was in that. "Cassi seems to be under the impression that you don't want her to take over because she's a woman." He braced himself for the fallout from that statement. It was a good thing Cassi wasn't here.

His dad pursed his lips. "She's the assistant manager. And she's a good one. She's been wanting to train Addy to help with management, but Addy's got her sights set on college and teaching—"

"That's a good thing, Dad."

"I know. Don't think I don't know it. But I've got a small staff with only a few who've been with me longer than a year, and I tell you what." He stuck his finger on the tabletop and stabbed at it to emphasize his words. "Leaving that diner for a seven-day cruise with your mom is one thing, but that's not the time—" He pressed his lips in a thin line and tried again. "That's not the time your mother is talking about. That's a blip compared to what she wants—what she's asking for after all of these years of asking for nothing. *Nothing.*" His dad swallowed and lowered his voice, though it was no less powerful. "And God will roast me alive if I don't give her what she wants now. She's in earnest, Jace. That look about her—"

His dad then did something Jace had never seen his dad do before. He quickly wiped a tear on his sleeve.

Liev swallowed. "She's in *earnest.* And I've got to pay attention to that. Because who knows how long we've got left." He took a moment to collect himself, then he nodded his head. "I know the timing is lousy. Cassi says you're moving up at that restaurant."

Jace made a small shrug.

"I just don't have anyone else I can lean on right now. And I'd be honored . . . I'd be humbled . . . if you would take on the diner. While I get my feet back under me and see what time has in store for us. While your mom and I try to figure out a plan for the future."

Jace had no words. The freedom he'd been determined to hold tight to in negotiating with his dad, the conversations and practiced declarations he'd run through his head during his trip down, now hung as limp as a wet flag. "Sure, Dad. I'll help."

* * *

A few days later, after enduring several hours of the retraining his dad considered necessary and two days of working side by side with the old man, Jace worked the grill at the diner solo, shouting back orders as Cassi read them off.

"Two BLATs, a bowl o' red, a crying Johnny, and give 'em shoes."

"Two BLTs with avocado, bowl of chili, quarter pounder extra onions to go."

She gave him a smile, and he appreciated it. He wiped his brow on his sleeve and turned back to flipping burgers and grilled-cheese sandwiches. His parents were home spending time together, preparing for their cruise. He guessed that meant his dad was asking a lot of questions about why they were being forced to do this and his mom was fussing over how much clean underwear to pack. Jace threw bacon on the grill with a sizzle, lowered a basket of home fries into the vat of boiling oil, and set the timer.

He pictured Georgie learning the bread ovens.

The diner's fries were like the restaurant's bread, and they went through a lot of them.

"Fish and chips," his sister called.

Nobody had come up with anything clever to call fish and chips. He smiled, then shook his head at himself. Somebody shouting "fish and chips" in his direction shouldn't fill him with a longing for home.

He paused. *Home.*

He frowned and set two full plates on the counter, and Paco, who still remained on staff, took them off to be delivered before Jace even rang the bell.

Cassi appeared at his side. "House is full today."

He nodded and lowered the fish into the fryer.

"I wonder why that is?" she asked pointedly.

"Why?" he lifted the fries out to let them drain.

"Oh, I don't know . . . Could be word's gotten out that a certain someone is back in town and working at the Boulder Buzz Diner."

"What? You're nuts."

"Go check the shake machine."

He shook his head. That had been a signal between all of them as teens if somebody worth checking out came into the diner. He wiped his hands, and she took over the grill.

"Addy should be coming in at the hour. Hasn't been this steady since The Coffee Cup had their day on Food Network."

The Coffee Cup was another diner across town. A TV show featuring diner food had run a spot on their pork chili verde omelet, and a lot of out-of-towners visiting Hoover Dam now saw The Coffee Cup as the only diner in Boulder City. It was a great place, but they weren't open for dinner. The Buzz was open for dinner.

Jace rounded the corner and glanced furtively at the crowded restaurant as he checked the milkshake machine for any adjustments.

"Yo, Jace!"

"Jace, there's my man."

"Welcome back, Jacey!"

Jace smiled, raised his chin, and gave a wave, not having a clue who these people were and not really wanting to investigate further. He refilled the cup dispensers and ducked back into the kitchen.

"Oh, no, you have to go out there and work the crowd." Cassi finished up an order and rang the bell. "Order up!" she yelled past him. Then back to him, she said, "We've got table campers out there, and for whatever reason, they're going to hang out until they talk to you, and that leaves my waitresses unable to turn tables. Now get out there, say hi to your admirers, and get your butt back in here."

"What? That's insane. What's the big deal?"

"You think I know? Just get out there and turn in circles a couple times, and then they'll leave when they're supposed to leave." She opened a couple of to-go bags.

"Ugh, I never had to do this at the restaurant." He turned to go back out.

"The sacrifices we make . . ." she mumbled after him.

As it turned out, a couple of acquaintances from high school and his old baseball coach were in the crowd. He visited briefly and checked on a few tables to see if patrons were enjoying their meals. He remembered bussing tables way back when and even garnering a few tips of his own.

When he thought he'd done a sufficient job of it, he turned to head back to the kitchen, passing a booth full of girls.

"Jace!" they called in chorus, then giggled.

He stopped. "Yes?" he asked, wondering if he knew any of them.

"We're Addy's friends," one of the girls said, flipping her hair.

He smiled. High school girls. Seniors. All grinning at him expectantly, leaning forward on their elbows; one was up on her knees.

"Can I do something for you, ladies? Have you ordered yet?"

A few of them giggled. "We're still deciding," their spokesperson said.

"I know what I want," one of them mumbled, and the table broke out in laughter.

Jace looked at his shoes and swallowed. He took a little breath and looked the girls over again, a smile still plastered on his face. "Would you like to hear my favorites?"

They all widened their eyes and nodded, and he tried to keep from laughing. He wondered what Georgie would say if she was witnessing this spectacle. Something about puppetry or gagging. He opened one of their menus, pointed out some favorites, tagged on some extras, then motioned for a waitress and turned the mob over to her.

He got back to the kitchen and found Addy tying on an apron. "Hey," he said, "I just met a table full of your friends."

Addy's brow furrowed, and she peeked out over the counter. "Ugh. They told you they were my friends? They don't even talk to me."

"Well, they talked to me," Jace said with a smirk.

Cassi laughed.

Addy made a face. "Oh, please." She got to work assembling baskets. "Just because you're cute."

"You think I'm cute?" he said, a big grin on his face. "Aww."

"That's not what I meant."

Jace took Cassi's place at the grill. "Crowd worked, my liege. Campers moving along."

She looked at him. "Thanks, Jace."

He shook his head. "The only thanks I ask is a bonus in my paycheck."

"Ha."

He winked at his older sister. Addy passed with a pile of plastic baskets lined with red-checked paper. He nodded his head toward her. "She thinks I'm cute."

Cassi laughed again as Addy made a disgusted sound and hid her smile.

Later, as he collapsed into bed at his parents' house, as he'd done every night since he'd arrived, he fought the urge to call Georgie and tell her about work. And just as he'd done every night, he stared at his phone, wondering why in the world she would want to hear it.

Chapter 22

GEORGIE LET DEACON BRING HER to work. He'd wanted to take a look at the restaurant and meet her coworkers, and he stayed for a few minutes, comfortably chatting with Reuben and Caleb. He'd always been outgoing in a reserved kind of way. People liked that, Georgie thought. Mai had immediately introduced herself and, if Georgie had observed correctly, had thrown in some flirt. The girl was subtle, but the way Deacon responded, suddenly becoming a fraction more smooth, his voice reaching a bit deeper, told Georgie her guess was spot on.

Huh. Didn't see that coming.

Speaking of flirting, Tyler had suddenly become chummy with a new waitress, an islander Georgie had spotted in the halls at church, probably from another ward. Maybe they would go to BYU together in the fall, get married, and have cute Tyler babies and—wow, she sounded bitter.

Georgie shook her head and walked outside for her break, joining Rhea on the picnic table. She sighed. "Hey there, Rhea."

"Hey." She smiled as she folded the paper bag that had held her dinner. "How's it going?"

"Good. And you? I never got to ask you about your date with John."

Rhea's smile widened. "It was fabulous. It was funny. It was really, really great."

"How was it funny?" Georgie asked.

Rhea's enjoyment of the date was apparent. She shook her head, considering. "Just . . ." She glanced at the back door before she went on. "John was kind of tripping all over himself making sure I was having a good time. It was pretty cute, you know? When we went walking later, in the rain, he was disappointed with the overcast skies because he wanted to show me the stars."

"The stars?"

"Yeah. He's kind of an amateur astronomer. Who knew, right? He's got a really nice telescope at his place. He can see planets and everything."

"Please tell me he didn't use that as some kind of pick-up line. 'Hey, baby, want to come up and see my telescope?'"

Rhea laughed, shaking her head. "We didn't go back to his place. But we drove out to the hills in north Seattle and parked—"

"Uh, TMI."

"No. Ha. We parked *the car*, and even though we couldn't see them, he showed me where all the constellations would be if we could. And he told me the stories about them, and it was so great, him just knowing all this stuff and wanting to show me." She looked down, her smile still on her face. "It was pretty romantic. I like it when a guy doesn't, you know, just take, take, take."

"Yeah," Georgie said, considering that. "So you had a good time."

She nodded.

"Are you going out again?"

She lifted her head. "Next clear night."

Georgie did smile, then. "I hope it comes soon."

"Me too." Rhea sighed. "Have you heard from Jace?"

Georgie's smile faded a little, and her heart skidded. But she didn't show that. "No. He did send me a text letting me know he got to Nevada safe." A very brief text. It had said, *Nevada*.

"Oh, that's good. It's too bad about him leaving. And just before the Tulip Festival. I hope his family stuff gets cleared up soon."

"Yeah."

Reuben had told the staff that Jace was helping out indefinitely with a family emergency.

"That was pretty smooth, by the way, getting my favorite flower like that. It's scary how much of a deal maker that was." Rhea laughed.

"I'm glad you liked it."

"So what's your favorite flower? If somebody needed to ask you out?"

Georgie shook her head. She looked out over the treetops and a little to the north. She hoped her smile still looked genuine. "Tulips," she said.

Rhea nudged her. "You came to the right place, then, huh?"

Georgie nudged her back but kept her answer to herself.

Rhea stood up from the table and brushed off her pants. "Well, my break's over. Enjoy the rest of yours." She gave Georgie one more grin, then hurried back to the kitchen.

Georgie picked up the foam cup she'd brought out and pulled the plastic spoon out of her pocket. She scooped up a spoonful of lobster bisque and tasted it, letting the creamy warmth slide down her throat as she swallowed. Haru had made the bisque today. It was good.

But not steal-the-last-bite good.

The following day, Sunday, rolled in gray and drizzly. With her mornings off, Georgie and Deacon and whomever else had been available throughout the week had gone to the zoo, the waterfront and Pike Place Market, and the Ballard Locks. She'd even cancelled her therapy session to have more time with her brother before he left. It was just good to be with people who had her complete trust. The world outside was flowering, greening up, and healing.

But this Sunday was perfect for staying in. After church they played Scrabble and Boggle, and Georgie found she could focus on letters and finding words. Not as fast as she'd like, but they came. She accused Deacon of going slower than he normally would to give her more time, and he simply beat her soundly the next three games. But her head didn't ache, and the words came.

The two of them decided to make dessert for their Sunday company, an older couple renting a house on the island for the month of the Tulip Festival. They made lopsided, drippy éclairs, but the process thrilled her, and they tasted much better than they looked. Naturally, she missed Jace. Anything with cooking made her miss him.

After a rainy walk, their company left, and Georgie, Deacon, and Tru settled in to watch the Food Network together. Deacon and Tru got into a discussion over past episodes of *The Bachelor*. Apparently Deacon was a fan.

That night Georgie pulled out her phone.

She typed, *Hey, remember me?*

Then erased it.

Then she typed, *It's raining here.*

Her thumb hovered over send.

It must have hovered too close because all of a sudden it sent. She gasped, feeling her face flush with heat. Her heart pounded as she tried to decide whether to follow it up with a quick apology or to act like it never happened. *What? Oh, I have no idea how that even got there. Why would I even text that? To you?*

She blew out a breath of frustration at herself. It's not like she'd written, *When it rains and everything is quiet, all I can hear is your voice and all I can feel is your kiss.* That would have been something to get all worked up about. But *It's raining here?* A weather report? *Calm down.* It wasn't like he would read between the lines.

Or would he?

Her stomach turned. He was smart. Insightful. And—her phone buzzed. She closed her eyes, grimacing, then forced one eye open.

Shocker.

A smile formed on her lips, and she let out a sigh of relief. He'd read it as a weather report after all. She grinned, feeling inexplicably giddy, holding in her hands a harmless text from Jace. A simple, friendly exchange.

Her grin slowly faded. A simple, friendly exchange unattached to any passionate, aching kiss he'd given her just before he'd left. Maybe he *had* read more into her message and was covering it. The humiliation slowly returned.

Then it occurred to her that this internal conflict might finally mark her inevitable descent into madness. She turned over, planted her face in her pillow, and yelled at the universe.

The following evening at work, Georgie sought out Tyler and pulled him off the sprayer and out the door.

"Georgie, what are you doing? I'll get fired."

"No, you won't; are you kidding me?" The door closed, and she folded her arms. "I just wanted to say something, and I wanted to say it now."

He looked at her like he was resigned to listen, so she moved ahead. "I'm sorry for being a jerk the other day. There's no excuse. You've been nothing but nice to me, and you didn't deserve me snapping at you like that. I hated how I felt afterward. Thank you for being my friend. Almost since I've been here, you've been a friend."

She waited for his response.

He toed the ground with his feet. He nodded. "Thanks."

She smiled, feeling lighter.

"You know," he said, still looking at the ground, "Megan told me that maybe I was coming on too strong. Which ticked me off because she kept setting things up." The corner of his mouth lifted. He finally shrugged. "Live and learn, right?"

Georgie nodded. "Are you seeing that cute waitress?"

He shrugged again, but his smile returned. "I'm trying to be more cool about it. You know, play the field."

"Sure." She tried in vain to imagine Tyler *playing the field*, but growing up was hard. Sometimes you just had to wing it. Or say you were winging it. "Just don't try too hard not to . . . try too hard."

He gave her a puzzled look, and she returned it.

"I'm pretty sure I meant something profound in there," she said.

That night she read through the Cordon Bleu pamphlet again. Deacon and Dar had held an animated conversation over what she could do with it. Dar even wondered aloud if there was some branch of restaurant law she could go into, should she be interested down the road. She'd laughed, but he was determined to look into it. Just to give her options.

Options felt great.

Later she held her phone close, thinking.

Is your dad glad to have you back? Send.

She was concerned. It was a friendly concerned question.

Seems like it.

So that was good. Things might not be too awful for him, then. Her phone buzzed again.

How are things at the restaurant?

How are things? Different. Quiet. Boring. Yech. All of those sounded like she was pining for him. And if he missed the restaurant, she wanted to sound positive.

The new dishes are popular. ☺

Smiley face? Really, Georgie?

What's it like working at the diner? she asked.

I'd forgotten how fun it is. Crazy but fun.

Her stomach knotted, and she rolled onto her side. *I'm glad.*

When a few minutes went by without any more from him, she put her phone away and pulled the quilt up over her head, squeezing her eyes shut.

She'd asked for that one.

* * *

Jace frowned. He slid his hand over his face and typed out one more text. *I wish I could show you.*

Then he erased it.

A few days later, Jace's parents were checked in and standing next to the airport security lines, ready to begin their seven-day Mexican Riviera cruise. At least his mom was ready.

"Remember to turn off those fryers every night. And lock both doors. I should have put up bars on the windows. I've been meaning to do that."

"Dad, we're not in Vegas."

"We're close. And don't let the mail pile up. Cassi knows what to do with the bills."

"Cassi knows everything. She should be running the place, Dad."

His dad paused whatever he was about to say, giving him a long look. He shook his head. "And make sure that dog of yours gets a walk. He likes that. If dogs get bored, they get into trouble. Digging holes in the lawn . . ."

Dad and Kit had bonded during their week at home together, but Dad wouldn't admit that.

"I'll make sure he gets a walk."

"Two, if you can manage. And don't forget the inspector's coming on Thursday." He placed his hand over his eyes and groaned. "What in Moses's wee little basket made me think I could go away for a week?"

"Liev?" his mother finally spoke, her voice sweet but firm.

He looked down at her.

"I'm the reason you think you can go. And I'm going to keep sowing that idea into your thick head until you are thrilled to be gone. Do you understand me?"

Jace smiled.

The lines in his dad's face softened. He patted his wife's hand, then took it in his own.

"The diner's in good hands, Dad," Jace said, meaning every word.

His dad glanced up at him, gave him a short nod, then turned, heading toward the security line.

His mom looked back at Jace. "Good-bye!" She blew him a kiss and lifted her shoulders, her face lit with anticipation.

He waved. "Have fun! Both of you!"

She winked at him, and then they were gone.

Step one, done.

Back at the diner, during the after-lunch lull, Jace met with his brother-in-law Dan, an accountant and their sometimes bookkeeper.

"Thanks for meeting with me. I just want a rundown of the numbers."

Dan sat across from Jace in the corner booth where Jace could keep an eye on things. Cassi and Addy were both at school, but a few staff members tended to chores and prepped for the next rush. Dan opened the ledgers and pulled up spreadsheets on his laptop.

"No problem. Cass and I have updated everything, so it's all on the computer, but Penny kept such accurate paperwork, we continue that as well. The original numbers go in the ledger as purchases are made, bills paid, etcetera, then we enter it all into the computer once a week."

Dan led him through purchases, site maintenance and mortgage, payroll, and everything else, saving overhead for last.

Jace squinted at the profit numbers. "Is that right?"

Dan shrugged. "Liev only has a couple more payments before he owns this building outright. They've been smart. Careful. Your dad can be a pain in the rear, but he knows his menu, he knows his vendors, and he knows the market. I've watched him forecast a day's sales simply by looking at the weather." He chuckled, rubbing his eyes. "I've seen Cass do the same thing."

"So . . . the diner is a sound investment."

"By somebody who knows what they're doing, yes. And by someone who's willing to commit to it. You've got prime real estate here, just down the street from a national landmark. And diners themselves are considered an American institution. Sentimental national pride in the form of, you know, little museums of food."

Jace smiled. "So all we'd need to find is a buyer."

Dan raised his brow. "Your dad won't agree to sell."

Jace narrowed his gaze. "Why is Cassi taking business classes?"

"Because she never finished her degree, and we thought it would be a useful thing for her to have."

"Have you seen her run this place?" Jace asked.

He could tell by the expression on Dan's face that he had. Sort of a resigned pride.

Jace leaned forward. "Why aren't you guys investing in this place? Why aren't you taking it over? Cassi already commits the time, and when she finishes school, it won't be such a stress on the family. On her."

"It's a stressful career anyway," Dan said.

"True. But I merely mentioned switching up the menu the other day, and she nearly tanned my hide. And have you heard her talk about this place? *My* waitresses. *My* marquis. *My* tables. Dan, have you asked her what she wants from this place? Have you asked her what she wants *for* this place?"

Dan sighed and let his gaze wander toward the kitchen. "I'm afraid to."

"Yeah," Jace said. "And I'm afraid to ask what she really thinks of Dad making it clear that he'd only leave it if *I* came back. That had to sting."

Dan rubbed his temples.

Jace continued. "I've got a job. With a pretty good future if I stick it out. I've got a place and a . . . Well . . . there are people."

"People?"

"Yeah. A someone. Maybe."

Dan's eyes focused on Jace. "Have you told the family this?"

Jace shook his head. "I came here to help. I'm committed to staying as long as I'm needed. But, yeah, I left stuff."

Dan turned the pages in the ledger from front to back. Finally he said, "We'd have to hire and train a new assistant manager."

"I'll help if I can," Jace said.

Slowly Dan let his forehead drop to the open ledger with a soft thud. "I have to buy my wife a restaurant," he told the pages.

Jace leaned across and rested his hand on Dan's shoulder. "You will be the husband of all husbands."

"I can use that, right?" he asked, still in the pages.

"Any chance you get."

Step two, done.

Jace put the key in the lock of his parents' house and turned it. He opened the door, flipped on the light, managed to shut the door, let Kit out back, and then stumbled to the sofa.

He groaned as he sat, his bag of dinner still clutched in his hand.

They'd scrubbed and mopped and bleached and shined and sorted and organized and stocked until the diner gleamed. Inspection was tomorrow, and Cassi had lorded over the staff like a madwoman. Jace was starving, but as he lay on the couch, he felt his eyes closing, and they were somehow winning out over his stomach.

I'll eat in a minute, he thought as he drifted off.

With the rattle of the front door knob, Jace opened one eye. He groped for his phone and peeked at the time. He'd slept for two hours.

The door burst open, and he sat upright, his now-cold bag of food sliding to the floor.

Cassi slammed the door behind her. Her expression was . . . not friendly. "Jace Christopher Lowe, what in Moses's wee little basket do you think you're doing talking to my husband behind my back about buying the diner?"

He scrunched his eyes tight and rubbed his face, trying to pull himself out of the depths of sleep he'd just been torn from. He blinked at his sister.

She stood with her hands on her hips, her eyes bulging.

"I just ran the idea by him."

"*Ran* the idea by him? Are you kidding me? He's ready to apply for a *loan*. Why couldn't you talk to me? Am I not smart enough or distinguished enough to be included in this decision? Do you think I am so completely incapable that I wouldn't be able to understand all your *man* vocabulary?" She puffed out her chest and dropped her voice. "Me Jace. Me sous-chef. You buy diner, everything A-okay."

"That doesn't sound anything like me."

She made an angry sound and stomped her foot.

"Do you not want the diner?" he asked.

"Of course I want the diner, but *that's not the point!*"

"So you do want the diner."

She paused, breathing hard. She nodded. "Yes."

He watched her calm down. Then her face crumpled, and he stood.

"Whoa, whoa, what's the matter?" he asked as she started to cry.

She took a breath. "You're just like Dad," she said, wiping her eyes.

He threw his hands up in the air and turned to the wall. "I don't *believe* this." He faced her again. Very calmly he placed his hands on her shoulders. "Cassi. I know what you can do. I know you have the brains and the drive and the ability to run that diner with one hand tied behind your back. I also know that Dad—being *Dad* and not *me*, Jace—is blind to that, and I am trying to do what I can to plant seeds, little, tiny, not-so-subtle seeds so that when the time comes for *you*—not *me*, Jace—to approach Dad about taking over the diner, he will be *A-okay* with that option."

She blinked at him. "But why couldn't you talk to both of us? Me and Dan together?"

Jace folded his arms. "Because Dad said something about Dan not supporting you in the idea, and I wanted to get the truth about that without you there influencing him. The last thing I'd want to do is drive a wedge between you and your husband."

"So . . . Dan was okay with the idea?"

Jace lifted his brow. "Hasn't he already told you he is?"

"Well, yeah, but . . . I thought you somehow—"

"Cassi, Dan admitted pretty quickly that he's known what you've wanted for a long time. He just happened to agree with me that the time was now."

"Oh."

"Oh? Are we A-okay?"

Slowly she smiled.

Jace began to sing. "You're gonna get the di-ner. You're gonna get the di-ner . . ."

She shook her head. "I have to talk to Dad still."

"Piece of cake. He'll be relaxed and tan and holding hands with Mom. You couldn't ask for better timing."

She smiled at him. Probably the best smile he'd ever gotten from her. "Thanks, Jace."

"I'm just a little cog in the great big Lowe machine."

"Well, thanks still," she said. "Oh, and one more thing." She slugged him hard on the arm.

"Ow! What was that for?" he asked, rubbing his arm.

"That's for not telling me you had a girl back in Washington. Holy crap, Jace. I told you you needed to think about being back here forever. And you came? What did you tell her? I feel like a first-class jerk. Don't keep stuff like that from family."

He was beginning to see a lot of Liev in his sister.

"First of all, I didn't say anything because it's complicated and I wasn't sure where things stood. And second of all, I spent most of the ride down here thinking of how to get back to her, so that kind of helped me with the first thing."

"Is it serious?"

"No." He moved his arm around, scowling. "But I'd like to find out if it could be. Someday."

Cassi went home happy, and Jace ate his warmed-up dinner. He rubbed his thumb over the surface of his phone. Georgie had texted him a few times since he'd been gone. Little things. He hadn't known how much response to give her. But tonight he felt like it was his turn.

Adam and Eve in a sombrero smokin' with whistleberries on the side.

It wasn't T. S. Eliot.

His phone beeped.

Do I even want to know what that is?

He smiled.

Juevos rancheros burrito, extra chilis, refried beans on the side.

He waited. She'd either laugh or roll her eyes.

Ha. Whistleberries.

She'd laughed.

He paused. This was where it got weird. The way he'd left and the time she needed to get beyond the demons she was fighting made it hard to say all the things that would be so easy to talk to her about. And he'd really rather just talk. A voice call. With voices.

But he'd left her, after that kiss out of nowhere, without a word.

He set his phone down.

You couldn't just pick up and talk about anything after doing something like that to somebody. After doing that to somebody like Georgie.

Chapter 23

DEACON CHECKED OUT HIS GOATEE in the hall mirror. "Do you think Mai would want to hang out with us tonight after work?"

Georgie gawked. "What?"

"You know, hang out. Get some ice cream. Play games. Watch a movie."

Georgie pulled on her jacket. "You are not dating my friends."

"Who said dating? I said 'hang out.' And I meant *friend*. Singular."

"And I said *no*. Singular." She waggled the car keys at him, and he followed her outside.

Deacon had been coming with her to work and hanging out in the kitchen for a few minutes before her shift started, then he'd leave and come back later to help close. This usually included some chatting with Tyler or Mai, and it interested Georgie to watch her brother field Mai's questions about his beliefs, his lifestyle, or his life plans.

"You know, you really can't tell me I can't invite Mai over," he said. "I'm older than you."

Georgie turned, and he stopped short. "I know."

"Then what's the deal? I'm only here a few more days. It's not like I'm pursuing a relationship. I just like her. I think she's interesting, and she asks good questions."

"And she's a Trekkie."

"Well, sh-yeah." He nodded.

She smiled. "I don't know. Maybe I'm just selfish. Like you said, just a few more days."

He grinned. "Who can blame you there?"

She rolled her eyes and got in the car.

He got in on the opposite side. "Just be warned, Mai might be coming over."

"Fine."

She started up the car. "Put your seat belt on."

"You are such a boss."

The day before, Reuben had left for the Northwest Food Service Expo in Oregon, leaving Haru and Caleb in charge of keeping the kitchens running and Mai and John in charge of waitstaff. With Jace gone too, the kitchen had a decidedly different feel to it. Not exactly a sense of freedom, because everyone in the kitchen remained intent on keeping up with the waitstaff and the orders, but more like a sense that the grown-ups were gone, so let's play grown-up. As soon as they got to work, Mai played by bringing Deacon a piece of day-old cake in a paper bag. Which, of course, led to more talking.

Talking, flirting, whatever they wanted to call it.

After a second warning from Georgie, Deacon finally excused himself with a promise to return.

After he left, Mai scrunched up her nose. "Your brother's pretty cute."

Georgie sighed. "He gets it from me."

Mai smiled and shook her head. "You've come a long way, baby."

"What do you mean by that?" Georgie asked.

Mai shrugged, then looked reluctant to say more.

"Oh, no. You flirt with my brother, you answer my questions."

Mai laughed out loud. "Fine. I was just noticing how much you've changed since you started working here. You're not afraid anymore."

Georgie dropped her gaze, knowing that wasn't true but liking how it sounded anyway. "Just go wait your tables."

Mai ignored her and lowered her voice. "And you definitely weren't so afraid of Jace anymore. I'm sorry he had to go. Maybe he'll be back. Reuben said it wasn't definite."

Georgie swallowed. "It's not definite."

Mai smiled, then left to organize the front.

But it feels so definite.

The evening flew by. Work was steady, and they kept up with it pretty well. When Deacon showed up, Georgie had to check the clock on the wall before she believed it was closing time. He immediately started helping Tyler by unloading the big industrial dishwasher. Those who were closing made themselves useful. The music was on, and the kitchen took on a celebratory-like atmosphere.

"Georgie, can you take over cleaning this grill?" Haru asked. "I've got to go help out front with the money."

"Oh, sure."

"Thanks."

Georgie poured the ice water on the griddle's surface and pushed it back and forth with the spatula, remembering the first time she'd done this with Jace standing next to her, carefully showing her what to do. And she realized how right Mai was. She had come a long way.

John and Rhea came in from the front with loads of dishes, talking lightheartedly. They reached the sink, and Deacon tried to send them away. Rhea laughed, but she and John prevailed in adding to the pile.

Tyler shook his head. "Nice try, Deak." He patted Deacon on the back with his wet hand and went back to spraying dishes.

Georgie smiled as she resumed cleaning the grill. *Deak? He is Deak now? Is that a name?*

The back door opened suddenly, and Anders stepped in, pulling the hood of his sweatshirt back. He held the hand of a little girl in jeans and a messy T-shirt. All sounds in the kitchen stopped. Somebody even reached for the music and turned it off.

Anders's brow was furrowed, but he didn't look angry. He looked tired. Maybe nervous. "Where's Reuben?" he asked quietly.

Georgie looked at John.

"He's not here," John said.

Anders turned his head away, grimacing in disappointment. Georgie hoped he would decide to leave, remembering the last time he was here. He didn't look high, but she wasn't an expert. She looked at the little girl, who had been watching her. The girl quickly withdrew behind Anders's leg.

"Do you know when he'll be back?" he asked.

John and Rhea exchanged glances. "He's gone through Sunday."

"What about Jace?"

"He's back in Nevada."

Anders swore and touched his forehead. He closed his eyes, his eyelids quivering slightly. "Well, can you give Reuben a message for me before then?"

"I can try," John said. "You can always leave a message at the office number too."

"Yeah, I've tried that. Look, I've got to get a job before Monday, or they take my little girl away, and he's kind of the only one who's given me a chance. He said he'd talk."

The little girl whimpered, and he looked at her. "C'mon, none of that."

Mai entered the kitchen from the dining area. She stopped short. "Hey, Anders." Her voice was tentative. "What are you doing here?" She looked at Georgie, confused.

Anders didn't seem to know how to answer her. The little girl continued to whimper.

Georgie's heart went out to her. "Would she like something to eat?"

Anders turned quickly to Georgie. He hesitated, but then he gave her a short nod.

Georgie held out her hand, and Anders nudged the little thing forward. "Go ahead, Linny."

She looked back at her daddy but took Georgie's hand.

Georgie led her to the walk-in fridge. "Would you like a sandwich?" She motioned for Mai to follow. As she did, Georgie spoke softly to Linny. "We have bread and cheese. Or we have chicken fingers. Do you like pie?"

The little girl nodded, finally taking her eyes off her daddy. Georgie pulled the walk-in door open. She turned her attention to finding something the little girl might like to eat.

"What's going on?" Mai asked quietly.

Georgie whispered as she looked over the shelves. "Anders wants his job back."

"What? Is he crazy? Reuben wou—" Mai stopped herself and looked down at the girl. "Well, he'd have to think about it, wouldn't he?"

Georgie nodded and sighed.

After Linny had chosen a ripe pear and a piece of pie, Georgie opened the door to raised voices. Her gut instinct was to close the door again, but she heard Deacon's calm voice under the shouting.

She looked down at the little girl, whose eyes had doubled in size as she clutched her pear. Georgie turned to Mai and gestured to ask if she had her phone. Mai shook her head. Georgie's was in her jacket with her keys and wallet. They weren't allowed to work with their cell phones on them. "Will you stay right here?" she asked Linny.

The little girl shook her head no, her gaze stuck in the direction of her father's voice.

Voices rose again—Anders's and John's and Tyler's now—shouting, "Wait! Wait a minute!"

Georgie heard an odd *thunk,* and Deacon and Rhea cried out at the same time.

Mai pushed past. "Anders? What in the—" She gasped.

Georgie stepped out to see the commotion and drew in a breath. John had a phone up to his ear and a hand out toward Anders. Deacon held his hand over his face as though hurt and was slowly sinking to the floor. Anders held the heavy sprayer nozzle, stretched on its long, snakelike cord. He had a knife out in his other hand, pointed at Tyler. Georgie looked back at her brother. He pulled his hand away, revealing a bloody gash over his eye. He knelt down on the floor as if his legs had given out, and swayed.

"Deacon?" As she stepped forward, Anders glanced her way, grabbed Tyler, and pulled him so Tyler faced everyone else. The sprayer nozzle bounced and hung swaying. Anders's knife was now pointed at Tyler's throat.

The fear in Anders's face was nothing like Georgie had seen before. The little girl hiding behind her whimpered.

"Anders," Mai said. "Let him go. Just let him go. You don't want to do this."

"All I asked," Anders spat at her, "was for my job back. I'd be good. Just wash the dishes better than this pretty boy." He gave Tyler a jerk, and Tyler grimaced.

Anders focused on John. "Just tell Reuben . . . to give me back my job, and I can keep my girl. I've been tryin', but nobody will listen. He said he'd talk. I can have my job back, and this turd"—he gave Tyler a shake—"can go back to workin' at Old Navy." Tyler was pale but remained calm, his eyes on Deacon.

John murmured into the phone. The phone. If Reuben was on the other side, he could have already called the police from where he was. They would be coming. He would have done that.

Carefully John held the phone out to Anders. "Reuben will talk to you, Anders. But you've got to give up Tyler."

Anders looked at the phone. He squeezed Tyler closer, the veins in his arm pulsing along his tattoos. Tyler winced.

Anders looked at John. "Give me my job back. I'll give you the kid if you'll give me my job back. I swear I'll be good. I swear it."

John slowly put the phone up to his ear. "Did you get that, Reuben?" He listened. He spoke again to Anders.

"Reuben will talk to you. Give up Tyler."

Georgie saw the conflict in Anders, and he began to breathe heavily. His voice rose. "Give me my job back." His eyes watered. Tyler sucked in his breath as the blade touched his skin. "I'll give you the *kid* . . . if you give me my *job back*!"

Dread pulsed through Georgie's veins like ice water, and she broke into a sweat, suddenly overcome with terror.

She saw him. Ian held the ring out as the car picked up speed. Too much speed, and he hugged the corner. She fought against the force of gravity pushing her against the door, the tires squealing.

"I'll slow down if you take the ring back! C'mon, Georgie, you decide." He laughed, and she heard the car accelerate on the black road, the scattered street lights flipping past.

"Slow down. Please, slow down," she pled.

"Take the ring back. We belong together, Georgie."

She shook her head, frantic. "No, Ian. Not anymore."

Briefly his foot eased off the accelerator, and she didn't dare move. *Please*, she prayed, *Please let me out.*

But he pressed down again, and the engine roared. His laughter was gone. "Take the ring back."

She braced herself as the headlights reflected off the guardrail on the curve ahead.

"It's a simple game we're playing, Georgie. You take the ring, I slow down." He still held the ring in front of her, his other hand on the wheel. He watched the road, a thrilled look on his face.

They screeched around the next curve, and she gripped her seat belt with one hand and the door with the other. She was going to be sick.

A game.

This was insane. "No, Ian," she yelled, angry now. The thrill vanished from his face. "Stop the car, and let me out."

The authority in her voice surprised her. Bolstered her.

He turned his head to look at her, his expression muddled.

"I'm done," she said.

Headlights from an oncoming car flashed in their faces, and the car's horn blared. Ian jerked his attention back to the road and swerved. Georgie screamed as they missed the car, but Ian overcorrected, still racing, and the car scraped against the guardrail, sparks flying.

"Slow down, Ian!"

He swore hard, and the car swerved in the other direction. They crossed the center line and careened toward the steep hill on the other side, and as Ian fought the wheel for control, the car shot back across the winding road, crashing through the guardrail head-on, and Georgie no longer knew if the bloodcurdling scream was hers or Ian's . . .

Georgie wasn't sure how much time had passed, but flashing lights through the restaurant back door and the sound of a police radio pulled her back to reality. She tried to steady her breathing. Everything blurred and swayed before it came into focus.

She was on the floor with a blanket around her, a cup of water in her hand. Mai sat with her arm around her shoulders. The little girl, Linny, sat near them, sniffling and wiping her nose as a paramedic spoke softly to her.

Across from Georgie, another paramedic tended to Deacon, wrapping his head as he sat on the floor. He attempted to motion away a stretcher, and as he did so, he caught Georgie watching. "You okay, Boss?" he asked.

Mai lifted her head.

Georgie nodded.

"You scared me for a few minutes there," he said weakly.

"I scared you?" Her voice sounded tinny. Like she spoke into a microphone.

He tried to nod, but the paramedic told him to hold still. "You're okay though?"

Her heart still hammered in her chest. "I think so." He was the one with the bandage on his head.

"Hey." He gestured toward the gash above his brow. "We'll be twins."

"It's a dream come true," she said as her voice stopped echoing in her ears. But she felt floaty, like she wasn't really a part of what was happening in this room.

He smiled but kept his eyes on her for several seconds before he seemed to believe she was okay.

He blinked then and looked at Mai. "I was going to ask if you wanted to hang out tonight."

"You were?"

"Yeah."

"That's sweet," Mai said.

"This isn't what I had in mind," he said.

Mai smiled. The paramedic seemed amused. Georgie wondered if she was supposed to say something but couldn't think of the words.

Deacon let the paramedic finish wrapping him on the stretcher.

Georgie looked around her, blinking slowly. Tyler, John, and Rhea were talking to police officers, and she tried to focus on what they were saying for a few minutes, but it was difficult.

Mai squeezed her shoulders. "Hey," she said. "You blanked out on us. They thought you were in shock." She tapped the cup, and Georgie lifted it and drank.

She wiped her lips and remembered the horrible scene in the kitchen. "Where's Anders?"

Mai peeked over at Linny and lowered her voice. "Back of the cop car. They busted in just after you screamed. You distracted the heck out of Anders, so Tyler knocked the knife away and threw his elbow into him, and then the cops came crashing in. It was over pretty fast."

The paramedic talking to Linny took the little girl's hand and gently led her out of the restaurant. She still held her pear.

"I wonder what will happen to her," Georgie said.

"I don't know. So sad." Mai pulled her arm from around Georgie and shivered. "Anders really lost it."

"He must have wanted her though."

"Yeah, or he brought her here for sympathy points."

Georgie picked at the edge of her blanket, considering that. Hadn't he been sincere? She put her head in her hand. She still hoped the best of people. Even if that left her wide open for disappointment. And hurt. "So . . . I screamed?"

Mai nodded. "Like Jack Nicholson had just put an ax through your door. Pretty smart move."

"Yeah." Georgie hadn't meant to scream. She hadn't meant to lapse into remembering the accident. Anders must have triggered the memory. Ripped it out of its hiding place.

Brains were weird.

The accident. She remembered every crisp, awful detail.

"Hey." Mai waved her hand in front of Georgie's face. "You still look pretty shaken. You okay? Everything happened pretty fast."

Everything had happened pretty fast. She felt a lump in her throat, remembering once more the thrilled look, then the fear, on Ian's face. He was just a kid. A spoiled, messed-up kid who had no clue how to love somebody. The jerk. What his parents had done to him, what his ego had done to him, they weren't her fault.

The accident wasn't her fault.

They'd both been victims in the end. Anger. Sadness. Relief. Each took their turn pulsing through her. She took a soft, deep breath and blew it out, feeling months of guilt rise off of her and dissipate into the air.

And without her bidding, something slipped in its place. Something she welcomed.

Assurance. Hope. Love.

She pushed away a tear. "I wish Jace were here." The words came out of nowhere, but as she said them, she was overcome with a longing for Jace's arms around her and his steady gaze and his presence in the kitchen. "I miss him."

Mai nodded. "We all do."

"I think he's the dragon," Georgie whispered.

Mai studied her a moment. "You know what a cage looks like from the inside, don't you?"

Georgie didn't answer. But she didn't have to.

"Have you escaped?" Mai asked.

"Maybe."

"With your own wings?"

Georgie met her gaze. "I've had some help."

Mai smiled. "So did the emperor's daughter." She drew her arm around her again, their heads touching.

"Does Jace know you miss him?" Mai asked.

Georgie shook her head.

"So let him know."

The thought of letting Jace know anything—everything—filled her with a sense of agitation . . . and hope.

But mostly agitation.

"And drink more of that." Mai pointed at the water and slowly stood. She surveyed the kitchen with her hands on her hips. "This is a crazy place, for sure. But I do love working here."

So did Georgie. And so had Jace.

At the hospital, Georgie filled out forms and got insurance information from her dad on the phone, answering her parents' questions about what had happened while defending her decision not to come home with Deacon. Her headache had returned full force while Deacon had been stitched up, cleaned, and given a new bandage. Now he was sitting on the edge of the bed, drowsy but ready to go.

Uncle Dar appeared, looking unruffled and in charge, and Georgie gratefully accepted his offer to talk to her parents. She directed them his way, and within a minute, he was fielding their questions on his own phone. She excused herself for a minute, handing the clipboard full of forms to Deacon. "Fill in the blanks," she said. Then she headed toward the lobby and outside.

Her phone rang, and part of her wanted to let it ring, but it was one of those nights where a phone call might mean something urgent.

She looked at the caller ID, then answered it breathlessly.

"Jace?"

"Reuben called. Are you okay?"

Her emotions began to crumble, and she sank to the curb as she fought the awful tide of fear finally tearing her down. "Yes."

And then the tears came, and she lowered her head, letting her hair fall over her face. She pressed her phone to her ear and sobbed silently. "Jace."

"Shhhhh. You did good. It's over."

He stayed on the line until she could breathe again.

* * *

The next evening, Georgie knocked on the door to the den.

"Come in," Dar said.

She pushed the door open and stepped into the room that served as Uncle Dar's office away from the office. He kept his older textbooks here, law books he didn't readily use at the firm, and file cabinets, and he sat at a great old mahogany desk, going through a stack of legal-looking papers.

He took off his bifocals. "Hello."

"Hi." Georgie was suddenly unsure. "I think I could use your help in a semilegal-counsel way. But I don't want to make more of it than it is. I want you to tell me how—or if—I should proceed. I'm not after anything, and I'm not sure I'm in trouble for anything, but—"

Dar cleared the stack of papers aside and hurriedly motioned for her to have a seat. "For heaven's sake, what is it?"

"I should have said that better." She hadn't meant to worry him. She sat down and squared her shoulders, determined to be more direct.

"I need your help writing a letter."

He frowned. "A letter? To whom?"

"Ian's mother. Shannon Hudson. I've remembered some things, important things I promised to tell her. But I think they could cause more pain for Ian's family. I don't want more pain for them. I just want to move on."

Dar folded his hands in front of him, ready to listen.

First she told him about Shannon's phone call, the veiled messages adding to Georgie's guilt at the time, then she told him everything she remembered about the night of the accident. He listened silently with a small frown. She ended with the new memory from the night before. "So now I know there was probably nothing I could have done. He chose. Again and again, he chose."

"And you've carried around that guilt for this long?" he asked, clearly concerned.

"I didn't know my part. I couldn't remember. Repeatedly I asked myself, what if I hadn't upset him? What if I'd waited? What if I'd given in? I had been made to believe my thoughts or actions were wrong if they weren't his. I'd learned that *he* made me matter. But that was wrong. That was so wrong."

Dar nodded. "Yes. And so was he. Only you can measure your self-worth. Only you decide who influences it."

She agreed. So much seemed clearer now. It was maddening, but she'd stopped wishing she could change the past.

"Now I'm not sure what to do," she said. "Ian's mom was acting so cryptic on the phone, determined to know why *I* was going so fast. Why *I* would have been driving through the canyon like that. She said she needed closure, but . . . what if they decide to throw all the blame on me? Or press charges or something?"

He drew his head back. "Ian was driving the car, was he not?"

"Yes, but—"

"He was driving."

"But his mom—"

"Georgie, whether they try to pass off a falsehood to elevate their son in others' eyes or are foolish enough to make some sort of legal battle over this—and they may, concerning the ring, at least—the fact is that Ian Hudson was driving the car. He was driving close to twice the speed limit, and there was no alcohol involved. He was driving. He was responsible for his vehicle, his passengers, his choices. That's it. That's the law."

She sat back, letting his solid, straightforward facts sink in. The knots in her stomach loosened. She felt a lightening of her spirit. "Why didn't somebody tell me this months ago?"

He took a deep breath and sighed. "My dear, you too were making choices. And, Lord bless you, you chose to remain very silent."

She nodded. "I did." She wouldn't make that mistake again.

"But no one will blame you for that. No one who really knows you." He smiled.

"Thank you," she said. "But what do I do now about Ian's mom? What do I tell her without making things worse?"

He pulled over a yellow legal notepad and picked up a pen. "Well, what is your first instinct?"

She thought a moment. "To tell her that Ian lost his temper and started speeding through the canyon, lost control of the car, and crashed."

"What if she asks what made him mad?"

Georgie had already gone through scenarios in her mind. She wasn't sure there was a right answer. She was either honest and threw herself to the Hudsons as the scapegoat for their son's death, or she lied and lived with that.

She shook her head. "I don't know. Most of me doesn't want her to know why Ian was so upset. But that feels dishonest."

"You're protecting yourself, and that's understandable."

"What if . . . what if in the letter I say, 'After the wedding reception, we had a serious talk. It was decided that we should call off our engagement. I gave Ian back the ring. It was upsetting for both of us, and he chose to accelerate through the canyon, picking up enough speed so quickly that he lost control of the car.' It will still be hard to hear, but it's not a lie. At least it's enough of the truth that I can live with it."

He nodded, glancing over his notes. "That might do. It is certainly kind to Ian."

"I think . . . I'm okay with that."

He studied her for a moment. "Good for you," he said.

Slowly she smiled.

Chapter 24

GEORGIE TOOK THURSDAY OFF WORK. It was Deacon's last day. He'd recovered pretty well, though he still wore a large bandage over his injury. Mai had visited a few times, and they even had a standing date for the next time he came into town. But now it was just Georgie and him. He had a late afternoon flight out of SeaTac, so he and Georgie left early and spent a couple hours at the Boeing Museum of Flight. Deacon geeked out at the space exploration exhibit. Then they grabbed lunch at the Wings Café, with a clear view of Boeing Field.

Then it was time to go.

Deacon hefted his suitcase onto the scale. After glancing at the weight, the airport attendant added it to the conveyor belt. Deacon turned, gave Georgie a look of resignation, then took her arm, and they walked slowly to the security lines.

After a week of leaning on Deacon, Georgie had to let him go back to his life. Stitches and all.

"You were kind of a lifesaver this week," she said.

"Don't be so dramatic," he said, but he smiled like he owned some of the truth in her statement.

Georgie took a deep breath, then put her arms around him, and he held her tight.

"You're going to amaze and astound," he said.

"You have to say that because I'm your sister."

He laughed. He pulled away and squared her in front of him. "I have one more for you."

She looked at him questioningly.

"*Per aspera ad astra.*"

"I don't know that one. Something with the stars?"

He nodded. "You can look up the rest." He glanced at the time. "I've got to get going."

She kissed his cheek. "Thank you for everything."

He smiled and hefted his backpack over his shoulder. "I hope you figure things out with Spock."

Georgie frowned. "He's not—"

"Shh." He laid his fingers over her mouth.

"Heef naw Sfock," she said behind his hand.

Deacon only grinned. "Love you, Boss." He turned and joined the end of the security line, already slipping off his shoes for the plastic x-ray bucket. He turned and gave her a last salute, with his shoe to his bandaged head.

She laughed, but she felt a fresh little hole inside her. Some good-byes did that.

Before she left the parking garage, she took out her phone and looked up the Latin phrase he'd given her.

Per aspera ad astra.

"Through hardships to the stars."

Back at home, the grown-ups were winding down. Georgie helped Faye shuck the clams they had dug the previous morning, and Dar peeled potatoes for the chowder.

Tru had come home from her job at the retirement center and disappeared to her room. Dean Martin crooned from the stereo as Faye hummed along.

Georgie smiled, a little bit sad, a little bit not.

Suddenly Tru came charging into the room. They all froze as she stopped and waited.

Tru straightened herself up and spoke loudly. "I have a friend who works with me in the kitchen at the retirement center. His name is Tommy Castallano, and I've asked him to Sunday dinner."

The silence was punctuated by Dino's song ending.

Faye shook out of her stupor. "That's wonderful."

"Yes. It is," Tru replied. "He's got a crooked tooth in the front, but he's very nice. I'm making gumbo. Because he's never had that. And my biscuits. And Georgie's going to make Jace's chocolate cake."

"Bu—" Georgie began, but a sharp look from Tru silenced her.

"So," Tru said, "that's gonna happen." She set her shoulders, then turned and walked back out of the room.

"Knock me down with a feather," Faye whispered.

Georgie glanced over at Dar, who was in a fit of silent laughter, gripping a potato and the peeler as he collapsed against the counter. He wiped at his eyes, grabbing a breath. "I guess . . . you better get that recipe, Georgie."

Georgie quickly looked at Faye for help. Faye stared back, wide-eyed, and then burst into laughter as well.

"You guys are a lot of help," Georgie said, then went back to shucking the clams, her heart pounding over Dino singing, "Everybody loves somebody sometime . . ."

The last time Georgie had spoken, sort of, with Jace was the night at the hospital when she'd broken down. He'd called her, and she'd heard his voice for the first time in weeks. And yet he hadn't called again. Neither had she. Maybe he was busy at the diner. Maybe she was chicken. But a text was easier. And she still needed easier as often as possible.

Hi. It's me. Tru invited a friend to dinner. She says I have to make the flourless chocolate cake. I have no idea how to make it. Could you send me the recipe? I understand if you can't.

Also, where do I get candied oranges?

She set the phone down and sighed, wondering what he would think of her request. Baking was not something they'd done together. She knew how to make cookies, but something told her the cake was a far cry from cookies. She picked up the new novel she'd chosen from Faye's shelves and continued to read.

Several minutes later, her phone buzzed.

Jace had taken a photo of the recipe in his notebook. Of his notes in his own writing. They were clear, and he had even scribbled where to find the oranges.

Good luck!

Seeing his notes pulled at her. A good pull. *Thank you*, she answered.

He replied immediately. *You're welcome. How are you?*

Oh, you know. Completely normal.

She paused over her phone, biting her lip. She was tired of the way they tiptoed over their words. Texting like they were balancing on the edge of a high-rise and the wrong phrase could send them hurtling.

Time to strap on those wings and see if they still worked.

I remembered the accident. Everything. It wasn't my fault. I want you to know.

She sent the text and set the phone down. She wasn't going to stare at the screen and wait for a response with her heart pounding out of her—

The phone buzzed, and she jumped and grabbed it.

Thanks for telling me. I don't know much about what happened, but this sounds important. Happy for you.

Okay. Okay, good.

That wasn't enough for her.

It is important. It means—what did it mean? Dang it. It meant moving on and being able to trust a little bit and then a little bit more. To accelerate instead of always checking her blind spot. To hope. To be herself and be comfortable in herself and have others be comfortable with her.

She couldn't write all that.

"Ugh, why is this so hard?" She flopped back on her bed.

It is important. It means I'm not so afraid anymore. And I wonder about things. I wonder about being brave.

Georgie paused, not sending it. She thought of Tru inviting Tommy Castallano to dinner. She thought of going to culinary school and seeing if it was part of her. She thought of what she'd just come through and not forgetting it but using it to see the world around her more clearly. She saw Jace pretty clearly.

She touched her finger to the keyboard.

. . . I wonder about you.

She hit send and held her breath.

And she realized she wanted it. Everything it should be. Everything in those stupid, lovely books she used to read mixed with what was real. What was hard. What she could hold on to and believe in and work for. She didn't need it to be whole. She *wanted* it . . . to see where it could take her. And she wanted it more than she'd let herself believe. To want something like that wasn't weakness. To want that, after everything, through everything to come . . . was courage.

Her phone buzzed.

Do you wonder about us?

Yes.

* * *

Jace grabbed the luggage and carried it back to his parents' room as the rest of the family greeted his mom and dad. Liev had entered the front door of his home, sunburnt, limping, and cranky.

Jace rubbed his hand over his face and told himself it didn't matter. Everything would work out. It had to. He returned to the room as Dan was ushering their boys out the back door to play with Kit. He gave Jace a doubtful look, and Jace shrugged in answer. Maybe now wouldn't be a good time to bring up a coup on the diner, which was what it suddenly felt like.

The others had sat in the front room.

"Jace." His mom reached for him, and he bent to give her a gentle hug.

"How are you feeling, Mom?"

"Wonderful," she answered, patting his back.

She looked in much better spirits than Dad, who was grumbling to Dan about a misstep on the pool deck and tweaking his ankle.

"Second-to-last day. The boat doctor had to look at it. I don't even want to guess how much that bill is going to be."

"Liev," his mom said, "it was less than forty dollars for the visit to the infirmary and the ankle wrap."

"How do you know?"

"I asked. You were very smart not to break anything. Then it would have been something astronomical. You told me just this morning it was feeling better."

"I did not."

"Yes, you did. I asked you if it was feeling better, and you grunted. I took that as a yes."

She turned and winked at Cassi, who, Jace noticed, was watching all this with a sort of greenish color in her face.

"But did you have a good time?" Jace asked.

His mom's face lit up. "We did. We laid in the sun. We swam. Your father is such a good swimmer. And until he hurt his ankle, we danced every night."

"You danced, Mom?" Cassi asked, showing some hope.

"I did. As well as I was able. Your father made sure I felt like I was floating on air." She smiled at Liev, and Jace found it interesting that his dad simply reached for her hand and held it, making no argument or complaint.

"It was heaven," Jace's mom said. "Such beautiful places and wonderful food. We were so spoiled." She grinned at her husband, and he gave in to a half smile.

"The bed was too small," he said. But he patted her hand. "But it was a good trip."

Cassi seemed to release her breath as though she'd been holding it. "Perfect," she said.

"Well," Jace asked, "would you do it again? A vacation like this, I mean?"

"Maybe," Dad said. "That depends on whether or not Cassi's ever gonna to get up the nerve to take over my diner." He raised his brow at Cassi, who gaped with her mouth open.

Mom clasped her hands together and grinned. She peeked at Jace, who leaned over and kissed her cheek. "Thanks, Mom," he whispered. "I knew you could do it."

Step three.

Later Jace heard a knock on the door to his room.

"Come in." He folded a pair of jeans and added them to the pile on his bed.

His dad entered.

"Hey, Dad. Have a good nap?"

"Sure."

Jace nodded.

"I know what you did."

Jace paused and turned. "What did I do?"

His dad simply raised his brow the tiniest fraction.

Jace turned back to folding his clothes.

"You really like it out there, don't you?" his dad asked.

"In Washington? Yeah, I do. But I like it here too, Dad."

"You know why that is?"

Jace paused and turned. "Because I grew up here."

His dad looked at him and pointed to the ground. "It's because here is where you learned to love what you do. And I'm proud of that."

Jace nodded, considering his words and their meaning. "Thanks, Dad."

"Don't you forget that."

"Which part?" Jace asked, partly teasing.

His dad paused. "Both."

Jace smiled.

Liev turned to go but paused at the door. "Oh, hey, I hear it only rains twice a year in Seattle."

Jace turned to him, frowning. "What?"

His dad smiled. "August to April, and May to July." He turned. "Don't forget your umbrella. You're headed into the rainy season."

Jace shook his head and laughed.

Chapter 25

AFTER DRIVING AROUND FOR TWENTY minutes, Jace spotted Georgie's car. She could have been anywhere, but her orange Kia—*burnt* orange Kia—stood out enough that he was fairly confident he could find it. Fortunately, this late in the season and this late in the day, the festival crowds had thinned. He pulled off the road. The compact he drove was a smooth ride, but he couldn't get over the feeling that he took up way too much space when he parked.

It had been weeks since he'd seen her. Since he'd heard her laugh. He hoped he'd made the right decision, that coming here wasn't some idea he'd regret later. But after the phone call on the night of Anders's meltdown, it really wasn't a decision.

Nope. Keep walking, Jace. Follow your gut. It's gotten you this far.

He rolled his eyes at himself but kept walking. He saw her looking away from him, her hands on her hips. His heartbeat picked up double time. He left the blacktop and stepped onto dirt. After he'd walked just a few more steps, she turned.

Slowly her eyes widened, her brow lifting in surprise.

He stopped and smiled nervously.

"Jace? What are you doing here?" she asked, slightly out of breath. "I thought you were in Nevada. I thought you had to . . . help your family."

He pulled his gaze from hers and looked out at the vivid stripes of color, like a quilt laid out beneath a patchy blue-and-gray sky. Georgie stood between the furrows of a tulip field in her winged rain boots and honey hair.

He returned to her waiting gaze. "I came to disturb the universe."

She considered that, an intense look in her eyes. Her knee bounced a little. "What about your dad? And the diner?"

He took a few steps closer as he spoke. "He's selling it to my sister. He's retiring with Mom. I'll be back at Peter and Andrew's on Monday." He waited, hoping to see relief or joy or something on her face. "After what happened, Reuben offered me a raise to come back now, which worked out pretty well because I was already on my way here."

She stepped toward him, her expression unreadable. "But I thought you weren't coming back."

He shook his head. "I didn't know, and then I did. I came back because"—cautiously he waved his finger between the two of them—"I'd like to see where this leads." He swallowed nervously. "I don't want to rush anything. I'm sorry . . . for leaving the way I did. I—"

She seemed to be having trouble breathing. "You're staying?"

He nodded.

She bit her lip before a smile spread widely over her mouth, but her eyes became glassy. "So you're home?"

He reached for her hand. She took it, wrapping her fingers in his. "I'm sorry you've been through so much," he said quietly.

"I'm okay," she said. And the way she said it, he almost believed her. "I'm glad you're back."

She was glad. He could see it. Good, she was glad. He'd take that.

"Did you know?" she asked. "I'm registered for classes. I'm going to Le Cordon Bleu."

He grinned. Reuben had told him. "That's really good news."

She squeezed his hand. "You know what we should do?" she asked. "We should go for a ride."

He grimaced. "Well . . . that's a great idea, but I don't have my bike."

She looked past him. "Where is it?"

He pressed his lips together. "I traded it in."

"For what?" The shock on her face was the first sign of fire in her he'd seen since he'd arrived. Somehow it flooded him with relief, and he gripped her hand more firmly.

The corner of his mouth drew up. "A car," he answered.

She blinked back at him. "But . . . what about your motorcycle?"

He swallowed hard, partly amused, partly frustrated, forgetting what he'd planned to say next. He was tempted to skip it all, pull her close, and never let her go because she was concerned about his stupid motorcycle.

"I needed something more practical—"

Her eyes widened in disbelief.

"Look, forget the car—" He tried to focus and remember what he wanted to say and what he wanted to do. *Stick to the plan.* It had worked for him so far.

He reached behind him for the tulip he'd stuck in the back of his jeans and held it in front of her as she stood in the field of color. His heart thumped in his chest. The stem was a little smashed.

She gasped as the flower drew her attention, and she met his gaze. "It's the Rhapsody."

He nodded. "I was thinking . . ." Dang, this was harder than he imagined. "I was wondering if you'd like to go out. For real, like a date. Of course like a date, you know, with food or a show or something." He knew he should have had something specific already planned. He was making a mess of things.

"With food or a show?" she repeated, looking up at him.

He nodded. "Or something."

She took the tulip and held it to her nose, spinning it just a bit so the petal edges brushed her skin. She looked up at him. "Can we cook something? Together?"

With that single question, his nerves calmed. "Yeah. Anything you want." He swallowed. "Do you have any ideas?"

She nodded. "I want to try sweet bacon peanut burg—"

He pulled her close, kissing her before she even finished. The rush of that kiss in the cooler returned, compounded by how much he'd missed her, how much he wanted to be in her life. She kissed him back with soft, sweet lips and a surprising determination in her embrace.

Yeah. Good decision.

She pulled away just for a moment. "Tru said tulips are given as a declaration of love. Did you know that?"

He stepped back, and she almost lost her balance. He steadied her. He shook his head, and she swallowed, blinking up at him.

"I would have brought you a truckload," he said honestly.

She smiled.

So much for not rushing anything.

But she didn't look worried. Something had changed in her. She no longer seemed . . . afraid. He stepped back to her and leaned in, slower this time.

"You're very close," she said, her gaze steady.

He nodded. She was beautiful, and he was going to spend a long time asking her questions. She reached for him, grasping the front of his shirt and drawing him closer.

Kissing Georgie was like . . . getting caught in a summer storm: a gentle rain soon rumbling with thunder and electricity.

"Jace." Her fingers had slid up his chest and found the nape of his neck. A few drops of rain had begun to fall.

"Yeah?" He pressed his lips to hers again and watched her through half-opened lids.

"You promised me you were safe." She was solemn but gently curled the hair at the back of his neck, sending currents beneath his skin.

He frowned, then nodded, not sure what she was getting at.

A smile played at her mouth like sun through clouds. She whispered, "Liar."

He grinned and grabbed her up, laughing along with her squeal. The clouds above them broke, and they gasped in the downpour. He took her hand to run to the car.

"No." She pulled him back. "No, it's perfect." She reached up and kissed him again.

And again.

And again.

About the Author

Nearly every one of Krista Lynne Jensen's elementary school teachers noted on her report card that she was a daydreamer. It was not a compliment. So when Krista grew up, she started putting those daydreams down on paper for others to enjoy. When she's not writing, she enjoys reading, cooking, hiking, her family, and sunshine. But not laundry. She never daydreams about laundry.

Until the age of ten, Krista lived in the Pacific Northwest and explored much of the Puget Sound with her family. The rain never stopped them. Later she returned, visiting her aunts' home on beautiful Camano Island. Her favorite time to visit was during the Skagit Valley Tulip Festival as everything was blooming and mostly dripping wet.

Krista is a member of LDStorymakers. Visit her blog at kristalynnejensen. blogspot.com and like her Facebook page at www.facebook.com/Author KristaLynneJensen.